The Devil of London

Copyright © 2025 Patti Petrone Miller All rights reserved

The characters and events portrayed in this book are fictitious. Any similarity to real persons, living or dead, is coincidental and not intended by the author.

No part of this book may be reproduced, or stored in a retrieval system, or transmitted in any form or by any means, electronic, mechanical, photocopying, recording, or otherwise, without express written permission of the publisher.

Cover design by: Grady Earls
Printed in the United States of America

Patti Petrone Miller

Introduction

In this gripping Gothic thriller set in Victorian London, we enter a world where darkness lurks beneath the veneer of polite society. The story follows Isabella Blackwood, a woman driven by revenge and ambition, as she becomes entangled with the mysterious and murderous Edward Hyde. Through moonlit streets and fog-shrouded alleys, we witness a deadly game of cat and mouse unfold between these two formidable characters. Hyde, a sophisticated monster who stalks London's elite, leaves a trail of mutilated bodies in his wake. His brutality is matched only by his cunning, as he manipulates the threads of power that bind London's high society. Isabella, far from being a helpless pawn, proves to be a worthy opponent, harboring her own darkness that rivals Hyde's malevolent nature.

The narrative weaves together multiple perspectives, from undertakers to aristocrats, creating a rich tapestry of Victorian London's underbelly. As alliances shift and betrayals mount, the story builds toward an inevitable confrontation between Isabella and Hyde, where the true nature of power, revenge, and darkness is revealed.

This tale of psychological suspense and Gothic horror explores the thin line between civilization and savagery, questioning whether one can fight monsters without becoming one. With its atmospheric prose and intricate plot, this novel pulls readers into a world where nothing is quite as it seems, and where the greatest dangers often wear the most charming smiles.

Welcome to a London where gaslight casts long shadows, where blood stains the cobblestones, and where a woman's revenge might just be more terrifying than the monster she hunts.

THE DEVIL OF LONDON

Excerpt

In the heart of London, where the fog crept through the cobbled streets like a spectral serpent, I, Sir Maximillion Worthington III, stood at the head of a grand table, a monolith of polished mahogany that stretched out before me like a battlefield. The room, a cavernous affair adorned with the trappings of wealth and power, was filled with the scent of beeswax candles and the faint tang of smoke from the nearby factories. The gas lamps cast a flickering light over the assembled faces, a mix of anticipation and skepticism etched into their features.

"Gentlemen," I began, my voice echoing through the chamber like a roll of thunder. "We stand on the precipice of change, a sweeping reform that shall cleanse our city of its moral decay." My hands, clasped firmly behind my back, hid the slight tremor that betrayed my inner turmoil. The gold pocket watch in my waistcoat ticked steadily, a comforting reminder of the passage of time, a constant in a world of variables.

I surveyed the committee members, their eyes glinting in the dim light like those of rats in a dark alley. There was Lord Harrington, his jowls quivering with each breath, a man more concerned with his next meal than the plight of the poor. Beside him sat Mr. Blackwood, a gaunt figure with sunken cheeks, his fingers stained with ink from countless hours poring over ledgers. His eyes held a gleam of curiosity, a willingness to be convinced.

"Our streets are rife with vice," I continued, my voice rising with the fervor of my convictions. "Prostitution, opium dens, the exploitation of the weak—it is a plague upon our society, a cancer that must be excised." The words tasted like ash in my mouth, a bitter reminder of my own hypocrisy. The image of my private dens, hidden away from prying eyes, flashed through my mind—a stark contrast to the moral high ground I now claimed.

The room was thick with tension, the air heavy with the weight of my words. I could feel the scrutiny of the gathered elite, their gazes boring into me like needles. Lord Harrington shifted uncomfortably in his seat, his doublet creaking with the strain. Mr. Blackwood leaned forward, his eyes narrowing as he considered my proposals.

"We must establish stricter regulations, enforce harsher penalties," I declared, my voice resonating with authority. "Our charitable institutions must be held accountable, their funds directed towards true reform, not lined pockets." The irony of my statement was not lost on me; my own pockets had grown heavy with the spoils of embezzlement, a secret shame that gnawed at the edges of my consciousness.

As I spoke, the memories of my private indiscretions threatened to surface, a dark undercurrent beneath my polished exterior. The opium dens, the whispered secrets, the blood—always the blood. The streets of London were stained with it, a grim testament to the violence that lurked in the shadows. The murders, brutal and senseless, had begun to haunt my dreams, a specter that refused to be silenced.

I pushed the thoughts aside, focusing on the task at hand. The committee members watched me with a mix of awe and doubt, their expressions a mirror of the conflict within me. I could see the wheels turning in their minds, the calculations and considerations that would determine the fate of my proposals.

"Gentlemen," I said, my voice dropping to a low, commanding register. "The time for idle talk has passed. We must act, and we must act now. The future of our city, of our very souls, depends upon it." The room fell silent, the only sound the distant rumble of the city beyond the walls. The weight of their gazes pressed down upon me, a physical force that threatened to crush my resolve.

But I stood firm, my hands clasped tightly behind my back, my chin held high. I was Sir Maximillion Worthington III, the honorable chairman, the reform champion—a man of contradictions, a study in calculated deceit. And as I looked out over the assembled faces, I knew that the true battle was not in the streets of London, but within the chambers of my own heart.

The grand table, a sprawling beast of polished mahogany, stretched out before me like a battleground, the committee members its reluctant soldiers. Their faces, a blur of powdered wigs and skeptical scowls, reflected the dancing flames of the chandelier above. The air was thick with tension, the scent of beeswax candles mingling with the sweet, cloying aroma of snuff and pipe smoke.

I had just finished outlining my proposals, the echo of my voice still lingering in the silence, when the heavy oak doors of the chamber creaked open with an ominous groan. The hairs on the back of my neck stood on end, a primal response to the sudden shift in atmosphere. All eyes turned to the entrance, where a figure stood, silhouetted against the dimly lit hallway.

Edward Hyde stepped into the light, his magnetic green eyes scanning the room with a predatory intensity. His gaze was like a physical force, drawing the attention of every man present, including myself. A shiver ran down my spine, an involuntary reaction to the aura of menace that surrounded him like a dark cloak.

He was dressed impeccably, his tall, elegant form swathed in a black frock coat that seemed to absorb the light around him. The lace at his cuffs and throat was as dark as a murder victim's blood, stark against the pale silk of his waistcoat. His breeches were likewise black, tucked into boots polished to a gleaming shine. The only colour about him was the emerald of his eyes and the silver that touched his temples, a distinguishing feature that did nothing to soften his harsh, aristocratic face.

A murmur rippled through the assembly, the committee members shifting uncomfortably in their seats as Hyde moved further into the room. His every step was deliberate, a panther stalking its prey, and I could not help but feel a frisson of unease as those hypnotic eyes met mine.

"Ah, Worthington," he purred, his voice a rich, melodious sound that seemed to wrap around my very soul. "A reform committee, how quaint. I trust you are discussing more than just the width of cobblestone streets and the placement of gas lamps?"

His words, though spoken in elegant tones, carried a hint of mockery that set my teeth on edge. I watched as he moved gracefully around the table, acknowledging the other members with a nod or a brief word. Each man he passed seemed to shrink into himself, their eyes following Hyde with a mix of fear and fascination.

My mind raced as I tried to discern his purpose here. Hyde was not a man to act without reason, and his presence at this meeting could bode nothing but ill. I had heard the whispers, the rumours of his involvement in the darker side of London's underbelly. Tales of bodies found in alleyways, throats slit from ear to ear, the cobblestones slick with blood that ran like rivers towards the Thames. And always, always, the faint scent of sandalwood and bergamot lingering in the air, a chilling calling card that spoke of Hyde's presence.

    As he continued his circuit of the table, I could not help but feel a growing sense of dread. His dark charisma was palpable, a tangible force that seemed to suck the very air from the room. I had faced many a formidable opponent in my political career, but none quite like Edward Hyde.

Patti Petrone Miller

Book List

Accidental Vows
A Krampus Christmas
Sin Takes A Holiday
Barking Up The Wrong Bakery, Thankgiving
Barking Up The Wrong Bakery, Christmas
Best Served Dead
Bewitching Charms
Christmas at Hollybrook Inn
Christmas on Peppermit Lane
Cabinet of Curiosities
Krampus
Hex and the City
Love in Stitches
Pies and Perps
Spectres and Souffles
Mamma Mia It's Murder
Once Upon A Christmas
The Fatman
The Frosted Felony
The Purr-fect Suspect
The Boogeyman
The Gingerdead Men
Vikings Enchantress
Welcome to Scarecrow Hollow
The Pendleton Witches
The Cabinet of Curiosities
Christmas In Pine Haven
Love in the Stacks
Once Upon A Christmas
Frosted Felony

For Harold and our late night chats
R.I.P

Chapter 1

The click of my boots against rain-slicked cobblestones echoed through Berkeley Square like the ticking of a funeral clock. Each step drew me closer to Lady Elizabeth Thornwood's gambling den, and to the devil himself—Edward Hyde. My fingers traced the outline of Father's journal through my reticule, its presence both a comfort and a curse. The January wind howled through the square's iron railings, but the shiver that ran through me had nothing to do with cold.

A carriage clattered past, its wheels throwing up dirty water that nearly stained my hem. I stepped back into the shadows, watching as various crests of nobility rolled by—Rutland, Pembroke, Sterling. Each one a reminder of those who had stood by, smiling behind their fans and glasses, as my family crumbled. The memory rose unbidden: Father's body swaying gently from our ballroom chandelier, the creak of rope against crystal, Mother's screams as they dragged her to Bedlam. Her last coherent words still haunted my dreams: "They're all connected, Isabella. All of them. The society..."

Before she could finish, they'd seized her, declaring her mad with grief. Perhaps she was, but that didn't mean she was wrong.

Through the fog, Lady Elizabeth's townhouse glowed with false warmth. I paused in the street, studying the elegant facade that concealed such depravity within. A group of gentlemen passed nearby, their voices carrying the precise accent of privilege. I turned slightly, letting the shadows hide my features. One of them—young Lord Frederick Pembroke, if I wasn't mistaken—glanced my way, but his eyes slid past without recognition.

Of course they did. The Isabella Wellington they remembered had been a diamond of the first water, all white muslin and pink roses, my chestnut hair arranged in perfect ringlets, my green eyes wide with affected modesty. That girl died the night they cut my father down. In her place stood a creature of darkness, clad in black silk that whispered against the cobblestones, my hair severely styled, my face half-hidden behind a delicate black lace mask.

The footman who admitted me wore the blank expression of one well-paid to forget faces. The gambling den's interior belied its respectable facade. Rich crimson wallpaper absorbed what little light escaped the crystal sconces, and the air hung heavy with Turkish tobacco and French perfume. Around the green baize tables, London's elite wagered their fortunes and reputations with equal abandon. I recognized more than a few faces behind their flimsy masks—a Cabinet minister's wife, her fingers trembling as she placed her bet; a young duke whose family's ancient name couldn't hide the desperation in his eyes.

Lady Elizabeth herself presided over the main salon like a copper-haired spider in her web. Her black silk gown caught the lamplight as she moved between tables, offering encouraging smiles to winners and losers alike. Our eyes met briefly across the room. Something like recognition flickered in her gaze before she turned away, though I was certain we had never met. Perhaps she simply recognized a fellow predator.

The crimson parlor lay beyond a hidden door concealed behind a Chinese screen. As I approached, the sounds of the gambling den faded, replaced by an oppressive silence that seemed to pulse with its own heartbeat. I had rehearsed this moment a thousand times in my mind, but nothing could have prepared me for the reality of Edward Hyde.

He stood by the marble fireplace, a snifter of brandy caught in the firelight like liquid amber in his hand. Tall and elegantly made, with dark hair touched by silver at the temples, he possessed a beauty that was almost painful to behold. But it was his eyes that arrested me—green as poison, they seemed to pierce through flesh and bone to read the secrets written on one's soul. Within their depths, I caught glimpses of something ancient and terrible, a darkness that called to the shadows in my own heart.

"Miss Wellington." His voice was rich as aged wine, with an undertone that made my skin prickle. "I've been following your... activities with great interest."

I forced myself to meet his gaze, though every instinct screamed to look away. "Then you know why I'm here."

"Indeed." He gestured to a high-backed chair upholstered in deep burgundy velvet. "Though I confess, I'm curious about your choice of timing. The Season is just beginning. Society's vultures are circling, eager to see if the infamous Miss Wellington will dare show her face at the opening balls."

The way he said my name sent shivers down my spine—half caress, half threat. I remained standing, my fingers tightening around my reticule. Through the thin leather, I could feel the edges of my father's journal pressing against my palm. Three years I'd kept it hidden, waiting for the perfect moment to unleash its secrets.

"Society's opinion ceased to matter the night they stood by and watched my family's destruction," I said, proud of how steady my voice remained. "I'm here because you, Mr. Hyde, have a particular talent for making powerful men suffer."

He moved then, with that peculiar grace that seemed almost inhuman. Setting his brandy aside, he circled behind me. I could feel his presence like a physical weight against my back, though he didn't touch me. His breath stirred the tiny hairs at my nape as he spoke.

"Suffering is an art form, Miss Wellington," he murmured, his voice dropping lower. "One that requires... patience." His fingers brushed my shoulder, so lightly I might have imagined it. "Tell me, how long did you watch them that night? The vultures who came to feast on your family's remains?"

The memory rose unbidden – myself hidden in the gallery above our ballroom, watching as London's finest filed past Father's body. They'd come under the pretense of offering condolences to Mother, but their eyes had gleamed with barely concealed satisfaction. Lady Pembroke's voice had carried clearly: "Well, really, what did they expect? Attempting to rise above their station..."

"Long enough," I whispered, my voice raw with suppressed emotion. "Long enough to memorize every face, every false word of

The Devil of London

sympathy. Long enough to understand that justice would never come through legitimate channels."

His laugh was dark as sin itself. "And so you've come to me, the devil of London's shadows. But what makes you think I would be interested in your little revenge scheme? I'm a busy man, Miss Wellington. The ton's appetite for sin keeps me quite occupied."

I turned then, meeting those poisonous eyes directly. "Because I offer something more valuable than money." From my reticule, I withdrew the small leather journal that had cost my father his life. "His last gift to me – proof of corruption that goes beyond mere scandal. Names, dates, coded letters... enough to bring down half the peers in England."

Hyde's eyes narrowed fractionally – the first genuine expression I'd seen from him. He took the journal with deliberate slowness, his fingers brushing mine in a touch that felt like electricity. The firelight caught his profile as he opened it, casting stark shadows across features that seemed carved from marble. For a moment, I could have sworn his skin rippled, as if something else moved beneath its surface.

"Fascinating," he murmured, thumbing through the pages. "Your father's hand, I presume? The man had a talent for detail... though perhaps not enough sense to keep such dangerous secrets properly hidden."

Anger flared in my chest. "He trusted the wrong people. A mistake I don't intend to repeat."

"No?" Hyde's smile was razor-sharp. "Yet here you are, trusting me with these very same secrets. Rather reckless, wouldn't you say?"

"Not at all." I allowed myself a small, cold smile. "That journal is insurance – copies of its most devastating contents are already in the hands of certain journalists, to be published in the event of my untimely death or disappearance. I may be reckless, Mr. Hyde, but I'm not a fool."

His laugh then was genuine, filling the crimson parlor with its dark music. "Oh, my dear Miss Wellington. You are absolutely delicious." He moved to his desk, withdrawing an envelope sealed with black wax. "Tell me, have you ever attended one of Lady Elizabeth's special gatherings? The ones where masks are not merely fashion, but necessity?"

"I haven't had the pleasure."

"Then consider this your invitation." He held out the envelope between two elegant fingers. "Tomorrow night. Wear red – it suits your coloring. And do try to remember that once you step through this door, there's no going back to the innocent young lady you once were."

I took the envelope, our fingers brushing for the briefest moment. The contact sent a jolt through me like touching a live wire, and in the flickering firelight, I could have sworn I saw something shift beneath his skin – as if the handsome face he wore was merely a mask over something far less human.

"That young lady died the night they cut my father down," I said softly. "What rises in her place... well, that remains to be seen."

His smile widened, showing teeth that seemed too sharp in the firelight. "Indeed it does, my dear. Indeed it does." He moved to pour another measure of brandy, the crystal decanter catching the light like blood. "Though I must warn you – Lady Elizabeth's gatherings have a way of... revealing one's true nature. Are you certain you're prepared for what you might discover about yourself?"

The question hung in the air between us, heavy with implications I wasn't entirely sure I understood. Through the walls, I could hear the muffled sounds of the gambling den – the soft clink of coins, scattered laughter, the rustle of silk and secrets. This world of shadows and sin was to be my new home, it seemed.

"I stopped fearing my own darkness long ago, Mr. Hyde." I tucked the envelope into my reticule, next to the space where Father's journal had been. "The question is, are you prepared for what I might become under your tutelage?"

He paused with the brandy snifter halfway to his lips, those poison-green eyes flickering with something that might have been approval – or hunger. "Oh, I do hope not, Miss Wellington. It would be such a shame to lose interest in you so quickly."

The implied threat should have terrified me. Instead, I felt a thrill of anticipation curl through my chest. "Then I shall endeavor to keep you entertained, sir."

As I turned to leave, his voice stopped me at the threshold. "One last thing, my dear. That clever insurance plan of yours, with the journalists?" When I looked back, his smile had turned cruel. "I've already taken care of it. The copies were destroyed within an hour of their delivery. Really, did you think you were the first to try such a gambit?"

My blood ran cold. "How did you—"

The Devil of London

"I make it my business to know everything that happens in my city." He raised his glass in a mocking toast. "Don't fret, though. I'm far more intrigued by your potential than your pathetic attempts at manipulation. Run along now. You'll need your rest for tomorrow night."

I forced myself to walk calmly from the crimson parlor, though my heart thundered in my chest. He'd known about the copies. Had probably known about them before I'd even entered his lair. The realization that I was now completely at his mercy should have sent me fleeing into the night. Instead, it felt strangely like freedom.

The gambling den's noise rushed back like a wave as I emerged from behind the Chinese screen. Lady Elizabeth caught my eye again, this time with a knowing smile that made me wonder just what sort of "gathering" tomorrow would bring. At a nearby table, I recognized Sir Maximillion Worthington III, the very picture of moral righteousness in his somber black evening dress. The same man who'd led the charge to deny my mother's claims of conspiracy.

He looked up as I passed, a flicker of recognition crossing his features before uncertainty set in. I gave him my sweetest smile, enjoying the way he paled slightly. Soon enough, he would learn exactly who I was – they all would.

The footman held my cloak ready as I reached the entrance hall. Through the fanlight above the door, I could see that the fog had thickened considerably, turning the gas lamps into ghostly orbs floating in the darkness. A hansom cab clattered past, its driver hunched against the chill. In the distance, a church bell tolled midnight, its somber notes echoing off the wet stones.

"Shall I call a cab for you, miss?" the footman inquired, though his tone suggested he already knew my answer.

"No, thank you. I prefer to walk."

Indeed, I had developed a taste for London's darkness these past three years. The night air carried the perpetual stench of coal smoke and rot, but beneath it, I caught a whiff of something else – the metallic tang of blood, real or imagined. It seemed fitting. After all, I had just made a bargain with the devil himself, and such contracts were always sealed in blood.

Mount Street lay ahead, though the fog had grown so thick I could barely make out the shapes of buildings. Gas lamps created halos in the mist, their light catching the occasional glint of a policeman's buttons or a prostitute's cheap jewelry. A group of young swells stumbled out of a nearby club, their laughter too loud, their evening dress disheveled. One of them – barely more than a boy, really – called out something lewd as I passed. I ignored him, though my hand tightened on the small derringer concealed in my cloak pocket.

"Oy, fancy piece! Didn't you hear the gentleman?" A rough hand grabbed my arm, spinning me around. The young swell's face was flushed with drink, his aristocratic features twisted into an ugly leer. "Come now, love, show us what's behind that mask—"

His words cut off in a gasp as he felt the derringer's barrel press against his ribs. "Remove your hand," I said softly, "or I shall be forced to redecorate your waistcoat with your insides."

The fog seemed to thicken around us, and for a moment, I could have sworn I saw a tall figure watching from the shadows – those unmistakable green eyes gleaming with amusement. But when the young man stumbled back, releasing me with a stream of curses, the figure was gone.

"Bloody hell, Charles, leave the crazy bitch be," one of his companions called. "Plenty of willing girls at Mother Watson's!"

They disappeared into the fog, their voices fading to echoes. I waited until the sound of their footsteps had completely gone before continuing on my way. The encounter had left me oddly energized, my blood singing with a dark sort of pleasure. Three years ago, such an interaction would have terrified me. Now it felt like a reminder of how far I'd come – and how much further I had yet to go.

A beggar woman huddled in a doorway caught my attention, her face hidden beneath a tattered shawl. As I passed, she began to sing in a cracked voice:

"The devil walks in London town, All dressed in silk and lace, He'll grant your heart's desire, my dear, But steal your soul with grace..."

I tossed her a coin, more for the appropriateness of her timing than any real charity. She caught it with surprising deftness, and as she looked up, I glimpsed features that seemed oddly familiar. But the fog swallowed her before I could place the resemblance.

The rest of my journey passed in a blur of shadows and half-glimpsed figures. A cat yowled somewhere in the darkness, the sound eerily like a child's cry. Through windows above, I caught fragments of domestic scenes – a couple arguing in silhouette, a lone figure writing at a

The Devil of London

desk, a woman brushing her hair with mechanical repetition. Each tableau seemed somehow sinister in the fog-diffused lamplight.

My own lodgings occupied the upper floor of a respectable if somewhat faded townhouse. Mrs. Harrison, my landlady, was a widow who asked few questions and turned a blind eye to my irregular hours. The arrangement suited us both – her need for additional income outweighing any concern for propriety.

"A package came for you, miss," she called from her parlor as I passed. "Most peculiar delivery man. Left it not an hour ago."

I paused, my hand halfway to my derringer. "Did he leave a name?"

"No, miss. But he had the strangest eyes..."

My heart skipped a beat. "Thank you, Mrs. Harrison. I'll collect it in the morning."

"It's on your dressing table, miss. He insisted it be taken up straight away."

I took the stairs two at a time, my mind racing. Hyde had known where I lived – of course he had. But to send something so quickly after our meeting? The implications were unsettling.

Sarah, my maid, was waiting up despite my instructions to the contrary. Her plain face showed relief at my arrival, quickly followed by concern as she noticed my agitation.

"Is everything alright, miss? That package—"

"Leave me," I ordered, already moving to my dressing table. "And Sarah? Under no circumstances am I to be disturbed until morning."

The package sat innocently among my cosmetics and hair pins – a box wrapped in black silk, tied with a red ribbon. No card, but then, none was needed. With trembling fingers, I untied the bow.

The silk fell away like water, revealing a lacquered box of deepest crimson. Inside, nestled on black velvet, lay a mask unlike any I'd seen before. It was crafted of what appeared to be red leather, so dark it was almost black in the shadows, worked into an intricate pattern of thorns and roses. But it was the material itself that made my breath catch – the leather had an odd, almost organic quality to it, as if it were still somehow alive.

Beneath the mask lay a note written in an elegant hand: "A proper mask for tomorrow's festivities. Do be careful – the thorns are quite real. - H"

As if compelled, I reached out to touch one of the decorative thorns. A sharp sting, and a bead of blood welled on my fingertip. I watched, transfixed, as the droplet fell onto the mask's surface. For a moment – though surely it was a trick of the lamplight – I could have sworn the leather absorbed it, the red growing deeper, richer.

"Will there be anything else, miss?" Sarah's voice made me start. I hadn't heard her return.

"No, I—" I turned, but the doorway was empty. Had I imagined her voice? The hour was late, my nerves perhaps not as steady as I'd thought.

I moved to my dressing table mirror, holding the mask up to my face without putting it on. The reflection that gazed back was a creature of shadow and sharp edges, barely recognizable as the girl who had once danced at Almack's. I thought of my first Season, how proud Father had been as he'd watched me navigate the social waters with what he'd called "natural grace."

Poor Father. He'd never understood that the very society he'd worked so hard to join was rotten at its core. The memories rose unbidden – finding his body, the note clutched in his lifeless hand: "I cannot bear the shame of what I've discovered. Forgive me." But there had been bruises on his neck that couldn't be explained by hanging, and Mother had sworn she'd heard voices in his study the night before...

A sudden gust of wind rattled the windows, making the lamp flames dance. In the mirror, the shadows seemed to move independently of the light, gathering in the corners like watching creatures. The mask in my hands felt warmer, almost pulsing with a life of its own.

I had long suspected there was more to London's darkness than mere human evil. In the years since Father's death, I'd heard whispers of ancient societies, of powers that moved behind the facade of polite society. Perhaps that's what Mother had glimpsed – the truth behind the masks that had driven her to madness. Or perhaps we were all mad, seeing patterns in chaos, monsters in shadows.

The clock on my mantel struck one, the sound unnaturally loud in the quiet room. Tomorrow – no, today now – I would attend Lady Elizabeth's gathering, wearing Hyde's gift. Whatever game he was playing, whatever web he was weaving, I was now irrevocably part of it.

I placed the mask carefully back in its box, noting how the thorn's prick had already stopped bleeding. In its place, I felt a curious warmth spreading through my veins, a sensation not entirely unpleasant. Moving to the window, I gazed out at fog-shrouded London. Somewhere out there, others would be receiving similar packages, preparing for whatever dark revelry awaited us.

A familiar figure caught my eye – a tall man in a black coat, standing perfectly still beneath a gas lamp across the street. Even through the fog, those green eyes were unmistakable. Hyde raised his hat to me, a gesture both courtly and mocking. When I blinked, he was gone, leaving only swirling fog.

Sleep would not come easily, I knew, but propriety demanded I at least go through the motions of preparing for bed. I rang for Sarah, though my fingers still trembled from the encounter. She appeared almost instantly – too quickly, I realized, for her to have come from the servants' quarters.

"You've been watching my door." It wasn't a question.

She dropped her eyes, fingers twisting her apron. "Begging your pardon, miss. It's just... there's been talk, in the servants' hall. About him. About what happens to those who..." She swallowed hard. "They say he's not natural, miss. That he's been walking London's streets for longer than should be possible."

"Nonsense." But even as I said it, I remembered the way his skin had seemed to shift in the firelight, how his shadow had moved against the laws of nature. "Help me undress."

Her hands were steady as she worked at my buttons, though I noticed she kept glancing at the window. The fog pressed against the glass like a living thing, occasionally parting to reveal glimpses of the street below. Each time, I half-expected to see that tall figure watching.

"Your evening gloves, miss." Sarah hesitated. "There's blood..."

I looked down at my right glove. A small dark stain marked where the mask's thorn had pricked me, but it seemed to have spread, creating a pattern that looked disturbingly like a rose. "It's nothing. Leave them on the vanity with the rest."

As she helped me into my nightgown, I caught our reflection in the mirror. The white cotton should have made me look innocent, girlish even. Instead, I appeared haunted, my eyes too bright, my skin almost translucent in the lamplight. For a moment, I could have sworn I saw another figure standing behind us – tall, elegant, with eyes that burned like fire.

"Will that be all, miss?" Sarah's voice seemed to come from very far away.

"Yes. Though Sarah..." I caught her arm as she turned to leave. "If I'm not myself tomorrow... if I seem changed after the gathering... burn the mask and run. Don't try to save me."

Her face paled, but she nodded. We both knew she wouldn't run – her loyalty, or perhaps her fascination with darkness, would keep her by my side no matter what horrors awaited.

Once alone, I extinguished all but one lamp and lay down upon my bed. The sheets felt unusually cold against my skin, though the prick on my finger burned like a brand. Outside, London's nocturnal symphony played on – the distant clatter of carriages, a drunk's song cut short by raucous laughter, the mournful howl of a dog that sounded almost human.

Sleep, when it finally came, brought dreams of masks and mirrors, of endless ballrooms where dancers whirled in dizzying patterns, their faces hidden behind leather masks that seemed to pulse with each turn. In every mirror I passed, I caught glimpses of Hyde watching me, his gaze burning brighter with each reflection.

The dream shifted, and I stood in Father's study on that fatal night. But this time, when I opened the door, it wasn't his body I found hanging from the ceiling. The figure suspended from the chandelier wore a red leather mask, and as it turned slowly in the draft from the window, I saw my own face beneath, eyes open and burning with an unholy fire.

I woke with a start to find my room bathed in the grey light of dawn. The fog had lifted somewhat, though London's ever-present smoke still turned the sunrise into a sickly yellow smear across the sky. My finger no longer hurt, but when I examined it, I found an odd mark where the thorn had pricked me – a tiny scar in the shape of a rose, its lines as delicate as if they'd been drawn in ink.

On my vanity, Hyde's mask seemed to watch me with eyeless anticipation. Tonight I would wear it to Lady Elizabeth's gathering, taking the first real step toward my revenge. But as I stared at my reflection, I wondered if vengeance was still truly my goal. The darkness Hyde offered whispered of something far more seductive – power, freedom, the chance to become something beyond the constraints of society and morality.

The Isabella Wellington who had watched her father's body cut down would have recoiled from such thoughts. But she was gone, replaced by this creature of shadow and steel who felt only anticipation at the horrors to come.

"Well, Father," I whispered to the empty room, "you always said I would make a remarkable match. I doubt this is quite what you had in mind."

The last of the fog cleared as if in response to my words. Across the street, a church bell began to toll, marking the start of another London day. Each sonorous note seemed to carry a warning, but it was far too late for those.

I had already chosen my path, signed my contract with the devil in blood. All that remained was to discover what sort of monster I would become in the unfolding of our dark dance.

Through the window, London awakened to its daily rhythm of commerce and propriety. But beneath the surface, I knew another city stirred – Hyde's London, a place of shadows and secrets, of masks and monsters. Tonight, I would finally step fully into that world, leaving the last traces of my old self behind.

The thought should have terrified me. Instead, I smiled, and in the mirror, my reflection smiled back with teeth that seemed just a little too sharp.

Chapter 2

The red silk of my gown whispered against my skin like a lover's caress, each rustle a reminder of the blood that would soon stain the streets of London. In the mirror's depths, my reflection was a creature of shadow and steel, barely recognizable as the innocent debutante I had once been. Sarah's hands trembled slightly as she laced my stays, though whether from fear or excitement, I couldn't tell.

"Tighter," I commanded, watching as my waist narrowed further, the pressure against my ribs a sweet torment. "Tonight's performance requires absolute perfection."

Sarah's eyes met mine in the mirror, her plain face drawn with concern. "There's talk below stairs, miss," she said softly, her fingers working at the laces. "About him. About what happens to those who... who cross him."

"Mr. Hyde, you mean?" I watched her reflection pale at the mere mention of his name. "Good. Let them talk. Fear can be a powerful ally."

Indeed, the rumors that swirled around Edward Hyde were part of his power. Some said he had destroyed entire families with a single whispered word in the right ear. Others claimed he kept a book of secrets that could bring down half the peers in England. All agreed that those who earned his enmity tended to meet unfortunate ends.

The Devil of London

The irony, of course, was that the truth proved far more devastating than any rumor. I had seen his methods firsthand during our careful planning sessions, had witnessed the way he orchestrated the complete undoing of his enemies, using their own sins as weapons against them. A shiver ran down my spine at the memory, though whether from fear or anticipation, I couldn't say.

My gaze drifted to Hyde's mask, lying innocently upon my dressing table. The red leather seemed to pulse in the candlelight, the pattern of thorns and roses more pronounced than before. The tiny wound on my finger where it had pricked me throbbed in response, the rose-shaped scar a constant reminder of my pact with darkness.

A sudden draft stirred the heavy curtains, though all the windows were sealed against the January chill. The candle flames flickered wildly, casting grotesque shadows upon the walls. Sarah crossed herself, a gesture that seemed pathetically inadequate against the forces we had unleashed.

"Will that be all, miss?" she asked, her voice barely above a whisper.

I studied my reflection once more - the severe styling of my dark hair, the blood-red silk of my gown, the shadows that seemed to gather around me like faithful servants. "Yes, Sarah. That will be all."

As Sarah's footsteps faded down the hall, I reached for Hyde's mask. The leather was warm to the touch, almost feverishly so, and I could have sworn I felt a pulse beneath its surface, like a living thing eager to bond with my flesh. The thorns gleamed in the candlelight, their points sharp enough to draw blood at the slightest touch.

A knock at my door startled me from my reverie. "Miss?" It was Mrs. Harrison, her voice tight with poorly concealed anxiety. "A... a gentleman has called for you. He's waiting in the parlor."

My heart skipped a beat. I hadn't expected Hyde to come here, to my sanctuary. "Tell him I'll be down directly."

The parlor was cast in shadow, the gas lamps turned low as if in deference to our visitor. Hyde stood by the window, his tall frame silhouetted against the fog-shrouded street. He turned as I entered, and I felt the familiar jolt of unease at the sight of his too-perfect features.

"My dear Miss Wellington," he purred, his eyes gleaming like a cat's in the dim light. "You look positively ravishing. The color of blood suits you."

I forced myself to meet his gaze. "You risk much, coming here. The neighbors—"

"The neighbors see what they wish to see," he interrupted, moving closer with that peculiar grace that seemed almost inhuman. "Just as society sees what it wishes to see. A grieving daughter, seeking solace in charitable works. How little they understand the darkness that burns within you."

His words sent a shiver down my spine, but I stood my ground. "You speak as if you know me, Mr. Hyde."

His laugh was low and rich, like aged brandy laced with poison. "Oh, but I do know you, Isabella. I know the rage that consumes you, the thirst for vengeance that drives you. I know how you lie awake at night, imagining the destruction of those who wronged you."

He was close now, close enough that I could smell his unique scent - sandalwood and something darker, metallic, like fresh blood. "Tonight," he continued, his voice dropping to a whisper, "you will take your first true step into my world. Are you prepared for what that means?"

I thought of my father's body, swaying gently from the chandelier. Of my mother's screams as they dragged her away. Of the smug faces of society as they watched our destruction with barely concealed glee. "I am prepared for anything," I said, my voice steady despite the trembling in my hands.

His smile was terrible to behold. "We shall see, my dear. We shall see."

The carriage ride to Lady Elizabeth's was a study in shadows, the fog pressing against the windows like ghostly hands seeking entrance. Hyde sat opposite me, his presence filling the small space with an almost physical weight. The mask lay between us on the leather seat, its thorns gleaming dully in the occasional flash of passing gas lamps.

"Tell me," Hyde said suddenly, his voice cutting through the silence like a blade, "do you remember the moment you first tasted darkness? The exact instant when innocence gave way to knowledge?"

The question caught me off guard, but the answer rose unbidden to my lips. "The night they cut Father down," I said softly. "Not when I first saw him hanging there, but after. When I watched the ton file past his body, their eyes gleaming with satisfaction barely hidden behind their masks of sympathy."

"Ah yes," Hyde murmured, leaning forward. "The moment when the veil was torn away, and you saw society for what it truly was - a nest of vipers, each one poised to strike." His eyes seemed to glow in the darkness. "And now you would become the serpent among them."

"Not become," I corrected him. "Reveal. The serpent was always there, merely waiting for the right moment to shed its skin."

His laugh was genuine this time, a sound of pure delight that sent shivers down my spine. "Oh, my dear Isabella. You continue to surprise me. Perhaps you are more ready for this than I thought."

The carriage came to a halt before Lady Elizabeth's townhouse. Through the fog, I could see other carriages arriving, their occupants hurrying inside like shadows flitting through the night. Each figure wore a mask, some elaborate confections of feathers and jewels, others simple dominos that spoke of deadlier purpose.

Hyde stepped down first, then turned to offer me his hand. As our fingers touched, I felt that same electric jolt, and for a moment - just a moment - I could have sworn his skin rippled, as if something else moved beneath its surface.

"Your mask, my dear," he said, retrieving it from the seat. "Shall I?"

I turned my back to him, feeling his fingers brush my neck as he secured the leather straps. The mask seemed to mold itself to my features, warm and alive against my skin. As it settled into place, I felt a curious sensation - as if my very blood was singing in response to its touch.

"There," Hyde murmured, his breath hot against my ear. "Now you truly look the part of a creature of shadow."

I turned to face him and saw his eyes widen slightly. "What is it?" I asked, reaching up to touch the mask.

"Nothing," he said, but his smile held a new edge of respect - or perhaps hunger. "Just admiring my handiwork. Shall we?"

As we approached the house, I caught our reflection in a window - my red silk gown a splash of blood against the night, the mask transforming my features into something both beautiful and terrible. And beside me, Hyde's form seemed to shift and change with each step, as if he were barely containing something far less human beneath his elegant exterior.

The door opened at our approach, spilling golden light onto the fog-shrouded steps. Within, I could hear music - not the usual waltzes and quadrilles of society balls, but something darker, more primal. A melody that spoke of ancient rites and forbidden pleasures.

"Remember," Hyde said softly as we crossed the threshold, "tonight is about more than mere revenge. Tonight is about embracing what you truly are."

"And what is that?" I asked, though part of me already knew the answer.

His smile was terrible and beautiful. "A monster, my dear Isabella. Just like me."

The masked figures that filled Lady Elizabeth's ballroom moved like specters in a dream, their elaborate costumes creating a kaleidoscope of color and shadow. The music that had seemed so strange from outside now pulsed through the air like a living thing, its rhythm matching the beat of my heart beneath the rose-thorned mask.

Lady Elizabeth herself stood at the top of the grand staircase, resplendent in a gown of deepest purple that seemed to swallow light. Her mask was a masterpiece of black lace and garnets, the stones catching the candlelight like drops of fresh blood. As we approached, I noticed how the other guests gave her a wide berth, as if sensing something dangerous beneath her carefully maintained facade of gracious hostess.

"Edward," she purred, extending her hand to Hyde. "How delightful of you to join us. And this must be your... protégé."

Her eyes met mine through our masks, and I felt a jolt of recognition. Not of her face - we had never met before - but of something deeper, more primal. She saw the darkness in me, just as I saw it in her.

"Miss Isabella Wellington," Hyde introduced me, his voice carrying a note of pride that made my skin prickle. "Though perhaps that name will soon be as outdated as the innocence it once represented."

Lady Elizabeth's laugh was like breaking glass. "Indeed? Well, my dear, you've chosen an interesting path." She leaned closer, her voice dropping to a whisper. "Do mind the thorns, won't you? They tend to draw more blood than one expects."

Before I could respond, the music changed, becoming something wild and ancient that made the very air vibrate with possibility. The masked dancers moved faster, their movements taking on an almost frenzied quality. Through the crowd, I caught glimpses of things that couldn't possibly be real - a woman's face becoming serpentine beneath her mask, a man's hands elongating into claws, shadows that moved independently of their owners.

"Shall we dance?" Hyde asked, his voice rough with anticipation.

I placed my hand in his, noting how his fingers seemed almost too long, too sharp against my skin. As he led me onto the dance floor, I felt the mask grow warmer against my face, its thorns pressing deeper though drawing no blood.

The other dancers parted for us, creating a circle of empty space that felt more like an arena than a ballroom. Hyde's hand at my waist was burning hot, even through the silk of my gown. As we began to move, I realized this was no ordinary waltz. The steps were ancient, primal, more ritual than dance.

"Look around you," Hyde murmured as we turned. "Really look. See them for what they are."

I did as he commanded, and the world seemed to shift. The masks the other guests wore no longer seemed like mere decorations, but revelations of their true natures. Here was a wolf in nobleman's clothing, there a serpent wearing a duchess's jewels. And everywhere, everywhere, the hungry eyes of predators watching us dance.

"What is this place?" I whispered, though I already knew the answer.

"This, my dear Isabella, is where society's masks slip. Where the monsters that lurk beneath silk and lace come out to play." His smile was razor-sharp. "Welcome to your true home."

As we spun faster, the room began to blur around us. The candlelight fractured into a thousand points of fire, and the music seemed to come from inside my own head. The mask grew hotter still, and I could feel something changing, transforming beneath its touch.

"Let go," Hyde whispered, his voice somehow inside my mind. "Let the darkness in. Become what you were always meant to be."

And I did. God help me, I did.

The transformation was exquisite agony. I felt the mask's thorns sink deeper, piercing not just flesh but soul. My blood sang with an unholy fire, and the world around me sharpened into terrible clarity. I could smell the fear beneath the guests' expensive perfumes, hear the racing of their hearts beneath their jeweled masks. Every sensation was heightened, every shadow held new meaning.

Hyde's grip tightened as the change took me, his own form shifting subtly beneath his perfect exterior. His eyes were flame-green now, pupils elongated like a cat's, and his smile showed teeth that were definitely sharper than any human's should be.

"Beautiful," he breathed, spinning me faster. "Oh, you are magnificent, my dear. Even better than I hoped."

Through the blur of motion, I caught our reflection in one of the ballroom's gilt-edged mirrors. The woman who stared back was both myself and a stranger - my features transformed by the mask into something wild and terrible. My eyes glowed like emerald fire, and shadows seemed to writhe around me like living things.

The music reached a fever pitch, and suddenly Hyde pulled me closer, his lips brushing my ear. "Now for your first test," he whispered. "Look there - by the punch bowl. Do you see him?"

I followed his gaze to where Sir Maximillion Worthington stood, his elaborate mask failing to hide his growing unease. He was watching us dance, his glass trembling slightly in his hand. Even from across the room, I could smell his fear.

"He was there that night, wasn't he?" Hyde's voice was soft, seductive. "When they took your mother away. He signed the committal papers himself, didn't he?"

The memory rose like bile in my throat - Sir Maximillion's satisfied smirk as Mother screamed and fought against the asylum attendants. His pompous voice declaring her unfit, dangerous, mad. The same voice that had led the chorus of whispers that destroyed my family's reputation.

"What would you do to him, if you could?" Hyde asked, his words like silk wrapped around a blade. "What darkness lurks in your heart, my dear Isabella?"

The answer came with frightening ease. "I would destroy him," I whispered. "Not just his body - his reputation, his standing, everything he holds dear. I would make him feel the same helplessness, the same despair he inflicted on my mother."

"Then do it." Hyde's voice held a note of command that resonated through my very bones. "The power is yours now. Take it. Use it. Show them all what happens to those who cross Isabella Wellington."

The mask seemed to pulse against my skin in agreement, its thorns singing with my blood. I felt power coursing through me, dark and heady as the finest wine. This was what I had been waiting for, what all those years of careful planning had led to.

As if sensing his doom, Sir Maximillion looked up and met my transformed gaze. I saw the moment recognition hit him, watched as the blood drained from his face. His glass slipped from nerveless fingers, shattering on the marble floor.

The sound was like a signal. The other dancers stopped, turning to watch as I moved toward my prey, Hyde's laughter following me like a dark blessing.

Sir Maximillion backed away as I approached, his feet crunching on the broken glass. The other guests formed a circle around us, their masks glinting in the candlelight, their silence expectant. They could sense what was coming - these creatures of shadow and secrets knew the scent of impending destruction.

"My dear Sir Maximillion," I said, my voice carrying an otherworldly resonance that surprised even me. "How wonderful to see you again. Tell me, do you remember the last time we met? When you had my mother dragged away in chains?"

"Miss Wellington," he stammered, his face pale beneath his mask. "I... I was merely doing my duty. The woman was clearly unwell—"

"Unwell?" The word came out as a snarl, and I felt the shadows around me writhe in response to my anger. "She was perfectly sane until you and your conspirators destroyed her. Until you murdered my father and covered it up as suicide."

A gasp rippled through the watching crowd. Sir Maximillion's eyes darted around wildly, seeking escape or allies, finding neither. "These are dangerous accusations, young lady. You have no proof—"

"Oh, but I do." I reached into my reticule, withdrawing a folded paper. "This document, for instance - in your own hand, ordering the payment to the men who staged my father's 'suicide.' How careless of you to keep such damning evidence."

His face went from pale to grey. "Where did you get that? Those papers were locked in my private safe—"

"I have friends now, Sir Maximillion. Friends in dark places." I smiled, feeling the mask's thorns pulse against my skin. "Friends who have taught me that revenge is an art form, best served with exquisite attention to detail."

From the corner of my eye, I saw Hyde moving through the crowd like a shark through water, his presence adding weight to my words. The other guests shifted uneasily, their own masks seeming to reflect their growing unease.

"What do you want?" Sir Maximillion whispered, his voice cracking.

"Want? Oh, nothing so simple as money or position." I stepped closer, close enough to smell the fear rolling off him in waves. "I want you to watch as everything you've built crumbles. I want you to feel your power slip away, piece by piece, until you're left with nothing but the knowledge that you brought this on yourself."

I turned to address the watching crowd, my voice carrying to every corner of the room. "Ladies and gentlemen, I hold in my hand proof that one of society's most respected members is nothing but a common murderer. A man who arranged my father's death, falsified evidence, and had my mother committed to hide his crimes."

The whispers started immediately, spreading through the crowd like wildfire. I could see reputations crumbling, alliances shifting, as London's elite processed this new development. Sir Maximillion's influence was already evaporating like morning mist.

"This," I continued, "is only the beginning. There are more secrets to be revealed, more masks to be torn away. Tonight marks the start of a new era in London society."

I felt Hyde's presence behind me, his approval radiating like heat from a furnace. The mask seemed to merge with my skin, its power flowing through my veins like liquid darkness. I was no longer simply Isabella Wellington, the ruined daughter of a disgraced family. I had become something else, something terrible and wonderful.

Sir Maximillion fled the ballroom, his departure marked by titters and whispers from the crowd. I watched him go, feeling no triumph, only a cold satisfaction and an hunger for more. This was just the first taste of the power I now wielded, the first step on a path that would lead to either glory or damnation.

As the music resumed and the dancers returned to their revels, Hyde's hand found mine. "Well done, my dear," he murmured. "Very well done indeed. But remember - this is only the beginning. There are so many more delicious games for us to play."

The Devil of London

    I turned to face him, seeing my own transformed reflection in his inhuman eyes. "Yes," I agreed, feeling the thorns of my mask pulse in time with my heartbeat. "So many more."

    The night spun on, a whirl of shadows and secrets, masks and monsters. And at its heart, I danced with the devil himself, no longer caring if the price of my revenge would be my soul. After all, what use is a soul to a creature of darkness?

    Through the windows, I could see the fog rolling in from the Thames, thick and grey as cemetery smoke. London's newest monster had risen, and she was hungry for more than just justice. The game of shadows had truly begun.

Chapter 3

The clock in my study chimed midnight as I, Thomas Harding, stood hunched over my ledger, its pages sticky with something darker than mere ink. My fingers trembled as I traced the latest entry: "Lady Margaret Winters, aged 26, cause of death..." I paused, pen hovering over the paper. How does one describe in clinical terms the transformation of flesh into nightmare?

Below, in my workroom, her body lay waiting, a grotesque tableau that defied my thirty years of undertaking experience. Her throat bore marks I had never seen before—punctures that seemed to pulse with a sickly phosphorescence, veins blackened as if filled with ink rather than blood. The wounds themselves appeared to shift when viewed directly, as if refusing to settle into any natural pattern of violence. Most disturbing were her eyes—still open, displaying the same otherworldly gleam I had witnessed in Isabella Wellington's gaze after Lady Elizabeth's gathering.

The thought sent a shudder through me. I had been there, watching from the shadows as Isabella emerged from that cursed party, her face transformed by more than just Hyde's rose-thorned mask. Something was spreading through London's elite like a contagion of the soul, turning human beings into... something else.

The Devil of London

The scent of lilies, deliberately cloying and thick, drifted up from below. They couldn't quite mask the other smell—not just blood and decay, but something older, something that made the primitive part of my brain want to flee. Each body that crossed my table was another weight upon my conscience. I had become Hyde's accomplice in death, arranging his victims into socially acceptable poses, crafting plausible explanations for wounds that defied explanation. How many families had I deceived with my carefully worded reports? How many monsters had I helped to hide?

A soft knock at the door interrupted my dark musings. "Enter," I called, hastily closing the ledger, though the wet ink left a mirror image on the opposite page—a Rorschach blot of my guilt.

Catherine Blackwood stepped into my study, her tall form wrapped in a cloak of deepest blue. Her dark hair was pulled back severely from her face, emphasizing the sharp intelligence in her gray eyes. Ink stains marked her gloved fingers—she had been documenting her own observations of London's descent into madness, I knew. Like her sister Isabella, she sought to understand the darkness that was consuming our city. Unlike Isabella, she had not yet embraced it.

"Mr. Harding," she began, her voice steady despite the lateness of the hour. "I trust I'm not disturbing you?"

I gestured for her to sit, noting how she chose the chair furthest from the door to my workroom. Even through the thick oak panels, the wrongness of Lady Margaret's corpse seemed to seep up like a miasma. "Not at all, Miss Blackwood. Though I confess, I'm curious about what brings you here at such an hour."

Her eyes met mine, direct and unflinching. "The same thing that keeps you awake, I imagine. Edward Hyde. Or rather, the creature that wears Edward Hyde's face."

The name hung in the air between us, heavy with implications. I fought the urge to look over my shoulder, half-expecting to see those poison-green eyes gleaming in the shadows. Instead, I reached for the brandy decanter on my desk, pouring us each a measure. The liquid caught the lamplight like blood. Catherine accepted hers with a slight nod but didn't drink.

"I have questions," she continued, her voice dropping lower. "About Lady Margaret's death. The official report will claim it was a robbery gone wrong, as they all do. But we both know the truth is far worse."

I took a long swallow of brandy, letting it burn away my hesitation. "What makes you so certain?"

"Because I saw him, Mr. Harding. The night she died. He was standing beneath her window, his face..." She paused, her composure cracking slightly. "His face was changing, shifting into something... else. The same way Isabella's does now, when she thinks no one is watching."

A chill ran down my spine as I recalled my own observations of Hyde's peculiar nature. The way his shadow sometimes moved independently of his body, how his reflection in mirrors seemed wrong somehow, distorted. And then there were the bodies—each one bearing marks that grew progressively less human. Lady Margaret's wounds were the worst yet, suggesting that whatever Hyde truly was, he was tired of maintaining his mortal masquerade.

"Miss Blackwood," I began carefully, "there are things in this city that defy rational understanding. Things that have always lurked in the shadows of our so-called civilized society, wearing human faces, waiting for the right moment to reveal themselves. Your sister—"

"Is becoming one of them," Catherine finished, her voice tight with suppressed emotion. "I see it happening, day by day. The way she moves, the way she speaks... even her scent is changing. And she's not the only one. Lady Elizabeth's gatherings grow stranger each time, I hear. More guests enter than leave."

I stood, moving to the window that overlooked the fog-shrouded street below. The gas lamps cast sickly halos in the mist, their light seeming to bend wrong around certain shadows. "Perhaps this was inevitable," I mused. "We built our empire on blood and darkness, spread our 'civilization' across the globe like a virus. Did we really think there wouldn't be... consequences?"

A sudden movement caught my eye—a tall figure standing perfectly still beneath the gas lamp across the street. Even through the fog, those green eyes were unmistakable. But now they held something ancient and alien, something that had grown tired of pretending to be human. Hyde raised his hat to me, a gesture both courtly and mocking. When I blinked, he was gone.

"He's watching us," Catherine said softly. She hadn't moved from her chair, but I could see her hands trembling slightly. "Always watching. But why? What game is he playing?"

I turned back to her, noting how the lamplight cast shadows across her face, making her appear older, more haunted. "I fear we're all players in his game, Miss Blackwood. Pawns to be sacrificed at his whim. Your sister's transformation, Lady Margaret's death, the strange metamorphosis spreading through London's elite—it's all connected. All part of some grand design we're only beginning to glimpse."

"No." Her voice was steel now, all trace of fear gone. "I refuse to be a pawn. If Hyde is orchestrating some grand design, then we must uncover it. We must understand what he truly is before we all become like him."

I thought of Lady Margaret's body below, of the inhuman savagery visited upon her flesh. The wounds that seemed to change when I looked at them directly, as if reality itself was becoming fluid, malleable. "Are you certain you want to know? Some truths are better left buried."

Catherine stood, her movements decisive. "Truth is our only weapon against him, Mr. Harding. Will you help me find it?"

I hesitated, weighing the risks. To oppose Hyde was to court destruction—I had seen the evidence of that fact laid out on my embalming table often enough. The progression of bodies told a story of increasing boldness, of a predator growing tired of hiding its true nature. Yet something in Catherine's determination called to me, awakening a resolve I had thought long dead.

"Yes," I said finally. "But we must be cautious. Hyde has eyes everywhere, and not all of them are human anymore. Look at what happened to your sister—"

A crash from the workroom below cut me off. We both froze, listening intently. The sound came again—the distinct clink of metal instruments being disturbed. But underneath that mundane noise was something else—a wet, sliding sound, like flesh moving of its own accord.

"Did you lock the door?" Catherine whispered.

"Always." But even as I spoke, I heard the creak of hinges. Something was coming up the stairs—something that moved with a rhythm that was not quite right, as if it had too many legs, or perhaps none at all.

The gas lamps flickered, their flames dancing wildly though there was no draft. Shadows seemed to coalesce in the corners of my study, taking on shapes that defied natural law. The temperature dropped sharply, our breath misting in the suddenly frigid air. And with that cold came a smell—the same otherworldly stench that rose from Lady Margaret's corpse.

"Mr. Harding." Hyde's voice came from everywhere and nowhere at once, rich with dark amusement. "How discourteous of you to discuss me behind my back. And Miss Blackwood—such dangerous questions you ask. Are you quite sure you want the answers?"

The shadows writhed and twisted, forming into a familiar tall figure. Hyde stepped out of the darkness as if being born from it, his elegant evening dress immaculate save for a few telltale drops of crimson on his cuffs. His smile showed too many teeth, and his eyes... his eyes were no longer even attempting to appear human. They were windows into something vast and ancient, something that had existed in the dark spaces between stars long before humanity crawled from the primordial ooze.

"Now then," he purred, "shall we have a proper conversation about truth and monsters?"

I moved to stand between him and Catherine, though I knew the gesture was futile. One did not shield a lamb from a wolf by merely standing in its way. Yet I had to try, had to maintain some semblance of the rational world I had once believed in.

"There's no need for violence," I said, striving to keep my voice steady. "We were merely—"

"Merely conspiring to uncover my secrets?" Hyde's laugh was like breaking glass. "Oh, my dear undertaker. You've seen what happens to those who pry too deeply into matters that don't concern them. Would you like to join them on your own embalming table? Though I must warn you—Lady Margaret is proving rather... restless."

As if in response, the wet sliding sound from below grew louder. Something was ascending the stairs, something that had once been Lady Margaret Winters but was now a demonstration of what human flesh could become when reality's laws grew fluid.

"If you meant to kill us," Catherine said suddenly, "we'd already be dead. You want something else."

The Devil of London

Hyde's smile widened impossibly, his face beginning to shift and flow like wax in a flame. "Clever girl. Indeed, I have a proposition for you both. A chance to satisfy your curiosity about my true nature. But I warn you—knowledge comes at a price. Are you prepared to pay it?"

I felt Catherine's hand grasp mine, her fingers ice-cold but steady. We both knew this was a turning point, a moment that would forever separate our lives into before and after. The sound on the stairs grew closer, accompanied now by a soft, wet breathing that no human throat could produce.

"We are," Catherine answered for both of us.

Hyde's eyes flared with an unholy light. "Excellent. Then let us begin your education in the true nature of monsters. I do hope you're taking notes, Miss Blackwood. There will be a practical examination later."

The shadows began to move again, coiling around us like living things. The last thing I saw before the darkness swallowed us completely was Hyde's face, his features shifting and flowing into something ancient and terrible. Something that had been wearing humanity like an ill-fitting mask, and had finally grown tired of the pretense.

The real game was about to begin.

CHAPTER 4

L ondon's morning fog carried the acrid scent of coal smoke and fear. I sat at my breakfast table, spreading marmalade on toast with deliberate precision while scanning the early edition of *The Times*. The story Hyde had threatened wasn't there—of course not. That would have been too obvious, too crude for his methods.

"Another cup, miss?" Sarah's hand shook slightly as she lifted the teapot, her gaze darting toward the other papers spread across the table—scandal sheets and society pages, each containing subtle hints of what was to come.

"Yes." I set down *The Times* and picked up *The Morning Post's* society column. Buried among the accounts of last night's balls and dinner parties was a small notice that made my breath catch: *Sir Maximillion Worthington III had been called away on urgent business to his country estate.* Most readers would see nothing significant in this, but I knew better. He was running.

A sharp rap at the door interrupted my reading. Through the parlor window, I caught a glimpse of a boy in a newsboy's cap—one of Hyde's street informants. Sarah returned moments later with a note written on expensive black paper.

My dear Isabella,

Sir Maximillion's hasty departure provides us with an interesting opportunity. It seems our upstanding moral crusader left certain documents unsecured in his haste. I've taken the liberty of arranging their retrieval.

More pressingly, your uncle appears to be arranging a private meeting with Colonel Harrison at his club this afternoon. I thought you might enjoy observing their desperate attempts to salvage their situation. The view from the ladies' tearoom across the street is quite excellent.

Yours in anticipation, H.

P.S.—Do watch tomorrow's papers for news of a tragic accident near the docks. It seems the Morning Star's captain was tragically careless with his evening brandy.

The rustle of grey silk accompanied me through London's fashionable shopping district, my path leading past the gentlemen's club where my uncle sought refuge. Through the tearoom's window, I watched him pace before the club's bay windows, repeatedly checking his pocket watch. His movements were quick, erratic. Desperation had set in.

"Quite the performance, isn't it?" Hyde's voice came from behind me, though I hadn't heard him approach. He seated himself at my table as if we had planned this meeting, every aspect of his appearance perfectly calculated for public consumption. "Colonel Harrison is already an hour late. His body was discovered in his study this morning—apparently, he suffered a fatal apoplexy while reviewing certain damaging documents."

My teacup paused midway to my lips. "Natural causes?"

"Entirely." Hyde's smile was subtle but chilling. "The human heart can be so fragile when faced with... unexpected revelations. I simply ensured the good Colonel had adequate privacy to review the evidence of his crimes. What happened after that was purely a matter of his own conscience."

Through the window, I watched my uncle receive what must have been the news of Harrison's death. His face went ashen, his fingers clenching the back of a nearby chair for support.

"How many others?" I asked quietly.

"The Morning Star's captain will be found tonight—a tragic case of drunken misadventure near the docks. By week's end, certain dock officials will meet with unfortunate accidents. Small players, each death seemingly unconnected." Hyde signaled for tea with an elegant flick of his fingers. "The art, my dear, lies in the pattern. Or rather, in ensuring no pattern is visible until it's far too late."

I thought of Colonel Harrison, alone in his study, evidence of his crimes spread before him. Had he understood, in those final moments, that the brandy Hyde had provided was merely a courtesy—not the actual instrument of his death?

"Sir Maximillion's flight complicates matters," I observed, studying Hyde's reaction.

"On the contrary." He stirred his tea with meticulous movements. "His panic serves our purposes beautifully. Even now, he's destroying evidence, severing ties, burning bridges—doing half our work for us. By the time he realizes his desperate actions have only isolated him further, he'll be perfectly positioned for… retirement."

"And my uncle?"

"Ah, Lord Chancellor Blackwood requires a more… deliberate approach. His position demands a certain delicacy. But watch him now. See how his hands shake? How he keeps looking over his shoulder?" Hyde's satisfaction was almost palpable. "Fear is a poison that works slowly but inexorably. By the time I pay him a personal visit, he'll be quite prepared to embrace whatever end I offer."

A commotion outside drew our attention. A messenger had arrived at the club, delivering urgent news. Even from across the street, I saw my uncle crumple the paper in his fist, his other hand gripping the wall for support.

"Ah." Hyde checked his pocket watch. "News of the Colonial Office's internal investigation has reached him. Amazing how quickly bureaucracy can move when properly motivated."

"The documents Harrison was reviewing?"

"Copies, of course. The originals are quite safe." Hyde's smile didn't reach his eyes. "Though I did ensure the Colonel's personal papers contained just enough evidence to implicate several of his colleagues. The investigation will keep your uncle quite occupied while we attend to other matters."

A police constable appeared outside the club, requesting a word with Lord Chancellor Blackwood. My uncle attempted composure, but the tremor in his hands betrayed him.

"How many more?" I asked softly.

"As many as necessary." Hyde's voice held no emotion. "Though some deaths serve us better than others. Sir Maximillion's flight, for instance, presents an interesting opportunity. A man running from imagined pursuers might meet any number of unfortunate ends."

He withdrew a small black leather notebook, consulting its pages with methodical precision. "At this moment, Sir Maximillion is traveling north by private coach, having paid an exorbitant sum for speed and discretion. He's changed horses twice, each time growing more paranoid about possible pursuit. By nightfall, he'll reach the coaching inn at Blackthorn Cross."

"You've been tracking his movements," I observed.

"My dear, I've been orchestrating them." Hyde's voice carried the ease of a man describing a well-executed play. "Each 'escape route' was carefully suggested by seemingly unconnected sources—a sympathetic clerk at his bank, a worried friend in Parliament, his own trusted secretary. All guiding him toward a specific destination."

Through the window, I saw two more police officers enter the gentlemen's club. My uncle had been moved from the cab to a private room for questioning. His increasingly agitated gestures were visible through the first-floor window.

"Shall we walk?" Hyde suggested, laying a coin on the table for our tea. "The weather is particularly suited to private conversation."

Under my parasol, we strolled through Mayfair's damp streets, the rain casting an eerie hush over the city. The usual afternoon shoppers had retreated indoors, leaving the pavements nearly empty. Ideal for discussions that should not be overheard.

"You seem troubled, my dear," Hyde observed, guiding me around a particularly deep puddle. "Having second thoughts about our methods?"

"No." I watched a police carriage rattle past toward the Colonial Office. "I'm merely... appreciating the complexity of your web. Each thread so carefully placed, yet invisible until too late."

He smiled, the expression sharp as a blade. "The best traps are the ones the prey walks into willingly. Speaking of which..." He paused, consulting his pocket watch. "I believe we have an appointment to keep. One that might interest you particularly."

I recognized the street ahead—the offices of my father's former solicitor. The very man who had handled the disgraceful proceedings after Father's death, ensuring our family's ruin was complete.

"Mr. Hartwell has been making inquiries," Hyde said casually. "Unwise ones. About shipping companies, banking records… even certain events three years ago."

My grip tightened on my parasol. "Has he indeed?"

"Oh yes," Hyde murmured, eyes gleaming. "And tonight, he will learn just how unfortunate curiosity can be."

Chapter 5

They found Hartwell's body the next morning, meticulously arranged in his office chair. His expression suggested he had seen something far worse than death in his final moments. The morning papers called it heart failure—an unremarkable end for a respectable solicitor. Only I noticed the faint marks on his throat, the slightly too-perfect positioning of his hands on the desk.

"Crude," Hyde remarked, studying the article over my shoulder. He had appeared in my parlor unannounced, immaculate as always in morning dress that somehow made other men's clothes look shabby by comparison. "The police surgeon is becoming careless. Those marks should have been better concealed."

"You killed him." It wasn't a question.

"Of course." He smiled, that terrible, gentle expression that meant someone else would die soon. "Though I'd say his heart did technically fail. Fear can do such interesting things to the human body, especially when one sees... impossible things."

I thought of that figure in the fog, the familiar way it moved, the wrongness about its features. "What I saw last night—"

"Was a carefully crafted illusion, nothing more." Hyde's voice held a warning edge. "Though Hartwell's reaction to it proved most illuminating. The guilty see such interesting things in their final moments."

Before I could press further, he held up a hand. "But come—we have an appointment to keep. Sir Maximillion has reached Blackthorn Cross, and I believe you'll want to witness what happens next."

The inn at Blackthorn Cross perched on the edge of a cliff, its windows overlooking a hundred-foot drop to jagged rocks below. We arrived just as dusk was falling, the heavy clouds promising another night of rain. Through the tavern's grimy windows, I could see Sir Maximillion at a corner table, flinching at every sound. His elegant clothes were travel-stained, his usually immaculate appearance disheveled by desperate flight.

"Watch," Hyde murmured, guiding me to a hidden vantage point. "See how he keeps looking toward the back door? Counting his escape routes. The brandy in front of him is his third—Dutch courage for the journey he thinks he's about to make."

A boy entered the tavern—one of Hyde's street informants, now dressed as a rural messenger. He handed Sir Maximillion a note, then quickly departed. Even from our position, I could see the man's hands shake as he read its contents.

"What news did you send him?"

Hyde's smile was predatory. "A warning that officers are approaching from London. And a suggestion of a 'safe' path through the cliffs—one that local smugglers supposedly use."

Thunder rumbled in the distance as we watched Sir Maximillion drain his glass with shaking hands. The brandy had brought a flush to his cheeks, but his eyes darted frantically between the inn's entrance and the back door leading to the cliffs.

"The brandy, of course, has been doctored," Hyde continued conversationally. "Nothing fatal—merely something to make his feet a little less steady, his judgment a touch more uncertain. Essential, when navigating treacherous paths in the dark."

As if on cue, hoofbeats sounded on the road from London. Sir Maximillion lurched to his feet, throwing coins on the table before hurrying toward the back door. The storm was breaking in earnest now, rain lashing against the windows.

"Shall we?" Hyde offered his arm, leading me through a side door and into the gathering darkness. The path he chose brought us to a vantage point above the cliffs, hidden from the main trail by a stand of twisted trees.

Below, we could see Sir Maximillion stumbling along the cliff path, one hand trailing against the rock face for balance. The rain had made the chalk treacherous, and the wind whipped his coat around his legs. Every few steps, he would pause, peering back toward the inn through the gloom.

"Watch carefully," Hyde murmured. "This is how justice truly works—not in courtrooms or prison cells, but in moments like these, when a man's own guilt drives him toward his doom."

A figure appeared on the path behind Sir Maximillion—another of Hyde's agents, I presumed, though distance and darkness made it hard to be certain. The sight of a pursuer had exactly the effect Hyde had predicted. Sir Maximillion's pace quickened, becoming more reckless with each step.

"The chalk here is particularly unstable," Hyde observed as our quarry approached a narrow section of the path. "Especially after rain. Local authorities have been warning about the danger of landslides for years."

Sir Maximillion reached the narrowest point, where the path curved around an outcropping. The drop below was sheer, waves crashing against razor-sharp rocks. He paused, swaying slightly as the drugged brandy took full effect.

Then I saw it—another figure, this one ahead on the path. Like the one I'd glimpsed in London, it moved with a terrible familiarity. Even through the rain, I could make out the distinctive posture of...

"Father?" I whispered.

Sir Maximillion saw it too. His scream of terror cut through the storm as he staggered backward, arms windmilling frantically. The rain-soaked chalk crumbled beneath his feet.

"Don't look away," Hyde's voice was hard. "This is what justice looks like, Isabella. This is what you wanted."

I forced myself to watch as Sir Maximillion fell, his cry fading into the crash of waves below. The figure that had appeared on the path was gone—if it had ever been there at all.

"An unfortunate accident," Hyde said with satisfaction. "The local authorities will find his body tomorrow or the next day, assuming the tide returns it. A tragic case of a desperate man taking a dangerous path in poor weather."

"And the… the figure he saw?"

Hyde's expression was unreadable in the darkness. "Guilt has many faces, my dear. Sometimes they wear familiar features." He checked his pocket watch by a flash of lightning. "Now, shall we return to London? We have another appointment to keep."

The journey back gave me time to contemplate what I'd just witnessed. Sir Maximillion's scream still echoed in my ears, but what disturbed me more was my own reaction to his death. I had felt no horror, no revulsion—only a deep satisfaction.

Hyde seemed to read my thoughts. "The first death is always the most… memorable. Though technically, I suppose Hartwell was your first."

"I didn't kill Hartwell," I protested, though even as I said it, I knew it wasn't entirely true.

"Didn't you?" Hyde's voice was soft in the carriage's darkness. "You knew what would happen. You could have warned him. Instead, you watched, and in watching, became part of it." His hand found mine. "Tell me, did you enjoy it? The moment when he realized there was no escape?"

I should have pulled away. Should have been horrified by the question. Instead, I found myself remembering Hartwell's expression before the end. "Yes," I whispered.

Hyde's satisfaction was almost palpable. "Good. Because our next target will require more… direct participation from you."

The carriage entered a darker part of the city. When we stopped, Hyde helped me down before a narrow house wedged between two larger buildings.

"Mr. Douglas Phillips," Hyde explained. "Former clerk to the East India Company. He was there the night your father died. Make him confess before the end."

The single light burning in the upper window felt like an invitation.

"Shall we?" Hyde murmured, his smile terrible in the lamplight.

CHAPTER 6

The wrought iron gates of the cemetery groaned as I, Thomas Harding, slipped through them. My footsteps sank into the damp earth, as if the ground itself sought to muffle my intrusion. The lantern in my grasp cast flickering light, animating the gravestones with grotesque shadows that twisted and stretched like grasping fingers. The air was thick with the scent of damp soil, decaying leaves, and something more elusive—a faint whisper of something long buried yet not forgotten.

Rows of tombstones stood like weary sentinels beneath a sky smeared with ink-black clouds. The twisted, skeletal branches of the oaks rattled overhead as though murmuring secrets among themselves. The wind howled through the graveyard, slipping between the mausoleums and crypts, carrying the echoes of the past. It was a place that thrived on silence, where time stretched long and thin, its fabric fraying at the edges.

The narrow paths between the graves were treacherous, slick with wet leaves and half-concealed roots that reached up like the grasping hands of the forgotten. Each step was a decision, every movement a risk. My breath was shallow, my heart a relentless drum against my ribs. The note from Edward Hyde burned in my pocket, a sinister promise pressed against my skin. "Beneath the stone lies the truth, Harding. Dare you seek it?"

A shadow of hesitation flitted across my thoughts. My professional discretion had shielded me for years, allowed me to walk the fine line between morality and necessity. But Hyde's message had disturbed something deep within me, unearthed a compulsion stronger than my own survival. This was not just curiosity; it was a compulsion, an inevitable descent.

A gust of wind moaned through the graveyard, rattling the wrought iron fence and sending a shower of brittle leaves tumbling over the graves. The lantern flickered wildly, shadows stretching long and sinister. I pressed forward, deeper into the heart of darkness.

The grave loomed before me, its limestone headstone worn and fractured, as though time itself had tried to erase it. "ELIZABETH FEATHERSTONE, Born 1765 - Departed 1791." A mere twenty-six years in this world. The inscription, though partially eroded, spoke of a life that had barely begun. The damp earth beneath my boots clung to my soles, as if the very ground conspired to hold me back.

A shudder of unease curled along my spine. I reached into my coat, fingers brushing against Hyde's note. "Beneath Featherstone's stone, you'll find what you seek. The key to Worthington's undoing and your redemption." The word haunted me—redemption. A glimmer of absolution dangled before me, tantalizing yet laced with peril. Could it be true? Or was I merely another pawn in Hyde's malicious games?

A rustle from behind froze me. My pulse hammered in my ears as I spun, lantern held high, heart leaping into my throat. A figure emerged from the shadows, her silhouette spectral in the lantern's glow. Isabella Blackwood, her gown the deep shade of a bruised sky, her piercing eyes reflecting the flickering light like polished onyx. The mist curled around her, as though reluctant to let her pass.

"Mr. Harding," she said, her voice smooth as silk yet edged with something sharper. "What an unexpected pleasure. I scarcely thought to find you in such a place at such an hour."

I swallowed hard, my throat dry as dust. "Lady Blackwood. You startled me."

She stepped closer, her movements graceful yet deliberate. "Clearly. But tell me, what brings a man of your profession to this grave under cover of darkness?"

My mind raced. How much did she know? Had she seen the note? Or was she merely acting on suspicion? Her composed demeanor revealed nothing, yet I knew the keen intelligence beneath her refined exterior.

"I might ask the same of you, my lady," I countered, my grip tightening on the lantern's handle.

A smirk ghosted across her lips. "Touché, Mr. Harding. But I believe you'll find my reasons pale in comparison to yours." She glanced at the headstone, then back at me. "Does this late-night excursion involve a certain Edward Hyde?"

The sound of his name sent a shiver down my spine. I could still see the last poor soul he'd sent my way, throat slit from ear to ear, blood soaking into the very cracks of my workshop floor.

I looked back at Isabella, the lantern trembling in my grasp. "Lady Blackwood, what do you know of Edward Hyde?"

Her smile widened, her teeth flashing white in the gloom. "More than I should. And certainly more than I care to. But I suspect that you, too, have knowledge of that man's dark deeds. And I would very much like to know what brings you here, to this grave, tonight."

Her voice was low, insistent. I felt like a mouse trapped in the gaze of a serpent, drawn in by her promise of shared secrets. And as I stood there, the lantern flickering between us, I realized that I had a choice to make—one that could lead me further into the abyss or offer a glimmer of salvation.

A gust of wind rattled the cemetery's iron gate. Isabella's eyes never left mine. "If you seek truth, Mr. Harding, we should not waste time. The night is not infinite."

I hesitated, then nodded. With slow, deliberate movements, I knelt and began clawing at the damp soil, my fingers sinking into the earth like flesh yielding to a blade. The wet ground resisted, as if it knew the secrets it held should remain buried.

Isabella knelt beside me, skirts billowing. "What do you suppose we shall find?"

I swallowed hard. "Something Hyde does not want us to see."

And then my fingers brushed against something solid. Ornate. Heavy. My breath caught in my throat. I brushed away the remaining dirt, revealing a small, carved box. The lantern light gleamed against its intricate designs, shifting in the damp air like living filigree.

Isabella leaned closer, her breath shallow. "It appears we have found our prize."

With a deep breath, I reached for the latch, hesitating only a moment before lifting the lid. Inside lay a collection of documents, edges yellowed with age, their surfaces covered in a spidery, elegant script. Beside them, folded neatly, was a handkerchief stained dark with dried blood.

A chill ran down my spine. The weight of the discovery settled over me like a shroud. "These papers... they implicate Worthington. And Hyde."

Isabella's expression did not change, but her fingers tightened around the edge of the box. "Then we must tread carefully, Mr. Harding. We have uncovered something dangerous. And men like Hyde do not let secrets go unanswered."

I exhaled, shaking off the cold dread creeping through me. The cemetery, shrouded in mist, seemed to watch as we exchanged a look of silent agreement.

"Then we proceed," I murmured. "But we do so with caution."

The iron gate groaned in the distance as if echoing my resolve. Without another word, Isabella and I parted ways at the cemetery entrance. She disappeared into the night, her silhouette swallowed by the mist. I turned down the slick streets, the shadows stretching long beneath the gaslights. My lodgings were in the older part of the city, where the air hung thick with the mingling scents of damp brick, soot, and the acrid tang of industry.

By the time I reached my door, exhaustion gnawed at me. Inside, I bolted the lock, my breath slow and heavy. The silence of my rooms was oppressive, yet comforting. I pressed my back against the door, heart still hammering. The weight of what I had discovered, what I had seen, settled over me. For now, I was safe. But for how long?

CHAPTER 7

In the heart of London, where the fog crept through the cobbled streets like a spectral serpent, I, Sir Maximillion Worthington III, stood at the head of a grand table, a monolith of polished mahogany that stretched out before me like a battlefield. The room, a cavernous affair adorned with the trappings of wealth and power, was filled with the scent of beeswax candles and the faint tang of smoke from the nearby factories. The gas lamps cast a flickering light over the assembled faces, a mix of anticipation and skepticism etched into their features.

"Gentlemen," I began, my voice echoing through the chamber like a roll of thunder. "We stand on the precipice of change, a sweeping reform that shall cleanse our city of its moral decay." My hands, clasped firmly behind my back, hid the slight tremor that betrayed my inner turmoil. The gold pocket watch in my waistcoat ticked steadily, a comforting reminder of the passage of time, a constant in a world of variables.

I surveyed the committee members, their eyes glinting in the dim light like those of rats in a dark alley. There was Lord Harrington, his jowls quivering with each breath, a man more concerned with his next meal than the plight of the poor. Beside him sat Mr. Blackwood, a gaunt figure with sunken cheeks, his fingers stained with ink from countless hours poring over ledgers. His eyes held a gleam of curiosity, a willingness to be convinced.

"Our streets are rife with vice," I continued, my voice rising with the fervor of my convictions. "Prostitution, opium dens, the exploitation of the weak—it is a plague upon our society, a cancer that must be excised." The words tasted like ash in my mouth, a bitter reminder of my own hypocrisy. The image of my private dens, hidden away from prying eyes, flashed through my mind—a stark contrast to the moral high ground I now claimed.

The room was thick with tension, the air heavy with the weight of my words. I could feel the scrutiny of the gathered elite, their gazes boring into me like needles. Lord Harrington shifted uncomfortably in his seat, his doublet creaking with the strain. Mr. Blackwood leaned forward, his eyes narrowing as he considered my proposals.

"We must establish stricter regulations, enforce harsher penalties," I declared, my voice resonating with authority. "Our charitable institutions must be held accountable, their funds directed towards true reform, not lined pockets." The irony of my statement was not lost on me; my own pockets had grown heavy with the spoils of embezzlement, a secret shame that gnawed at the edges of my consciousness.

As I spoke, the memories of my private indiscretions threatened to surface, a dark undercurrent beneath my polished exterior. The opium dens, the whispered secrets, the blood—always the blood. The streets of London were stained with it, a grim testament to the violence that lurked in the shadows. The murders, brutal and senseless, had begun to haunt my dreams, a specter that refused to be silenced.

I pushed the thoughts aside, focusing on the task at hand. The committee members watched me with a mix of awe and doubt, their expressions a mirror of the conflict within me. I could see the wheels turning in their minds, the calculations and considerations that would determine the fate of my proposals.

"Gentlemen," I said, my voice dropping to a low, commanding register. "The time for idle talk has passed. We must act, and we must act now. The future of our city, of our very souls, depends upon it." The room fell silent, the only sound the distant rumble of the city beyond the walls. The weight of their gazes pressed down upon me, a physical force that threatened to crush my resolve.

But I stood firm, my hands clasped tightly behind my back, my chin held high. I was Sir Maximillion Worthington III, the honorable chairman, the reform champion—a man of contradictions, a study in calculated deceit. And as I looked out over the assembled faces, I knew that the true battle was not in the streets of London, but within the chambers of my own heart.

The grand table, a sprawling beast of polished mahogany, stretched out before me like a battleground, the committee members its reluctant soldiers. Their faces, a blur of powdered wigs and skeptical scowls, reflected the dancing flames of the chandelier above. The air was thick with tension, the scent of beeswax candles mingling with the sweet, cloying aroma of snuff and pipe smoke.

I had just finished outlining my proposals, the echo of my voice still lingering in the silence, when the heavy oak doors of the chamber creaked open with an ominous groan. The hairs on the back of my neck stood on end, a primal response to the sudden shift in atmosphere. All eyes turned to the entrance, where a figure stood, silhouetted against the dimly lit hallway.

Edward Hyde stepped into the light, his magnetic green eyes scanning the room with a predatory intensity. His gaze was like a physical force, drawing the attention of every man present, including myself. A shiver ran down my spine, an involuntary reaction to the aura of menace that surrounded him like a dark cloak.

He was dressed impeccably, his tall, elegant form swathed in a black frock coat that seemed to absorb the light around him. The lace at his cuffs and throat was as dark as a murder victim's blood, stark against the pale silk of his waistcoat. His breeches were likewise black, tucked into boots polished to a gleaming shine. The only colour about him was the emerald of his eyes and the silver that touched his temples, a distinguishing feature that did nothing to soften his harsh, aristocratic face.

A murmur rippled through the assembly, the committee members shifting uncomfortably in their seats as Hyde moved further into the room. His every step was deliberate, a panther stalking its prey, and I could not help but feel a frisson of unease as those hypnotic eyes met mine.

"Ah, Worthington," he purred, his voice a rich, melodious sound that seemed to wrap around my very soul. "A reform committee, how quaint. I trust you are discussing more than just the width of cobblestone streets and the placement of gas lamps?"

His words, though spoken in elegant tones, carried a hint of mockery that set my teeth on edge. I watched as he moved gracefully around the table, acknowledging the other members with a nod or a brief word. Each man he passed seemed to shrink into himself, their eyes following Hyde with a mix of fear and fascination.

My mind raced as I tried to discern his purpose here. Hyde was not a man to act without reason, and his presence at this meeting could bode nothing but ill. I had heard the whispers, the rumours of his involvement in the darker side of London's underbelly. Tales of bodies found in alleyways, throats slit from ear to ear, the cobblestones slick with blood that ran like rivers towards the Thames. And always, always, the faint scent of sandalwood and bergamot lingering in the air, a chilling calling card that spoke of Hyde's presence.

As he continued his circuit of the table, I could not help but feel a growing sense of dread. His dark charisma was palpable, a tangible force that seemed to suck the very air from the room. I had faced many a formidable opponent in my political career, but none quite like Edward Hyde.

He paused at the end of the table, his eyes locked onto mine, a knowing smile playing at the corners of his mouth. "You have our undivided attention, Worthington," he said, his voice laced with a chilling amusement. "Do continue."

I swallowed hard, my mouth suddenly dry as the Sahara. The room seemed to tilt beneath my feet, and I grasped the edge of the table for support. The committee members watched me, their expressions a mix of anticipation and unease. I knew I must regain control, steer the conversation back to my proposals, but the words seemed to stick in my throat, held captive by the power of Hyde's gaze.

The grand table, a slab of polished mahogany, stretched out before me like a chasm, the committee members mere shadows along its edges, their faces a blur of anticipation and skepticism. My hands, clasped behind my back, betrayed the slightest tremor, a secret battle against the opium's withdrawal, a condition I prayed remained hidden from prying eyes. The wavering flames of the gas lamps cast eerie dances on the wood-paneled walls, as if the very room anticipated the storm that Hyde's entrance had promised.

Hyde lowered himself into the leather chair at the far end of the table, his movements deliberate and unhurried. His dark coat, tailored to perfection, seemed to absorb the light, giving him the appearance of a specter, a phantom conjured from the shadows. I felt a flicker of apprehension, a cold finger tracing my spine, as his hypnotic eyes remained fixed upon me.

His voice, smooth and controlled, cut through the silence like a honed blade. "You paint a most noble picture, Worthington," he began, his lips curling into a semblance of a smile. "A London freed from the shackles of vice and corruption. Yet, I cannot help but wonder if your... enthusiasms are not perhaps born from a desire to exorcise your own demons."

I felt the blood drain from my face, my cheeks growing cold as his words struck home. A vision flashed before my eyes—a dimly lit opium den, the air thick with smoke and the scent of sweet oblivion. The memory of my own weakness gripped me, a vice around my heart.

His eyes never left mine, his gaze a physical force, pinning me in place. "After all," he continued, his voice barely above a whisper, yet commanding the room, "we are all slaves to our passions, are we not? Some of us merely hide them better than others."

His words were laced with subtle hints, a dance around the truth that only I understood. The room seemed to grow darker, the shadows encroaching, as if drawn by his presence. I could see it then, the faint outline of his true nature, the monster lurking beneath the polished veneer. I had heard the whispers, the tales of blood-soaked cobblestones and the scent of sandalwood and bergamot lingering in the air like a chilling calling card.

My composure began to falter, the carefully constructed facade of Sir Maximillion Worthington III crumbling under the weight of his scrutiny. I felt a bead of sweat trickle down my spine, a cold rivulet that seemed to trace the path of my own impending downfall. His words were a noose, tightening around my neck, threatening to expose the rot that festered beneath my polished exterior.

I thought I saw it then, a flicker of red in his eyes, a reflection of the blood that stained his hands. The room seemed to tilt, the gas lamps flickering like dying stars, as I grappled with the reality of the monster before me. He was a predator, a wolf in sheep's clothing, and I was his prey, frozen in his sights, my own sins binding me in place.

His smile widened, a grotesque parody of mirth, as if he could see the very thoughts that raced through my mind. "But perhaps, dear

Worthington," he said, his voice a low purr, "you are the exception. Perhaps you are the saint that can save us all."

His words were a challenge, a gauntlet thrown, and I knew then that this was a battle for my soul, a fight for my very survival. And as I stood there, my hands trembling and my heart pounding, I knew that I was fighting for more than just my political ambitions—I was fighting for my life.

The grand table, once a platform for my unshakeable confidence, now felt like a fragile barrier between me and the encroaching darkness. Hyde's words still hung in the air, a foul miasma that seemed to taint the very atmosphere of the room. I could feel the weight of his gaze, those hypnotic green eyes boring into me, as if he could see the very secrets that I had so carefully buried. My hands, clasped behind my back, trembled like autumn leaves, the slight tremor that I had always been able to hide now growing into a storm that threatened to consume me.

"Gentlemen," I began, my voice faltering like a worn-out phonograph. I cleared my throat, attempting to regain the authoritative tone that had once come so naturally. "We must not allow ourselves to be distracted from the task at hand. Our purpose here is to forge a new path for our great city, to sweep away the corruption and decay that has taken root in its streets."

I could hear the hollow ring in my own words, the faint echo of desperation that belied my attempt at command. My eyes flicked to the other committee members, their expressions a mix of concern and unease. They could see it too, the cracks in my facade, the chinks in my armor that Hyde had so expertly exploited.

I felt a bead of sweat trickle down my spine, a cold and clammy sensation that made me shiver despite the warmth of the room. My collar, once crisp and white, now felt like a noose, tightening around my neck, threatening to choke the very life from my body. I could feel the panic rising within me, a dark tide that threatened to overwhelm my senses.

As I struggled to maintain my composure, I could see Jonathan Hartwell from the corner of my eye. His tall, lean frame was poised like a bird of prey, his keen, analytical gaze darting between Hyde and myself. His aristocratic features were a mask of calm, but I could see the subtle signs of his own agitation—the slight tremor in his normally steady hands, the shadows that lurked beneath his eyes, the nervous tic that played at the corner of his mouth.

The Devil of London

I could almost see the cogs turning in his mind, the wheels of his intellect spinning as he calculated the threat and opportunity that Hyde presented. His dark hair, perfectly groomed as always, seemed to gleam in the gaslight like the feathers of a raven, a harbinger of doom or a symbol of cunning, I could not tell which.

His eyes, sharp and piercing, seemed to miss nothing, taking in every nuance of the exchange, every flicker of emotion that played across my face. I could see the ambition that burned within him, the ruthless drive that had carried him to the heights of his profession, but I could also see the paranoia that gnawed at his edges, the fear that he was losing control of the game that he had played for so long.

I could see the images that haunted his thoughts, the blood-soaked memories of Hyde's victims, the twisted bodies that littered the streets of London like discarded dolls. I could see the faces of the dead, their glassy eyes and gaping wounds, the crimson trails that led back to the monster that sat before us, his hands stained with the blood of the innocent.

I could see the struggle within him, the battle between his desire for power and his growing unease at the cost of his dealings with Hyde. I could see the shadows that lurked in the corners of his mind, the dark whispers that threatened to consume him, the same shadows that now threatened to consume me.

As I stood there, my heart pounding and my breath coming in ragged gasps, I knew that I was not alone in my fear, not alone in my struggle against the darkness that Hyde embodied. But I also knew that I was running out of time, that the sands of my hourglass were slipping away, that the noose around my neck was growing ever tighter. And as I looked out at the sea of faces before me, I knew that I was fighting for more than just my political ambitions—I was fighting for my life, for my soul, for my very sanity.

The grand table, a sprawling beast of polished mahogany, stretched out before me like a chasm, separating me from the rest of the Reform Committee. The room, heavy with tension, seemed to close in around us, the very air thick with the scent of beeswax candles and the tangible unease that had settled like a pall upon the gathering. Worthington, his face a mask of barely concealed distress, stood at the head of the table, his knuckles white as he gripped the edge, his voice echoing through the chamber like a distant thunder, struggling to maintain its erstwhile authority.

I, Jonathan Hartwell, observed this spectacle with a keen, analytical eye, my mind racing as I weighed the implications of Hyde's presence. The man was a conundrum, a dark enigma who had swept into our midst like a chill wind, his hypnotic green eyes missing nothing, his every movement calculated, precise. He was a predator, a shark amidst minnows, and the blood in the water was ours. Yet, amidst the fear, there lurked opportunity, a chance to harness the power he wielded, to steer the course of this storm.

Hyde, seated with an almost casual elegance, his dark form a stark contrast to the nervous energy that surrounded him, watched Worthington with an amused, almost indulgent expression. I could see the faint curve of his lips, the knowing smile that played at the corners of his mouth, as if he were privy to some secret jest. The committee members, their faces a tableau of unease, exchanged furtive glances, their discomfort palpable.

I leaned forward, my elbows resting on the table, my fingers steepled before me, a pose that conveyed calm consideration, even as my mind raced. "Mr. Hyde," I began, my voice measured, each word carefully chosen, a lawyer's weapon in the dance of rhetoric. "You speak of... changes. Of reform, as it were. Pray, enlighten us as to your particular... interests in this endeavor. What, sir, is your stake in this grand game of politics?"

Hyde turned his gaze to me, his eyes meeting mine with a force that was almost physical. His smile never wavered, yet seemed to deepen, as if he welcomed the challenge, the thrust and parry of verbal sparring. "Ah, Mr. Hartwell," he replied, his voice a smooth, cultured purr. "Ever the astute observer. My interests, you ask? Let us say that I have a... vested stake in the well-being of this great city. Its streets, its alleys, its dark corners, they are all dear to me. I wish to see them... prosper."

His words, laced with ambiguity, did little to clarify his intentions. Instead, they served only to deepen the mystery that surrounded him, to cast longer shadows on the already murky waters of his motives. I could feel the tension in the room ratchet up, like the turning of a screw, as the committee members exchanged uneasy glances, their faces pale, their eyes wide with barely concealed apprehension.

I could see it then, the flicker of images, the echoes of Hyde's dark deeds, the crimson trails that led back to him, the blood that stained his hands, the shadows that clung to him like a shroud. I could see the bodies, the discarded dolls that littered the streets, their glassy eyes and gaping wounds, the silent testimony to Hyde's brutal efficiency. And I could see the fear, the creeping terror that gnawed at the edges of our minds, the dark whispers that threatened to consume us all.

Yet, amidst the fear, there burned a spark of ambition, a flame that refused to be extinguished. For in Hyde's presence, in the face of his dark charisma, his sophisticated menace, there lay opportunity. A chance to harness his power, to bend it to my will, to ride the storm and emerge triumphant. It was a dangerous game, a dance on the edge of a blade, but I was no stranger to risk, no novice to the machinations of power. And so, with a calm I did not feel, I met Hyde's gaze, his hypnotic green eyes, and I smiled, a silent acceptance of the challenge, a tacit acknowledgement of the game afoot. The dance had begun, the pieces were in motion, and I, Jonathan Hartwell, would play my part, come what may.

The grand table, a slab of polished mahogany, stretched out before me like a battlefield, the committee members my reluctant soldiers. I stood at its head, my hands clasped behind my back to still the slight tremor that threatened to betray my nerves. The room, a cavernous affair with walls adorned with the gilt-framed portraits of my predecessors, seemed to close in around me, the air thick with tension and the sweet scent of beeswax candles.

"Gentlemen," I began, my voice echoing in the chamber, a desperate edge creeping into my measured tone. "We must not waver from our course. Our city cries out for reform, her streets choked with the destitute and the depraved. We must sweep away the filth, banish the shadows that lurk in her alleys and courts." I could feel the weight of their gazes upon me, the mix of anticipation and skepticism that hung in the air like a miasma. My waistcoat, a garment of rich brocade, suddenly felt too tight, my cravat a noose about my neck.

I could see it in their eyes, the flicker of doubt, the nagging worm of uncertainty that Hyde's presence had planted. Lord Ashbury, a corpulent man with a penchant for snuff, avoided my gaze, his plump fingers drumming a nervous tattoo on the table. Sir Reginald, usually my staunchest ally, looked away, his eyes fixed on the middle distance, his lips pursed as if he had tasted something sour.

"We must not allow ourselves to be distracted by... baser elements," I continued, my voice rising, a hint of desperation seeping in like blood through a bandage. "Our cause is just, our purpose pure. We shall not be swayed by those who would seek to drag us down into the mire, who would have us wallow in the gutters with the whores and the murderers."

Hyde's words echoed in my mind, his silken threats coiling about my thoughts like a serpent. The bodies in the streets, the glassy eyes, the gaping wounds... the blood that stained his hands. I could see it, crimson and vivid, a stark contrast to the white lace at his cuffs, the elegant cut of his coat. A shiver ran down my spine, a phantom chill that gnawed at my bones.

I could feel my control slipping, my authority ebbing like the tide. The committee members shifted in their seats, their bodies turning inward, away from me, a subtle but unmistakable sign of their waning confidence. Lord Blackwood, his gaunt face a map of shadows, leaned back in his chair, his fingers steepled before him, his eyes narrowed in thought. Or calculation.

"We must stand united," I declared, my voice ringing out, a clarion call that fell on deaf ears. I could hear the pleading note that undercut my words, the faint whiff of desperation that clung to them like the stink of the Thames. "Together, we shall forge a new path, a brighter future for our city, for our people."

But my impassioned speech fell flat, my words empty vessels that clattered to the floor, hollow and meaningless. The unease that gripped the room was palpable, a living thing that squirmed and writhed, feeding on the doubts that Hyde had sown. I could see it in their faces, the subtle shifts in their expressions, the tightening of a jaw, the furrowing of a brow. They were questioning, not just my leadership, but my very stability.

I felt a pang of despair, a bitter taste on my tongue. My vision of reform, my grand designs for the city, were slipping through my fingers like sand, the grains falling away, lost to the shadows that Hyde had cast. I was losing them, my committee, my championed cause, my carefully cultivated image. And all I could see, as I looked out over the battlefield of the table, were the glassy eyes of the dead, their silent testimony to Hyde's brutal efficiency, and the creeping terror that gnawed at the edges of my mind.

The grand table, once a platform for my unshakable vision, now stretched before me like a chasm, swallowing the echoes of my faltering voice. The room, heavy with the stench of beeswax candles and the tangible doubt of my colleagues, seemed to close in around me. The gilded walls, adorned with the portraits of my august forebears, now felt like a mausoleum, their eyes following me with what I imagined to be reproach.

Hyde, the serpent who had slithered into our midst, now rose from his seat with a sinuous grace that made my stomach churn. His eyes, those hypnotic green orbs, swept over the assembly with a cool detachment, as if he were already dismissing us from his thoughts. "Gentlemen," he said, his voice like velvet, "I fear I have other... engagements to attend to." He paused, his gaze lingering on me, a cruel smile playing at the corners of his mouth. "But do give my regards to the good people of the city. I am certain they will appreciate your... reforms."

As he turned to leave, the candlelight caught the silver threads at his temples, and the bloody ruby at his throat seemed to wink like a malevolent eye. His cloak, as dark as a moonless night, billowed behind him like a shroud, and I could not help but recall the tales of his nocturnal prowls, the bodies left in his wake, throats slit from ear to ear, their lifeblood drained like that of a pig at slaughter.

The door clicked shut behind him, but the sense of dread that had entered with him lingered like a malignant fog. I could feel it, cold and clammy against my skin, seeping into my very bones. The room seemed darker, the shadows longer, as if Hyde's departure had robbed the very air of its vitality.

I looked out over the committee, their faces a blur of pale skin and worried eyes. They seemed to waver, like reflections in a pool of blood, their confidence in me, in our cause, hemorrhaging like a wound that would not close. I could see it in Lord Blackwood's tightened jaw, in Sir Reginald's furrowed brow, in the way Lady Harrington's gloved hands twisted in her lap.

I grasped the edge of the table, the polished wood slick beneath my damp palms. "Gentlemen, Lady Harrington," I began, my voice sounding distant and strange to my own ears. "We must not allow ourselves to be swayed by... outside influences. Our cause is just, our purpose true." I heard the pleading note in my voice, tasted the bitterness of desperation on my tongue.

"Our city is a festering wound," I continued, "its streets teeming with vice and corruption. We have the power to cauterize that wound, to burn away the rot and build something new, something better." I looked from face to face, searching for a spark of conviction, a glimmer of the passion that had once united us.

But all I saw was uncertainty, a shadow that seemed to grow larger, darker, with every passing moment. Hyde's influence, like a stain spreading on silk, threatened to engulf us all. I felt a shiver run down my spine, a cold sweat break out on my forehead. The room seemed to tilt, the floor shifting beneath my feet like the deck of a ship in a storm.

"We must stand together," I implored, my knuckles white as I gripped the table. "We must not let this... this shadow divide us. We must fight, must strive for the light, for the dawn of a new age."

But even as I spoke, I could feel the darkness closing in, Hyde's chilling whisper echoing in my mind like the laughter of the damned. And I knew, with a terrible, sinking certainty, that our cause, our grand vision, was balanced on the edge of a blade, and that blade was held in the hand of Edward Hyde.

CHAPTER 8

The carriage rumbled to a halt, and I, Annabelle Blake, stepped out onto the cobblestone drive, my heart aflutter with a mix of anticipation and trepidation. Before me loomed the grand entrance of Thornwood Mansion, its imposing facade a stark silhouette against the moonlit sky. The soft glow of candlelight spilled from the windows, casting elongated shadows that danced macabrely on the stone exterior. The mansion seemed to leer at me, its countless windows like eyes that bore into my very soul.

I took a deep breath, the crisp autumn air filling my lungs as I approached the entrance. The heavy oak doors were adorned with ornate carvings that twisted and writhed in the flickering light, depicting scenes of ancient hunts and battles. The craftsmanship was exquisite, yet unsettling—the figures seemed almost to shift in the candlelight, whispering untold stories of triumph and betrayal. A shiver ran down my spine, as if the very doors whispered tales of darkness and deceit. The closer I got, the more aware I became of the weight of unseen eyes, the presence of something lurking just beyond the veil of light and civility.

As I crossed the threshold, warmth enveloped me, carrying with it the hum of conversation and the clinking of glasses. The vibrant atmosphere of the soirée was a stark contrast to the chilling exterior, and I found myself immediately immersed in a sea of elegantly dressed guests. The ladies were resplendent in silk gowns, a symphony of rich colors and shimmering fabrics that caught the light with every movement. The gentlemen, likewise, were attired in fine tailcoats and breeches, their polished boots reflecting the glow of the chandeliers above. Their laughter was easy, yet their eyes were sharp, watchful, calculating. Every flicker of an eyelash, every measured pause in conversation carried layers of meaning, a silent game being played beneath the surface.

I took a moment to compose myself, drawing on the lessons imparted by Isabella Blackwood. Her voice echoed in my mind, a steady guide amidst the whirlwind of sensation. "Maintain your poise, Annabelle," she would say, her deep blue eyes holding a knowing darkness. "Observe, listen, and never let them see your true intentions."

With a careful, measured step, I moved further into the grand entrance hall. The air was thick with the scent of perfumes and the sweet aroma of wine. Above, the grand chandelier cast a kaleidoscope of light upon the gathered assembly, illuminating the intricate social dance that unfolded around me. The golden glow reflected off polished wood and gleaming silverware, lending a dreamlike quality to the scene, as if I had stepped into another world. I could feel the weight of numerous gazes upon me, some curious, others calculating. The tension beneath the pleasantries was palpable, a simmering current beneath the polished veneer.

"Ah, Miss Blake, what a delight to see you this evening," remarked a gentleman to my left, his eyes lingering a touch too long on my pale gown. His voice was smooth, practiced, his smile charming but hollow. I offered him a demure smile, my voice as melodious as a lullaby.

"The pleasure is mine, sir. Thornwood Mansion is truly a sight to behold," I replied, my eyes drifting to the grand staircase that swept upwards to the shadowed balcony above. There, in the dim light, I could make out the figure of a man, his form half-hidden in the darkness. A shiver ran down my spine as I recognized the distinctive profile of Edward Hyde, his eyes fixed on someone in the crowd below. The stories surrounding him were too dark to ignore, whispers of violence and brutality wrapped in an air of unrelenting control. The flickering candlelight cast deep shadows across his face, giving the illusion of something inhuman lurking beneath his polished exterior.

I turned my attention back to the gentleman before me, though my thoughts remained on Hyde. Rumors of his dark deeds had reached my ears, whispers of blood and gore that painted a chilling portrait of the man. I could not help but wonder what secrets lay hidden within the shadows of Thornwood Mansion, and what role Hyde played in the dangerous game unfolding around me. The walls themselves seemed to hold their breath, waiting for some inevitable disaster to unfold.

As I navigated the crowded hall, I caught snippets of conversation, each revealing a layer of intrigue and hidden agendas. The air was thick with tension, a palpable undercurrent that belied the elegant facade of the gathering. I could feel the weight of secrets pressing in around me, fueling my curiosity and determination to learn more.

"Did you hear about the latest victim?" whispered a lady nearby, her fan concealing her mouth as she spoke to her companion. "They say he was found in an alley, his body mutilated beyond recognition."

Her companion shuddered, her eyes wide with a mix of horror and fascination. "And they say Hyde was seen nearby, his clothes stained with blood."

I felt cold, as if someone had just walked over my grave, the image of Hyde's shadowed figure etched in my mind. The murmurs of the crowd seemed to fade away, replaced by the pounding of my own heart as I contemplated the dark secrets that lurked within the walls of Thornwood Mansion. I had stepped into a world far more dangerous than I had anticipated, and yet, some part of me thrilled at the challenge. The danger was intoxicating, a force that both terrified and enthralled me.

Drawing on Isabella's teachings, I maintained my composure, my demure appearance masking the turmoil within. I knew that I must tread carefully, for the path I walked was fraught with danger and deceit. Yet, amidst the shadows and whispers, I could not deny the thrill that coursed through my veins, the intoxicating allure of power and darkness that called to me like a siren's song.

As I moved deeper into the heart of the soirée, I could not help but feel a sense of empowerment, a burgeoning awareness of my own potential to influence the very dynamics I once found intimidating. The lessons of Isabella Blackwood echoed in my mind, a steady guide amidst the whirlwind of sensation and intrigue that surrounded me. I was no longer just an observer—I was becoming a participant.

With each step, I grew more determined to uncover the truth that lay hidden within the shadows of Thornwood Mansion, to become a player in the dangerous game that unfolded around me. For in the heart of London's elite society, I had found a darkness that called to my very soul, a world of secrets and power that I could not resist. And so, with a careful, measured step, I ventured forth into the night, my heart aflutter with anticipation and trepidation, ready to embrace the challenges and opportunities that lay ahead.

    The night was young, and the game had only just begun.

CHAPTER 9

In the sullen heart of London, where the fog choked the alleys and gas lamps flickered like dying candles, I, Edwin Barrett—Flash to them what knows me—slid through the gloom like a specter. The gentleman's club loomed before me, a monolith of decadence and secret whispers. I slipped in through the servants' entrance, my boots soft on the worn stone steps. The corridor stretched out, dimly lit and thick with shadows. My heart pounded a steady rhythm, a drumbeat to my dance with the devil.

The air was thick with smoke and the cloying scent of expensive perfumes, a stark contrast to the reek of the streets. I moved with practiced ease, my shoulders rolled forward, hands in constant motion, ready to snatch a coin or lift a watch—old habits die hard. My clothes, a dull waistcoat and breeches, blended with the livery of the servants. I was a shadow, unseen, unnoticed.

The patrons, bloated with wealth and wine, paid me no heed. Their laughter echoed through the halls, grating and false. I sidestepped a lumbering footman, his tray laden with empty glasses and the dregs of expensive liquor. His eyes slid over me, dismissive. I was nothing to him, just another rat in the walls.

My destination was a private room, tucked away from prying eyes. I knew the layout well; Hyde had seen to that. The man had a knack for being everywhere at once, his influence like a stain on the city. I approached the door, my steps silent on the thick carpet. The wood was polished to a high sheen, reflecting the flickering light of the sconces. I pressed myself against the wall, listening.

"...the documents are in order, Hartwell." A woman's voice, smooth and cultured, but with an edge that spoke of streets and alleys. Rose Whitechapel, the madam with a mind like a steel trap. "The property is yours, as agreed."

"And the other matter?" Hartwell, his voice tight, nervous. I could picture him, tall and lean, his dark hair perfectly groomed, but his eyes—his eyes would be darting, anxious. He was in deep, and he knew it.

"Hyde assures me it will be taken care of." Rose's voice was cool, dismissive. "The obstacle will be... removed."

Removed. A polite word for what Hyde did. I'd seen his handiwork, the blood and gore that painted the streets. A shiver ran down my spine, but I pushed it away. This was no time for fear.

I leaned closer, my ear almost touching the door. My heart pounded in my chest, but my mind was clear, sharp. I was a tool, honed and ready. Hyde had seen to that, too.

"The timing is crucial," Hartwell insisted. "If anything goes wrong —"

"It won't." Rose's voice was firm, brooking no argument. "Hyde is... thorough."

Thorough. Another polite word. I'd seen thorough. I'd seen the bodies, the blood, the entrails strewn like garlands. I swallowed hard, my mouth dry. This was the game, the dance. And I was a pawn, moving across the board.

But a pawn could become a player, if he played his cards right. I filed away the snippets of conversation, the hints of conspiracy. Knowledge was power, and I intended to wield it. For Hyde, yes, but also for myself. Survival was a fickle mistress, and I served her first.

The conversation inside the room died down, the voices dropping to murmurs. I strained to hear, but the words were lost to the thick wood and the distant hum of the club. I lingered a moment longer, then slipped away, melting back into the shadows. My heart pounded with the thrill of discovery, the rush of the game.

As I retraced my steps, the club's opulence faded to a blur of gold and velvet. My mind was racing, the gears turning, the pieces falling into place. This was the dance, the deadly waltz of power and deception. And

I, Edwin "Flash" Barrett, was a master of the steps. Or so I told myself, as I moved through the gloom, a shadow in the night.

The door, a barrier of polished mahogany, separated me from the secrets within. I pressed my ear against the cool wood, the murmurs from the other side vibrating against my skin. The scent of beeswax and cigar smoke filled my nostrils, the distant hum of the club a mere whisper compared to the pounding of my heart.

"...the bodies, Hartwell. You promised a swift resolution." A woman's voice, sharp and insistent. Rose Whitechapel. Her tone was like a blade, honed by years of survival in the grimy streets of London. I could picture her, dark eyes flashing, her scar a silent testament to her past.

"And I have delivered, Miss Whitechapel. The constables have been... taken care of." Hartwell's response was clipped, his usual eloquence strained. I imagined his practiced poise, the subtle tremor of his hands as he spoke. "Hyde's... indiscretions have been swept under the rug, so to speak."

A rustle of fabric, the snap of a document unfurling. "And the money?" Rose's voice was a low purr, dangerous as a tiger's.

"All here, as agreed." Hartwell's voice was barely audible, a whispered assent to their shared secret. "The deed to the property, and the funds for... cleanup."

I risked a glance through the keyhole, my breath held tight in my chest. Hartwell, tall and lean, his dark hair gleaming in the candlelight. He held out a thick envelope, his fingers trembling slightly. Rose, elegant and composed, her striking features set in a mask of calculation. She took the envelope, her fingers brushing against his. A transaction, a pact sealed in the dim light of the private room.

My mind raced, the gears turning like a well-oiled clock. This was more than a mere business deal; this was a conspiracy, a dance of power and deception. And I, Edwin "Flash" Barrett, was privy to it all. The blood, the entrails, the stench of death - all swept under the rug, all part of Hyde's bloody game.

I thought of Hyde, his eyes wild with a hunger that chilled me to the bone. The bodies, the blood... it was all part of his plan, his mad quest for power. And here, in this room, were the puppets, playing their parts in his twisted theatre.

But knowledge was power, and I had it in spades. I could use this, turn it to my advantage, to Hyde's advantage. Or could I? A flicker of doubt gnawed at the edges of my mind. This was a dangerous game, and the stakes were higher than ever. The blood, the bodies... they were real, not just pawns in a game. And I was a part of it, a cog in the machine, a servant of the monster that was Edward Hyde.

But a cog could turn the wheel, couldn't it? A pawn could become a player, if he played his cards right. I filed away the details, the exchange of money and documents, the whispered conspiracies. This was leverage, pure and simple. And I intended to wield it, for Hyde, yes, but also for myself. Survival was a fickle mistress, and I served her first.

The conversation inside the room died down, the voices dropping to murmurs. I strained to hear, but the words were lost to the thick wood and the distant hum of the club. I lingered a moment longer, then slipped away, melting back into the shadows. My heart pounded with the thrill of discovery.

The door creaked open, a sliver of light cutting into the dim hallway as Hartwell and Whitechapel emerged, their faces etched with the weight of their conspiracies. I pressed myself against the wall, heart pounding like a drum in my chest. The flickering gas lamps cast eerie shadows on the paneled walls, distorting the silhouettes of the two figures as they parted ways, each vanishing into the labyrinthine corridors of the gentleman's club.

I counted to ten, breath held, before daring to move. The plush carpet beneath my feet muffled my steps as I retraced my path, eyes darting from shadow to shadow. The club's opulence, once a comfort, now felt stifling, the air thick with cigar smoke and the cloying scent of expensive perfumes. Each doorway I passed revealed glimpses of London's elite, laughing and drinking, oblivious to the dark undercurrents swirling around them.

My heart thudded in my ears, a relentless beat urging me forward. The thrill of discovery coursed through my veins, sharpening my senses. The details of the exchange—the rustle of banknotes, the crisp fold of documents—were seared into my memory. This was power, raw and untapped, waiting to be wielded.

I slipped past a group of gentlemen, their laughter booming like thunder. One of them, a portly fellow with a ruddy complexion, clapped a hand on my shoulder. "Here, boy! Fetch us another round, would you?"

I forced a grin, the picture of youthful innocence. "Right away, sir!" I ducked away, quick as a flash, melting back into the crowd. My pulse raced, but I kept my movements smooth, unhurried. Invisible, just as Hyde had taught me.

As I neared the grand staircase, a figure stepped into my path. A woman, tall and elegant, her honey-blonde hair swept up in a modest but elegant style. Her clear blue eyes met mine, and she smiled, a natural warmth that put me instantly on guard.

"Pardon me, young man," she said, her voice soft yet authoritative. "I couldn't help but notice your haste. Are you here for the reform meeting as well?"

I blinked, taken aback. Reform meeting? I quickly schooled my features into a neutral expression, my mind racing. "Reform meeting, miss?" I asked, affecting a respectful tone.

She nodded earnestly. "Yes, I was told it would be held here tonight. I am Victoria Sterling," she extended a gloved hand, her gown of fine quality, muted in color, but fashionable. "And you are?"

I hesitated for a fraction of a second before taking her hand, bowing slightly. "Edwin Barrett, miss. At your service." My mind whirred, calculating the best course of action. This was an unexpected complication, but one that could perhaps be turned to my advantage.

Her smile widened, genuine and trusting. "A pleasure to meet you, Mr. Barrett. I must admit, I am relieved to find a fellow reformer in this den of... indulgence." She gestured discreetly to the lavish surroundings, her nose wrinkling slightly.

I chuckled nervously, playing along. "Indeed, miss. One must go where the need is greatest, after all." My words were a careful dance, a blend of truth and deception. I was a chameleon, adapting to the role required of me.

As we stood there, her earnestness clashing with my pragmatism, I couldn't help but feel a twinge of admiration for her sincerity. It was a rare quality in the world I inhabited, a world stained with blood and shadowed by Hyde's dark deeds. The image of the latest victim, a poor wretch left in a pool of his own blood, flashed through my mind. The contrast was stark, a grim reminder of the duality of my existence.

But for now, I pushed those thoughts aside, focusing on the task at hand. Victoria Sterling was a puzzle piece I hadn't anticipated, but one that could fit neatly into the ever-shifting landscape of my loyalties.

The opulent chandeliers cast a fractured glow upon the maroon carpets, stretching the shadows of the club's patrons into grotesque echoes of their owners. I, Edwin Barrett, slipped through the labyrinth of debauchery, my heart a drumbeat against my ribs. The thrill of discovery coursed through my veins like opium, as intoxicating as it was dangerous. My clothes, a forgettable blend of servant and street, allowed me to glide unnoticed through the gilded halls.

"You seem in an awful hurry, sir." A voice, clear and melodic, interrupted my careful retreat. Victoria Sterling stepped into my path, her tall, graceful form clad in a conservative gown of muted blue. Her honey-blonde hair caught the dim light, a halo framing her earnest face.

I started, my nerves already taut. "Indeed, miss, I've matters to attend to," I replied, my tongue adapting to the proper English of her class. My hands, ever in motion, fluttered nervously at my sides.

Her blue eyes held mine, unblinking. "Matters of reform, I hope." She mistook my hurried departure, assuming me an ally in her crusade. "I overheard your conversation earlier. It's refreshing to find someone who shares my beliefs in this place."

My mind raced, quick as a rat through a sewer. She'd overheard me? My thoughts flew to Hyde, to the blood-slicked cobbles and the stench of death that clung to his name. I saw the latest victim, a man whose face was barely more than a bloody pulp, swallowed by the shadows of Whitechapel. Play along, I thought. Gather more information. "Ah, yes, reform," I agreed, my grin disarming. "A noble cause, indeed."

Victoria's face lit up, her passion igniting like a flame to a wick. "Isn't it, though? There's so much injustice, so much suffering. We must strive to make a difference, Mr. Barrett." Her vocabulary revealed her education, but her sincerity stripped it of condescension.

I nodded, my thoughts a whirlwind. Could this idealistic young woman be of use to Hyde? Or was she a hindrance, a complication in his bloody plans? My loyalties wavered, a scale tipping back and forth with every beat of my heart. "Indeed, we must," I echoed, my voice a hollow mimicry of her fervor.

She stepped closer, her voice dropping to a conspiratorial whisper. "I have plans, Mr. Barrett. Plans to expose the corruption that plagues our city. But I need allies. Men of courage and conviction." Her eyes searched mine, seeking a kindred spirit.

My laughter was nervous, a habit born of unease. "I'm afraid I'm but a humble servant, miss. I hardly think I'm the champion you seek." My words were a careful dance, a blend of truth and deception.

The Devil of London

Her smile was gentle, her persuasion soft as a summer's breeze. "Every man can be a champion, Mr. Barrett. It's not the station that makes the man, but the heart that beats within him."

My heart hammered against my ribs, a traitor to my careful composure. I thought of Hyde, of the power he wielded, the fear he inspired. But I also thought of the blood, the endless river of red that flowed through the streets of Whitechapel. Was there a way to serve both masters - the devil I knew and the angel I didn't?

Victoria's eyes shone with unshed tears, her passion a palpable force. "Won't you help me, Mr. Barrett? Won't you stand with me against the darkness?"

My thoughts raced, calculations spinning like the cogs of a machine. To align with Victoria was to risk Hyde's wrath, but to spurn her was to lose a potential ally, a tool to be wielded in the ever-shifting landscape of my loyalties. My survival instincts screamed at me to play this carefully, to keep my options open.

"I will consider it, miss," I replied, my voice steady despite the tempest within me. "After all, every man must do his part." My words were a careful balance, a promise and a hedge, all wrapped in one.

As I stood there, my pragmatism clashing with her earnestness, I couldn't help but feel a twinge of admiration for her sincerity. It was a rare quality in the world I inhabited, a world stained with blood and shadowed by Hyde's dark deeds. But admiration was a luxury I couldn't afford. Not when survival was the game, and my life the wager.

The gas lamps flickered, casting eerie shadows that danced macabrely on the cobblestones, as if the very streets of London were alive with whispers of Hyde's dark deeds. I could still see the remnants of his last grim calling card—a splatter of blood on the alley wall, a grim reminder of the brutality that lurked in the city's underbelly. Victoria, her eyes ablaze with fervor, seemed oblivious to the sinister surroundings, her focus solely on the battle she waged with words.

"You speak of reform, Miss Sterling," I said, my breath misting in the chill air, "but have you truly seen the depths of depravity that plague this city? The blood that flows through these gutters is not merely a metaphor."

Victoria's gaze did not waver. "I have seen enough, Mr. Barrett," she replied, her voice steady and clear. "I have walked these streets, tended to the wounded, and listened to the tales of the downtrodden. I know the darkness that lurks here, and it is precisely why I fight for change."

Her sincerity was like a beacon in the gloom, a stark contrast to the duplicitous world I inhabited. There was a purity in her conviction that I had not encountered before, a genuine belief in the possibility of redemption for these forsaken streets. It stirred something within me, a flicker of doubt about the path I had chosen, the allegiance I had sworn to Hyde.

"Your passion is commendable, Miss Sterling," I admitted, my voice softening. "But passion alone cannot vanquish the evil that stalks these alleys. Hyde's reach is vast, his influence insidious. To stand against him is to invite his wrath, and believe me, it is a wrath that knows no bounds."

Victoria's eyes widened slightly, but she did not falter. "Then we must stand together, Mr. Barrett," she insisted, her voice taking on that compelling intensity that made it hard to resist. "Together, we can be a force for good, a light in the darkness. Surely, you must see that there is strength in unity."

Her words resonated within me, echoing a long-buried longing for something more than mere survival. I had always prided myself on my adaptability, my ability to shift and change as the situation demanded. But this...this was different. This was a call to something higher, a summons to a battle that transcended the petty struggles of my daily existence.

I looked at Victoria, her face illuminated by the faint glow of the gas lamps, her eyes shining with unshed tears. In that moment, I saw not just an idealistic young woman, but a warrior, a beacon of hope in a world that had long forgotten the meaning of the word. And I knew, with a sudden clarity, that I wanted to stand beside her, to be a part of her crusade.

"You are right, Miss Sterling," I said, my voice steady despite the tempest within me. "Together, we can achieve more than either of us could alone. I will stand with you, not just as an ally, but as a friend."

As I spoke the words, I felt a shift within me, a subtle realignment of my loyalties. It was a risk, a gamble that could cost me dearly if Hyde ever discovered my duplicity. But it was a risk worth taking, a chance to be part of something greater than myself.

The Devil of London

Victoria's face lit up with a smile that was like the dawn breaking through the darkness. "Thank you, Mr. Barrett," she said, her voice filled with gratitude. "Together, we shall bring light to the shadows of this city."

In that moment, as we stood amidst the squalor and despair of Whitechapel, I felt a sense of purpose that I had never known before. The path ahead was fraught with danger, the risks immense, but I was ready to face them, to stand beside Victoria and fight for a better future. The devil I knew might be formidable, but the angel I didn't was a force to be reckoned with, and I was willing to bet my life on her.

The flickering glow of the gas lamps cast eerie, dancing shadows upon the gilded walls of the gentleman's club, as if the very light itself conspired to keep our secrets. Victoria walked beside me, her chin held high, eyes alert. Her elegant silk gown, the color of a summer's dawn, rustled softly with each step, a stark contrast to the dark, forgettable attire I had donned for the evening's clandestine activities.

"We must meet tomorrow, at the old bookshop on Chancery Lane," she whispered, her voice barely audible above the distant hum of the club's patrons. "Father knows the proprietor, a discreet man who will allow us to speak privately."

My heart pounded in my chest like a drummer's urgent beat, each strike echoing the thrill and danger that hung heavy in the air. "Aye, I know the place," I replied, my voice low. "But we must be cautious. Hyde's eyes and ears are everywhere, and if he catches wind of our meeting..." I let the sentence hang, the implication clear. I had seen firsthand the bloody consequences of crossing Hyde; the vivid crimson of a throat laid open, the dull gleam of lifeless eyes. My stomach turned at the memory.

Victoria nodded, her blue eyes steely with resolve. "Caution is our watchword, Mr. Barrett. We cannot hope to challenge the darkness that grips this city if we ourselves are consumed by it."

Her words sent a shiver down my spine, not of fear, but of admiration. Her conviction was infectious, her determination a beacon that cut through the fog of my own uncertain loyalties. As we made our way through the labyrinthine corridors, I could not help but compare her to Hyde, who wielded his power like a blade, carving through the lives of others with cold precision. Victoria, on the other hand, sought to lift people up, to shine a light on the injustices that festered in the shadows.

I felt a pang of guilt as I considered my own role in Hyde's machinations. How many lives had I helped to ruin, all in the name of loyalty and self-preservation? The thought sat heavy in my gut, a stone of regret that threatened to drag me down into the mire of my past actions.

But now, walking beside Victoria, I felt a glimmer of hope, a spark that ignited a desire for redemption. Perhaps, with her guidance, I could find a way to make amends, to use my skills and knowledge to bring about change, rather than merely serving the whims of a madman.

As we approached the grand entrance of the club, the doorman, resplendent in his crimson livery, offered Victoria her cloak. She draped the garment around her shoulders, the deep blue fabric adorned with intricate silver embroidery that shimmered in the light like moonbeams upon the Thames.

I leaned in, my voice barely a whisper. "Tomorrow, then. At noon. I shall ensure I am not followed."

Victoria smiled, her eyes reflecting the warmth of her spirit. "Until tomorrow, Mr. Barrett. May God watch over us both."

With that, we stepped out into the foggy London night, the thick mist swirling around us like a living thing. The cobblestones glistened with the recent rain, and the air was filled with the familiar scent of smoke and damp earth. The city was alive with sound, the distant clatter of carriage wheels, the laughter of drunkards spilling out of nearby taverns, and the haunting melody of a lone street musician's fiddle.

As we parted ways, I could not shake the feeling that this night marked a turning point, a crossroads at which I had chosen a new path. The road ahead was shrouded in mist, fraught with danger and uncertainty, but I was resolved to see it through, to stand beside Victoria and fight for a better future.

Yet, as I made my way through the darkened streets, I could not help but think of Hyde, of the web of deceit and violence that he had spun throughout the city. What would he make of my newfound allegiance, of my betrayal of his trust? A shudder ran through me as I considered the potential consequences, the bloody retribution that he was sure to exact.

But there was more to it than that. As I walked, I could not escape the nagging sensation that there was something greater at play, a conspiracy that stretched far beyond the confines of Hyde's twisted games. The meeting between Hartwell and Whitechapel, the exchange of money and documents, the whispered promises of power and influence –

it all pointed to a deeper, darker truth, one that threatened to consume not only Hyde, but the very heart of London itself.

I quickened my pace, my heart pounding in time with my steps. The night was far from over, and the challenges that lay ahead were daunting indeed. But I was ready to face them, to embrace the uncertainty and forge a new path, one step at a time.

For in that moment, as I strode through the foggy streets, I was no longer merely Edwin "Flash" Barrett, street urchin and servant to a monster. I was something more, something greater. I was a partner in the fight for justice, a warrior against the encroaching darkness, a beacon of hope in the shadowy heart of London. And I would not go down without a fight.

CHAPTER 10

The grandeur of Lady Elizabeth Thornwood's dining room was a spectacle to behold, a cavernous chamber illuminated by the flickering light of a hundred candles. The opulence was almost suffocating—gilded mirrors reflecting the dance of flames, heavy velvet drapes in deep jewel tones, and a table laid with such an abundance of silver and crystal that it seemed to groan under the weight of its own splendor. The scent of beeswax and fine perfumes intertwined, creating an air of aristocratic decadence. As I, Edward Hyde, stepped into this resplendent arena, the subtle tension in the air was palpable, like the first whispered notes of a symphony yet to crescendo.

Lady Elizabeth, ever the consummate hostess, greeted each guest with a practiced smile that never quite reached her ice-blue eyes. Her copper-red hair was arranged in an elaborate coiffure, adorned with pearls that caught the light as she moved. She wore a gown of rich emerald velvet, the color of old blood, which complemented her alabaster skin and commanded attention. Her strategic placement of the guests was a masterstroke of social engineering; I found myself seated between Isabella Blackwood and the formidable Sir Maximillion Worthington. The stage was set for an evening of intricate maneuvers and subtle power plays.

The Devil of London

As the first course was served—a delicate consommé that steamed gently in the cool air—I turned my attention to Isabella. She was a vision of classical beauty, her deep blue eyes holding a knowing darkness that belied her youth. Her gown, a shimmering silk of midnight blue, clung to her graceful form with an almost liquid quality. The candlelight illuminated the delicate curve of her collarbone, accentuating her controlled poise. I could not help but admire the contrast between her outward composure and the calculating intelligence that lurked beneath.

"Miss Blackwood," I began, my voice a rich, melodious purr that seemed to resonate in the very air around us. "You are a vision this evening. That gown—it reminds me of the night sky just before the first stars appear. There is a certain... anticipation in its darkness, is there not?"

Isabella turned to me, her eyes meeting mine with a cool appraisal. "Mr. Hyde, you are too kind. Though I must admit, the night sky often holds more than mere anticipation. It conceals countless secrets, does it not?"

I smiled, a slow, predatory curve of my lips. "Indeed, it does. And like the night sky, you possess a depth that invites exploration. One might find themselves lost in such darkness, were they not careful."

Her eyebrow arched ever so slightly, a silent acknowledgment of the undercurrent in my words. "And what of you, Mr. Hyde? Do you not fear becoming lost in the darkness you so admire?"

My smile widened, revealing a hint of the predator within. "Fear, Miss Blackwood? No, I do not fear the darkness. I revel in it. It is, after all, where the most interesting games are played."

As I spoke, my mind drifted to the shadows of London's alleys, where the cobblestones were slick with more than just rain. The memory of blood, dark and viscous, pooling around the lifeless forms of those who had crossed me, was a vivid tableau in my mind's eye. The scent of it, metallic and thick, mingled with the damp earth and the acrid smoke of the city. It was a world away from the opulence of Lady Elizabeth's dining room, yet it was a part of me, a dark tapestry woven into the very fabric of my being.

Sir Maximillion, seated to my right, shifted uncomfortably in his chair. His silver beard was meticulously groomed, his tailoring impeccable, yet there was a slight stoop to his shoulders that betrayed the weight of his secrets. He cleared his throat, a gruff sound that seemed to echo in the suddenly quiet room. "Hyde, you have a peculiar way with words. One might almost think you enjoy playing with fire."

I turned to him. "Ah, Sir Maximillion, fire is but one element among many. It is the darkness that truly fascinates me. It is where the most interesting truths are hidden, would you not agree?"

His gray eyes narrowed, a flicker of unease passing over his features. "I would advise caution, Hyde. Some truths are best left undisturbed."

I leaned back in my chair, a picture of elegant nonchalance. "And yet, Sir Maximillion, it is often those very truths that hold the key to our deepest desires. Would you not agree, Miss Blackwood?"

Isabella's lips curved in a faint, enigmatic smile. "Desire, Mr. Hyde, is a double-edged sword. It can cut both ways if one is not careful."

I raised my glass, the crystal catching the light of the candles. "Indeed, it can, Miss Blackwood. But where would be the fun in always playing it safe?"

As the consommé was cleared away, I could not help but feel a sense of satisfaction. The evening was young, and already the delicate dance of words and intentions had begun. The night held promise, a dark and intoxicating allure that called to the very core of my being. And as the shadows lengthened and the candles burned lower, I knew that the true game was only just beginning.

The grand chandelier above flickered, casting eerie shadows that danced macabrely across the suddenly silent dining room. The crystalline echo of glasses meeting in toast seemed to linger, suspended in the air like the sword of Damocles. Hyde's words, smooth as poisoned honey, had stilled every tongue and frozen every heart.

Lady Elizabeth, seated at the head of the table like a queen upon her throne, maintained a rigid smile, but I could see the slight tightening around her eyes, the whitening of her knuckles as she gripped her glass. Her carefully laid plans were unraveling like a badly stitched tapestry, and she knew it. "Well," she said, her voice a trifle too bright, "Mr. Hyde certainly knows how to command an audience. But let us not forget our desserts, gentlemen. They are, after all, the sweetest part of the meal."

Her words fell flat, a desperate attempt to steer the conversation back to safer shores. The mood had shifted, as palpably as the changing of the tide. The gentle hum of conviviality had been replaced by a tense silence, broken only by the distant ticking of the grandfather clock in the hall.

And as I looked into Hyde's eyes, I saw reflected there the grim knowledge that the night was far from over, and that the true horrors were yet to come.

CHAPTER 11

In the gloom of Harding & Sons Funeral Services, I stood hunched over the day's ledger, the scent of polished wood and faded lilies clinging to the air like a shroud. My hands, those traitorous appendages, trembled slightly as I grasped the pen, the nib scratching out figures and names that danced before my weary eyes. The glass of brandy beside me remained untouched, a silent testament to my resolve, or perhaps my despair.

The soft rustle of skirts announced her arrival, a sound as familiar as it was unexpected at this late hour. I looked up to see Catherine Blackwood sweep into the parlor, her tall, slender form garbed in a dress of somber gray, the color of her eyes—eyes that missed nothing and now fixed upon me with an intensity that was almost physical. Her dark brown hair, pulled back severely from her face, accentuated the keen intelligence that radiated from her gaze.

"Mr. Harding," she began, her voice precise and measured, yet laced with an undercurrent of urgency. "I find myself in need of your assistance, though I daresay the matter is of a delicate nature."

I set down my pen, giving her my full attention. "Miss Blackwood," I replied, my voice carefully modulated, a habit of my profession. "How might I be of service?"

The Devil of London

She stepped closer, her ink-stained hands clasped before her. "It is regarding my sister, Isabella. I have reason to believe she has become entangled with a man of dubious repute—one Edward Hyde."

The name sent a shiver down my spine, conjuring images of the gruesome tableaux I had been forced to attend in my professional capacity. Bodies ripped asunder, blood spattered like morbid art upon the cobblestones, the stench of death and terror lingering in the air. I had seen Hyde's handiwork, the brutal calling card of a man who dealt in violence and fear.

"I see the name is not unfamiliar to you," Catherine observed, her gaze sharpening. "Then you are aware of the danger Isabella may be in. I have it on good authority that she has been seen in his company, and her behavior of late has been... troubling."

I thought of Isabella, her laughter and her light, and the shadow that Hyde would cast over her life. The images of his victims flickered through my mind like a grotesque gallery: the baker's wife, her throat slit from ear to ear, her eyes wide with terror; the young man from the docks, his body broken and twisted, his face a bloody pulp; the countless others, their lives snuffed out with brutal efficiency.

"Miss Blackwood," I began, my voice barely above a whisper, "the company your sister keeps is indeed a cause for concern. But I must tread carefully, for the sake of all involved."

Catherine's eyes flashed, a silent challenge. "I understand your position, Mr. Harding, but I implore you—if you know anything, anything at all, that might help me extricate Isabella from this situation, I beg of you to share it."

Her words hung in the air, a plea that was almost a demand. I felt the weight of her expectations, the silent burden of knowledge that I carried, and the delicate balance that I must maintain. For in the world of shadows and secrets that Edward Hyde inhabited, one false step could prove fatal.

The flickering flame of the candle cast grotesque shadows upon the wall, mirroring the dance of indecision within my mind. Catherine's eyes, sharp as a raven's, bore into me, and I felt the weight of her gaze as keenly as the chill from the draft that whispered through the room. Her skirts, the color of a bruised sky, rustled softly as she shifted, impatient for my response.

"Mr. Harding," she pressed, her voice a low, insistent murmur, like the first rumblings of a storm. "You know something of Isabella's dealings with that man, do you not? I can see it in your eyes."

I struggled to meet her gaze, my hands clammy as I clasped them together to still their trembling. The scent of lilies, once sweet, now cloyed and sickened, much like the secrets that festered within me. My professional discretion demanded silence, yet my conscience screamed for release.

"Miss Blackwood," I began, my voice barely audible, as if the very air conspired to smother my words. "It is not so simple as you might think. There are... considerations."

Her eyebrows lifted, a silent challenge. "Considerations, Mr. Harding? Or fears?"

The image of the baker's wife flashed before my eyes, her throat a gaping maw, blood pooling like a obscene collar about her neck. The stench of her terror filled my nostrils, and I could taste the metallic tang of her lifeblood as it ebbed away. And there, always there, loomed Hyde, his eyes wild and hungry, his hands dripping with gore.

Catherine leaned closer, her voice barely above a whisper, yet urgent as a scream. "I know you see things, Mr. Harding. Things that haunt you. I see them now, reflected in your eyes. But I implore you, if Isabella is to be saved from whatever darkness she courts—"

I shuddered, the echo of a memory tugging at my conscience. Isabella, her laughter like silver bells, her eyes sparkling as she danced with Hyde at the assembly rooms. The same hands that had spun her in delighted circles were the ones that had torn the life from the young man at the docks, his body broken and twisted, face beaten to a bloody, unrecognizable pulp.

Feeling the weight of Catherine's expectations, I took a shaky breath. "I have seen them together, Miss Blackwood. At the assembly rooms, and... and once, outside the theatre. She seemed... taken with him."

Catherine's lips pressed into a thin line, her eyes never leaving mine. "And?"

I hesitated, the delicate balance of discretion and integrity teetering on the edge of a blade. "And I have seen Hyde, Miss Blackwood. Seen him in the dark of night, his clothes stained with blood and filth. I have seen the results of his... predilections. To speak of it is to risk—"

The Devil of London

To risk what? My reputation? My life? Or worse, Isabella's? The shadows in the room seemed to lengthen, their tendrils reaching for me, as if to drag me into their depths. Yet, Catherine's gaze anchored me, her urgency a beacon in the gloom.

"To risk what, Mr. Harding?" she asked, her voice steady, relentless. "For if Isabella is lost to us, what then? What price will your silence command?"

I felt a chill, as if the grave itself breathed down my neck. The echoes of Hyde's laughter mingled with the screams of his victims, a symphony of horror that only I could hear. And there, amidst the cacophony, a small, insistent voice. The voice of my conscience, urging me to speak, to act, before another life was lost.

"Very well, Miss Blackwood," I said, my voice barely above a whisper. "I will tell you what I know. But mark me, the path we tread is dark and treacherous, and once begun, there is no turning back."

The dim light of the funeral parlor flickered like a dying man's gaze, casting eerie shadows that danced macabrely on the polished wood of the caskets. The air was thick with the cloying scent of lilies, their funereal perfume mingling with the ever-present dust of the deceased. I, Thomas Harding, stood rooted to the spot, the weight of Catherine Blackwood's expectations pressing down upon me like a shroud.

As I opened my mouth to reveal what little I knew of Isabella's entanglement with that fiend, Edward Hyde, a sharp, authoritative click echoed through the room. The sound of boots, polished to a militaristic gleam, struck the floor with a precision that demanded attention. Lord Frederick Pembroke had arrived.

His tall, athletic frame cast a long shadow as he entered, his dark blonde hair catching the faint light, his steel-blue eyes reflecting the dancing flames of the candles. The scar above his right eyebrow lent an air of rugged distinction to his otherwise aristocratic mien. His suit, impeccably tailored and conservative, spoke of his diplomatic station, while his bearing screamed of his military past.

Catherine turned sharply at his entrance, her gray eyes flicking from me to Lord Pembroke, her keen intelligence assessing the situation with the swiftness of a striking serpent. I felt a pang of envy at her composure, wishing I could maintain such calm in the face of the storm that was surely coming.

"Mr. Harding," Lord Pembroke began, his voice measured and precise, each word chosen with the care of a diplomat navigating a treaty. "I find myself in need of your particular skills. A matter of some delicacy and urgency has arisen, and I am afraid I must insist on your cooperation."

I felt a chill run down my spine, a sensation not unlike the cold touch of the corpses I tended to. "Lord Pembroke," I replied, my voice barely steadier than my trembling hands. "I am, of course, at your service. Pray, tell me what you require."

His eyes met mine, unwavering and steady. "I have been tasked with a military inquiry, Harding. A matter of life and death, you might say." He paused, his gaze flicking briefly to Catherine before returning to me. "I require the exhumation of a body. A man who died under... suspicious circumstances. His name was Captain Albert Hogan. I believe you are familiar with him?"

The name sent a jolt through me, conjuring images of the poor wretch as he had been brought to me. His throat had been slashed, a grotesque smile carved from ear to ear, his eyes wide and staring, frozen in a perpetual state of terror. His entrails had spilled forth like bloody serpents from his abdomen, the work of a madman—or something worse. I had seen many a grisly sight in my line of work, but the memory of Captain Hogan haunted me, a specter that refused to be laid to rest.

"I remember him," I said, my voice barely above a whisper. The echoes of Hyde's laughter seemed to ring in my ears, a chilling accompaniment to the grim tableau painted in my mind.

Lord Pembroke nodded, his expression grave. "Then you understand the gravity of my request. The fate of more than one life may hang in the balance, Harding. I need not remind you of the potential repercussions should this task not be carried out with the utmost discretion and expediency."

His words hung heavy in the air, a palpable weight that settled over the room like a pall. I felt the noose tightening, the delicate balance between my professional discretion and personal integrity threatening to snap like a taut wire. And all the while, Catherine watched, her silent observation a stark reminder of the stakes involved. The path we tread was dark indeed, and the shadows seemed to grow ever longer, their tendrils reaching out to ensnare us all.

The Devil of London

The flickering flames of the candles cast eerie, dancing shadows upon the walls of my funeral parlor, as if the very room itself writhed in the throes of some unseen agony. The air, thick with the cloying scent of lilies and polished wood, seemed to press in around me, constricting my breath as I stood there, frozen in the grip of indecision. Lord Pembroke's request, uttered with such steadfast resolve, had plunged my mind into a chaotic storm of conflicting loyalties and fears.

My hands, those tools of my grim trade, trembled slightly as I clasped them behind my back, their usual pallor now a stark, bloodless white. The knuckles protruded like the peaks of some gaunt mountain range, a testament to the tension that coursed through my veins. The brandy, once a tempting distraction, now sat forgotten, its amber depths unable to quell the tempest within.

"Mr. Harding," Catherine began, her voice a soft, measured intrusion into the whirlwind of my thoughts. I met her gaze, those penetrating gray eyes seeming to strip away the facade of my composure, laying bare the struggle that raged within. "I understand the gravity of Lord Pembroke's request, but consider this—Isabella's well-being, and perhaps even her life, may depend upon the choices we make here and now."

Her words, spoken with such quiet conviction, served only to deepen the chasm that yawned before me. My promise to Isabella, a whispered vow uttered in the hallowed silence of this very room, hung heavy around my neck, a millstone threatening to drag me down into the abyss of broken trust. And yet, Lord Pembroke's authority, the weight of his military bearing and the unmistakable importance of his request, pressed down upon my shoulders like the hands of some unseen, implacable force.

My mind's eye conjured forth the grisly spectacle that was Captain Hogan's fate—his body, a grotesque parody of human form, splayed open like a macabre blossom upon the cold stone slab. The memory of his viscera, gleaming and obscene beneath the harsh glare of the examination lamps, sent a shudder coursing down my spine. Hyde's handiwork, a bloody testament to his depraved genius, had left an indelible stain upon my soul, a haunting reminder of the evil that lurked within the shadows of our city.

Catherine watched me, her analytical mind processing the situation with a clarity that I could not help but envy. Her presence, a silent sentinel amidst the storm, served as both a reminder of the stakes involved and a source of quiet support. Her dark dress, severe in its simplicity, seemed to absorb the dim light of the room, as if she were a shadow given form, a phantom conjured forth by my guilt-ridden conscience.

"The path we tread is dark indeed, Mr. Harding," she murmured, her voice barely audible, yet cutting through the cacophony of my thoughts like a knife. "But tread it we must, for the sake of those who cannot walk it themselves."

Her words struck a chord deep within me, resonating with the same unyielding determination that had first drawn me to this grim profession. The dead deserved justice, and the living deserved the truth—no matter how painful or terrifying it may prove to be.

And so, with a heavy heart and a spirit bowed beneath the weight of my decision, I turned to face Lord Pembroke, the resolve in my eyes mirroring his own steely determination. The die was cast, the Rubicon crossed—and may God have mercy upon our souls.

In the gloom of my study, the ticking of the grandfather clock echoed like a death knell, each swing of the pendulum another shovelful of earth upon my conscience. Lord Pembroke loomed before me, his steel-blue eyes fixed and unyielding, the scar above his brow a stark reminder of his unshakeable resolve. His gloved hands, clasped behind his back, bore the impress of his signet ring, a symbol of his family's legacy and the weighty expectations he carried.

"Harding," he began, his voice steady and measured, "I understand the gravity of my request. Yet, I must insist upon the exhumation. The fate of more than one soul rests upon your decision this night." His words, though calm, bore an undercurrent of urgency, like the swift movement of a river beneath a frozen surface. "I have reason to believe that the body in question may hold the key to a matter of national security. A matter that, if left unresolved, could lead to the loss of countless lives."

My heart pounded in my chest, a drumbeat of anxiety. The decision before me was akin to choosing between the devil and the deep blue sea. My mind's eye flashed with images of Isabella's trusting gaze, Catherine's determined expression, and the cold, hard truth etched onto Lord Pembroke's face. The pressure mounted, a physical force that threatened to crush me.

"Lord Pembroke," I stammered, my voice barely recognizable, "I am bound by professional oaths, by promises made to the deceased and their families. What you ask... it is not a simple matter."

He leaned in, his voice dropping to a low, intense register. "Neither is the preservation of English lives, Harding. I would not ask this of you if there were any other way. But time is of the essence, and the shadows are closing in."

A shiver ran down my spine, a sensation akin to the feeling of a coffin lid being slid into place. I knew, with a dreadful certainty, that my decision would have consequences that echoed far beyond the walls of my funeral parlor.

I turned away from his gaze, seeking solace in the familiar sight of my study. The heavy velvet curtains, drawn against the chill of the night, seemed to sway slightly, as if stirred by an unseen hand. The flickering flame of the single candle cast dancing shadows upon the polished wood of the desk, where the open ledger lay forgotten, its columns of figures a stark reminder of the world of order and reason that now seemed so far away.

As I wrestled with the demons of my conscience, the room seemed to grow darker still, the very air thick with portent. The decision before me was akin to stepping off a precipice, a plunge into unknown depths. And yet, I knew that there was no turning back. The die was cast, and the only path forward was through the darkness.

With a heavy heart, I turned to face Lord Pembroke once more, the words of consent bitter upon my tongue. But before I could speak, a sudden draft extinguished the candle, plunging the room into darkness. The curtains billowed inward, revealing a glimpse of the street beyond— and the figure that stood across the way.

Edward Hyde, his tall, elegant form partially obscured by the shadows of the alley, was a statue carved from the night itself. His eyes, those magnetic green orbs, seemed to glow with an infernal light, fixed upon the funeral parlor with an intensity that made my blood run cold. His hands, encased in fine leather gloves, were stained with a darkness that I knew was not merely the play of shadows. I had seen those hands before, in the grim aftermath of his violent passions, the blood and gore that marked his path like a trail of breadcrumbs leading straight to the gates of Hell.

In the dim recesses of my memory, I saw again the carnage he had wrought: the lifeless bodies, their throats slit from ear to ear, the crimson tide that stained the cobblestones, the entrails steaming in the cool night air. His victims, their faces contorted in eternal screams, were a testament to his savagery, their mutilated forms a grotesque tableau of his twisted artistry.

And now, as I stood on the brink of a decision that would forever alter the course of my life, Hyde's presence loomed like a specter, a silent threat that chilled me to the very marrow of my bones. The choice before me was no longer merely a matter of professional ethics or personal loyalties—it was a dance with the devil himself, and the price of a misstep was more than I dared to contemplate.

The gas lamps flickered feebly, their meager light barely piercing the thick fog that choked the streets. Across the way, Hyde lingered like a statue carved from the night itself, his eyes glinting like a cat's as they reflected the dim glow. His fine wool greatcoat, the color of obsidian, melted into the shadows, but the red silk lining flickered like fresh blood each time the wind caught it.

His gaze bore into me like an auger, and I felt the sickening sensation of his influence seeping into the funeral parlor, a poisonous tendril snaking through the air. The very atmosphere grew heavy, as if the ghosts of his victims had entered the room, their mangled specters whispering grim warnings. I could see them in my mind's eye, their entrails glistening like eels in the moonlight, their limbs twisted and broken, marionettes in a grotesque dance of death.

The memory of the last poor soul I had seen in his wake assailed me—a prostitute, her shift torn and bloody, her body splayed open like a gutted fish. Her glassy eyes stared up at me, accusing, and her intestines spilled out like slippery serpents onto the cobblestones. The smell of her, the cloying stench of blood and voided bowels, filled my nostrils as if I were once again kneeling beside her corpse.

I tore my gaze from Hyde's, my heart pounding like a drumbeat in my chest. Lord Pembroke stood before me, his blue eyes steady and unblinking, awaiting my answer. His military bearing was evident in his stiff stance, his broad shoulders squared, and his scar a stark reminder of battles fought and won.

The Devil of London

"Mr. Harding," he pressed, his voice a low rumble, urgent yet controlled. "I must insist. The fate of more than one soul rests upon your cooperation."

I swallowed hard, my mouth dry as cotton. The ledger lay open before me, the figures swimming in my vision. I could feel the weight of Hyde's gaze, the silent threat that hung in the air like the blade of a guillotine. My hands trembled slightly as I closed the book, the sound of the pages thudding softly like a coffin lid closing.

"Very well, Lord Pembroke," I said, my voice steady but tinged with the bitterness of resignation. "I shall assist you in this matter. But mark my words, this may unravel the carefully maintained facade of my professional life."

As I spoke, I could feel the threads of my existence beginning to fray, the delicate balance I had maintained for so long threatening to topple into chaos. The scent of lilies and polished wood seemed suddenly cloying, the air thick with the sickly sweet perfume of decay. I was acutely aware of the danger lurking outside, the dark forces that Hyde embodied, and the blood-soaked memories that stained my conscience.

The flickering flame of the solitary candle cast grotesque shadows upon the wall, the dance of light and dark a grim reflection of the turmoil within me. I watched as Lord Pembroke, his tall figure ramrod straight, turned on his heel, the clicking of his polished boots echoing through the parlour like the ticking of a clock, counting down to some inevitable doom.

Catherine stood silent, her gray eyes reflecting the candlelight like twin moons. Her hands, stained with ink, were clasped tightly before her, the only outward sign of her inner turmoil. Her dark brown hair, pulled back severely, emphasized the paleness of her skin, the sharp contrast reminding me of the marble effigies that adorned the tombs in the churchyard.

"Mr. Harding," she began, her voice a soft, measured tone, yet laced with an undercurrent of steel. "I am grateful for your cooperation. Truly, I am." Her eyes met mine, and I saw within them a mix of relief and concern, like the first rays of sunlight struggling to pierce the thickest fog. "But I fear that this is only the beginning. The path ahead is fraught with peril, and we must tread carefully."

I nodded, my mouth dry as dust. The scent of lilies, once comforting, now seemed oppressive, a cloying reminder of the decay that lurked beneath the surface of my world. I could feel the weight of my secrets, the countless confessions of the dead and the dying, pressing down upon me like a shroud.

"Indeed, Miss Blackwood," I replied, my voice barely above a whisper. "The game is afoot, and we are but pawns in its playing."

As Lord Pembroke reached the door, he paused, turning back to us. His eyes, cold and hard as flint, bore into mine. "I shall expect your full cooperation, Mr. Harding. The fate of more than one soul rests upon it." With that, he swept out of the room, the heavy door closing behind him with a resounding thud.

I turned back to Catherine, her figure framed by the dim light, the rustle of her skirts the only sound in the silence. Her eyes searched mine, and I felt a pang of guilt, knowing that I had drawn her into this web of deceit and danger.

My mind was a whirlwind of thoughts, a tumultuous sea of fears and regrets. I thought of Isabella, her laughter echoing through the halls of her family's estate, her eyes sparkling with life. And now, she was entangled in the machinations of that monster, Edward Hyde. I thought of the bodies I had seen, the gruesome tableaux of his handiwork. The blood, so much blood, pooling on the cobblestones, the stench of death heavy in the air. The limbs, twisted and broken, the flesh torn and mangled, the eyes, wide and staring, reflecting the horror of their final moments.

I swallowed hard, the bile rising in my throat. The weight of my secrets, the knowledge of the darkness that stalked the streets of London, was a heavy burden to bear. And now, Catherine was a part of it, her fate intertwined with mine, her life hanging in the balance.

As I looked into her eyes, I saw a reflection of my own fears, my own doubts. But I also saw determination, a steely resolve that burned like a flame in the darkness. And I knew, in that moment, that we were bound together, drawn inexorably into the heart of the storm.

The shadow of Edward Hyde loomed large over us, his presence a chilling reminder of the dark forces at play in our world. The path we had chosen was treacherous, the outcome uncertain. But we had taken the first step, and there was no turning back. The die was cast, and we could only pray that we would emerge from the shadows, our souls intact.

CHAPTER 12

The grand doors of the ballroom swung open, and in swept a figure that commanded the gaze of every soul present.

Edward Hyde, disguised in a demonic mask that seemed to amplify rather than conceal his chilling allure, paused at the threshold. The orchestra's lively melody faltered, as if the very air had been sucked out of the room. His eyes, visible through the mask, were a piercing green that seemed to gleam with an otherworldly light. He was dressed in an elegant black suit, the crisp white shirt beneath stark against his dark waistcoat, with a silver-tipped cane that tapped ominously against the marble floor.

"Lord have mercy," whispered a lady nearby, her fan fluttering rapidly. "Who is that?"

The crowd parted before him like the Red Sea before Moses, a mixture of awe and fear etched on their faces. The air grew thick with tension, the scent of beeswax candles and expensive perfumes cloying in the sudden heat. Hyde moved with the grace of a panther, his every step calculated, his every gesture measured. As he passed, the revelers leaned in, drawn to him like moths to a flame, yet recoiling from the latent menace that radiated from his person.

My own eyes were drawn to him, unable to look away. There was something about him—a dark allure that sent a shiver down my spine.

Isabella, I warned myself, do not be taken in by such a man. Yet, I could not tear my gaze from his form. His mask was a grotesque thing, horned and twisted, yet it was the bloodstains on his cuffs that truly caught my attention. Rumors of his brutal exploits had reached even my sheltered ears—tales of bodies found in alleys, throats slit from ear to ear, entrails spilled onto the cobblestones like grim offerings to some unholy deity. It was said that he had a particular fondness for the sound of begging, for the music of desperation that played out as his blade traced patterns of agony on helpless flesh.

"Good God, man," someone muttered, "he looks as though he's stepped straight from the abyss."

Hyde turned, his eyes meeting mine, and I felt a jolt of something primal and unsettling. His lips curved into a slow, predatory smile, and he began to move towards me, the crowd melting away in his path. My heart pounded in my chest, a drumbeat of warning and anticipation.

What does he want with me? I thought, my mind racing. I had heard the whispers, the stories of his manipulations, his delight in exploiting the weaknesses of others. Yet, as he approached, I found myself drawn to him, captivated by the darkness that clung to him like a shroud.

"Miss Blackwood," he murmured, his voice a low rumble that seemed to resonate within my very soul. "A pleasure to make your acquaintance."

I offered him my hand, my gloves concealing the slight tremor of my fingers. He took it, his grip firm, his thumb tracing a subtle pattern on my knuckles. His touch was warm, almost feverish, and I could not suppress the shiver that ran through me.

"Mr. Hyde," I replied, my voice steadier than I felt. "I must admit, your reputation precedes you."

His smile widened, a flash of white teeth behind the grotesque mask. "Indeed?" he said, his voice laced with amusement. "And what, pray tell, have you heard of me?"

I hesitated, my mind flashing back to the whispered tales of his brutality. I had heard that he had once disemboweled a man, leaving his entrails strewn about like morbid decorations. That he had flayed another, the skin peeled back to reveal the glistening muscle beneath. That he had taken a particular delight in the torment of his victims, their screams echoing through the dark streets like a symphony of suffering.

"Only that you are a man of... considerable influence," I said, choosing my words carefully. "That you have a certain... appetite for power."

He chuckled, a sound like distant thunder. "You are quite correct, Miss Blackwood," he said. "I do indeed have an appetite. And I always get what I want."

His words sent a chill down my spine, even as a dark thrill coursed through me. This man was dangerous, a predator in every sense of the word. Yet, I could not deny the fascination that stirred within me, the desire to dance on the edge of the abyss, to taste the darkness that he offered.

As he led me to the dance floor, I could not shake the feeling that I was stepping into a game of shadows and deceit, a game that I was not sure I wanted to play, yet one that I was powerless to resist. The orchestra struck up a waltz, the music swelling around us like a dark tide, and as we began to move, I could not help but feel that I was being swept away, caught in the current of Edward Hyde's twisted desires.

The grand chandeliers cast a flickering glow over the masquerade ball, the air thick with the scent of wax, perfume, and the faint undernote of decay that seemed to permeate all things in London. The orchestra played a lilting melody, but the sweetness of the music was lost on me, Lady Elizabeth Thornwood, as I observed the scene from my vantage point near the grand staircase. My copper-red hair was piled high, adorned with jewels that matched my emerald gown, a stark contrast to the pallid faces and muted tones of the other widows who lingered at the edges of the ballroom.

As the revelers twirled and chattered, the atmosphere shifted abruptly, as if a chill wind had swept through the room. The cause was immediate and unmistakable: Edward Hyde had made his entrance. His demonic mask, a grotesque visage of black and red, seemed to leer at the assembly, and his commanding presence drew both admiration and unease from the crowd. The sea of masked faces turned towards him, some with fascination, others with palpable dread.

I watched as the throng parted for him, the way rats scatter from a burning building. His tall, elegant form cut through the crowd, his dark coat swaying with a predatory grace. There were whispers, of course—whispers of his deeds, of the bodies found in the rookeries, throats slit from ear to ear, entrails spilling onto the cobblestones like bloody ribbons.

The papers had screamed of the brutality, the pools of congealing blood reflecting the grimy moonlight. Yet here he was, moving among the elite as if he owned them. And perhaps, in a way, he did.

My gaze shifted to Isabella Blackwood, her dark hair and pale complexion a stark contrast to the vibrant colors of the ballroom. Her eyes were fixed on Hyde, a mixture of intrigue and wariness playing across her features. I could see the internal conflict raging within her, the fascination with the darkness he embodied warring with the instinctive caution that such darkness warranted.

As Hyde approached her, the air seemed to grow thicker, the tension palpable. The crowd parted for him as if by instinct, a silent acknowledgment of the power he wielded. I watched as he stood before her, his psychotic eyes gleaming behind the mask, a hypnotic intensity that made the hairs on the back of my neck stand on end.

"Miss Blackwood," he said, his voice a rich, melodious purr that carried just enough to reach my ears. "You look positively enchanting this evening."

Isabella's smile was a delicate thing, a blend of charm and caution. "Mr. Hyde," she replied, her voice steady despite the turmoil I knew must be churning within her. "You have a knack for making an entrance."

He chuckled, a sound like distant thunder. "I find that a touch of theatricality can be quite effective in setting the tone for an evening."

Their exchange was a dance in itself, a subtle battle of wits and wills. I could see the charged undercurrents, the magnetic pull between them. It was a game of shadows and deceit, a game that I was all too familiar with.

"And what tone do you intend to set this evening, Mr. Hyde?" Isabella asked, her eyes never leaving his.

Hyde leaned in slightly, his voice dropping to a conspiratorial whisper. "Why, Miss Blackwood, I intend to set the tone of... revelation. Of truths laid bare and secrets unearthed."

Isabella's eyebrow arched slightly, a silent challenge. "And what truths do you hope to reveal, Mr. Hyde?"

His smile was a slow, predatory curve. "All in good time, my dear. All in good time."

I watched their interaction with a calculating gaze, my mind racing with the implications of Hyde's words. He was a master manipulator, a puppeteer pulling strings in the shadows. But I was no

The Devil of London

mere pawn in his game. I had my own agenda, my own desires, and I would not let him disrupt the delicate balance I had so carefully cultivated.

As the orchestra struck up a new melody, I stepped forward, my skirts rustling softly against the polished floor. It was time to remind Mr. Hyde that he was not the only player in this game of power and deceit.

"Mr. Hyde," I said, my voice a cool interjection. "How delightful to see you again."

His eyes turned to me, a gleam of amusement in their depths. "Lady Thornwood," he replied, a mocking bow accompanying his words. "Always a pleasure."

For in the shadows of Mayfair, power was a fickle mistress, and I would not be bested by the likes of Edward Hyde.

The grand chandeliers cast a kaleidoscope of fractured light across the ballroom, illuminating the revelers in a dance of shadow and glow. The orchestra's melody swelled like a pulsating heart, resonating through the marble floors and gilded walls. Hyde's hand, gloved in black leather, enveloped mine as he led me onto the dance floor. His touch was firm, almost possessive, and I could feel the suppressed strength in his grip. The crowd parted for us, their eyes following our every movement, a sea of silken masks and whispered curiosities.

"You dance with the devil, Miss Blackwood," Hyde murmured, his voice a low rumble that seemed to vibrate through me. His free hand settled on my waist, drawing me closer. The scent of him, a mix of sandalwood and something darker, more primal, filled my senses.

"And what makes you the devil, Mr. Hyde?" I replied, my voice steady despite the turmoil within me. His devilish eyes bore into mine, and I felt an unsettling sensation, as if he could see through my carefully crafted facade.

"Because, my dear, I know the sins that lurk in the hearts of men," he said, his voice barely above a whisper. "I have seen them, indulged them, and left them bleeding in the streets."

His words painted a grotesque image in my mind: cobblestone alleys slick with rain and blood, the gutter running red like a river of sin. I could see him there, his elegant form stark against the squalor, his hands dripping with gore as he stood over his victim, a rictus grin of triumph on his face. The thought should have repelled me, but instead, it sparked a dark fascination, a morbid curiosity that I could not suppress.

Our dance was a macabre ballet, each step measured and precise, yet charged with an undercurrent of danger. His hand at my waist was a brand, his eyes never leaving mine, even as we twirled and spun with the music. I felt like a moth drawn to a flame, aware of the risk, yet unable to resist the allure.

"You speak of sins as if you are not tainted by them," I countered, my breath coming slightly faster than I would have liked. "But I see the blood on your hands, Mr. Hyde. I see the shadows that cling to you like a shroud."

His smile was a slow, predatory curve, and he leaned in, his lips brushing my ear. "Indeed, Miss Blackwood," he whispered. "But my sins are not mere stains on my soul. They are trophies, badges of honor in the game of power and deceit."

As the dance drew to a close, Hyde released me, his gloved hand lingering on mine a moment longer than necessary. The absence of his touch left me feeling strangely bereft, a sensation I quickly pushed aside. As I stepped back, I noticed Lady Elizabeth approaching, her eyes fixed on Hyde with a calculating gaze.

"Mr. Hyde," she said, her voice a cool interjection. "I believe it is my turn to dance with the devil."

Hyde's eyes gleamed with amusement as he turned to Elizabeth, a mocking bow accompanying his words. "Lady Thornwood, always a pleasure."

As they took to the floor, I watched, my heart still pounding from our dance. Their interaction was a study in contrasts—Elizabeth's poise and strategic mind against Hyde's dark charisma and manipulative intelligence. They moved with the elegance of predators circling each other, each testing the other's resolve.

"You play a dangerous game, Mr. Hyde," Elizabeth said, her voice soft yet laced with steel. "But I am no mere pawn in your machinations. I have my own agenda, and I will not be swayed by your charm or your threats."

Hyde's laughter was a low, throaty sound, akin to the purr of a jungle cat. "Ah, Lady Thornwood, ever the strategist. But tell me, what good is a game if there is no risk, no thrill of the unknown?"

Their dance was a battle of wits, a duel fought with words and subtle movements. Elizabeth's eyes never wavered from Hyde's, her expression a mask of calm composure. Yet, I could see the tension in her shoulders, the slight tightening of her jaw—signs of the internal struggle she fought to maintain control.

As they spun past me, I caught a glimpse of Hyde's face, his eyes alight with a dark excitement. In that moment, I saw the true extent of his power, the depth of his manipulations. He was a master puppeteer, pulling strings in the shadows, and we were all mere players in his game.

The thought sent a shiver down my spine, a mix of fear and exhilaration. For in the twisted world of Mayfair's elite, power was a fickle mistress, and I was determined to navigate its treacherous waters, even as I remained ensnared in Hyde's web of intrigue.

In the throes of the masquerade, I, Sir Maximillion Worthington, stood amidst the revelry, my eyes fixed upon the figure of Edward Hyde as he danced with Lady Elizabeth. My hands, clasped behind my back, betrayed the slightest tremor, a telltale sign of the agitation that roiled within me. The grandeur of the ballroom, with its gilded mirrors and resplendent chandeliers, seemed to close in, the air thick with the scent of perfumes and the undercurrent of intrigue.

Hyde moved with a predatory grace, his dark hair glinting under the candlelight, his mask doing little to conceal the sharp, aristocratic features that had become the talk of Mayfair. His every step, every turn, was a calculated move in a game only he seemed to understand. I watched as he leaned in to whisper something to Elizabeth, her eyes never wavering from his, her expression a mask of calm composure. Yet, I could see the tension in her shoulders, the slight tightening of her jaw—signs of the internal struggle she fought to maintain control.

My own facade, meticulously constructed over years of political maneuvering and private indulgences, felt increasingly fragile. Hyde's presence was a threat, a dark shadow looming over the carefully cultivated image I presented to the world. His every word, every gesture, seemed to peel back the layers of my deceit, exposing the rot that lay beneath.

I could not stand idly by, watching as he wove his web of manipulation. With a determined stride, I made my way through the crowded ballroom, the silks and satins of the revelers brushing against me like whispers of conspiracy. The cool night air hit me like a slap as I stepped out into the secluded garden, the din of the ball fading to a distant hum.

Hyde was already there, standing beneath a ancient oak, its gnarled branches casting eerie shadows in the moonlight. He turned to face me, his eyes gleaming with that same dark excitement I had seen on the dance floor.

"Sir Maximillion," he greeted, his voice a rich, melodious sound that sent a chill down my spine. "I had a feeling you would seek me out."

"Hyde," I acknowledged, my voice steady despite the turmoil within me. "I must speak with you."

He raised an eyebrow, a slight smirk playing at the corners of his mouth. "Oh, indeed? And what could the esteemed Sir Maximillion Worthington possibly have to discuss with a man like me?"

I took a deep breath, steeling myself for the confrontation. "You pose a threat, Hyde. To me, to my position, to everything I have built."

Hyde laughed, a low, throaty sound that was more chilling than any shout. "A threat? My dear Sir Maximillion, I am merely a humble servant of the people, seeking to expose the truth that lurks in the shadows of our fair society."

"Truth?" I scoffed, my hands clenching into fists behind my back. "You deal in lies and manipulation, Hyde. You twist people to your will, playing them like pawns in your sick game."

Hyde's smile widened, his teeth gleaming like a predator's in the moonlight. "And what of you, Sir Maximillion? Are you not a master of manipulation yourself? Do you not hide behind a facade of morality while indulging in the darkest of pleasures?"

His words struck like a physical blow, the truth in them cutting deep. I thought of the bodies I had left in my wake, the blood that stained my hands—both literally and metaphorically. The memory of my last victim surfaced unbidden, her lifeless eyes staring up at me, her throat a bloody, gaping maw. I had taken pleasure in her pain, in the feel of her life draining away at my hands. And Hyde knew. Somehow, he knew.

"You speak of things you know nothing about," I growled, taking a step closer to him.

Hyde did not flinch, his gaze steady and unyielding. "On the contrary, Sir Maximillion. I know more than you could possibly imagine. I know about the girls, the ones who disappear in the dead of night, their bodies left to rot in the filthy alleys of London. I know about the blood on your hands, the darkness that stains your soul."

"You know nothing," I hissed, my voice barely more than a whisper.

Hyde's smile vanished, his expression turning cold and hard. "I know enough to destroy you, Sir Maximillion. I know enough to tear down your carefully constructed facade and expose you for the monster you truly are."

"And why have you not done so?" I challenged, my heart pounding in my chest.

Hyde's smile returned, a cruel, twisted thing. "Because, my dear Sir Maximillion, you are far more useful to me alive. For now, at least."

The threat in his words was clear, the underlying promise of violence sending a shiver down my spine. I was a man accustomed to power, to control, yet in that moment, I felt utterly helpless, a puppet dancing to Hyde's twisted tune.

"What do you want, Hyde?" I asked, my voice barely more than a whisper.

Hyde's smile widened, his eyes gleaming with a dark, malevolent joy. "All in good time, Sir Maximillion. All in good time."

From my hidden vantage point behind the ivy-covered trellis, I watched the tableau unfold like a macabre dance. The moon cast a sickly glow upon Sir Maximillion and Hyde, their figures locked in a silent battle of wills. The air was thick with tension, the scent of blooming roses doing little to mask the underlying stench of decay that seemed to follow Hyde like a shroud.

Sir Maximillion's face was a study in barely contained rage, his jaw clenched so tightly I could see the muscles working beneath his skin. His hands, encased in fine white gloves, were balled into fists at his sides. Hyde, by contrast, appeared almost languid, his posture relaxed as he leaned against the marble statue of some long-forgotten deity. His eyes, however, belied his casual stance. They gleamed with a dark intensity that sent a shiver down my spine, even from my concealed position.

"You speak of monsters, Sir Maximillion," Hyde said, his voice a low purr that carried through the still night air. "But you have no idea what true monstrosity looks like. I've seen it, you know. I've walked amongst the bodies of those poor, unfortunate souls who've crossed my path."

He paused, his lips curling into a cruel smile. "I've painted the streets of London with their blood, watched as their entrails steamed in the cold night air. I've heard their screams, their pleas for mercy. And do you know what I've done?"

Sir Maximillion said nothing, his breath coming in harsh gasps. I could see the pulse pounding in his neck, a sign of his mounting fear.

Hyde leaned in closer, his voice dropping to a conspiratorial whisper. "I've laughed, Sir Maximillion. I've laughed as I've torn them apart, as I've bathed in their blood and reveled in their pain. That is what a monster looks like. That is what you should fear."

My heart pounded in my chest as I listened to Hyde's words, my breath coming in shallow gasps. I should have been horrified, disgusted by his graphic descriptions. Yet, I felt a strange thrill coursing through my veins, a dark excitement that I could not deny. This was the power I had longed to understand, the darkness I had yearned to explore.

Hyde's gaze shifted slightly, his eyes seeming to meet mine through the leaves of the trellis. I froze, my heart leaping into my throat. But he said nothing, his smile merely widening before he turned his attention back to Sir Maximillion.

"But you need not fear me, Sir Maximillion," he said, his voice once again smooth and charming. "For I am your ally, your partner in this dance of deceit. Together, we shall remake this world in our image, a world where the weak cower before the strong, where the darkness is embraced rather than feared."

With that, he turned and strode away, leaving Sir Maximillion standing alone in the garden. I watched as the older man sagged against the statue, his face a picture of defeat. Then, with a sigh, he pushed himself upright and made his way back towards the ballroom, his steps heavy with resignation.

I waited until he had disappeared from view before emerging from my hiding place, my mind racing with all that I had witnessed. As I made my way back towards the ballroom, I could not help but feel a sense of exhilaration, a thrill of anticipation for the games yet to come.

The ballroom was a buzzing hive of whispered conversations and shifting alliances as I slipped back inside. The elite of Mayfair moved like colourful pawns on a chessboard, their silk gowns and embroidered waistcoats a stark contrast to the dark secrets that lurked beneath their polished exteriors.

Lady Henrietta and Lord Blackwood stood in a corner, their heads bent together in urgent conference. I could see the flash of diamonds at

Lady Henrietta's throat as she nodded sharply, her eyes darting around the room as if fearful of being overheard. Nearby, the Duke of Somerset held court, his laughter booming out as he regaled his companions with some witty anecdote. Yet, even his joviality seemed forced, his eyes betraying a wariness that had not been present earlier in the evening.

I moved through the crowd, my senses heightened as I took in the subtle shifts in power dynamics. There, in the far corner, Margaret Winters stood alone, her eyes scanning the crowd with a look of thinly veiled disdain. Her hands were clasped tightly before her, her knuckles white with tension. As I watched, she was joined by Thomas Harding, his gaunt figure cutting a stark contrast to her tall, elegant form. They exchanged a few words, Margaret's expression growing increasingly anxious as Harding spoke in low, urgent tones.

As I continued my circuit of the room, I could hear snippets of conversation, whispers of scandal and intrigue that sent a thrill of excitement down my spine.

"Did you hear about Lady Catherine's youngest daughter?" one matron whispered to another, her fan fluttering wildly before her face. "Rumour has it she's been secretly engaged to that scoundrel, Lord Rutherford."

"No!" her companion gasped, her eyes wide with shock. "But he's old enough to be her father!"

"Indeed," the first woman replied, her voice dripping with scandalized delight. "But they say he's promised her a fortune in jewels and silks. Not to mention the title, of course."

I smiled to myself, filing away the information for future use. Such secrets were the currency of our world, the keys to unlocking the hidden desires and fears of those around us. And I intended to collect as many as I could, to wield them like weapons in the games yet to come.

As I reached the edge of the dance floor, I caught sight of Isabella, her dark eyes meeting mine across the crowded room. She looked away quickly, but not before I saw the flash of unease that crossed her face. I could not help but wonder what secrets she hid behind her enigmatic smile, what darkness lurked beneath her carefully crafted facade.

But such musings would have to wait, for at that moment, the orchestra struck up a lively quadrille, and the room was filled with the swirling colours of the dancers' gowns. As I took my place among them, I

The grand chandelier overhead flickered, casting eerie, dancing shadows upon the gilded walls as the night wore on. The once-jovial atmosphere had soured, turning into a palpable unease that hung heavy in the air like the smoke from a hundred candles. The guests, once united in their merriment, now fragmented into tight knots of tense whisperings and furtive glances. The shifting alliances were almost palpable, like the changing winds before a storm.

Standing near the grand staircase, I observed this spectacle with a growing sense of disquiet. The silk of my gown, a deep burgundy reminiscent of dried blood, rustled softly as I shifted my weight, my eyes scanning the crowd. The elaborate wigs and painted faces that had once seemed so festive now appeared garish, grotesque even, under the flickering light.

Lady Worthington and her coterie huddled near the punch bowl, their fans fluttering like nervous birds. I could hear snippets of their conversation, voices low and urgent.

"Have you seen the way Lord Blackwood watches Hyde?" one of them murmured, her eyes darting towards the gentleman in question. "Like a hawk eyeing its prey."

"Indeed," another replied, her voice barely audible. "And did you hear about the murder in Covent Garden last night? They say the victim was torn apart, limb from limb. The cobblestones were slick with blood and... other things." She shuddered delicately, her fan snapping shut.

My stomach churned at the image, but I filed it away nonetheless. Such gruesome tidbits were valuable, especially given Hyde's reputation. I had heard the whispers, the rumors that followed him like a dark cloud. They said he had a taste for blood, for violence. That he had once torn a man's heart from his chest with his bare hands.

Across the room, Margaret Winters stood stiffly, her gloved hands clenched around her sister's arm. Her eyes, usually so calm and collected, darted around the room like a trapped animal seeking escape. I could see the pulse fluttering in her neck, a telltale sign of her anxiety. She leaned down, whispering something in her sister's ear. The younger girl paled, her eyes widening in fright.

Suddenly, the orchestra fell silent, their last note hanging in the air like a dying breath. The chatter died down, the whispers faltering as all eyes turned towards the grand staircase. My heart pounded in my chest as Edward Hyde ascended, his boots echoing ominously on the marble steps.

The Devil of London

His eyes, those hypnotic green orbs, surveyed the crowd with a cold, calculating gaze. He looked every inch the predator, from his sharply tailored coat to the gleam of his polished boots. A shiver ran down my spine as his gaze passed over me, lingering for just a moment too long.

"Ladies and gentlemen," he began, his voice resonating through the ballroom like a funeral toll. "I trust you are enjoying the evening's... entertainments." His lips curved into a cruel smile, and I felt a wave of nausea wash over me.

"However," he continued, his voice dropping to a low, dangerous purr, "I fear the night is not yet over. In fact, it is just beginning."

A gasp rippled through the crowd, the sound echoing off the vaulted ceiling like a ghostly whisper. Hyde paused, his eyes gleaming with malicious delight as he surveyed the sea of shocked faces.

"You see," he said, his voice barely above a whisper, yet carrying through the silent room like a shout, "I have come to make an announcement. One that will change the very fabric of our dear society."

The air was thick with tension, the silence so complete that I could hear the rapid beating of my own heart. Hyde's smile widened, his teeth gleaming like a wolf's grin in the candlelight.

"I intend," he said, his voice dripping with malice, "to expose each and every one of your secrets. To lay bare the rotten core that festers beneath your fine silks and powdered wigs."

The room erupted into chaos, the guests' faces a blur of shock and outrage. The air filled with the sound of gasps and murmurs, the rustle of silk as people turned to one another in disbelief. I stood frozen, my heart pounding in my chest as I stared at Hyde, his eyes gleaming with triumph as he surveyed the pandemonium he had unleashed.

As the night wore on, the unease that had permeated the room congealed into a thick, choking fog of fear and anticipation. The games had only just begun, and we were all pawns in Hyde's twisted play.

The grand chandelier overhead flickered, its crystals casting eerie shadows that danced macabrely across the suddenly pale faces of the assembly. The ballroom, once a buzzing hive of feigned gaiety, now hummed with a discordant melody of whispers and anxious titters. I, Isabella Blackwood, stood rooted to the spot, my heart a drumbeat of dread within my breast.

Hyde's announcement had plunged the room into chaos, and now the air was thick with the scent of fear, a cloying perfume that mingled with the sweat and pomades of the nobility. Around me, silks rustled like dry leaves as the elite of Mayfair shifted uncomfortably, their eyes darting from one to another, as if the very words they spoke might betray the secrets they so desperately clutched to their bosoms.

"Dear Lord, what shall we do?" muttered a nearby countess, her fan fluttering rapidly, a vain attempt to cool her suddenly flushed cheeks. Her companion, a portly baron, mopped his brow with a lace-edged kerchief. "This is an outrage!" he blustered, though his voice trembled. "Who does this Hyde think he is?"

I could not help but steal a glance at the man himself, standing tall and implacable amidst the tempest he had stirred. His green eyes gleamed with a malevolent delight, his lips curved in a cruel smile as he surveyed the havoc. He was a conductor, I realized, and we his orchestra, playing our discordant symphony to his whim.

Lady Elizabeth Thornwood stood across the room, her copper-red hair a beacon amidst the pastel wigs and powdered coiffures. Her expression was one of calculated contemplation, her ice-blue eyes narrowed as she regarded Hyde. I knew that look; she was plotting, scheming, trying to turn this sudden shift to her advantage.

"Lady Elizabeth seems unruffled," a voice murmured at my side. I turned to find Sir Maximillion Worthington, his usually jovial face etched with worry. "But what of you, Miss Blackwood? You are pale as a ghost."

I forced a smile, a brittle thing that felt more like a grimace. "I am merely taking in the spectacle, sir," I replied, my voice steady despite the turmoil within me. "After all, it is not every day one sees the foundations of society so... vigorously shaken."

Sir Maximillion frowned, his gaze flicking nervously to Hyde. "This is no spectacle, miss. This is a bloodbath waiting to happen. Mark my words, there will be bodies in the streets before this is done."

His words sent a shiver down my spine, conjuring images of blood-slicked cobblestones and lifeless eyes staring blankly at the cold London moon. I had heard the whispers, the rumors of Hyde's brutal ascension to power. They said he had left a trail of corpses in his wake, that he had carved his way through the underbelly of London like a plague, leaving only ruin and rot behind him.

The Devil of London

I stole another glance at Hyde, his elegant frame and sharp features belying the monster that lurked beneath. I could almost see it, the beast within, its claws dripping with blood, its teeth bared in a snarl of triumph. I shuddered, my stomach churning at the thought of the carnage he was capable of unleashing.

Elizabeth, ever the strategist, began to move through the crowd, her head held high, her poise unshaken. She paused here and there, leaning in to whisper to this lord or that lady, her words too soft to catch, but her intent clear. She was rallying, consolidating her power, shoring up her defenses against the storm that was Hyde.

I knew I should do the same, should weave my own web of alliances and assurances, but I felt rooted to the spot, transfixed by the horror and the fascination that warred within me. Hyde, as if sensing my gaze, turned to me, his eyes locking onto mine. His smile widened, a grotesque parody of pleasure, and he raised his glass in a mocking salute.

I tore my gaze away, my heart pounding, my breath coming in short, sharp gasps. I would not be a pawn in his game, I resolved, nor a plaything for his amusement. I would navigate these treacherous waters, would chart my own course through the chaos. But even as I steeled myself for the trials ahead, I could not shake the feeling of unease, the sense that I was already ensnared, a fly caught fast in Hyde's web.

As the night wore on, the ballroom began to empty, the nobility fleeing like rats from a sinking ship. Those who remained huddled in tight knots, their voices low, their eyes wide with fear and speculation. The chandelier overhead flickered again, its light casting eerie shadows that seemed to twist and writhe, a grim portent of the darkness to come.

And through it all, Hyde stood tall and unyielding, his eyes gleaming with malice and delight, the conductor of our symphony, the puppet master pulling our strings. The games had only just begun, and we were all, every one of us, dancing to his tune.

The fog rolled in from the Thames, a choking miasma that clung to the cobblestones and wrapped the gas lamps in a sickly halo. I walked briskly, my boots clicking sharply against the damp stones, the hem of my greatcoat sweeping the filth from the streets. The night air was thick with the stench of decay and the acrid tang of coal smoke, the ever-present odor of London's relentless industry.

My mind was a whirlwind of thoughts, a chaotic jumble of images and words from the night before. Hyde's announcement had left the ballroom in shambles, the elite of Mayfair scattering like frightened mice. But I, Isabella Blackwood, would not be so easily shaken. I had resolved to face whatever horrors Hyde unleashed, to navigate the treacherous waters he stirred.

A sudden noise from an alleyway snapped me from my thoughts. A low, guttural moan echoed through the fog, raising the hairs on the back of my neck. I paused, straining my ears, my heart pounding in my chest. The sound came again, a choked, desperate cry that spoke of untold agony.

I stepped cautiously towards the alley, my hand reaching into my coat to grasp the cold steel of a small pistol. The fog was thicker here, a cloying shroud that clung to my skin and caught in my throat. As I rounded the corner, my eyes widened in horror at the sight before me.

A man lay sprawled in the filth, his body twisted at an unnatural angle. His fine clothes were torn and bloodied, his silk waistcoat slashed to ribbons. His face was a mask of terror, eyes wide and staring, mouth frozen in a silent scream. But it was his chest that drew my gaze, a gaping wound that laid his insides bare, a grotesque parody of a surgeon's incision.

I choked back a wave of nausea, my grip tightening on the pistol. This was Hyde's work, of that I had no doubt. The precision of the cut, the sheer brutality of the act, it bore all the hallmarks of his twisted genius. I turned to leave, eager to escape the sight of such butchery, when a voice stopped me in my tracks.

"A gruesome sight, is it not?"

I spun around, my pistol raised, to find Hyde standing at the mouth of the alley. His eyes gleamed in the faint gaslight, a malevolent spark that sent a shiver down my spine. He stepped closer, his boots clicking on the cobblestones, his hands clasped behind his back as if he were taking a casual stroll.

"You did this," I hissed, my voice barely more than a whisper. "You butchered him like an animal."

Hyde smiled, a slow, lazy curve of his lips that held no warmth. "Indeed, I did," he replied, his voice a low purr. "But tell me, dear Isabella, do you not find a certain... artistry in my work?"

I stared at him, revulsion churning in my gut. "Artistry?" I spat. "This is madness, Hyde. Sick, twisted madness."

He chuckled, a sound like distant thunder. "Madness, perhaps," he conceded. "But there is a method to it, dear girl. A purpose behind the bloodshed."

I shook my head, my pistol still trained on his heart. "You are a monster, Hyde," I whispered. "A beast that feeds on the suffering of others."

His smile widened, a grotesque parody of pleasure. "Indeed, I am," he agreed. "But tell me, Isabella, are you so different? Do you not hunger for power, for control? Do you not yearn to bend others to your will, to shape the world to your design?"

I hesitated, his words striking a chord deep within me. I thought of the ballroom, of the shifting alliances and whispered conversations, of the power plays and manipulations that defined my world. Was I so different from Hyde? Did I not, in my own way, crave the same control, the same dominion over others?

Hyde stepped closer, his voice dropping to a low, intimate murmur. "You and I, Isabella, we are two sides of the same coin," he said. "We understand the true nature of power, the sacrifices it demands. We know that to gain control, one must be willing to spill a little blood."

I stared at him, my heart pounding in my chest, my mind a whirlwind of doubt and uncertainty. And as I stood there, the fog swirling around us, the stench of death heavy in the air, I could not help but wonder: was Hyde truly the monster he appeared to be? Or was he merely a reflection of the darkness that lay within us all?

As I lowered my pistol, I knew that the days ahead would bring more bloodshed, more horror, more twisted games of power and manipulation. But I also knew that I would face them head-on, that I would navigate the treacherous waters of Hyde's world, and that I would emerge from the chaos stronger, more ruthless, more determined than ever.

For I was Isabella Blackwood, and I would not be a pawn in anyone's game. I would be the queen, the puppet master, the architect of my own destiny. And heaven help anyone who dared to stand in my way.

CHAPTER 13

The heavy oak door of The Crimson Lantern creaked open, revealing a den of iniquity that even the devil himself might shy away from. I, Jonathan Hartwell, stepped inside, my eyes adjusting to the dim light as the stench of cheap perfume and even cheaper liquor assaulted my senses. The flickering gas lamps cast eerie shadows on the worn velvet wallpaper, creating a dance of light and dark that seemed to mirror the battle raging within my own mind.

My heart pounded a steady, calculated rhythm as I scanned the room. The patrons here were a motley crew of thieves, prostitutes, and cutthroats, their laughter and chatter a grating cacophony that set my teeth on edge. Among them, I sought two familiar faces: Rose Whitechapel and Edwin "Flash" Barrett.

As I weaved through the crowded tables, my mind raced, calculating and strategizing like a general preparing for battle. The stakes were high, and the path I trod was treacherous, lined with the bloody remnants of Hyde's victims. I had seen their mutilated corpses, the flesh flayed from their bones, organs glistening like obscene jewels amidst the crimson gore. The images haunted me, fueling my ambition and my desperation.

Finally, I spotted them, tucked away in a secluded corner, their forms shrouded in a thick haze of tobacco smoke. Rose, regal and composed, her dark eyes reflecting the dance of the flames. Her gown, a rich burgundy silk, shimmered in the low light, the expensive lace at her throat concealing the thin scar that betrayed her past. Beside her, Flash, his sandy hair tousled, fingers drumming nervously against the table. His clothes were plain, unassuming, designed to blend in, to be forgotten.

I approached their table, my steps measured, my demeanor calm and composed. As I sat, the chair scraped against the worn wooden floor, the harsh sound echoing like a judge's gavel. "Good evening, Rose. Flash." I nodded to each in turn, my voice steady, betraying none of the turmoil within.

Rose's lips curved into a slow, calculating smile. "Mr. Hartwell," she acknowledged, her voice a low purr. "You're looking...driven."

Flash offered me a nervous grin, his laugh a staccato burst of tension. "Evenin', guv'nor. Quite the night, ain't it?" His fingers continued their dance, his gaze darting between Rose and myself.

I allowed myself a small, guarded smile, a mere twitch of my lips. "Indeed, Flash. Quite the night." My mind whirred, sifting through strategies, weighing each word before it crossed my lips. The negotiation was a delicate dance, a battle of wits and wills. And I was determined to emerge victorious, no matter the cost.

The flickering flame of the solitary candle cast grotesque shadows upon the worn tabletop, the dim light barely illuminating the rough faces of those gathered. I leaned in, my voice low and measured, like the steady ticking of a clock counting down to some inevitable end. "Ladies and gentlemen of the jury," I began, as if addressing a courtroom, "allow me to paint a vision of our future. A future where the streets of London are not merely ours to walk, but ours to command."

I steepled my fingers, my gaze shifting from Rose to Flash, drawing them in as I would a jury. "Consider, if you will, the power we hold in our collective grasp. Rose, your establishment is the heart of society's secrets. Every whisper, every indiscretion, flows through The Crimson Pearl like blood through veins. And Flash," I turned to him, "your knowledge of the underground is unparalleled. You are the pulse of the streets, the eyes that see all."

I allowed myself a pause, letting my words sink in like a fine blade. "Together, we can consolidate our influence. With your intelligence and my legal acumen, we can manipulate the law, the press, the very fabric of society. We can turn whispers into weapons, silence our enemies, and elevate our allies."

As I spoke, I could see the scenes unfolding in my mind's eye. The cobblestone streets slick with rain and blood, the echoes of Hyde's victims' screams bouncing off the cold brick walls. A severed hand, pale and lifeless, discarded in the gutter like so much trash. The power we could wield would be absolute, the consequences be damned.

Rose listened, her expression inscrutable. Her eyes, dark and knowing, reflected the candlelight like polished obsidian. She was a statue, a monument to calculated thought, her silence a chasm into which my words tumbled. "And what of Hyde, Mr. Hartwell?" she asked finally, her voice a low, melodic rumble. "What role does that...creature play in your grand design?"

I smiled, a slow, careful curve of my lips. A trap, baited and set. "Hyde is a tool, my dear. A brutal, blood-soaked tool. He is the terror that stalks the night, the monster that keeps the populace cowering. With him, we have a force that operates outside the law, beyond morality. He is the blade that strikes in the dark, the fear that ensures compliance."

Rose's eyebrow arched, a delicate shift of her features. "And who wields this...blade, Mr. Hartwell? Who controls the monster?"

I leaned back, my fingers tracing the cool metal of my pocket watch. "Why, we do, Rose. Together. United, we form a triumvirate of power. Society's sins flow through your establishment, the streets whisper to Flash, and I...I am the law that binds or frees them."

Her lips curved, a faint, enigmatic smile. "A bold vision, Mr. Hartwell. But what of the cost? What toll will this dance with the devil exact from us?"

I waved my hand, dismissing her concerns like so much smoke. "Progress always demands sacrifice, Rose. The blood spilled is a necessary evil, a means to an end."

Even as I spoke, I could see the bodies. The limbs torn asunder, the entrails steaming in the cool night air, the eyes wide and staring, glassy with terror and pain. A necessary evil. A means to an end.

Rose's gaze bore into me, a relentless, probing force. "And what of your ambition, Mr. Hartwell? What role does it play in this alliance?"

I met her stare, my composure unshaken. "My ambition, Rose, is the engine that drives us all forward. It is the relentless force that will see this plan through, that will not shy from the hard choices, the necessary sacrifices."

In my mind, the streets ran red, the screams echoed, and the power, the sweet, intoxicating power, coursed through my veins. This was my vision, my future. And I would see it made real, no matter the cost.

The Crimson Lantern's dimly lit confines enveloped me, a choking miasma of smoke and shadows that seemed to seep into my very soul. My eyes flitted from Hartwell's calculated gaze to Rose's inscrutable expression, their words washing over me like a tide of filth. I could feel it, the familiar chill that accompanies Hyde's presence, creeping up my spine. I pulled at my collar, the once-comforting disguise of servitude now a noose, constricting, suffocating.

Hartwell's voice droned on, a low and steady rumble, like the ceaseless roll of distant thunder. "Consider, Rose," he purred, "the benefits of consolidated power. With your influence over the streets and my command of the law, we shall be unstoppable." His fingers danced through the air like a puppeteer's, pulling at invisible strings.

Rose, her features cast in stark relief by the flickering candlelight, sat as still as a statue, her eyes twin pools of shadow. Her gown, a rich velvet the colour of blood, seemed to absorb what little light dared to venture near. She was a vision, a dark madonna, and I, a lowly sinner, torn between salvation and damnation.

"And what of Hyde?" I blurted, the words escaping my lips before I could contain them. My hands, traitorous appendages that they were, trembled slightly as I clasped them before me. I could see him, Hyde, his form shrouded in the night, a brutal silhouette framed by the gaslit streets. The cobblestones slick with blood, the air thick with screams, and there, in the heart of it all, Hyde, his eyes ablaze, his hands, those terrible hands, dripping with gore.

Hartwell's gaze shifted to me, his eyes narrowing as if seeing me for the first time. "Hyde is a means to an end, Barrett," he said, his voice barely above a whisper. "A tool to be wielded, nothing more."

The images assailed me, a grotesque parade of Hyde's victims. The woman from Whitechapel, her entrails strewn about like so much discarded rubbish. The man from the alley, his face a bloody pulp, bone gleaming wetly in the moonlight. The children... dear God, the children. Their tiny bodies broken, twisted, their innocent faces frozen in eternal terror.

I swallowed hard, my mouth dry as ash. "He's more than that," I rasped. "He's... he's a monster."

Hartwell's lips curved, a slow, sinister smile. "Exactly, Barrett," he said, his voice like silk. "And monsters, by their very nature, inspire fear. Fear that we, as his... associates, shall capitalize upon."

Rose's gaze shifted to me, her eyes softening ever so slightly. "And what of your associations, Barrett?" she asked, her voice a low purr. "What of Sterling? Where does her influence fit into this sordid affair?"

I felt it then, that familiar tug, the allure of Victoria Sterling. Her image rose unbidden in my mind, a beacon of purity amidst the squalor. Her eyes, so full of hope, of promise. Her touch, gentle, soothing, a balm to my tormented soul. But there, on the periphery, lurked Hyde, his shadow looming, ever-present, a stain that could not be washed away.

Hartwell, sensing my indecision, leaned forward, his eyes gleaming with barely concealed desperation. "Consider, Barrett," he said, his voice a low growl. "The power we could wield, the change we could effect. With Rose's influence, Sterling's wealth, and Hyde's... persuasion, we could reshape this city in our image."

His words painted a picture, a grotesque tapestry woven from the threads of my darkest fears. I could see it, the streets running red, the bodies piled high, and there, atop the bloody throne, Hartwell, his eyes wild, his laughter echoing through the empty halls of my mind.

I shuddered, my resolve wavering. The line between salvation and damnation blurred, the chasm yawning wide, threatening to consume me whole. I was a man torn, my loyalties frayed, my soul laid bare. And as the night wore on, the shadows deepened, and the bloody tide of Hyde's reign rose ever higher.

The door to The Crimson Lantern swung open with such force that the candle flames guttered, casting macabre shadows on the already grim tableau. In strode Victoria Sterling, a vision of elegance and virtue amidst the squalor. Her honey-blonde hair, though modestly styled, seemed to catch what little light there was, forming a halo around her resolute face. Her blue eyes blazed with a fervor I had seen before, but never directed at me with such intensity. Her dress, a muted blue, was of fine quality, the hem slightly muddied from the filthy streets outside, a stark reminder of the world beyond this den of iniquity.

My heart pounded in my chest as I took her in, a stark contrast to the blood-soaked images that had been dancing in my mind's eye mere moments before. I had been envisioning the streets running red with blood, the cobblestones slick with the entrails of Hyde's victims. I had seen the bodies piled high, their limbs contorted in the final throes of agony, their faces frozen in eternal screams. The stench of death and decay had been almost palpable, the air thick with the coppery tang of blood.

But now, Victoria's presence cut through the gloom like a beacon, her righteous indignation a palpable force. Her gaze swept over the room, taking in the dimly lit corners, the shadowy figures hunched over their drinks, and finally, our secluded table. Her eyes widened slightly as she recognized me, her expression a mix of disappointment and determination.

"Edwin Barrett," she said, her voice filled with a quiet authority that commanded attention. "I had hoped to find you here, though not, I must admit, in such company." Her gaze flicked briefly to Hartwell and Rose, her disapproval evident.

I shifted uncomfortably in my seat, my hands fidgeting with the worn fabric of my breeches. My heart pounded in my ears, a drumbeat of guilt and shame. I could feel Hyde's shadow looming behind me, his presence a dark stain on my soul. Yet, Victoria's gaze held a promise, a lifeline thrown to a drowning man.

"Miss Sterling," I stammered, my voice barely above a whisper. "You shouldn't be here. It ain't safe."

She stepped closer, her skirts rustling softly. "Safe?" she repeated, her voice barely above a whisper. "And what of the safety of those poor souls who fall victim to your... associates? What of the women and children who live in fear of the very streets they call home?"

Her words cut deep, a knife twisted in my gut. I could see them, the victims, their faces pale, their eyes wide with terror. I had seen the aftermath of Hyde's wrath, the bodies torn asunder, the blood pooling in the gutters. I had heard the screams, the pleas for mercy that fell on deaf ears. And I had done nothing.

"I... I ain't got a choice, Miss Sterling," I said, my voice barely audible. "Hyde... he'd kill me if I crossed him."

Victoria's expression softened, her eyes filled with a compassion that threatened to undo me. "There is always a choice, Edwin," she said gently. "You can choose to do what is right, what is just. You can choose redemption."

Her words hung in the air, a promise, a challenge. I could feel the weight of my decisions bearing down on me, the line between salvation and damnation blurring once more. And as I looked into Victoria's eyes, I saw a glimpse of the man I could be, the man I wanted to be. But the path to redemption was steep, and the shadows of my past threatened to consume me whole.

The crimson lantern cast a sickly glow upon the table, its blood-red hue painting our faces like grotesque masquerade masks. The air was thick with tension, a palpable miasma that clung to the worn velvet of my waistcoat like the fog on the Thames. Victoria turned from Barrett, her gaze piercing through the gloom, and fixed her stare upon Hartwell and myself. Her eyes, clear and blue as a summer's day, held a storm that chilled me to the marrow.

"And what of you, Mr. Hartwell? Ms. Whitechapel?" she began, her voice steady and resonant, a beacon of righteousness in this den of iniquity. "Have you too been swayed by the promises of power and wealth, whilst the good people of London live in terror?"

Hartwell shifted in his seat, his normally composed demeanor fracturing like the first cracks of ice upon a frozen lake. He laughed nervously, a sound like the rattle of dry bones. "Miss Sterling," he said, his voice a study in false calm, "you misunderstand our intentions. We seek only to... to stabilize the situation. To bring order—"

"Order?" Victoria interjected, her voice sharp as a surgeon's blade. "You speak of order whilst Hyde's victims lie in pieces, their blood washed into the gutters like so much rainwater!"

I could see them then, the remnants of Hyde's grisly work. A severed hand, its fingers curled like a dead spider, wedged in a narrow alley. The stench of rotting flesh, thick and cloying, mingling with the heavy scent of cheap perfume and cheaper gin. A woman's torso, flayed open like a butcher's cut, organs glistening beneath the pale moonlight. Her eyes, staring wide and unseeing, filmed over with the milky sheen of death.

Hartwell's lips thinned into a bloodless line, his knuckles white as he gripped the edge of the table. "You cannot comprehend the complexities of the situation, Miss Sterling," he said, his voice taking on a desperate edge. "Sometimes, sacrifices must be made for the greater good."

The Devil of London

Victoria did not flinch. "The greater good, Mr. Hartwell?" she challenged, her voice low and fierce. "Or your own ambition? How many more must die before you admit the truth—that you have sold your soul for naught but empty promises and bloody coin?"

Hartwell's composure cracked further, his eyes darting between Victoria and myself like a cornered animal. "You know nothing of the world, Miss Sterling," he snapped, his eloquence dissolving into terse syllables. "Nothing of the hard choices that must be made."

I watched, silent and still, as Hartwell's carefully constructed facade crumbled. His hands trembled slightly, the gold of his pocket watch glinting dull in the crimson light. He was a man on the precipice, his ambition aflame, yet his conscience gnawing at his heels like a hungry cur.

Victoria's gaze shifted to me, her eyes searching, questioning. I felt a shiver run down my spine, a cold finger tracing the length of my vertebrae. "And you, Ms. Whitechapel?" she asked, her voice softer but no less intense. "Have you too been blinded by the lure of power?"

I met her gaze, my expression inscrutable, even as my mind whirled with calculations and assessments. I had seen the depths of human depravity, had built an empire upon the backs of the fallen. Yet, as I looked into Victoria's eyes, I saw a reflection of something I had long thought lost—a flicker of conscience, a spark of humanity amidst the ashes of my past.

But I pushed the thought away, burying it deep within the dark recesses of my mind. This was not the time for sentimentality, not the time for weakness. Not when the stakes were so high, and the path forward so treacherous.

"We all make choices, Miss Sterling," I replied, my voice cool and measured. "And we all must live with the consequences, be they heaven or hell."

Hartwell, seizing the moment, attempted to rally, his voice regaining a semblance of control. "Precisely, Ms. Whitechapel," he said, his words a thin veneer over his growing doubts. "We must look to the future, to the stability of London, and not be swayed by emotion or—"

"Stability, Mr. Hartwell?" Victoria interjected, her voice a whip-crack, sharp and unyielding. "Or complicity? You speak of choices, of consequences, yet you would see this city burn in Hyde's bloody reign rather than admit your own culpability."

Hartwell paled, his lips parting as if to speak, but no words came forth. He was a man drowning, his plans unraveling like a shroud in the wind. And as I watched him flail, I could not help but feel a sense of satisfaction, a cold and bitter pleasure in his discomfort.

For in that moment, as Victoria's quiet authority cut through the tension, I saw the truth—that Hartwell's ambition, once a beacon of strength, was now his undoing. And as the shadows of The Crimson Lantern closed in around us, I knew that the night was far from over, and the true test of our mettle was yet to come.

The Crimson Lantern's air was thick with tension, the dim light flickering over the worn tables and casting macabre shadows on the patrons' faces. I, Rose Whitechapel, sat with my back straight, my eyes fixed on the dance of flames in the hearth. Victoria's words still hung heavy in the air, a challenge that had shifted the very ground beneath our feet.

My mind raced, calculating the risks and rewards of the path Hartwell proposed. I had seen the bodies left in Hyde's wake, their limbs torn asunder, entrails steaming in the cold London air. The cobblestones slick with blood, the stench of death clinging to the fog like a shroud. A man eviscerated in Whitechapel, his screams echoing through the night until his lungs were silenced by the monster's hand. A woman in Spitalfields, her flesh flayed, bones gleaming like ivory in the moonlight. Hartwell offered stability, but at what cost? Would I trade my soul for safety, become a pawn in his game?

I glanced at Hartwell, his composure crumbling like a rotten facade. His cravat was askew, his coat rumpled, the very picture of a man unraveling. Beside him, Flash Barrett fidgeted, his fingers dancing a nervous jig on the table. The boy's eyes darted between Victoria and Hartwell, his loyalties torn.

"Rose," Hartwell began, his voice a thin veneer over desperation, "consider the power we could wield, the order we could impose—"

"Order?" I interjected, my voice a low purr. "Or complicity? You speak of power, Jonathan, but I've seen the price of it. The streets run red with blood, the gutters clogged with flesh. Hyde's reign is bloody, brutal. And you would have us join him, sanction his madness."

Hartwell paled, his lips thinning into a harsh line. "It is not madness, Rose. It is control. A means to an end."

The Devil of London

I leaned back, my gaze shifting to Victoria. Her eyes were fierce, her conviction palpable. She stood like a beacon in the gloom, her cloak a stark contrast to the shadows, her bonnet framing her face in a halo of righteousness. She was a formidable opponent, her quiet authority a blade cutting through the mire of Hartwell's ambition.

Flash's nervous laughter cut through the silence, a jarring note in the symphony of tension. "It ain't right, Mr. Hartwell," he said, his voice barely above a whisper. "The things 'e does... the screams..." He shuddered, his eyes haunted. "I can't... I won't be a part of it no more."

Hartwell's eyes widened, his grip tightening on the table's edge. "Barrett, think about what you're saying. Think about the consequences —"

"I am, sir," Flash interjected, his voice gaining strength. "I am thinkin' about 'em. And I can't live with 'em no more." He turned to Victoria, his expression a mix of fear and determination. "I'll 'elp you, miss. I'll testify, do whatever you need. Just... just make it stop."

Victoria offered him a small, encouraging smile. "You're doing the right thing, Edwin."

My mind whirred, the calculations shifting, the scales tipping. Flash's defection was a blow to Hartwell, a chink in his armor. The power dynamics were changing, the alliances shifting like sand beneath our feet. I could almost taste the tang of blood in the air, the coppery scent of opportunity and risk.

I looked at Hartwell, his eyes wild, his plans unraveling like a poorly spun tapestry. He was a drowning man, grasping at straws, his ambition a millstone around his neck. And as I watched him flail, I made my choice.

"I'm out, Jonathan," I said, my voice a low, decisive purr. "I won't be a party to Hyde's reign. I won't sanction his madness. Not for power. Not for stability. Not for anything."

The words hung in the air, a gauntlet thrown, a line drawn in the sand. The Crimson Lantern seemed to hold its breath, the shadows closing in, the night far from over. The true test of our mettle was yet to come, the consequences of our choices a bloody tangle of risk and reward.

The Crimson Lantern's air grew thick with tension, a palpable miasma that seemed to cling to the very walls. The flickering gas lamps cast eerie shadows, dancing like macabre puppets against the faded velvet drapes. My heart pounded in my chest, a relentless drumbeat echoing the turmoil within. Victoria's presence had stirred a tempest, forcing us all to confront the dark recesses of our souls.

Hartwell's eyes, once calm and calculating, now burned with a wild desperation. His perfectly groomed facade crumbled, revealing the ruthless ambition beneath. "You cannot simply walk away, Rose," he hissed, his voice a low, dangerous growl. "You know too much. You've seen too much. Hyde will never let you go."

I could see it then, the gruesome tableau of Hyde's wrath. The cobblestone alleys slick with rain and blood, the air heavy with the coppery stench of slaughter. Bodies torn asunder, entrails steaming in the cold night air, their cries of agony echoing through the fog. A shudder ran down my spine, but I held my ground. "I won't live in fear, Jonathan," I retorted, my voice steady despite the churning in my gut. "Nor will I be a party to such... such grotesqueries."

Victoria stood tall and resolute, her blue eyes ablaze with righteous fervor. "You speak of power, Mr. Hartwell," she said, her voice cutting through the tension like a knife. "But at what cost? Look around you. See the blood on your hands, the shadows in your eyes. Is this the legacy you wish to leave?"

Hartwell's gaze flicked to his hands, trembling slightly as he gripped the edge of the table. The shadows under his eyes seemed to deepen, the tremor in his hands growing more pronounced. His once-immaculate suit now appeared rumpled, his cravat askew, a stark contrast to Victoria's composed elegance. "You don't understand," he rasped, a note of pleading in his voice. "The things I've done... the things I've seen... I can't turn back now."

Barrett, his cheerful facade stripped away, looked from Hartwell to Victoria, his eyes haunted. "I've seen it too, miss," he said, his voice barely above a whisper. "The bodies... the blood... It's like a nightmare, it is. But Miss Victoria, she's right. We can't keep silent. Not no more."

Hartwell's laugh, a brittle, desperate sound, echoed through the room. "Silence?" he cried. "There is no silence in the world Hyde has created. Only the screams of the damned." His eyes met mine, a chilling emptiness in their depths. "You think you can escape, Rose? You think any of us can?"

I felt a pang of pity, seeing the man he once was crumbling under the weight of his ambition. But I steeled myself, remembering the horrors he had helped unleash. "I won't be a pawn in your game, Jonathan," I said, my voice firm. "Nor will I stand by and watch as Hyde turns London into a charnel house."

The confrontation reached its zenith, the air thick with the stench of fear and desperation. Alliances shifted like quicksand, loyalties tested and frayed. Hartwell, once the embodiment of calm control, now teetered on the brink of ruin, his ambition a noose around his neck.

As the night wore on, the reality of his unraveling plans seemed to crash down upon him. His eyes, once bright with cunning, now held a glassy sheen, his breath coming in ragged gasps. He looked around the room, his gaze flicking from me to Victoria, to Barrett, his lips moving soundlessly, as if trying to formulate a plan, a argument, anything to regain control.

But it was too late. The seeds of doubt had been sown, the cracks in his armor widening into chasms. His ambition, once his driving force, now threatened to consume him, a wildfire burning out of control. As I watched him struggle, I couldn't help but feel a sense of grim satisfaction, mixed with a twinge of pity. The great Jonathan Hartwell, brought low by his own hubris.

The night was far from over, the true test of our mettle yet to come. But as I stood there, amidst the shadows and the blood, I knew one thing for certain. I would not fall with him. I would not be consumed by the darkness. I would fight, tooth and nail, to forge my own path. To reclaim my soul from the clutches of Hyde's madness.

The Crimson Lantern's heavy door creaked open, expelling us into the chill of a London night, the cobblestones slick with rain and worse. The air was thick with the smell of smoke and decay, a stark contrast to the tense atmosphere we left behind. My heart pounded in my chest, echoing the tumultuous events of the evening, as I stepped out onto the deserted street.

Victoria walked beside me, her chin held high, her eyes reflecting the dim glow of the gas lamps. Her cloak, a deep crimson, billowed behind her like a battle standard. "We have set events in motion, Margaret," she said, her voice barely above a whisper. "There is no turning back now."

I nodded, my thoughts a whirlwind. The image of Hartwell, his face contorted with the realization of his crumbling plans, was etched into my mind. His once impeccable cravat was disheveled, his waistcoat stained with the red wine he had spilled in his distress. The memory sent a shiver down my spine, a mix of revulsion and satisfaction.

Barrett trailed behind us, his usually jovial demeanor replaced with a somber silence. His hands, shoved deep into his pockets, clenched and unclenched, a visible sign of his internal struggle. His coat, a vibrant blue earlier in the evening, now appeared dull and worn, matching the conflicted spirit within.

Rose, ever the enigma, had slipped away into the night, her departure as silent as her arrival. Her final words to me echoed in my thoughts, "The game is not yet over, Margaret. Remember, the darkest hour is just before dawn." Her gown, a shimmering black, had blended with the shadows, leaving only her piercing eyes visible as she disappeared.

The streets were far from empty, despite the late hour. Beggars huddled in doorways, their hollow eyes watching our procession with a mix of envy and despair. Drunkards stumbled home, their raucous laughter echoing through the narrow alleys. And in the shadows, the faint sounds of struggle, of violence, hinted at Hyde's continued reign of terror.

As we turned a corner, the scent of blood, fresh and metallic, assailed my senses. A body lay crumpled in the alley, the white shirt stained a grotesque red, the flesh torn and mangled. The sight turned my stomach, bile rising in my throat. Yet, I could not look away. The victim's eyes, wide and accusing, seemed to bore into my very soul.

"We must stop this, Victoria," I murmured, tearing my gaze away from the grisly sight. "Hyde's madness must end."

Victoria's expression hardened, her lips pressing into a thin line. "Indeed, it must," she agreed, her voice steely with resolve. "But the path will not be easy, Margaret. We must prepare for the darkness to deepen before the light."

Barrett, pale and shaken, looked back towards The Crimson Lantern, his eyes haunted. "I never wanted this," he muttered, almost to himself. "I never wanted any of this."

As we continued through the labyrinthine streets, the weight of the night's events settled heavily upon my shoulders. The alliances we had forged were tenuous, the paths before us shrouded in uncertainty. Yet, amidst the doubt and the fear, a spark of determination burned within me.

We reached my lodgings, the warm glow of the windows a stark contrast to the darkness we left behind. As Victoria and Barrett bid me goodnight, their faces etched with the same resolve I felt, I knew that the true test of our mettle was yet to come. The night's events had set us on a path from which there was no return, the repercussions of our confrontation with Hartwell yet to fully unfold.

With a final glance at the shadowed streets, I stepped inside, the door closing behind me with a soft click. The night was far from over, the true battle for our souls yet to commence. But as I stood there, the horrors of the evening fresh in my mind, I knew one thing for certain. I would not yield to the darkness. I would fight, with every fiber of my being, to forge my own path. To reclaim my soul from the clutches of Hyde's madness.

For in the depths of the night, amidst the blood and the terror, a spark of hope remained. A beacon against the encroaching darkness, a promise of the dawn yet to come. And so, with a deep breath, I stepped forward, ready to face whatever the morrow might bring.

CHAPTER 14

In the flickering light of the drawing room, I, Lady Elizabeth Thornwood, swept towards Isabella Blackwood with a practiced smile, my copper-red hair a flame against the gloom. Her figure was draped in a modest yet elegantly cut mourning gown, the black bombazine a stark contrast to her pale skin. As we exchanged pleasantries, my eyes roved over her, searching for any chink in her armor, any hint of weakness I could exploit.

"Isabella, dear, how kind of you to call upon me," I said, my voice a sweet poison. My gloved hands reached out, grasping hers in a gesture of false warmth.

Her smile was soft, almost distracted. "Elizabeth, the pleasure is mine."

I could see the faint shadows under her eyes, the slight tightening of her jaw—signs of a restless night, perhaps a troubled mind. I filed these observations away, like precious jewels to be examined later.

"Come, sit by the fire," I purred, guiding her towards a pair of ornate chairs that flanked the hearth. The fire cast macabre shadows on the walls, the dancing flames a stark reminder of the hellish secrets I kept hidden. As we walked, the rustle of our skirts whispered like conspirators against the polished floor.

The Devil of London

I gestured for her to sit, my movement a careful ballet of grace and calculation. Her eyes followed me, watchful and wary. I could see the questions lurking in their depths, the curiosity that was her Achilles' heel.

As she settled into the chair, I couldn't help but recall the sight I had witnessed earlier that day. The alley behind St. Giles, slick with rain and blood, the cobblestones gleaming like black ice. The body—what was left of it—had been sprawled in a grotesque parody of sleep, the limbs akimbo, the flesh ripped and torn. The stench of death and offal had clung to the air like a miasma, choking and thick.

Hyde's work, no doubt. The savagery, the brutal delight in the destruction of human flesh—it was his signature, his art. A shiver of revulsion and fascination coursed through me as I remembered the vivid red of the blood, the stark white of bone, the glistening coils of viscera steaming in the cold air.

I arranged my skirts carefully, the rich velvet a sensuous caress against my fingers. I leaned forward slightly, my voice low, a conspirator's whisper. The dance was beginning, the delicate minuet of words and silences, the subtle battle of wills. And I, Lady Elizabeth Thornwood, was a master of the game. Little did Isabella know, she was merely a pawn in my grand design, a fly caught in my careful web.

But even as I prepared to steer the conversation, to shape it to my will, I could not shake the image of Hyde's victim, the raw, screaming violence of his death. It was a stark reminder of the monster that stalked our streets, the dark heart of London's underbelly. And it was a testament to the power of Edward Hyde, the man who held the city in his thrall, a puppet master pulling strings of blood and terror.

The fire cast grotesque shadows on the walls, dancing like demons like those in the darkness of London's alleys where Hyde's latest masterpiece lay. My silken skirts rustled like dry leaves as I shifted, turning my attention to Isabella. Her profile was lit by the firelight, her eyes reflecting the dance of the flames, a distant stormy sea churning with unspoken thoughts.

"You have been quite the social butterfly of late, Isabella," I began, my voice a sweet poison dripping with feigned interest. "I trust you have been enjoying the diversions of the season?"

Isabella turned to me, her deep blue eyes holding a world of secrets. "Indeed, Lady Elizabeth," she replied, her tone polite yet detached, as if her mind were far from the warmth of my drawing room.

"The opera was most entertaining. 'The Marriage of Figaro,' a delightful farce."

Her words were measured, her gaze drifting back to the fire. I could see the faint crease between her brows, a telltale sign of preoccupation. She was a million miles away, wandering down some darkened path where, no doubt, Edward Hyde lurked.

"A farce, indeed," I agreed, my laughter tinkling like broken glass. "And what of the other entertainments? I hear the streets of London have been... lively."

I watched her closely, my heart pounding like a ticking clock, counting out the seconds until my trap was sprung. At the mention of the streets, her eyes flickered, a spark of intrigue igniting within them.

"The streets, Lady Elizabeth?" she asked, her voice barely above a whisper, a shiver running through her like the first rustle of autumn leaves.

"Mmm," I murmured, leaning back slightly, my gaze never leaving her face. "A gruesome tableau, I am told. The work of our mysterious newcomer, Mr. Edward Hyde."

I let the name hang in the air between us, a dark spell woven from silk and shadows. Isabella's reaction was minute, a slight widening of the eyes, a sharp intake of breath, but I saw it. I saw the flicker of intrigue, the spark of fascination. She was drawn to the darkness, to the bloody canvas Hyde had painted on the cobblestones.

My mind flashed back to the alley, the stench of blood and offal thick in the air. The body had been barely recognizable, a grotesque parody of a human form. The throat slashed, the eyes wide, staring up at the indifferent stars, the chest... My stomach churned at the memory. The chest had been torn open, the ribs cracked and splintered like broken porcelain, the heart... The heart had been ripped out, leaving a gaping, bloody maw.

A shiver ran down my spine, a twisted dance of revulsion and morbid fascination. Hyde's work was brutal, visceral, a stark testament to the monster that stalked our streets. And yet, there was something almost... artistic about it. A savage beauty in the destruction, a primal power that called to something deep and dark within me.

I looked back at Isabella, her eyes shining with a dark curiosity that mirrored my own. She was not repulsed by the darkness; she was drawn to it, just as I was. Just as we all were, moths circling a flame, dancing with the devil himself. And in that moment, I knew: Isabella Blackwood was not a pawn in my game. She was a player, a kindred spirit, a fellow dancer in this macabre waltz. And the dance had only just begun.

The fire cast a flickering glow upon Elizabeth's face, her eyes reflecting the dance of flames as she leaned in, her voice dropping to a conspiratorial whisper. "You know, I have heard the most troubling rumors about Mr. Hyde," she began, her fingers delicately tracing the rim of her teacup. "They say he is not merely a man of eccentric tastes, but one of dangerous appetites."

I watched her lips curve around each word, her tongue darting out like a serpent's, tasting the air before striking. "Indeed?" I replied, my voice steady despite the quickening of my pulse. "And what, pray tell, makes these appetites so dangerous?"

Elizabeth's eyes narrowed, her gaze locked onto mine as if searching for a way in. "They say he has a penchant for... darkness," she said, her voice barely above a whisper. "That he finds pleasure in the pain of others. There are whispers of secret meetings, of rituals performed under the cloak of night, where the only light comes from the gleam of a blade and the only warmth from the spilling of blood."

Her words painted a vivid image in my mind's eye: Hyde, his elegant form silhouetted against the moonlit night, a knife glinting in his hand. The blade slicing through flesh, the warm rush of blood, the glistening organs laid bare. A shiver ran down my spine, a twisted dance of revulsion and morbid fascination.

"There are rumors of bodies found in the alleyways, Isabella," Elizabeth continued, her voice a soft, insistent pressure. "Bodies barely recognizable, their throats slashed, their chests torn open, their hearts... ripped out. The work of a monster, they say. A savage beast walking among us in the guise of a man."

I could see it all too clearly: the broken, twisted forms lying in the filthy streets, the blood pooling in the cobblestones, the vacant stare of the dead. And Hyde, standing amidst the carnage, his green eyes ablaze with a primal, feral hunger. My stomach churned, but I could not look away.

"And you believe these rumors?" I asked, my voice barely a whisper. I leaned in, drawn to the darkness like a moth to a flame.

Elizabeth's smile was slow, calculated. "I believe there is no smoke without fire, my dear," she said, her voice laced with false sympathy. "And where Mr. Hyde is concerned, there is a veritable inferno."

The fire cast a lurid glow upon Elizabeth's face, her copper hair shimmering like a demon's halo as she leaned in, the silk of her gown rustling with the urgency of her movement. Her voice cut through the air, sharp and insistent. "Isabella, you must heed me. Hyde's connection to Sir Maximillion Worthington is not mere coincidence. The scandal that enshrouds them both is as thick as London fog and as dark as the Thames at midnight."

I felt a chill creep up my spine, yet my curiosity was a flame that would not be extinguished. The image of Hyde, his green eyes burning with that feral intensity, was seared into my mind. I could see him, standing in the dimly lit alley, his coat gleaming with the blood of his victims. The cobblestones slick with crimson, the air thick with the coppery tang of slaughter. A shiver ran through me, but it was not revulsion alone; there was a thrill, a morbid excitement that quickened my pulse.

"Pray, Elizabeth," I said, my voice steady despite the tumult within me, "elaborate upon this connection. What manner of scandal binds Hyde to Sir Worthington?"

Elizabeth's eyes narrowed, her gaze fixed upon me with an intensity that was almost unsettling. "They say Sir Worthington's fortune is built upon the misery of others, his wealth stained with the blood of the innocent. Hyde is his instrument, his shadow in the night, silencing those who would speak against him."

Her words painted a grim tableau in my mind: Hyde, his hands gloved in crimson, standing over the mutilated corpse of some hapless soul who had dared to cross Sir Worthington. The throat slashed wide, the chest cavity yawning open like a grotesque maw, the heart torn out and cast aside like so much offal. I could see the entrails steaming in the cold night air, the blood congealing in dark pools upon the filthy stones.

"And what of the bodies, Elizabeth?" I pressed, my voice barely above a whisper. "The ones found in the alleyways, their hearts ripped out? Are those the work of Hyde as well?"

Elizabeth's lips curled into a grim smile, her voice barely more than a hiss. "Indeed, they are. They say he takes trophies from his victims, keeps them locked away in his chambers. God knows what manner of dark rituals he performs with them."

The Devil of London

The image was gruesome, yet I could not turn away from it. I saw Hyde, his hands dripping with gore, holding a still-beating heart aloft like some pagan offering. His eyes wild, his lips curled back in a snarl of savage triumph. The room around him was a charnel house, the walls adorned with the remnants of his grisly work, the air thick with the stench of death and decay.

"And yet," I murmured, my voice barely audible even to myself, "you speak of rumors, of whispers in the dark. Have you any proof of these horrors, Elizabeth?"

Elizabeth's eyes flashed, her voice sharp as a blade. "Proof? I have seen the fear in the eyes of those who dare to speak his name, Isabella. I have heard the tales of those who have glimpsed his work and lived to tell of it. What more proof do you need?"

The fire crackled in the hearth, casting long, dancing shadows across the drawing room. Elizabeth's face, once a picture of composure, now contorted in a grimace of frustration. Her hands, delicate and usually so controlled, gripped her silk skirts—the rich jewel tone now crumpled within her tense fingers. Her knuckles shone white as the embroidered lace that adorned her collar.

"Isabella," she began, her voice no longer the smooth, melodic sound I was accustomed to, but sharp and urgent. "You do not seem to grasp the gravity of the situation. Hyde is not some romantic figure from a gothic tale. He is a monster, a butcher. They say he has a chamber filled with the rotting hearts of his victims, each one a testament to his depravity."

She leaned closer, her breath hot on my cheek. "His hands, Isabella, are stained with the blood of the innocent. He does not merely kill; he eviscerates, he dismembers. He bathes in the blood of his victims, painting grotesque murals on the walls with their entrails."

Her words were meant to repel, to shock me into compliance. Yet, with each vivid description, I found myself drawn deeper into the dark allure of Edward Hyde. I could see him now, his form silhouetted against the dim light of a candle, his arms dripping with crimson as he meticulously arranged the organs of his victims like some macabre artist. The room around him was a symphony of carnage, the air thick with the metallic tang of blood and the sweet, cloying scent of decay.

"Elizabeth," I replied, my voice steady despite the gruesome images flooding my mind, "you presume too much. I am not some naive debutante, easily swayed by tales of horror. I understand the risks, the danger. But there is something intoxicating about Hyde, something that draws me to him like a moth to a flame."

I leaned back in my chair, my fingers tracing the cool, smooth surface of the armrest. "You speak of chambers filled with rotting hearts, of walls adorned with entrails. But have you ever considered the power that comes with such darkness? The control, the freedom?"

Elizabeth's eyes widened, her desperation now tinged with fear. "Freedom? Isabella, you speak of madness. Hyde is a psychopath, a killer. He knows no restraint, no mercy. He will drag you down with him, and God knows what will become of you then."

Her words were meant to scare me, to paint Hyde as a figure to be avoided at all costs. Yet, each one only served to fuel my fascination. I could feel the darkness within me stirring, reaching out towards the enigmatic figure of Edward Hyde. I wanted to understand him, to uncover his secrets and immerse myself in the dark world he inhabited.

The fire crackled in the hearth, casting a macabre dance of shadows upon the ornate wallpaper as I, Lady Elizabeth Thornwood, sat across from Isabella, her eyes reflecting the same flames that seemed to burn within her. The room, once filled with the tense energy of our verbal sparring, now held a heaviness, a resignation that settled upon my shoulders like a shroud. Her words, her defiance, had left me with naught but a bitter taste upon my tongue.

"Isabella," I began, my voice barely above a whisper, the fight drained from it. "I see that my warnings fall upon deaf ears. I have shown you the dark heart of Edward Hyde, the blood-soaked path he treads, and yet you persist in this...this morbid fascination." I leaned forward, my corset creaking softly like the binding of a forgotten tome. "I implore you, consider the fate of those who have crossed his path."

My mind's eye conjured the gruesome tableaux I had described earlier, the memories of Hyde's atrocities clinging to my consciousness like the stench of a plague pit. The cobblestones of Whitechapel slick with blood, the entrails of some poor wretch strewn about like some obscene celebration of death. The air thick with the coppery tang of blood and the hum of fat, blue-bottle flies feasting upon the remains of Hyde's victims.

A shiver ran through me as I recalled the most recent discovery, a prostitute from the rookery of St. Giles. Her body had been found in an alley, her limbs arranged with a grotesque precision, her abdomen emptied of its contents. Her heart, torn from her chest, was found in her mouth, a grisly parody of a lover's kiss. The newspapers had screamed of the 'Monster of Mayfair,' but I knew the truth. Edward Hyde was more than a monster; he was death incarnate.

Isabella's gaze met mine, her deep blue eyes holding a knowing darkness that sent a chill through my very soul. She rose from her chair, the silk of her gown rustling like the first stirrings of a storm. Her decision was made; I could see it in the set of her jaw, the cold determination in her eyes.

"Lady Elizabeth," she said, her voice a melody of politeness that did little to conceal the steel beneath. "I appreciate your concern, truly I do. But I am not some fainting violet, easily swayed by tales of blood and horror." She paused, her fingers tracing the cool, smooth marble of the mantelpiece. "I see the darkness in Hyde, but I also see the power. And I would have that power for my own."

Her words sent a jolt of fear through me, a primal response to the predator before me. I had underestimated her, underestimated the depth of her obsession with Hyde. I had come to this meeting with the intention of steering her from her path, of saving her from the darkness that threatened to consume her. But I saw now that she did not want to be saved. She wanted to embrace the darkness, to wrap it around her like a lover's embrace.

"Isabella," I tried once more, my voice tinged with a desperation I could no longer hide. "You speak of power, of control. But Hyde knows no control, no restraint. He is a beast, a killer. He will destroy you, as he has destroyed so many others."

But she merely smiled, a slow, chilling curve of her lips that held no warmth, no humor. "Perhaps," she said, her voice barely more than a whisper. "But perhaps, in the destruction, I will find my true self. Perhaps, in the darkness, I will find my light."

And with that, she turned, the train of her gown whispering against the polished floor as she made her way to the door. I watched her go, my heart heavy with the knowledge of my failure. I had tried to save her, tried to warn her of the path she was treading. But she had chosen her fate, chosen to embrace the darkness that was Edward Hyde. And I, Lady Elizabeth Thornwood, mistress of manipulation, had been powerless to stop her.

The echo of Isabella's footsteps faded, leaving me alone in the cavernous silence of the drawing room. The scent of her perfume lingered, a cloying reminder of her presence, now replaced by a void that seemed to mock my failure. My gaze fell upon the shattered remnants of a once-pristine teacup, its fragments scattered across the parquet floor like a constellation of defeat. Each jagged piece reflected the harsh reality of my loss, a visual testament to the irreparable rift that had torn through the delicate fabric of our discourse.

I stood there, frozen in the stillness, the weight of my failure settling upon my shoulders like a shroud. The room, once a sanctuary of civility and control, now felt alien, its opulence a hollow mockery of my intended triumph. The grandeur of the drawing room—with its ornate moldings, sumptuous draperies, and polished surfaces—only served to highlight the stark contrast of my inner turmoil.

My mind raced, a whirlwind of thoughts and calculations as I grappled with the implications of Isabella's departure. The social landscape of Mayfair, so meticulously cultivated and maintained, was now shifting beneath my feet like quicksand. The carefully constructed facade of genteel refinement that I had worn like armor was crumbling, revealing the desperate vulnerability that lay beneath.

I paced the length of the room, my heels clicking sharply against the floor, each step a staccato rhythm of frustration and despair. The fire in the hearth cracked and hissed, casting eerie shadows that danced macabrely across the walls. The flickering light illuminated the portraits of my ancestors, their stern faces seeming to judge me from their gilded frames.

My thoughts turned to Edward Hyde, the enigmatic figure who had so captivated Isabella's imagination. The mere mention of his name conjured images of blood and carnage, a grotesque tableau of his brutal handiwork. I had heard the whispers, the tales of his savagery whispered in dark corners and hushed parlors. The bodies he left in his wake were not merely victims but grim testaments to his depravity.

I recalled the gruesome details with a shudder: the lifeless forms strewn like broken dolls, their limbs twisted at unnatural angles; the crimson pools of blood congealing on cobblestone streets; the vacant stares of eyes glazed over in eternal horror. The streets of London, already steeped in shadows and mystery, had become a hunting ground for this monster, a labyrinth of terror where innocence was but a fleeting illusion.

Yet, despite the revulsion that churned within me, I could not deny the allure that Hyde held for Isabella. His darkness was a siren's call, a seductive melody that promised power and corruption. She had chosen to embrace that darkness, to dance with the devil himself, and I had been powerless to stop her.

A bitter laugh escaped my lips, a sound devoid of humor or joy. I had underestimated her, misjudged the depth of her fascination with the macabre. Her words echoed in my mind, a chilling refrain that sent a shiver down my spine: "Perhaps, in the destruction, I will find my true self."

The realization of my miscalculation was a bitter pill to swallow, but it was one I could not afford to ignore. The game had changed, the rules irrevocably altered by Isabella's defiance. I could no longer rely on the tried and true methods of manipulation and deceit that had served me so well in the past. No, I would need to adapt, to evolve, if I were to maintain my position and influence in this ever-shifting landscape.

I paused before the hearth, the heat of the flames licking at my skin as I stared into the dancing fire. The embers glowed like the eyes of some ancient beast, watching, waiting. A resolve began to form within me, a steel-like determination that hardened my heart and sharpened my mind.

I would not be defeated so easily. I would not allow Isabella's fascination with Hyde to undermine my carefully laid plans. I would find a way to turn this to my advantage, to use her obsession as a tool for my own gain. The game was far from over, and I, Lady Elizabeth Thornwood, would not go down without a fight.

As I stood there, the fire casting a fierce glow upon my face, I knew that the path before me would be fraught with danger and uncertainty. But I was ready. I would adapt, I would strategize, and I would emerge victorious. For in the world of Mayfair's social elite, there was no room for weakness, no place for the faint of heart. And I was anything but weak.

With a final glance at the shattered teacup, I turned and left the drawing room, my steps purposeful and determined. The door closed behind me with a resounding thud, sealing away the remnants of my failure and ushering in a new era of calculation and cunning. The game had changed, but I was ready to play. And this time, I would not be so easily bested.

In the grimy labyrinth of London's streets, where the fog curled like a spectral serpent, I found myself ensconced in the shadows, my heart a drum of dread within my breast. The cobblestones glistened with the day's rain, reflecting the sickly yellow of gas lamps that did little to pierce the gloom. My once-pristine silk gown, the color of a bruised plum, now bore the grime of my desperate journey, the hem tattered from the jagged edges of this city's rotten teeth.

I had ventured far from Mayfair's refined avenues, far from the drawing room where the shattered teacup lay in state, a monument to my failure. The air here was thick with the stench of poverty and despair, a stark reminder of the world beyond my carefully cultivated existence. Yet, it was in these squalid depths that Edward Hyde held sway, and where I must needs confront the truth of his allure.

A rough voice, like gravel crunching underfoot, echoed through the mist. "Ye lost, milady?"

I turned to face a man, his features obscured by the brim of his cap, his clothes stained and torn. "I seek an audience with Mr. Hyde," I declared, my voice steady despite the quiver in my stomach.

The man grunted, spat upon the ground, and jerked his head towards an alleyway. "Down there. But ye be warned, he ain't one for polite company."

I pressed on, the alley walls closing in around me like a stone vice. The stench grew fouler still, the smell of rotting flesh and human waste assailing my senses. A rat scuttled past my feet, its eyes gleaming in the dim light. I fought the urge to retch, to flee this godforsaken place, but I could not turn back. Not until I understood the power Hyde wielded.

A door creaked open at the alley's end, revealing a room bathed in a bloody crimson light. Within, a figure stood, his back to me, his coat tails swaying gently as if stirred by some unseen breeze. He turned, and I beheld Edward Hyde in all his chilling glory. His eyes, those magnetic green orbs, fixed upon me, and I felt a shiver run down my spine, a primal response to the predator before me.

"Lady Thornwood," he purred, his voice a velvet caress that belied the monster within. "How delightful to find you in my humble abode."

I steeled myself, met his gaze, and stepped into the devil's lair. The room was a chamber of horrors, the walls adorned with the tools of his bloody trade. Knives, saws, and implements of torture I dared not name gleamed in the sanguine light. In the corner, a heap of rags stirred, revealing a man, his face a pulpy mess of bruised flesh and congealed blood. He moaned, a pitiful sound that turned my stomach.

Hyde smiled, a cruel twist of his lips. "Pay him no mind, dear lady. He is but a plaything, a means to pass the tedious hours."

I tore my gaze from the wretch, focusing on Hyde. "You take pleasure in their suffering," I stated, my voice barely above a whisper.

He chuckled, a sound like distant thunder. "Pleasure? Oh, indeed. But it is more than that. It is power, Lady Thornwood. The power to control, to dominate, to hold another's life in your hands and squeeze until it runs through your fingers like sand."

His words painted a vivid image, one that should have repulsed me, yet I found myself drawn to the darkness in his voice, the promise of control it held. I thought of Isabella, of her fascination with this beast, and I understood. This was the allure, the dance with death that set the blood afire.

But I could not succumb. I would not.

"You are a monster, Mr. Hyde," I said, my voice steady despite the turmoil within me. "A beast that preys on the weak and the innocent."

He laughed then, a full-throated sound that echoed through the chamber. "Innocent? There is no such thing, dear lady. We are all of us corrupted, our souls stained with sin. I merely peel back the layers, reveal the rotten core beneath."

He stepped closer, his voice dropping to a conspiratorial whisper. "You know this, Lady Thornwood. You have seen it, lived it. The game of society is but a mirror to the game I play. We are not so different, you and I."

I recoiled, my heart pounding in my chest. "No," I breathed, the word a denial, a plea.

He smiled, a slow, knowing curve of his lips. "Ah, but yes. You have tasted power, Lady Thornwood. You have reveled in it, bathed in it. You cannot turn back now. You cannot unknow what you know."

I thought of Mayfair, of the drawing rooms and ballrooms, the whispered secrets and veiled threats. I thought of the power I wielded, the lives I held in my hands. And I knew, with a chilling certainty, that Hyde was right.

I turned, fled the chamber, the alley, the stinking streets. But I could not flee the truth. I was a part of this world, this dance of death and deceit. And I would play my part, or be consumed.

As I stepped back into the familiar streets of Mayfair, the fog closed in around me, a shroud of uncertainty and dread. For I knew now the dark allure of Edward Hyde, the power he held, the beast he was. And I knew, with a sickening twist of my heart, that I was not so different from him.

The game had changed, the rules rewritten in blood and shadow. And I would play, would adapt, would strategize. For there was no other choice. Not for me. Not anymore.

And so, with a heavy heart and a steadfast resolve, I stepped back into the gilded cage of society, the echo of Hyde's laughter ringing in my ears, a haunting melody that would not be silenced. The chapter closed, but the story was far from over. And the night held terrors yet unseen.

CHAPTER 15

In the throes of a dreary London evening, I, Lord Frederick Pembroke, strode through the gilded doors of the gentleman's club, the weight of my military past etched into every precise step. The opulent surroundings—a symphony of velvet drapes, mahogany panels, and flickering gas lamps—could not distract from the tempest brewing within my mind. Each thought was a stark reminder of the confrontation that lay ahead, a dance with the devil himself.

I paused at the entrance to the main room, the hubbub of voices and clinking glasses washing over me like a discordant melody. My eyes scanned the crowd, a sea of powdered wigs and tailored frock coats, until they narrowed in on the figure I sought. Edward Hyde sat with an air of casual dominance, his darkly charismatic presence a stark contrast to the club's elite patrons. He was a striking figure, his magnetic green eyes gleaming with predatory intelligence, and his dark hair, touched with silver at the temples, lending him an air of distinguished menace.

As I observed him, a chill ran down my spine, recalling the gruesome tales that had reached my ears. Whispers of Hyde's nocturnal escapades, where the cobblestones of London's alleys were painted with the blood of his victims. I had heard of the mutilated corpses, their throats slit from ear to ear, entrails spilling onto the cold stone like some macabre offering to the night. The images haunted me, the stench of death and decay clinging to my nostrils as if I had witnessed the carnage myself.

Hyde's victims were not merely killed; they were eviscerated, their bodies reduced to grotesque tableaux of flesh and bone. The thought of such brutality sickened me, yet I could not ignore the perverse fascination that gripped my soul. It was as if Hyde's darkness called to some hidden part of me, a part I dared not acknowledge.

I steeled myself, my military bearing a shield against the horrors that threatened to consume me. Hyde's presence was a poison, seeping into the very air of the club, tainting it with an almost palpable malevolence. Yet, I could not turn back. Duty and honor compelled me forward, my steps echoing with the weight of my moral convictions.

As I moved closer, the chatter of the patrons seemed to fade, replaced by the pounding of my own heart. Hyde's eyes met mine, and for a moment, time stood still. In that fleeting instant, I saw the depths of his depravity, a void of darkness that threatened to swallow me whole. Yet, I could not look away. The battle lines were drawn, and I was helpless to resist the pull of this deadly dance.

The grandeur of the gentleman's club enveloped me like a velvet shroud, the air thick with the scent of tobacco and the distant clink of crystal. The opulent surroundings, a stark contrast to the grim thoughts that plagued my mind, seemed to mock the turmoil within me. As I approached Hyde's table, the room's ambient chatter dimmed, as if the very air held its breath in anticipation of the storm to come.

Hyde, ever the picture of dark elegance, looked up from his seat, his magnetic green eyes meeting mine with an intensity that sent a shiver down my spine. A subtle smile played on his lips, a nod that was both respectful and mocking, a silent acknowledgment of the complex history that bound us. His dark hair, touched with silver at the temples, framed his aristocratic features, casting him in an almost ethereal light despite the shadows that clung to him like a second skin.

I took a seat opposite him, my posture rigid with controlled tension. The weight of my moral convictions pressed down upon me, a burden I bore with military precision. "Hyde," I began, my voice steady but edged with the gravity of our impending confrontation, "the unrest in Mayfair grows ever more disturbing. The bodies found in the alleys, their entrails strewn about like some grotesque artistry—it reeks of your handiwork."

Hyde's smile widened, a predatory gleam in his eyes that sent a chill through my veins. "Ah, Pembroke," he replied, his voice a rich, melodious sound that belied the darkness within him. "Ever the vigilant guardian of Mayfair's virtues. But tell me, what makes you so certain that these... incidents are the work of my hand?"

The images of the mutilated corpses flashed before my eyes, their flesh torn asunder, blood pooling in sickening rivulets on the cobblestones. The stench of decay clung to my nostrils, a phantom scent that refused to dissipate. "The precision of the cuts," I said, my voice a low growl, "the arrangement of the entrails—it is as if each victim were a canvas for your twisted art. No common criminal could achieve such... perfection in their depravity."

Hyde leaned back in his chair, his eyes never leaving mine. "You flatter me, Pembroke," he said, his voice a silken purr. "But tell me, what drives you to seek me out? Is it duty? Or perhaps something more... personal?"

The room seemed to grow colder, the shadows creeping closer as if drawn by Hyde's dark aura. I could feel the weight of the patrons' gazes upon us, their ears keenly attuned to the unfolding drama despite their feigned disinterest. "It is my duty to protect the innocent," I said, my voice steady but laced with a quiet fury. "And I will not stand idly by while you turn Mayfair into your personal slaughterhouse."

Hyde's smile never wavered, his eyes gleaming with a predatory intelligence that saw through my words to the core of my being. "Ah, Pembroke," he said, his voice a soft whisper that carried the weight of centuries. "Ever the noble warrior, fighting for a cause that may already be lost. But tell me, what will you do when you realize that the darkness you seek to vanquish resides not in the shadows, but within yourself?"

The room fell silent, the weight of Hyde's words hanging heavily in the air. I could feel the tension building, a storm on the horizon, ready to unleash its fury upon the unsuspecting world. And as I sat there, locked in a silent battle of wills with the man who embodied the very darkness I sought to destroy, I could not help but wonder if Hyde's words held a grain of truth—if the darkness I fought so desperately to vanquish was not an external foe, but a part of my own soul, waiting to be awakened.

The room seemed to hold its breath as I sat, ramrod straight, my eyes locked onto Hyde's. The gentleman's club, with its opulent trappings and gilded mirrors, felt more like a den of vipers than a sanctuary for London's elite. The air was thick with smoke and tension, the murmurs of the patrons reduced to a faint hum, like the distant buzzing of flies over a corpse.

Hyde, resplendent in a waistcoat of deep burgundy, the color of dried blood, leaned back in his chair. His fingers, long and pale, drummed a silent rhythm on the polished mahogany tabletop. "Ah, Pembroke," he began, his voice a low purr, like the distant thunder that heralds a storm. "Ever the staunch defender of the helpless. Tell me, does the lion of Kandahar still roar with the same ferocity, or has time dulled your claws?"

His words were laced with a double edge, a blade concealed in velvet. I felt a chill run down my spine, a shiver that I hoped did not show. The patrons around us feigned disinterest, their eyes on cards or newspapers, but their ears were pricked, senses attuned to the drama unfolding. I could see it in the tense set of their shoulders, the furtive glances cast our way.

"Your words are as forked as ever, Hyde," I retorted, my voice steady despite the turmoil within. "But I will not be drawn into your games. I am here for one reason alone—to put an end to the terror that grips Mayfair."

Hyde's smile widened, a grotesque parody of mirth. "Games, Pembroke? You wound me. I merely speak the truth. And the truth, as they say, shall set you free." He leaned in, his voice dropping to a conspiratorial whisper. "Or, in your case, bind you in chains of your own making."

A shadow crossed my vision, a memory of Kandahar—the stench of blood and death, the screams of the dying echoing in my ears. Hyde's eyes bore into mine, and I knew he saw it too, the shared horror that bound us together, even as it tore us apart.

"You speak of truth, Hyde?" I countered, my voice rising despite my best efforts. "Then let us speak of the truth of your recent activities. The bodies piling up in the alleys, the blood flowing like rivers through the streets. Is that the truth you wish to discuss?"

I had seen the carnage firsthand, the entrails strewn like garlands, the eyes staring blankly, accusingly. The stench of death clung to me still, a phantom scent that haunted my every waking moment. And Hyde sat there, his smile never wavering, his eyes gleaming with a dark, malevolent glee.

"Ah, the murders," he said, his voice a soft sigh, as if he were remarking on the weather. "Such a messy business, isn't it? All that blood, all that screaming. It's enough to make one lose their appetite." He paused, his tongue darting out to wet his lips, a serpent tasting the air. "But then, you know all about messy business, don't you, Pembroke? After all, we shared quite the adventure in Kandahar, did we not?"

My composure faltered, a crack in the stoic facade I had so carefully cultivated. The memories threatened to overwhelm me, the sights and sounds and smells of that godforsaken place. But I could not afford to show weakness, not here, not now. Not with Hyde.

"Kandahar was a lifetime ago, Hyde," I growled, my hands clenched into fists beneath the table. "And I will not let you use it to distract from the matter at hand. I know it is you behind these murders. I know it is your hand that wields the knife."

Hyde's laughter was a soft, chilling sound, like the rustling of dry leaves. "Prove it, Pembroke," he whispered, his eyes never leaving mine. "Prove that I am the monster you believe me to be. But be careful, my old friend. For in your quest to vanquish the darkness, you may find that it is you who is consumed."

The room seemed to darken as Hyde leaned forward, his eyes gleaming like a cat's in the dim light of the club. His voice, when it came, was a low, insidious purr, a sound that seemed to slip beneath my skin and coil about my spine. "Ah, Pembroke, ever the noble crusader," he began, his lips curling into a semblance of a smile. "But tell me, how fares your wife these days? Does she still weep for the child she lost, or has time begun to dull that particular pain?"

I felt as if he had reached across the table and struck me, a physical blow that left me reeling. My wife's grief was a sacred, private thing, not to be bandied about in this den of vipers. I could feel the eyes of the other patrons on us, their curiosity a palpable thing, yet I could not tear my gaze from Hyde's face.

"You go too far, Hyde," I growled, my voice low with warning.

He ignored my protest, his voice dropping to a conspiratorial whisper. "And what of your brother? Does he still bear the scars of his... indiscretions? Does he still wake in the night, screaming for mercy, begging for forgiveness?"

My hands clenched into fists, the knuckles white with strain. How could he know such things? What dark magic had he employed to peer into the inner workings of my family?

Hyde's smile widened, as if he could sense my discomfort and fed upon it. "And you, Pembroke," he continued, his voice like silk drawn over a blade. "Do you still see the faces of those you killed in Kandahar? Do you still hear their screams echoing in your dreams?"

I could see them then, the men I had killed in the heat of battle, their faces contorted in agony, their bodies twisted and broken. I could smell the blood, the stench of death, the acrid tang of gunpowder. It was as if Hyde had reached into my mind and plucked forth my darkest memories, laying them bare for his amusement.

From the corner of my eye, I saw Thomas Harding and Catherine Blackwood exchange a glance. Harding's face was pale, his eyes wide with concern, while Catherine's expression was one of intrigue, her eyes sharp and calculating. They leaned closer, their attention focused on Hyde, absorbing his every word.

Hyde, ever the showman, did not disappoint. His voice dropped to a hushed, intimate tone, forcing the others to strain to hear him. "But perhaps it is not the ghosts of Kandahar that haunt you, Pembroke. Perhaps it is something closer to home. Something... fresher."

He paused, his tongue darting out to wet his lips, a serpent tasting the air. "Tell me, Pembroke, do you ever think of the girl? The one who screamed so prettily as she died? The one who begged for mercy, who pleaded for her life as you stood by and watched?"

I felt the blood drain from my face, my heart pounding in my chest like a drum. He could not know of that. It was impossible. I had told no one, had carried the burden of that night alone.

Hyde's smile was a twisted, grotesque thing, a parody of mirth. "Ah, I see you remember," he said, his voice a low, gloating purr. "I must admit, I was impressed. You stood there, so stoic, so unmoved, as I carved her like a roast. As I peeled back her skin and bathed in her blood. You watched as I sliced her open, as I laid bare her insides, steaming and wet. You did nothing as I reached inside and pulled forth her still-beating heart."

His words were a vivid, horrifying tableau, a nightmare come to life. I could see it all, the blood, the gore, the sheer, brutal savagery of it. And at the center of it all, Hyde, his eyes gleaming with malevolent glee, his hands dripping with the blood of the innocent.

I felt a wave of nausea wash over me, my stomach churning at the memories his words evoked. I could feel the bile rising in my throat, the

The Devil of London

bitter taste of guilt and shame. I wanted to look away, to deny the truth of his words, but I could not. I was transfixed, held captive by the sheer, brutal power of his gaze.

The room seemed to close in around me, the opulent decor of the gentleman's club suddenly garish and obscene. The air was thick with the scent of tobacco and the cloying perfume of the elite, a sickening contrast to the stark horror of Hyde's words. I could feel the sweat beading on my brow, my cravat tightening like a noose around my neck as I struggled to maintain my composure.

"You lie," I managed to choke out, my voice rising with a mix of anger and desperation. "You twist the truth to suit your own ends, Hyde. I knew you were a monster, but I never thought you capable of such...such depravity."

Hyde's smile never wavered, his green eyes gleaming with a cold, predatory intelligence. He leaned back in his chair, his posture relaxed, the very picture of calm control. "Depravity, Pembroke?" he repeated, his voice a low, melodious purr. "You wound me, sir. I merely recount the events as they transpired. You were there, after all. You saw what I did to that poor, helpless creature."

His words were like a physical blow, each one striking at the heart of my moral code. I could see it all again, the blood, the gore, the sheer, brutal savagery of it. The memory of that night was a festering wound in my mind, a dark stain on my soul that I could not scrub clean.

"You speak of that night as if it were a mere trifle," I spat, my hands clenched into fists on the table before me. "As if you did not bathe in the blood of an innocent, as if you did not...did not..." I could not bring myself to say the words, the bitter taste of bile rising in my throat.

Hyde's eyebrow arched, a subtle, mocking gesture. "Did not reach into her chest and pull forth her still-beating heart?" he finished for me, his voice barely above a whisper. "Did not hold it aloft, the blood dripping from my fingers like the juices of a ripe fruit? Oh, Pembroke, you do me a disservice. I thought you a man of the world, not some squeamish maiden afraid of a little blood."

The patrons around us shifted uncomfortably, their eyes darting from Hyde to me and back again. They could sense the escalation of tension, the charged atmosphere that crackled like lightning between us. I could feel their gazes like a physical weight, their judgment and speculation a tangible thing.

"You are a monster, Hyde," I growled, my voice low and harsh. "A beast in human form. You revel in the suffering of others, you delight in the pain and the terror. You are a sickness, a plague upon this city, and I will not rest until you are brought to justice."

Hyde's smile widened, a twisted, grotesque thing that sent a shiver of dread down my spine. "Justice, Pembroke?" he repeated, his voice a low, gloating purr. "You speak of justice as if it were a tangible thing, as if it were not merely a construct of the weak, a crutch for the masses to lean upon. But I will humor you, Pembroke. I will give you your precious justice."

He leaned forward, his eyes gleaming with a malevolent glee that sent a jolt of fear through my veins. "You think me a monster, a beast in human form? You are not wrong, Pembroke. But tell me, have you ever stopped to consider that perhaps the beast is the true form, and the man merely a disguise? Have you ever wondered what lies beneath the surface, what dark desires and hidden appetites lurk in the hearts of men?"

His words were a chill wind, a whisper of madness that threatened to engulf me. I could feel the tendrils of doubt creeping in, the insidious whispers that questioned the very foundations of my beliefs.

"You speak in riddles, Hyde," I snapped, my voice sharp with impatience. "You seek to confuse and obfuscate, to twist the truth to suit your own ends. But I will not be swayed. I will not be turned from my path. I will see you brought to justice, no matter the cost."

Hyde's smile never wavered, his calm, controlled demeanor a stark contrast to my own rising agitation. "Very well, Pembroke," he said, his voice a low, silken purr. "If it is justice you seek, then it is justice you shall have. But tell me, are you prepared to pay the price? Are you willing to make the sacrifices necessary to see your precious justice done?"

His words were a challenge, a gauntlet thrown down before me. I could feel the weight of his gaze, the cold, calculating intelligence that seemed to strip me bare, to lay open my very soul. I swallowed hard, my mouth suddenly dry, my heart pounding in my chest like a drum.

"I will do whatever is necessary," I vowed, my voice steady and sure. "I will not be swayed from my path, Hyde. I will see you brought to justice, no matter the cost."

Hyde's smile widened, a twisted, grotesque thing that sent a shiver of dread down my spine. "Very well, Pembroke," he said, his voice a low, gloating purr. "Then let us see how far you are willing to go in the name of your precious justice. Let us see how much you are willing to sacrifice in the name of your principles."

He leaned back in his chair, his posture relaxed, his eyes gleaming with a cold, predatory intelligence. "You speak of that night as if it were a mere trifle, Pembroke," he said, his voice barely above a whisper. "But tell me, have you ever stopped to consider that perhaps it was not an isolated incident? Have you ever wondered if perhaps there were other nights, other victims, other hearts beaten and stilled by my hand?"

His words were a chill wind, a whisper of madness that threatened to engulf me. I could feel the tendrils of doubt creeping in, the insidious whispers that questioned the very foundations of my beliefs.

"You lie," I managed to choke out, my voice rising with a mix of anger and desperation. "You seek to confuse and obfuscate, to twist the truth to suit your own ends. But I will not be swayed, Hyde. I will not be turned from

In the gloom of the gentleman's club, the air thick with smoke and the stench of human frailty, I sat rigid in my seat, Hyde's words still ringing in my ears like the peal of a funeral bell. The room seemed to close in around me, the gilded walls and ornate ceiling suddenly oppressive, as if the very building conspired to crush me under the weight of my own hubris.

"You speak of justice, Pembroke," Hyde had said, his voice a low, insidious purr, "as if it were a tangible thing, a bauble to be clasped in your hand. But I see it, Pembroke. I see the blood on your hands, the shadows that cling to your soul."

His words had conjured images in my mind, vivid and grotesque: the cobblestone streets of London slick with rain and blood, the alleys echoing with the desperate cries of Hyde's victims. I had seen the bodies in my mind's eye, their throats slit from ear to ear, their entrails steaming in the cold night air. I had seen the lifeblood of innocents pooling in the gutters, the dark red tide lapping at the feet of Hyde's shadowy form.

I could bear it no longer. I rose abruptly, my chair scraping against the polished floor like a shriek of protest. My face felt hot, a mask of barely contained fury, and I could feel the eyes of the room upon me, their gazes a physical force that threatened to crush me.

"You shall not have the last word, Hyde," I growled, my voice low and trembling with barely suppressed rage. "I shall see you brought to heel, mark me. I shall see justice done."

Hyde merely smiled, a slow, serpentine curve of his lips that made my blood run cold. "I look forward to it, Pembroke," he murmured, his voice a low, mocking purr. "Indeed, I do."

I stormed out of the club, my boots striking the floor with a sharp, staccato rhythm that echoed like the ticking of a clock, counting down to some unseen doom. The door swung shut behind me with a resounding thud, a public acknowledgment of my tarnished reputation, a blow to my carefully maintained image.

As I stepped out into the night, the cold air slapped me like an open palm, the shock of it bringing me back to myself. The streets of London stretched out before me, a labyrinth of shadows and secrets, the cobblestones slick with more than just rain. I could feel the weight of Hyde's words still heavy upon me, the insidious whispers that questioned the very foundations of my beliefs.

Behind me, in the warmth and light of the club, I knew that Hyde reclined in his chair, exuding an air of triumph. I could picture him, his magnetic green eyes gleaming with predatory intelligence, his dark hair touched with silver at the temples, a distinguished monster holding court amidst the elite of Mayfair.

I could imagine the patrons, now abuzz with whispered speculation, casting furtive glances at Hyde, recognizing his growing influence over their ranks. I could see them, their faces flushed with wine and intrigue, their eyes wide with the thrill of the scandal that hung heavy in the air.

My mind churned with the implications of Hyde's revelations, the bloody tableaux that his words had painted in my thoughts. I could see the victims, their faces pale and lifeless, their bodies mutilated and broken, the streets of London running red with their blood.

And above it all, I could see Hyde, his elegant form standing tall and triumphant amidst the carnage, his eyes gleaming with a cold, predatory intelligence, his hands stained with the blood of the innocent.

As I strode through the streets of London, the night closing in around me like a shroud, I knew that I must bring Hyde to justice, no matter the cost. For if I did not, if I faltered in my resolve, then the streets of London would run red with the blood of the innocent, and the name of Pembroke would be naught but a bitter taste on the tongue, a faded memory in the annals of a forgotten city.

The Devil of London

In the wake of Pembroke's hasty retreat, the gentlemans club bubbled with a tense excitement, the air thick with the scent of cigars and the tang of spilled wine. I, Thomas Harding, remained seated, my fingers tracing the cool silver of my pocket watch, a morbid ticking echoing in my mind. The watch, a gift from my late wife, was a comforting weight in my palm, a stark reminder of the passage of time and the urgency of the situation that was unfolding. Catherine Blackwood sat beside me, her back straight as a rod, her pen suspended over a small notebook, her ink-stained fingers trembling slightly.

"Mr. Harding," she murmured, her voice barely audible over the hum of the crowd, "the shift we have just witnessed... it is unsettling, is it not?"

I nodded, my eyes fixed on the blood-red liquid swirling in my glass. "Indeed, Miss Blackwood. Hyde's influence is akin to a malignant tumor, spreading insidiously amongst the elite of Mayfair." My mind's eye flashed with images of the corpses I had seen, their flesh rent and torn, their lifeless eyes staring accusingly. I could see the sinews and muscles, the viscera spilling forth from abdomens like some grotesque parody of birth. The killer's modus operandi was brutal, primal, a testament to his savage nature.

Hyde still sat, a dark king holding court amidst his unwitting pawns. His eyes gleamed with a feral intelligence, his lips curled in a faint, enigmatic smile. He seemed to bask in the whispered speculations, the furtive glances cast his way.

Catherine's voice drew me from my grim reverie. "His knowledge of Lord Pembroke's past... it is clear that his reach extends far beyond what we initially suspected." Her gaze was fixed on Hyde, her eyes narrowed in intense concentration.

"Indeed," I agreed, my grip tightening on my glass. "His allusions to Kandahar... it speaks of a history shared in blood and violence." I could see it then, the hot sun beating down on the desert sands, the bodies of soldiers lying twisted and broken, their blood soaking into the parched earth. Hyde stood amidst the carnage, his uniform pristine, his saber dripping crimson. The image shifted, the sands giving way to the cobblestones of London, the bodies now those of innocent civilians, their throats slashed, their entrails steaming in the cool night air.

Hyde rose then, his movements fluid and predatory. The room fell silent, all eyes drawn to his commanding presence. He buttoned his coat, a fine black wool that seemed to absorb the light, his fingers lingering on the silver fastenings. His eyes met mine, and he offered a nod, a slight tilt of his head that spoke volumes. It was an acknowledgment, a silent recognition of our roles in this grim dance.

Beside me, Catherine drew in a sharp breath, her eyes wide with a mix of fear and determination. "He means to draw us into his web," she whispered, her voice barely audible. "We must tread carefully, Mr. Harding. The path we walk is treacherous, the destination uncertain."

I nodded, my resolve hardening. "Indeed, Miss Blackwood. But tread it we must, for the sake of those who cannot speak for themselves." The victims, their voices silenced, their bodies desecrated, deserved justice. And I, Thomas Harding, undertaker and unwilling confidant to a monster, would see that justice served, no matter the cost.

I felt a chill as I looked back at the man who was a murderer in our midst. I saw the blood on his hands and the sneer on his face. I had seen his victims, their throats slashed ear to ear, their entrails ripped from their bodies, their eyes gouged from their sockets. I had seen the aftermath of his brutality, the bloody tableaux that he left in his wake. And I knew, with a cold certainty, that I must bring Hyde to justice, no matter the cost.

The heavy oak door of the gentleman's club swung shut behind Hyde, sealing his exit with a resonant thud that echoed through the chamber like a judge's gavel. The patrons, myself included, watched as the ripples of his departure undulated through the room. Conversations resumed, yet the air remained thick with tension, a palpable miasma that clung to our throats like the London fog.

I shifted in my seat, the velvet upholstery suddenly coarse against my skin. My cravat, once loose, now constricted my breath, as if Hyde's mere presence had tightened it into a noose. The crystal glass in my hand, still half-full of port, reflected the flickering gaslights, casting blood-red shadows on the linen tablecloth. I could not help but recall the vivid hue of crimson that had painted the cobblestones of Mitre Square, where one of Hyde's victims had been discovered, her entrails steaming in the cold night air.

"Quite the spectacle, wasn't it, Mr. Harding?" Sir Reginald, a portly gentleman with mutton chops and a penchant for gossip, leaned in from his adjacent seat. His eyes gleamed with a morbid curiosity that made my stomach churn.

"Indeed," I murmured, my gaze fixed on the empty seat where Hyde had held court. "A spectacle of power and manipulation."

Sir Reginald chuckled, his jowls quivering. "You give him too much credit, Mr. Harding. He's merely a man, not some demon from the pit."

I turned to him, my expression grave. "You've not seen what I have, Sir Reginald. The bodies... the sheer brutality..." I let my words trail off, the images of Hyde's victims flashing before my eyes. The woman in Miller's Court, her body flayed like a cadaver in a medical theatre, her heart missing, as if torn from her chest by a ravenous beast.

Sir Reginald blanched, his laughter fading. "Good God, man. Spare me the gruesome details."

I offered him a grim smile. "Gruesome indeed. Yet we must not shy away from the truth, no matter how unpleasant."

Catherine, seated beside me, laid a gloved hand on my arm. Her touch was gentle, yet firm, a silent reminder of our shared purpose. "We must be vigilant, Mr. Harding," she said softly, her voice barely audible amidst the hum of conversation. "For who knows what shadows lurk in the hearts of men?"

I nodded, my resolve strengthening. Around us, the club's patrons continued their discussions, their words a meaningless drone. The atmosphere remained charged, an electric current that prickled my skin. The scent of cigars and brandy, once comforting, now cloyed in my nostrils, mixing with the phantom stench of blood and death that seemed to linger in Hyde's wake.

As I looked around the room, I saw the unease reflected in the eyes of the other patrons. Their laughter was too loud, their gestures too animated, as if they sought to convince themselves that all was well. Yet the shadow of Hyde's presence lingered, a testament to his mastery of manipulation and control.

I took a deep breath, steeling myself for the tasks ahead. The path we walked was treacherous, the destination uncertain. But walk it we must, for the sake of those who could not speak for themselves. The victims, their voices silenced, their bodies desecrated, deserved justice. And I, Thomas Harding, undertaker and unwilling confidant to a monster, would see that justice served, no matter the cost.

Even as the club's patrons attempted to lose themselves in their usual revelries, the specter of Edward Hyde loomed large, a dark stain on their collective consciousness. The scene closed with a lingering sense of unease, a silent acknowledgment that none present would forget the events of this night, nor the chilling reminder of the predator in their midst.

CHAPTER 16

In the chill grip of a London evening, I, Annabelle Blake, found myself traversing the cobblestone streets, each step echoing with a resolve that had long been simmering within my breast. The gas lamps cast eerie, elongated shadows that danced macabrely on the damp walls, as if the very city itself whispered secrets of its dark underbelly. My destination loomed ahead, a grand townhouse nestled within the heart of Mayfair, its facade adorned with ornate carvings that seemed to sneer at the lesser edifices surrounding it.

As I approached, my thoughts were a whirlwind of determination and calculation. Too long had I been underestimated, dismissed as a mere ornament by the elite of Mayfair. They saw only the porcelain doll, the golden curls, the doe-eyed innocence—a facade I had cultivated with meticulous care. Beneath that veneer, however, stirred an ambition as dark and relentless as the Thames at midnight. Tonight, I vowed, they would begin to see the true Annabelle Blake.

The heavy oak door swung open at my touch, revealing a drawing room that was the epitome of opulence. Velvet drapes the color of clotted cream framed towering windows, while the walls were adorned with gilt-framed portraits of stern-faced ancestors. A chandelier dripping with crystals cast a shimmering light over the polished mahogany furniture, each piece a testament to the wealth and taste of its owners.

I stepped into the room, my heels clicking softly on the parquet floor. My gown, a confection of pale blue silk with darker embroidery snaking up the bodice, rustled gently with each movement. I had chosen it with care, knowing that the delicate hue would enhance my apparent innocence while the subtle touches of darkness hinted at the truth lurking beneath.

My demeanor was one of subtle confidence, a demure smile playing on my lips as I greeted those already present with a nod. Yet behind that facade, my mind was a whirr of calculation. Each gesture, each word, was a piece on the chessboard of society, moved with precision to further my aims.

As I took my seat, I couldn't help but recall the grisly scenes that had unfolded in the shadows of this very district. Edward Hyde's handiwork was whispered about in hushed tones, the details growing ever more grotesque with each retelling. I had heard of the butcher's wife found in her own shop, her throat slit from ear to ear, blood pooling on the cold stone floor like a macabre offering. Her eyes, it was said, had been gouged out, leaving empty sockets that stared accusingly at the ceiling.

And then there was the young gentleman, his body discovered in an alley behind a gambling den, his entrails spilling from a gaping wound in his abdomen. The stench of his decaying flesh had drawn rats, their beady eyes gleaming in the dim light as they feasted on his remains.

These images, gruesome as they were, held a morbid fascination for me. They were a stark reminder of the darkness that lurked just beneath the surface of our polite society. And tonight, I intended to harness that darkness, to wield it as a weapon in my quest for power.

As I settled into my chair, I couldn't help but feel a thrill of anticipation. The game was afoot, and I was ready to play.

As I stepped into the drawing room, the heavy scent of beeswax candles and expensive perfumes enveloped me, a stark contrast to the putrid stench of death that lingered in the alleys I had traversed. The opulence of the room was overwhelming, the flickering flames of the candelabra casting eerie shadows on the gilded mirrors and ornate moldings. My reflection stared back at me from a distant mirror, a petite figure cloaked in a modest gown of lavender silk, the color of twilight—a stark contrast to the grandeur surrounding me.

My demure appearance was a mask, a facade carefully cultivated to disarm those who underestimated me. Beneath the delicate lace and innocent smiles, a serpent stirred, coiling and ready to strike. I was no longer the naive girl who had once trembled at the thought of navigating

Mayfair's treacherous waters. I was a woman reborn, forged in the fires of ambition and tempered by the chill of calculation.

As I moved further into the room, my eyes met those of Isabella Blackwood. She was already present, her tall, graceful figure draped in a gown of deep crimson, the color of fresh blood—a stark reminder of Hyde's gruesome deeds. Her dark hair framed her face like a raven's wings, and her deep blue-gray eyes held a knowing darkness that sent a shiver down my spine. She observed me with a sharp, calculating gaze, her subtle smile never reaching her eyes.

"Ah, Annabelle," she purred, her voice a velvety whisper that seemed to slither through the air like a poisonous mist. "How charming to see you here. I must admit, I was rather curious to see if you would attend."

I returned her smile with one of my own, a delicate tilting of my lips that concealed the turmoil within. "Isabella," I acknowledged, my voice soft yet steady. "I could not very well miss such an... illuminating gathering, could I?"

Her eyebrow arched, a subtle hint of her own agenda playing at the corners of her mouth. "Indeed, one would not wish to miss the spectacle that is sure to unfold."

Before I could respond, the rustle of silk and the click of heels on polished wood announced the arrival of Lady Elizabeth Thornwood. She swept into the room with an air of genteel refinement, her tall, elegant figure commanding attention. Her copper-red hair was piled atop her head in an intricate coiffure, and her ice-blue eyes surveyed the room with a practiced smile that concealed a steely determination.

"Good evening, ladies," she greeted, her voice a melodious lilt that belied the sharpness of her gaze. "I trust I have not kept you waiting overlong?"

Isabella's smile widened, a predator's grin that sent a chill down my spine. "Not at all, Lady Elizabeth. We were merely enjoying a moment of... anticipation."

As Lady Elizabeth took her seat, I couldn't help but recall the grisly tales of Hyde's handiwork. The images of the butcher's wife, her throat slit and eyes gouged out, flashed before my eyes. The young gentleman, his entrails spilling from his abdomen like a grotesque offering, haunted my thoughts. The stench of decay and the gleam of rats' eyes in the dim light sent a shudder through me, a morbid fascination that fueled my determination.

Tonight, I would harness that darkness, wield it as a weapon in my quest for power. And as I looked at Isabella and Lady Elizabeth, I knew that I was not the only one with secrets and ambitions lurking beneath the surface. The game was indeed afoot, and I was ready to play—ready to claim my place among Mayfair's elite, no matter the cost.

The flickering flames of the candelabra cast eerie shadows upon the opulent drawing room, where the heavy scent of beeswax and the faint undernote of decay seemed to linger. I, Annabelle Blake, stood with an air of delicate poise, my pale blue gown adorned with subtle black lace trimmings—a nod to the darkness I intended to embrace. The room, a symphony of gilded mirrors and velvet drapes, felt charged with an electric tension, as if the very air hummed with the secrets and ambitions of those present.

"I must confess," I began, my voice as soft and melodious as a lullaby, "the masquerade revealed much about the hidden desires of our esteemed company. Would you not agree, Lady Elizabeth?"

Lady Elizabeth Thornwood, seated with regal elegance, raised an eyebrow ever so slightly. Her gown, a rich burgundy that evoked images of fresh blood, rustled as she shifted. "Indeed, Miss Blake? And what, pray tell, did you glean from such an evening of debauchery?"

I smiled sweetly, my eyes widening with feigned innocence. "Why, merely that the masks we wear in society are but a thin veneer over our true selves. For instance, I heard whispers of a certain lord's indiscretions that could prove... compromising."

Isabella Blackwood, her deep blue eyes gleaming with a predatory light, leaned forward. "You speak of Lord Harrington, perhaps? His dalliances are hardly a secret, Annabelle."

I turned to her, my expression one of mild surprise. "Oh, Isabella, I had not realized you were so well-acquainted with his affairs. But then, your own connections to certain gentlemen of ill repute are likewise intriguing."

The room seemed to grow colder, the tension palpable as each woman measured her words like poison. Lady Elizabeth's smile never wavered, but her eyes narrowed imperceptibly. "And what of you, Miss Blake? What secrets do you harbor beneath that demure facade?"

I felt a thrill of excitement, a dark energy coursing through me. "Me? Why, I am but a humble observer, learning from the masters of the game." I paused, allowing a moment of silence to hang heavy in the air. "Though I must admit, the tales of Mr. Hyde's... exploits... have piqued my curiosity. The butcher's wife, her throat slit like a second smile, her eyes gouged out and left for the rats—such brutality is almost artistic, is it not?"

Isabella's lips curled into a smirk, her voice dripping with sarcasm. "Artistic? Or merely the work of a madman?"

I tilted my head, my tone thoughtful. "Ah, but is there not a fine line between madness and genius? The young gentleman, his entrails spilling forth like a grotesque offering—it is as if Hyde paints with blood and viscera, creating a tableau of terror that cannot be ignored."

Lady Elizabeth's gaze sharpened, her voice cutting through the air like a blade. "You speak of these horrors with a disturbing familiarity, Miss Blake. One might wonder at your motivations."

I met her stare with a calm, unyielding gaze. "My motivations are simple, Lady Elizabeth. I seek to understand the darkness that drives men like Hyde. To harness it, perhaps even to wield it."

The room fell silent, the tension a living thing that coiled around us, ready to strike. Each word was a carefully placed piece on a chessboard, each pause a strategic maneuver. I could feel the power shifting, the delicate balance of control teetering on the edge of a knife.

As the conversation unfolded, the air grew thick with unspoken threats and veiled accusations. Each woman was a predator, circling, waiting for the slightest sign of weakness. The room seemed to close in, the shadows growing darker, the candles flickering as if in anticipation of the storm to come.

In that moment, I knew that I had set the stage for a dance of death and deception, a game where the stakes were not just power, but survival itself. And as I looked into the eyes of Isabella and Lady Elizabeth, I saw reflected back at me the same hunger, the same ambition—the same darkness that I knew lurked within my own soul.

The room had become a powder keg, the air thick with tension and the acrid taste of secrets held too long. The grandeur of the drawing room, with its opulent furnishings and gilded mirrors, seemed to mock our whispered conspiracies. The very walls, adorned with ancient tapestries, appeared to lean in, eager to bear witness to the unfolding drama.

As I prepared to deliver another calculated barb, the heavy oak doors creaked open with a groan that echoed through the chamber like a dying man's last breath. The atmosphere shifted abruptly, as if the very air had been sucked from the room. In strode a figure that commanded instant attention, a man whose darkly charismatic aura filled the space like a tangible force. Edward Hyde had arrived.

His striking form, tall and elegantly built, moved with a predatory grace that belied the danger lurking beneath his polished exterior. His magnetic green eyes, possessing an almost hypnotic quality, scanned the room with a cold, calculating gaze. His dark hair, touched with silver at the temples, added to his distinguished appearance, yet there was an indefinable quality about him that made one instinctively uneasy.

Hyde's attire was impeccable, a tailored black coat that hugged his frame, accentuating his broad shoulders and narrow waist. His waistcoat, a deep crimson, seemed to shimmer in the candlelight, as if still wet with the blood of his latest victim. I could not help but recall the whispers of his nocturnal activities, the gruesome tales of bodies found in alleyways, their throats slit from ear to ear, organs spilled onto the cobblestones like some grotesque offering to the gods of the underworld.

His eyes locked onto mine, and I felt a shiver run down my spine, as if his gaze had physically penetrated me. He smiled, a cold, knowing smile that seemed to strip away my carefully cultivated facade, laying bare my ambitions and insecurities. "Ah, Miss Blake," he purred, his voice a rich, melodious sound that wrapped around me like a silken noose. "Always a pleasure to encounter such...ambition."

He turned his attention to Isabella, his eyes narrowing as he took in her sharp, calculating expression. "Miss Blackwood," he acknowledged with a slight nod, his lips curling into a smirk that hinted at some shared secret. Isabella's eyes flashed with a mix of defiance and fear, her hands clutching the fabric of her gown as if seeking an anchor in the storm of Hyde's presence.

Finally, his gaze settled on Lady Elizabeth. Her practiced smile faltered under his scrutiny, her steely determination momentarily rattled. "Lady Thornwood," he murmured, his voice dropping to a low, intimate tone. "Ever the paragon of refinement." His words hung in the air, a subtle challenge that seemed to shake the very foundations of her carefully constructed world.

The Devil of London

As Hyde moved closer, the candles flickered wildly, casting eerie shadows that danced macabrely on the walls. I could not help but imagine those shadows as the tormented souls of his victims, their silent screams echoing through the room. His boots, polished to a mirror shine, clicked against the marble floor, each step measured and deliberate, a predator stalking his prey.

He circled us like a vulture, his eyes never leaving our faces, assessing our reactions, our vulnerabilities. I felt a strange mixture of revulsion and fascination, drawn to him like a moth to a flame, knowing full well the danger he posed. His presence was a dark, intoxicating force, a whirlpool threatening to drag us all under.

As he completed his circuit, coming to stand before us, I could not help but feel a sense of dread wash over me. The game had changed, the stakes raised to a level none of us could have anticipated. Hyde's arrival had thrown everything into chaos, his presence a catalyst for the darkness that lurked within us all. And as I looked into his hypnotic green eyes, I knew that the true dance of death and deception had only just begun.

The opulent drawing room, once a sanctuary of civilized discourse, now teemed with an undercurrent of darkness, as if the very air was infused with Hyde's malevolent presence. The heavy brocade curtains, drawn against the encroaching fog, seemed to shudder as he stepped closer, his tall, elegant figure cutting through the tense atmosphere like a blade.

My heart pounded in my chest as Hyde insinuated himself into our circle, his sharp, aristocratic features illuminated by the flickering candlelight. His magnetic green eyes held a cold, calculating gleam, and I could not help but recall the rumors of his brutal exploits—bodies found in alleys, throats slashed so deeply that the heads were barely attached, entrails spilled onto the cobblestones like grotesque offerings to the devil himself.

"Ladies," he began, his voice a low, seductive purr that seemed to wrap around us like a silk noose. "I must confess, I find it most invigorating to be in the company of such... formidable women." His lips curled into a smile, but it held no warmth, only a chilling promise.

Lady Elizabeth, her ice-blue eyes flashing, was the first to respond. "Mr. Hyde, your reputation precedes you. I must admit, I am curious as to what brings you to our humble gathering." Her voice was steady, but I noted the slight tightening of her fingers on her fan, a whisper of nervousness betrayed.

Hyde's smile widened, a shark scenting blood. "Reputation, Lady Elizabeth? Pray, tell me, what do they whisper of me in your gilded halls?" He moved with a predatory grace, his dark hair, touched with silver at the temples, catching the light as he circled her like a wolf.

Isabella, ever the calculating observer, watched their exchange with a subtle smile playing on her lips. Her deep blue-gray eyes held a knowing darkness, and she seemed to be weighing Hyde's words, searching for the double meaning hidden within.

I felt a shiver run down my spine as Hyde turned his attention to me, his eyes locking onto mine with an intensity that made me feel as if he could see straight through to my soul. "And you, Miss Blake," he said, his voice dropping to a conspiratorial whisper. "What dark secrets do you harbor beneath that demure exterior?"

I swallowed hard, my mouth suddenly dry. "I assure you, Mr. Hyde, I am nothing more than I appear," I lied, my voice steadier than I felt.

He laughed, a low, throaty sound that sent a chill through me. "Oh, Miss Blake, we are all more than we appear. Would you not agree, Lady Elizabeth?" He turned back to her, his eyes gleaming with malice. "After all, who among us does not hide a multitude of sins beneath our silks and laces?"

Lady Elizabeth's cheeks flushed, her grip on her fan tightening until her knuckles were white. "You speak in riddles, Mr. Hyde. I find it most unbecoming."

Hyde's smile never wavered, but his eyes hardened, a flash of steel beneath the velvet. "Riddles, Lady Elizabeth? Or perhaps you find the truth too harsh for your delicate sensibilities?" He leaned in, his voice dropping to a murmur. "I wonder, how many of your admirers know the true extent of your... ambition?"

The tension in the room ratcheted up, the air thick with unspoken threats and promises. Isabella, her eyes gleaming with fascination, seemed to be enjoying the spectacle, her gaze flicking between Hyde and Lady Elizabeth like a spectator at a gladiatorial contest.

Hyde turned back to me, his eyes softening, his voice taking on a gentler, almost sympathetic tone. "And you, Miss Blake. You seek to assert your influence, to rise above the petty constraints of society. But tell me, are you prepared for the sacrifices that such ambition demands?"

His words struck a chord within me, a dark resonance that set my nerves on edge. I thought of the bodies left in his wake, the blood spilled in his relentless pursuit of power. Was I truly prepared to walk that path?

As if sensing my discomfort, Hyde reached out, his fingers brushing against my cheek in a gesture that was both tender and threatening. "Do not fear, Miss Blake," he murmured. "The darkness can be most... liberating."

I felt a shiver run through me, a mixture of revulsion and fascination. This was the true dance of death and deception, a twisted waltz of power and manipulation. And as I looked into Hyde's eyes, I knew that there was no turning back. The game had changed, and we were all pawns in his deadly play.

The room seemed to close in around me, the air thick with tension and the cloying scent of expensive perfumes. The grand clock in the corner ticked away the seconds like a countdown to some inevitable doom. Hyde stood at the center of our circle, his eyes gleaming with malice and amusement as he surveyed each of us in turn.

"Lady Elizabeth," he began, his voice a low purr that seemed to slither beneath my skin. "Your husband's seat in Parliament is not as secure as you might believe. There are whispers of scandal, of secrets that could topple his power like a house of cards."

Lady Elizabeth's face paled, but her voice remained steady. "Mere rumors, Mr. Hyde. You should know better than to put stock in idle gossip."

Hyde's smile widened, a shark's grin that sent a chill down my spine. "Indeed, rumors can be such fickle things," he replied. "But when they are backed by evidence... well, that is another matter entirely."

Isabella watched the exchange with avid interest, her eyes sharp and calculating. "And what of you, Mr. Hyde?" she interjected. "What secrets do you hide beneath that polished exterior?"

Hyde turned to her, his gaze hardening. "My dear Miss Blackwood, you should know better than to ask such questions. After all, we each have our skeletons, do we not?"

I felt a cold sweat break out on my brow as Hyde's attention shifted back to me. His eyes seemed to pierce through my very soul, laying bare my deepest fears and insecurities. "And you, Miss Blake," he said softly. "What would the fine ladies and gentlemen of Mayfair say if they knew the truth about your family? About the blood that stains your hands?"

My heart pounded in my chest, a drumbeat of panic and dread. How could he know? The secrets I had buried so deep, the past I had fought so hard to escape—he wielded them like a blade, cutting through my carefully constructed facade.

Lady Elizabeth's eyes narrowed, her voice like ice. "You go too far, Mr. Hyde. We will not be intimidated by your threats."

Hyde laughed, a sound that sent a shiver down my spine. "Threats, Lady Elizabeth? I merely speak the truth. And the truth, as they say, shall set you free."

Isabella's lips curled into a smirk. "Or bury you six feet under."

The tension in the room was palpable, a living thing that seemed to crackle in the air like lightning. Each word, each glance, was a carefully calculated move in a deadly game of chess. And Hyde, the master puppeteer, pulled our strings with ruthless precision.

Suddenly, Hyde's expression darkened, his eyes flashing with a cold, murderous light. "But perhaps you need a reminder of the stakes we play for," he said, his voice barely above a whisper.

Before any of us could react, he moved with the speed of a striking viper. His hand shot out, grasping Lady Elizabeth by the throat. She gasped, her eyes wide with shock and terror as he lifted her effortlessly from the ground.

"Mr. Hyde!" Isabella cried out, her composure shattering. "Release her at once!"

But Hyde paid her no heed. His grip tightened, Lady Elizabeth's face turning a sickly shade of purple as she struggled for breath. I stood frozen, horror rooting me to the spot as I watched the life drain from her eyes.

Then, with a brutal twist, Hyde wrenched her head to the side. The sickening crack of breaking bone echoed through the room, and Lady Elizabeth's body went limp, her lifeless eyes staring accusingly at the ceiling.

Hyde let her fall to the floor, her corpse landing with a sickening thud. Blood pooled beneath her, a crimson stain spreading across the polished wood. I stared in mute horror, my mind struggling to comprehend the gruesome tableau before me.

The Devil of London

Isabella's scream shattered the silence, a primal sound of terror and despair. She stumbled back, her hands clasped over her mouth as she stared at Lady Elizabeth's broken body.

Hyde turned to us, his eyes wild and feral. "Now you see the true face of power," he growled. "The price of ambition. Are you prepared to pay it, Miss Blake? Miss Blackwood?"

I felt bile rise in my throat, the coppery tang of blood and fear filling my mouth. This was the true dance of death and deception, a twisted waltz of power and manipulation. And as I looked into Hyde's eyes, I knew that there was no turning back. The game had changed, and we were all pawns in his deadly play.

The room seemed to spin around me, the walls closing in like a coffin. The grand clock ticked on, its steady rhythm a mocking reminder of the fleeting nature of life. And as I stared at Lady Elizabeth's lifeless form, I knew that the darkness Hyde had spoken of was not liberating—it was a prison from which there was no escape.

The grand clock's pendulum swung back and forth, its steady ticking a grim counterpoint to the chaos that had erupted in the drawing room. My gaze remained fixed on the grisly sight before me, the once-pristine floor now marred by a spreading pool of crimson. Lady Elizabeth's body lay broken and twisted, her lifeless eyes staring accusingly at the ceiling. The air was thick with the coppery scent of blood, mingling with the cloying perfumes of the ladies present, creating a nauseating miasma that clung to the back of my throat.

Isabella's screams had subsided into wracking sobs, her body shaking as she turned away from the gruesome spectacle. Her usually immaculate coiffure had come undone, dark tendrils falling around her face like a shroud. I could see the calculations behind her tears, the wheels turning in her mind as she sought to turn this tragedy to her advantage.

Hyde stood tall and unmoving, his breath coming in ragged gasps, a stark contrast to his usual composure. His eyes, those hypnotic green orbs, were now wild and feral, locked onto my face with an intensity that made my heart race. Blood flecked his cheeks and cravat, a stark reminder of the violence he had just inflicted. His hands, those powerful instruments of death, were clenched at his sides, the knuckles white with tension.

"You...you monster," Isabella choked out between sobs, her voice barely above a whisper. "You've killed her...you've killed Lady Elizabeth."

Hyde's lips curled into a snarl, his voice a low growl. "She was a pawn, nothing more. Her death is a mere stepping stone to greater power." His eyes never left mine, and I felt a shiver run down my spine, a mix of fear and exhilaration.

Margaret, who had been standing silently by the pianoforte, suddenly sprang into action. She rushed to Lady Elizabeth's side, her skirts swishing around her like a dark cloud. Her hands fluttered over the broken body, her face a picture of horror and disbelief. "We must send for a doctor," she murmured, her voice shaking. "Perhaps it is not too late—"

"It is too late, Miss Winters," Hyde interjected, his voice cold and dismissive. "Her neck is broken, her spirit fled. No doctor can bring her back."

Margaret looked up at him, her eyes wide with shock and anger. "You did this," she whispered, her voice barely audible. "You are a monster, Mr. Hyde."

Hyde's laughter filled the room, a harsh and brutal sound that sent a shiver down my spine. "Indeed, Miss Winters," he replied, his voice laced with mockery. "I am a monster. And I suggest you remember that."

As the others reeled from the violence, I found myself strangely detached, my mind racing with the implications of what had just occurred. I had seen death before, had witnessed the gruesome aftermath of Hyde's handiwork, but this was different. This was a deliberate act, a brutal display of power that had forever altered the dynamics of our little gathering.

I looked down at my hands, surprised to find them steady, my gloves pristine and unmarked by the carnage that surrounded me. A sense of calm washed over me, a realization that I had crossed a threshold from which there was no return. I had played my part in this dance of death, had sown the seeds of discord and mistrust that had led us to this bloody conclusion.

As I looked up at Hyde, his eyes locked onto mine, I felt a strange kinship with him, a bond forged in blood and darkness. He had shown me the true face of power, the price of ambition, and I knew that I was forever changed. The girl who had entered this room, her heart filled with dreams of influence and control, was gone, replaced by a woman who understood the true cost of her desires.

The Devil of London

The grand clock continued its steady ticking, its pendulum swinging back and forth like the scythe of the Grim Reaper himself. The sound filled my ears, a constant reminder of the fleeting nature of life and the permanence of death. I knew that I would never forget this moment, this baptism by blood and violence.

As I turned to leave the room, my skirts rustling softly around me, I knew that I had irrevocably changed the balance of power in Mayfair. The old order was crumbling, and a new era was dawning, an era forged in blood and darkness. And I, Annabelle Blake, would be at the heart of it, my hands stained with the blood of the old regime, my eyes fixed firmly on the future.

The future was uncertain, a yawning chasm of possibilities and pitfalls, but I was ready to face it. I had looked into the abyss and seen the true face of power, and I would not shy away from it. The game had changed, and I was a player now, a pawn no longer. The darkness had claimed me, and I would rise from the ashes, a phoenix reborn in blood and fire.

As I stepped out into the cold night air, the streets of London stretching out before me like a labyrinth of shadows and secrets, I knew that I was ready to embrace the darkness, to dance with the devil himself if need be. For I was Annabelle Blake, and I would not be underestimated again.

As I stepped out into the cold night air, the streets of London stretching out before me like a labyrinth of shadows and secrets, I knew that I was ready to embrace the darkness, to dance with the devil himself if need be. For I was Annabelle Blake, and I would not be underestimated again.

My heart still pounded with the thrill and horror of the night's events. The opulent drawing room, now a tableau of chaos and bloodshed, was a stark contrast to the quietude of the street. The cobblestones glistened under the faint moonlight, reflecting the eerie silence that had descended upon Mayfair.

The image of Edward Hyde, his green eyes gleaming with a wild, almost feral intensity, was burned into my memory. His entrance had shifted the atmosphere, his dark charisma filling the room like a palpable force. And then, the violence—swift, brutal, and utterly transformative.

Isabella Blackwood, her sharp eyes now wide with shock, had watched in stunned silence as Hyde's blade flashed through the air. Lady

Elizabeth Thornwood, her genteel refinement shattered, had recoiled in horror as blood spattered her pristine gown. The room had erupted into a symphony of screams and gasps, the air thick with the coppery scent of blood.

Hyde had moved with a terrible grace, his every action calculated to maximize terror and chaos. The sight of him, his hands dripping with the lifeblood of his victims, was a grotesque spectacle that would haunt my dreams. Yet, amidst the carnage, I felt a strange exhilaration. This was the power I had sought, the power to reshape the world according to my will.

As I walked through the deserted streets, the echoes of the night's violence followed me like a spectral procession. The clatter of carriage wheels over cobblestones, the distant cries of night watchmen, and the rustling of unseen creatures in the shadows all seemed to whisper of the upheaval I had set in motion.

My thoughts turned to Margaret Winters, her gray eyes filled with a mixture of fear and determination. She had stood frozen, her ash-blonde hair escaping its severe style, as Hyde's blade had flashed mere inches from her. Her dedication to propriety had been shaken to its core, and I wondered how she would navigate the treacherous waters ahead.

The uncertainty of the future hung heavy in the air, a yawning chasm of possibilities and pitfalls. The alliances and rivalries forged in blood and violence would shape the days to come, and I knew that I was at the heart of it all. The game had changed, and I was a player now, a pawn no longer.

As I approached my residence, the grandeur of the facade seemed to mock the turmoil within me. The flickering lamps cast long, dancing shadows, and I imagined the whispers that would soon spread through the halls of Mayfair. Whispers of blood and betrayal, of power and ambition.

I paused at the threshold, my hand resting on the cold brass handle. The future was uncertain, but I was ready to face it. I had looked into the abyss and seen the true face of power, and I would not shy away from it. For I was Annabelle Blake, and I would dance with the devil himself if need be.

With a deep breath, I stepped inside, leaving the night's chaos behind. But the echoes of violence and the lingering sense of uncertainty followed me, a constant reminder of the new era I had ushered in. An era forged in blood and darkness, where the old order crumbled and new alliances were forged in the fires of ambition and fear.

And so, with a heart both heavy and exhilarated, I embraced the darkness, ready to face whatever lay ahead. For I was Annabelle Blake, and I would not be underestimated again.

CHAPTER 17

The cobblestones were slick with rain and something more sinister. The metallic tang of blood clung to my nostrils. I had seen Hyde's handiwork tonight—a grisly tableau of flesh and viscera painted across the alley behind The Ten Bells. The man had been more than just killed; he'd been eviscerated, his entrails strung up like morbid bunting, his eyes staring wide with a terror that refused to fade even in death. I shook the image from my mind and focused on the dim gaslight flickering ahead, marking the safehouse where Victoria awaited.

The streets were too quiet, as if the city itself held its breath. I slipped through the shadows, my nondescript waistcoat and breeches blending into the night. My hands trembled slightly as I reached for the door.

The safehouse was little more than a hovel, tucked away in a forgotten corner of Whitechapel. The dim light from within cast eerie shadows that danced macabrely. Victoria Sterling sat by the hearth, her tall, graceful form silhouetted against the feeble fire. Her honey-blonde hair gleamed in the glow, and the deep blue of her gown stood in stark contrast to the squalor around us.

The Devil of London

Her clear blue eyes met mine as she rose, her hands outstretched in welcome. "Edwin, I'm so glad you've come. Please, sit. You look as though you've seen a ghost."

I forced a smile. "Something like that, Miss Sterling," I replied, my voice barely above a whisper. I perched on the edge of the chair, ready to flee at a moment's notice.

Her gaze was unwavering. "You have something to tell me, Edwin. Something important. You can trust me."

I hesitated. The image of the eviscerated man flashed before my eyes again, his blood pooling in grotesque halos. Hyde's laughter had echoed through the alley, reveling in his gruesome masterpiece. My breath hitched. Victoria sensed my hesitation, her hand covering mine, warm and reassuring.

"Take your time," she said softly. "You are doing the right thing. I believe in you."

I took a deep breath. "Hyde is not who you think he is," I began. "He's a monster. A psychopathic killer who revels in the blood of his victims."

The words hung heavy in the air. Victoria's grip on my hand remained firm. She did not flinch, nor did she let go. Encouraged by her steady presence, I continued.

"I've seen things... unspeakable things. He doesn't just kill, Miss Sterling. He plays with them, takes his time. The screams... they echo through the streets, but no one comes. No one ever comes when Hyde is on the hunt."

Victoria's face paled, but she nodded. "We must stop him."

Just as I was about to reveal Hyde's lair, the door to the safehouse swung open abruptly. Rose Whitechapel and Jonathan Hartwell stood in the doorway, their expressions tight with urgency. Rose, her dark eyes sharp, scanned the room with a practiced elegance. Hartwell, tall and imposing, his aristocratic features grim, betrayed a slight tremor in his normally steady hands.

Their arrival sent a shockwave through the room. The safehouse, once a sanctuary, now crackled with unspoken tension.

"Well, Flash," Rose said, stepping forward, her velvet gown whispering against the floor. "I do hope we've not interrupted something delicate."

Hartwell's voice was as cold as iron. "I trust you've not been divulging anything... sensitive. It would be most unfortunate."

My mouth went dry. Hyde's twisted trust in me had been my shield, but now it felt like a noose tightening around my neck. Victoria stiffened beside me, but her faith in me remained palpable.

Then, the door swung open again.

Nathaniel Wake strode in, his massive frame filling the doorway, his scarred face set in grim determination. The room, already fraught with tension, now felt on the verge of collapse.

Wake's eyes bore into me. "You've found yourself in a bit of a mess, haven't you, Barrett?"

My stomach churned. The memories of Hyde's atrocities swarmed my mind. The alley behind the Ten Bells, the cobblestones slick with blood, the mutilated bodies. The twisted glee in Hyde's eyes.

"I... I don't know what you mean, Mr. Wake," I stammered.

Wake stepped forward, his boots heavy on the floorboards. "Don't play the fool, Barrett. I've seen Hyde's work. The bodies, the rivers of blood. It has to end."

Victoria gasped, her hand flying to her mouth. Rose, however, remained unreadable, calculating. Hartwell, ever the strategist, merely observed.

Wake's gaze never wavered. "I choose to put an end to this madness."

Hartwell's lip curled. "And what do you intend to do?"

Wake looked at me. "I intend to see justice done. True justice."

The words settled over the room like a hammer blow. The lines had been drawn. There was no going back.

Victoria's eyes shone with unshed tears, her belief in me unwavering. I thought of Hyde, of the horrors he had unleashed, the countless victims left in his wake. And I made my choice.

"I'll stand witness," I said, my voice steady. "I'll testify against Hyde. I'll see justice done."

The air shifted. Rose's mask slipped, fury flashing in her eyes. Hartwell merely nodded, ever the tactician.

Wake inclined his head. "Well played, Barrett. Well played."

Rose took a step forward, her voice a venomous whisper. "You cannot fathom the depths of Hyde's depravity. His reach is long. His vengeance, swift."

I swallowed hard. "I know what I've done. I know what I must do."

Rose's eyes darkened. "Then you have signed your own death warrant."

With a swirl of velvet, she turned, sweeping from the room. Hartwell lingered a moment before following, leaving behind only the echoes of their unspoken threats.

As the door clicked shut, the tension ebbed. Victoria turned to me, eyes brimming with gratitude. "You have done the right thing, Edwin."

I managed a small smile, though dread curled in my gut. The die was cast. Hyde would come for me.

But for now, in this quiet moment, I allowed myself a sliver of peace. I had made my choice. Perhaps, amidst the ruins of my past, I could find redemption.

The candle flickered. The shadows danced. And somewhere in the dark, the true horror was only just beginning.

CHAPTER 18

In the gloom of the Blackwood townhouse drawing room, I, Thomas Harding, cut a spectral figure, pacing back and forth like a phantom bound to its haunt. The room, a cavern of shadow and faded opulence, seemed to echo with the whispers of the secrets that had long gnawed at my conscience. The faint scent of beeswax candles and the ticking of the mantel clock were the only signs of life within, save for the relentless tread of my feet upon the worn carpet.

My mind was a whirlwind of guilt and fear, a tumult that threatened to consume me. For years, I had kept the dark confidences of the dead, their silent accusations a weight upon my shoulders. But now, the secrets of the living had become an even greater burden, one that I could no longer bear alone. I wrung my hands, the skin pale and bloodless, like that of a corpse. The very thought of revealing what I knew sent a shiver down my spine, as if the icy tendrils of the grave had reached out to claim me.

The flickering candlelight cast grotesque shadows upon the wall, twisted doppelgängers of myself that seemed to mock my cowardice. I could almost hear the sneering laughter of Edward Hyde, the psychopathic killer who had left a trail of blood and terror through the streets of London. The memories of the crime scenes I had been forced to attend rushed back to me, unbidden and unwanted.

The cobblestones slick with blood, the air thick with the coppery stench of death. Bodies torn asunder, limbs akimbo, entrails steaming in the cool night air. Hyde's victims were not merely murdered, but desecrated, their forms rendered into bloody parodies of humanity. I had seen the dark heart of man, and it was a twisted, malevolent thing.

I paused in my pacing, my breath coming in ragged gasps. The room seemed to spin around me, the shadows coalescing into monstrous forms. I could feel the panic rising within me, threatening to overwhelm my senses. It was then that a soft, measured voice cut through the fog of my despair.

"Mr. Harding, I trust you have not forgotten the purpose of our meeting."

I turned to find Catherine Blackwood seated upon the chaise, her back straight and her eyes fixed intently upon me. Her dark brown hair was pulled back severely from her face, emphasizing her penetrating gray eyes. Those eyes seemed to bore into my very soul, as if she could see the secrets that writhed within me.

Her hands, ink-stained and quick-moving, were folded neatly in her lap. Her dress, a simple gown of deep blue, was unadorned save for a small silver brooch at her throat. She was the very picture of composure, a steadying force amidst the storm of my emotions.

"Miss Blackwood," I said, my voice barely more than a whisper. "I fear that I have been remiss in my duties. The secrets that I have kept... they have become a burden too great to bear."

Her expression did not change, but I could see the intensity in her eyes, the quiet determination that lay beneath her controlled exterior. "We all have our burdens to bear, Mr. Harding," she said. "But it is only by confronting them that we may find any measure of solace."

I felt a shiver run down my spine, as if the very air had grown colder. The shadows seemed to press in around me, the weight of my secrets a physical force that threatened to crush me. But Catherine's presence was a beacon in the darkness, a steadying hand that guided me back from the brink of despair.

"You are right, of course," I said, my voice gaining a measure of strength. "I have seen things, Miss Blackwood. Things that would chill the blood of any sensible man. But I cannot keep silent any longer. The truth must be revealed, no matter the cost."

Catherine nodded, her eyes never leaving mine. "And I will be here to help you bear the burden, Mr. Harding. Together, we shall see this through to the end, no matter what horrors may await us."

In that moment, I felt a spark of hope amidst the gloom. The path before me was shrouded in darkness, the shadows thick with the whispered threats of Edward Hyde. But with Catherine Blackwood by my side, I knew that I could face whatever terrors lay ahead. For the truth, no matter how grim, was a light that could pierce even the deepest shadows. And in that light, I found the strength to continue, to reveal the secrets that had haunted me for so long, and to bring the monstrous Hyde to justice.

The flickering candlelight cast macabre shadows upon the drawing room walls, as if the very flames were conspiring to paint the gruesome images that haunted my mind. I could see them still, the mutilated corpses, the blood pooling like spilled ink on the cobblestones, the echoes of screams silenced by the thick London fog. I took a deep breath, the air heavy with the scent of beeswax and the faint, underlying tang of my own fear.

Catherine sat before me, her back straight as a rod, her eyes fixed upon me with an intensity that was almost unnerving. Her dark dress blended with the shadows, save for the stark white collar that framed her throat, emphasizing the paleness of her skin. Her hands, stained with ink, rested calmly on her lap, yet her gaze was anything but tranquil. It was a gaze that saw more than I wished it to, that seemed to pierce the very depths of my soul, laying bare the secrets I had kept buried for so long.

I reached into my coat pocket, my fingers brushing against the cool metal of the locket. The mere touch of it sent a shiver down my spine, as if the very object was tainted with the evil it had witnessed. I withdrew it, the silver surface glinting ominously in the candlelight, like a malevolent eye winking in the darkness.

"I have seen things, Miss Blackwood," I began, my voice trembling slightly despite my best efforts to steady it. "Things that would turn the stomach of even the most hardened of men." I took a deep breath, the air shuddering in my lungs. "Hyde... he is not a man, but a monster. A beast that walks among us, cloaked in the guise of a gentleman."

The Devil of London

Catherine's eyes never left mine, her expression one of calm determination. Yet, I could see the curiosity burning in her gaze, the hunger for the truth that she sought. I prayed she was ready for the horrors I was about to reveal.

I opened the locket, the hinge creaking softly, as if protesting the revelation of its secrets. Inside lay a folded note, yellowed with age and stained with... I shuddered, unable to complete the thought. With careful, almost reverent hands, I removed the note, unfolding it to reveal the spidery scrawl that adorned its surface.

"It is a list, Miss Blackwood," I said, my voice barely above a whisper. "A list of names, each one a member of London's elite. Beside each name is a date, a time... and a method." I swallowed hard, the bile rising in my throat as the images flooded my mind once more.

"A method, Mr. Harding?" Catherine asked, her brow furrowing slightly. "A method for what?"

I met her gaze, my voice steady as I delivered the grim truth. "For murder, Miss Blackwood. For the most brutal, most grotesque of murders."

Her expression shifted then, the curiosity replaced by shock, then horror. I could see the realization dawning in her eyes, the comprehension of the depravity we were dealing with. I pressed on, the words tumbling from my lips like a confession, a purging of the sins that had weighed so heavily upon my soul.

"I have seen the aftermath of Hyde's work, Miss Blackwood. I have seen the bodies, torn and mutilated, the blood splattered like some obscene painting on the walls. I have seen the entrails, the organs, the... the pieces of what were once living, breathing human beings, scattered like so much rubbish on the streets of our fair city."

I took a deep breath, the air shuddering in my lungs as I fought to maintain my composure. "And I have seen the way he looks at them, Miss Blackwood. The way he admires his handiwork, his eyes gleaming with a satisfaction that is almost... sexual in its intensity."

Catherine's hand flew to her mouth, her eyes wide with horror. I could see the revulsion in her gaze, the stark realization of the evil we were dealing with. I knew then that she understood, that she saw the true face of Edward Hyde, the monster that lurked beneath the surface.

I handed her the note, my hands trembling slightly as I did so. She took it, her eyes scanning the list, her expression growing grimmer with each passing moment. I knew what she was seeing, what she was feeling. I had felt it myself, the first time I had seen that list, the first time I had understood the true extent of Hyde's depravity.

As she read, I could see the determination in her eyes, the steely resolve that I had come to admire in her. I knew then that she would not rest until Hyde was brought to justice, until the monster that stalked the streets of London was stopped once and for all. And I knew, too, that I would be by her side, every step of the way, no matter what horrors awaited us. For we had seen the face of evil, and we could not turn back now.

The door to the drawing room creaked open, and in swept Isabella Blackwood, her tall, graceful form cloaked in a gown of deep midnight blue. The silk rustled like dead leaves underfoot, whispering secrets only she understood. Her eyes, a piercing blue-gray, surveyed the room with an unsettling intensity, lingering on Catherine's pallid complexion and my trembling hands. I felt a shiver run down my spine as her gaze met mine, her slight smile barely concealing the calculating whir of her thoughts.

"Mr. Harding," she acknowledged me with a nod, her voice cool and measured. "I see I've arrived just in time for the revelations." Her eyes flicked to the locket still clutched in Catherine's hand, the silver chain dripping through her fingers like a poisonous vine.

I swallowed hard, my mouth dry as cotton. "Lady Isabella," I began, my voice barely above a whisper. "I was just—""No need to recap, Mr. Harding," she interjected, her eyes scanning the note Catherine held. "I can see quite plainly that you've unearthed something...unsavory."

She glided closer, her skirts brushing against the faded opulence of the drawing room. Her sharp gaze fell upon the list, her eyes narrowing as she scanned the names. "Lord Harrington, Sir Reginald, Mr. Abernathy..." Her voice trailed off, her brow furrowing slightly. "All pillars of our society, yet here they are, entwined in Hyde's web."

I watched as her expression shifted, her fascination becoming increasingly apparent. She reached out, her fingers tracing the edge of the note, her touch almost reverent. "Tell me, Mr. Harding," she said, her voice barely above a whisper. "What has Hyde promised them? What could possibly tempt them to align with such...darkness?"

My mind flashed with images of the crime scenes I'd witnessed—the blood, the gore, the stench of death. Lord Harrington's study, awash with crimson, the walls spattered with blood and brains. Sir Reginald's body, slumped in his chair, his throat slit from ear to ear, the gaping wound like a grotesque, grinning mouth. Mr. Abernathy, his entrails strewn about like some macabre garland, his eyes glassy and vacant.

I shuddered, my voice trembling as I spoke. "He offers them their deepest desires, Lady Isabella. But in return, he demands their souls."

Isabella's eyes gleamed with a dark intensity. "And what of you, Mr. Harding?" she asked, her voice soft yet probing. "What has Hyde offered you, that you find yourself so entangled in his affairs?"

I hesitated, my heart pounding in my chest. "He...he offered me release," I admitted, my voice barely a whisper. "Release from the guilt, the pain...the memories."

Isabella's eyes narrowed, her gaze piercing through me. "And what does he ask in return, Mr. Harding?" she pressed, her voice barely audible. "What price does he demand for such...freedom?"

I felt a cold sweat break out on my brow, my hands trembling slightly. "He asks that I bear witness," I said, my voice choked with emotion. "That I document his...his crimes, his conquests. That I chronicle his descent into darkness."

Isabella's eyes widened slightly, her breath hitching in her throat. "And have you, Mr. Harding?" she asked, her voice a hushed whisper. "Have you borne witness to his...work?"

I nodded, my mind awash with the gruesome tableaux I'd been forced to endure. "I have," I admitted, my voice heavy with guilt. "I have seen things, Lady Isabella...things that would haunt your dreams, that would chill your very soul."

Isabella's eyes gleamed with a dark fascination, her lips curving into a slow, unsettling smile. "Then share them, Mr. Harding," she urged, her voice barely concealing her eagerness. "Share your nightmares, your horrors. For if we are to combat this darkness, we must first understand it."

I hesitated, my mind a whirl of blood and gore, of screams and shadows. But as I looked into Isabella's eyes, I saw a reflection of my own darkness, my own fascination with the macabre. And so, I began to speak, my voice a haunted whisper, my words painting a portrait of horror and depravity, of a monster who walked among us, his true face hidden behind a mask of civility and charm. And as I spoke, I watched as Isabella's fascination grew, her eyes gleaming with a dark hunger, a hunger for the very darkness that threatened to consume us all.

The heavy oak door creaked open, and in stepped Sir Maximillion Worthington, his silver beard gleaming in the dim candlelight like the edge of a freshly sharpened blade. His penetrating gray eyes swept over the room, pausing briefly on each of us, his eyebrows raised in an expression of mingled incredulity and disdain. I could feel the weight of his judgment, the power of his presence, like a physical force pressing down upon me.

"Worthington," Isabella acknowledged, her voice cool and measured. "How good of you to join us."

Sir Maximillion's lips curled into a faint sneer as he took in the scene before him. His gaze lingered on me, and I felt a shiver run down my spine as I saw the skepticism writ large in his eyes. "Harding," he said, his voice like the crack of a whip. "I should have known you would be at the center of this...whatever this is."

I swallowed hard, my mouth suddenly dry as dust. "Sir Maximillion," I began, my voice barely more than a croak. "I have...that is, there are things you must know. About Hyde, about the murders—"

He cut me off with a sharp gesture, his hand trembling slightly as he did so. "Murders?" he scoffed. "You speak as if you have knowledge of such things, Harding. I should think your profession would have taught you the value of discretion."

Isabella interjected, her voice like ice. "Discretion has its place, Sir Maximillion, but so too does the truth. And the truth, in this case, is that a monster walks among us, a monster who has left a trail of blood and terror in his wake."

Worthington's eyes narrowed, and he looked from Isabella to me, his expression one of growing unease. "A monster, you say?" he murmured, his voice barely audible. "And what manner of monster is this?"

I took a deep breath, steeling myself for what was to come. I thought of the bodies, the blood, the stench of death that clung to my clothes and my skin like a shroud. "The victims," I said, my voice steady despite the turmoil within me. "They are not mere corpses, not simple murders. They are...disassembled, their limbs and organs scattered like the pieces of some grotesque puzzle." I could see it all in my mind's eye, the blood-slicked floors, the walls spattered with gore, the stench of death and decay. "He takes trophies, Sir Maximillion," I continued, my voice barely more than a whisper. "Fingers, toes, eyes...he keeps them, like the spoils of some grisly war."

Worthington's face paled, and he reached out a hand to steady himself against the back of a nearby chair. "Good God," he breathed, his voice barely audible. "What manner of beast are you describing, Harding?"

Isabella's eyes gleamed with a dark intensity as she leaned forward in her seat. "A beast in human form, Sir Maximillion," she said, her voice barely concealing her eagerness. "A man who walks among us, hidden behind a mask of civility and charm. A man who has left a trail of death and destruction in his wake, a trail that leads directly to his door."

Worthington's eyes widened in horror as the implications of our words became clear. "You speak of Hyde," he said, his voice barely more than a whisper. "Edward Hyde."

Catherine, who had been silent until now, spoke up, her voice steady and determined. "We do," she said, her eyes fixed on Worthington's face. "And we must stop him, Sir Maximillion. We must put an end to his reign of terror, before more innocent lives are lost."

Worthington's eyes flicked from Catherine to Isabella, then finally to me, his expression one of growing dread. "And how do you propose we do that, pray tell?" he demanded, his voice shaking slightly. "How do you suggest we bring this...this monster to justice?"

Isabella's lips curved into a slow, unsettling smile. "We must fight fire with fire, Sir Maximillion," she said, her voice barely concealing her eagerness. "We must use his own weapons against him, use his own darkness to bring him down."

Worthington's eyes widened in horror as he took in her words, his mind already racing with the implications. "You speak of madness," he breathed, his voice barely audible. "You speak of descending into the very abyss we seek to escape."

I could feel the tension in the room, the air thick with the weight of our collective fear and uncertainty. I thought of the bodies, the blood, the stench of death that clung to me like a second skin. I thought of Hyde, of his eyes, gleaming with predatory intelligence, his hands stained with the blood of his victims. And I knew, with a sickening certainty, that Isabella was right. We must fight fire with fire, descend into the abyss, if we were to have any hope of bringing Hyde to justice.

"It is a risk we must take, Sir Maximillion," I said, my voice steady despite the turmoil within me. "For if we do not act, if we do not stand against this darkness, then we are surely lost."

Worthington's eyes met mine, and I saw the fear in them, the dread that mirrored my own. But I saw something else as well, a spark of determination, a glimmer of the strength that had made him the man he was. "Very well," he said, his voice barely more than a whisper

As I, Thomas Harding, stood in the dimly lit drawing room of the Blackwood townhouse, the air thick with the weight of my confession, the heavy mahogany door creaked open. In strode Sir Maximillion Worthington, his tall, imposing figure silhouetted against the faint glow of the hallway. His silver beard, meticulously groomed, did little to soften the harsh lines of his face, and his penetrating gray eyes swept over the room with an air of authority and unease. I felt a shiver run down my spine as his gaze settled on me, his hands clasped behind his back, perhaps to hide the slight tremor that betrayed his inner turmoil.

"Worthington," Isabella acknowledged with a nod, her sharp gaze never leaving the man. Catherine remained seated, her composure unwavering, though her eyes held a newfound wariness.

Worthington's voice, formal and authoritative, filled the room. "I must admit, I find this gathering most irregular. Harding, you have summoned us here with cryptic messages and dire implications. I trust there is a valid reason for this... melodrama?" His skepticism was palpable, but I could see the hint of dread lurking behind his stern facade.

I took a deep breath, my voice trembling as I continued my confession. "Indeed, Sir Maximillion. The matter at hand is of the utmost gravity. As I was revealing to the ladies, I have in my possession a locket that contains a cryptic note. A note that hints at a conspiracy involving the highest echelons of London's elite."

Worthington's eyebrow arched, his skepticism evident. "A conspiracy, you say? And what proof do you have of this... allegation?"

I reached into my coat pocket and produced the ornate silver locket, its surface glinting ominously in the candlelight. "Within this locket lies a note, written in a code known only to a select few. A code that I have seen before, in the correspondence of Edward Hyde."

At the mention of Hyde's name, a visible shudder passed through Worthington. His voice dropped to a low growl. "Hyde, you say? That man is a menace, a blight upon our society. But what could he possibly have to do with this... conspiracy?"

Isabella leaned forward, her eyes gleaming with a fascination that sent a chill down my spine. "Indeed, Sir Maximillion. Hyde's involvement is what makes this matter all the more intriguing. Tell us, Harding, what do you know of Hyde's... activities?"

I swallowed hard, the images of Hyde's gruesome deeds flashing before my eyes. The blood-soaked alleyways, the mutilated bodies, the stench of death that clung to the very stones of the city. "Hyde's activities are... unspeakable. He delights in the suffering of others, in the spilling of blood. I have seen his handiwork, the bodies left in his wake. Limbs torn asunder, entrails strewn about like some grotesque tapestry. He is a monster, a psychopathic killer who revels in the darkness."

Catherine's face paled, but her voice remained steady. "And yet, you have kept this knowledge to yourself, Harding. Why?"

I felt a pang of guilt, a bitter taste in my mouth. "Fear, Madam. Fear of retribution, fear of the scandal that would ensue. Fear of the darkness that Hyde embodies. And yet, I can no longer remain silent. The secrets I have kept have become a burden too heavy to bear."

Worthington's voice cut through the tension, sharp and efficient. "And what of this conspiracy? What does Hyde seek to gain?"

Isabella's voice was thoughtful, her mind already calculating the potential ramifications. "Power, Sir Maximillion. Hyde seeks power, influence. He seeks to control the very heart of London, to bend it to his will. And he will stop at nothing to achieve his goals."

The room fell silent, the weight of our words hanging heavy in the air. The flickering candlelight cast eerie shadows on the walls, the darkness seeming to close in around us. I could feel the dread, the fear, the uncertainty that gripped each of us. And yet, amidst the turmoil, there was a sense of determination, a resolve to uncover the truth, no matter the cost.

Worthington's voice, now laced with a growing sense of dread, broke the silence. "Then we must act, and act swiftly. We must uncover the truth behind this conspiracy, and put an end to Hyde's reign of terror. For the sake of London, for the sake of our very souls, we must stand against the darkness."

And so, in that dimly lit drawing room, our fates became intertwined, our paths inexorably linked to the dark machinations of

Edward Hyde. The night was still young, the shadows still deep, and the horrors yet to come were beyond our wildest imaginings. But we were determined, steadfast in our resolve. And as the candlelight flickered and the shadows danced, we steeled ourselves for the battle that lay ahead.

The air in the drawing room had grown thick with tension, the shadows cast by the flickering candles seemed to writhe and twist as if alive, reflecting the turmoil within each of us. The once comforting scent of old parchment and aged wood now mingled with an acrid undernote of fear, a tangible reminder of the secrets that had been laid bare. My heart pounded in my chest like a funeral drum, each beat echoing the growing dread that gripped my soul.

Worthington's face, once a picture of skepticism, now bore the pallor of a man staring into the abyss. His eyes darted from Harding to Catherine, then to Isabella, seeking some semblance of reason in the whirlwind of madness that had enveloped us. "But if what you say is true, Harding," he said, his voice hoarse with dread, "then the very foundations of our society are at stake. The ramifications... they are unthinkable."

Harding's hands trembled as he clutched the locket, his knuckles white with strain. "I have seen it with my own eyes, Worthington," he insisted, his voice barely above a whisper. "The bodies... the blood... Hyde's brutality knows no bounds."

Catherine, her composure steadfast amidst the storm, leaned forward, her eyes ablaze with determination. "We must not falter," she declared. "If Hyde's influence extends as far as you claim, then it is our duty to expose him, to bring his reign of terror to an end."

Isabella, her sharp gaze fixed on the locket, interjected, "But at what cost? Are we prepared to sacrifice everything - our reputations, our lives - to bring this monster to light?" Her words hung heavy in the air, a stark reminder of the personal stakes involved.

The room seemed to grow darker, the shadows deeper, as if the very house was reacting to the horrors we spoke of. I could see it all too vividly - the cobblestone alleys slick with rain and blood, the lifeless eyes of Hyde's victims staring accusingly into the night. The stench of death and decay clung to my nostrils, a phantom scent carried on the wings of memory.

Harding's voice trembled as he recounted the gruesome details. "I saw him, with my own eyes, tear the very heart from a man's chest, his laughter echoing through the streets as he did so. The blood... it flowed like a river, staining the cobblestones, a grim testament to his savagery." His eyes were haunted, the memories etched deep into his soul.

Worthington paled visibly, his hand clutching at his collar as if it had suddenly grown too tight. "Good God," he murmured, his voice barely audible. "This is madness. Utter madness."

The tension in the room was palpable, a powder keg ready to ignite. Each word spoken was like a spark, threatening to set the room ablaze. The emotions that simmered just below the surface were a volatile mix of fear, anger, and determination, each of us grappling with the horrifying reality that had been revealed.

Suddenly, the door to the drawing room swung open with a force that sent the candles flickering wildly. The shadows danced macabrely on the walls as a chill swept into the room, a palpable cold that seemed to grip the very marrow of my bones. Standing in the doorway was Edward Hyde, his tall, elegant figure cloaked in a black greatcoat that billowed dramatically behind him. His eyes, those magnetic green orbs, gleamed with a predatory intelligence that sent a shiver down my spine.

His lips curled into a smile that was equal parts charming and chilling, a contradiction that seemed to embody the very essence of the man. "Forgive the intrusion," he said, his voice a rich, melodious sound that seemed to fill the room. "But I couldn't help but overhear your... discussion." His gaze swept over each of us, lingering just long enough to convey a silent, unsettling message.

The room seemed to hold its breath, the tension that had been simmering now frozen in a tableau of shock and fear. Hyde's presence cast a pall over the gathering, his sophisticated menace a stark reminder of the darkness that lurked just beneath the surface of our world. As he stepped into the room, the door swinging shut behind him with an ominous finality, I couldn't shake the feeling that we had just invited the devil himself into our midst.

The once-charged atmosphere now hung heavy and still, as if the very air was afraid to stir in Hyde's presence. The candles flickered seeming to twist and writhe in time to some unheard symphony of the damned. I could feel the blood draining from my face, leaving me as pale as the moon that hung like a specter in the night sky outside the window.

Hyde removed his greatcoat with an eerie calm, revealing a waistcoat of deep burgundy, the color of dried blood. He folded the coat with meticulous care, as if performing a ritual, and laid it across the back of a chair. His eyes never left us, his prey, as he moved with the grace of a panther stalking its next meal.

Catherine, who had been the picture of composure, now sat rigid in her seat, her knuckles white as she gripped the arms of the chair. Her eyes, wide and filled with a frightening understanding, followed Hyde's every movement. Isabella, ever the calculating one, watched Hyde with a mix of fascination and terror, her mind no doubt racing to comprehend this new dynamic. Sir Worthington stood frozen, his earlier bluster replaced with an almost comical expression of disbelief and fear.

"Ah, the esteemed company of Mayfair," Hyde began, his voice a silken purr that slithered through the room. "How fortunate I am to find you all gathered here, like moths drawn to a flame." He cast a glance at the locket, still clutched in Harding's hand, and smiled. "And what secrets have we been discussing, I wonder?"

Harding, his voice barely above a whisper, replied, "A conspiracy, Hyde. One that involves London's elite and reaches the highest echelons of power."

Hyde raised an eyebrow, a gesture that seemed to mock our fear. "Conspiracy, you say? Such weighty matters for such a delicate gathering." He moved closer to Catherine, his eyes locked onto hers. "And what, pray tell, does the lovely Catherine Blackwood make of such... intrigue?"

Catherine's voice was steady, but I could see the pulse at her throat quicken. "I make of it what any sensible person would, Mr. Hyde. That it is a matter of grave concern."

Hyde chuckled, a sound like distant thunder. "Grave concern, indeed." He turned to Isabella, his eyes gleaming with an unsettling intensity. "And you, dear Isabella? What dark thoughts dance behind those sharp eyes of yours?"

Isabella met his gaze, her voice cool and collected. "I think, Mr. Hyde, that you know more than you let on. And that you take a certain... pleasure in the darkness that surrounds you."

Hyde's smile widened, revealing a row of perfect white teeth. "Ah, Isabella, ever the perceptive one." He turned to Sir Worthington, his expression shifting to one of mocking respect. "And Sir Maximillion Worthington, pillar of society, defender of the crown. What say you to these whispers of conspiracy?"

Sir Worthington's voice was barely audible, his earlier bravado replaced with a palpable unease. "I say that it is a matter for the authorities, Hyde. Not for... parlor games."

Hyde laughed, a sound that sent a shiver down my spine. "Parlor games, indeed. But tell me, Sir Worthington, what do the authorities know of the dark heart of London? Of the blood that runs in its veins, the sinew that binds it together?"

He leaned in, his voice dropping to a conspiratorial whisper. "Do they know of the bodies that lie rotting in the alleys, their throats slit from ear to ear, their entrails spilled out like silk ribbons? Of the whores who disappear without a trace, their screams echoing through the night like a grim lullaby?"

He turned to me, his eyes boring into mine. "Or of the secrets that lie buried in the minds of men, festering like corpses in a shallow grave?"

I felt a wave of nausea wash over me as images of Hyde's victims flashed through my mind. The stench of decay, the sight of blood pooling in the gutters, the sound of flies buzzing around lifeless eyes. I had seen the results of Hyde's handiwork, the brutal tableaux he painted with the lives of the innocent.

Hyde's voice cut through the fog of memory, his words laced with a venomous charm. "But enough of such unpleasantries. We are here to discuss more pressing matters, are we not?" He gestured to the locket, his eyes never leaving mine. "And I must say, the contents of that locket... well, let us just say that it would be most unfortunate if they were to fall into the wrong hands."

The candle flames flickered as if cowering before the chill that had settled in the drawing room. Hyde's presence had transformed the once cozy atmosphere into a tableau of dread. My heart pounded against my ribs like a trapped beast, my breaths shallow and quick. I could feel the sweat gathering beneath my wig, the powder itching my scalp as if my very skin was trying to escape Hyde's scrutiny.

Harding stood frozen, his face a pallid mask, while Isabella's eyes darted between Hyde and the locket, her mind visibly racing. Catherine, bless her stoic soul, maintained her composure, but her fingers gripped the armrests of her chair so tightly that her knuckles shone white as bleached bone.

Hyde paced slowly around the room, his boots clicking against the wooden floor like the ticking of a countdown clock. He paused behind

Catherine, leaning down to whisper in her ear, "Your grace under pressure is admirable, Lady Blackwood. But tell me, does your husband know of your late-night visits to Whitechapel? I daresay he would find them most... intriguing."

Catherine's eyes widened, but she held her tongue. I could see the pulse in her neck quicken, her breath hitch slightly. Hyde's mere presence was a poison, seeping into our veins, paralyzing us with fear.

Harding's voice cut through the silence, tremulous but determined. "Hyde, you cannot continue this. Too many have died. The locket... it implicates you, implicates us all. It must end."

Hyde turned to Harding, a cold smile playing on his lips. "End? Why, Mr. Harding, whatever do you mean? Do you refer to the unfortunate souls who met their end at the hands of... shall we say, persons unknown? The maid whose intestines were wound around her neck like a grotesque necklace? Or perhaps the footman whose eyes were gouged out, his sockets left as bloody pits of despair?"

Isabella gasped, her hand flying to her mouth. I felt bile rise in my throat as images of Hyde's victims flooded my mind. The stench of decay seemed to fill the room, the coppery tang of blood mixing with the sickly sweet scent of rotting flesh.

Hyde continued, his voice a velvety purr. "Or perhaps you refer to the secrets that bind us all, Mr. Harding? The indiscretions, the lies, the sins that would see us all ruined if they were to come to light?"

Harding's hands trembled visibly now, his resolve crumbling under Hyde's relentless assault. I could see the battle raging within him, the desperate urge to flee warring with the knowledge that he was already ensnared.

Hyde turned to me, his eyes gleaming with malice. "And you, Sir Worthington. The paragon of virtue, the beacon of justice. How would your peers react if they knew of your... proclivities? The darkness that lurks beneath your shining armor?"

I felt a cold sweat trickle down my spine, my stomach churning. Hyde's words were like a knife twisting in my gut, his insinuations cutting too close to the truth. I could see the carefully constructed facade of my life crumbling, the respect and admiration of my peers turning to disgust and condemnation.

The tension in the room was palpable, a powder keg ready to explode. Each of us grappled with our own demons, our own secrets, as

Hyde's presence forced us to confront the darkness within ourselves. The stakes were clear: confess our sins and face ruin, or remain silent and be complicit in Hyde's machinations.

Catherine was the first to break the silence, her voice steady despite the fear in her eyes. "You speak of ruin, Mr. Hyde, but there is also the potential for redemption. We are not beyond saving, not yet."

Hyde laughed, a sound like shattering glass. "Redemption? My dear Lady Blackwood, there is no redemption in the face of truth. Only acceptance... or annihilation."

His words hung in the air like a guillotine's blade, poised to fall and sever the delicate threads of our lives. The room seemed to darken, the shadows deepening as if Hyde's presence was extinguishing the very light around us. The chill in the air was no longer merely physical; it was the icy grasp of dread, the paralyzing touch of fear.

In that moment, I understood the true horror of Hyde's power. It was not his wealth or his influence, nor even the brutal violence he inflicted on his victims. It was his ability to strip away our pretenses, to lay bare our vulnerabilities and exploit them with surgical precision. He was a puppet master, pulling our strings with a cruel and practiced hand.

The reality of our situation was stark and inescapable. We were bound to Hyde, our fates intertwined with his dark machinations. To defy him was to court ruin, to invite the exposure of our deepest, most shameful secrets. And yet, to comply was to condemn ourselves to a life in his shadow, forever at the mercy of his whims.

As I looked around the room, meeting the eyes of my companions, I saw the same realization dawning in their faces. We were trapped, caught in Hyde's web like flies in a spider's silken snare. And like those hapless creatures, we could only wait, hearts pounding, as the predator approached, his eyes gleaming with malicious intent.

The flickering flame of a nearby gas lamp cast eerie shadows upon the cobblestones as I stumbled out of the Blackwood townhouse, the night air clawing at my throat like a chilled specter. My heart pounded a staccato rhythm against my ribs, echoing the tumultuous storm of thoughts that raged within my mind. The evening's revelations had left me shaken, the grim tableau of Harding's confession and Hyde's sinister influence playing out in my mind's eye like a grotesque pantomime.

Catherine had remained behind, her porcelain complexion drained of all color, her eyes haunted by the specter of uncertainty. Isabella, ever the calculating strategist, had retreated into a silence that spoke volumes of her inner turmoil. And Sir Maximillion... his blustering facade had crumbled, revealing the frightened, indecisive man beneath. We were all pawns in Hyde's twisted game, our fates dangling precariously from the puppet master's strings.

As I walked, the once-familiar streets of Mayfair now seemed alien, the grand townhouses looming like monolithic tombstones, their windows staring down at me like empty eye sockets. The wind whistled through the narrow alleys, carrying with it the faint, unsettling scent of decay, as if the very air was tainted by Hyde's corruption.

Turning a corner, I found myself on a narrow, deserted lane, the cobblestones slick with a substance that glistened black in the dim light. A sense of unease prickled at the back of my neck, and I slowed my pace, my breath misting in the cold air. As I approached the murky puddle, the coppery tang of blood assaulted my nostrils, and I recoiled, my stomach churning with revulsion.

"By Jove," I muttered, my voice barely audible as I took in the grisly sight before me. A man lay sprawled in the filth, his body contorted at unnatural angles, as if he had been discarded like a broken marionette. His throat had been slashed from ear to ear, the gaping wound a dark, glistening maw that seemed to leer at me in morbid triumph. His eyes, wide and glassy, reflected the dim glow of the gas lamp, their surface already dulled by the creeping veil of death.

I stumbled back, my hand clutching at my mouth to stifle the bile that rose in my throat. The man's clothing, though torn and bloodied, bore the unmistakable signs of quality tailoring. This was no common street thief or beggar; this was a gentleman, a member of London's elite, cut down like an animal in the grimy back alleys of Mayfair.

As I stood there, frozen in horror, a chilling realization washed over me. This was Hyde's doing. The brutal, precise nature of the killing bore all the hallmarks of his sickening prowess. It was a message, a gruesome reminder of the power he wielded and the fate that awaited those who dared to defy him.

"You should not linger here, my friend."

The voice, smooth and cultured, sliced through the fog of my revulsion like a knife. I turned to find Hyde standing mere feet away, his tall, elegant form swathed in a cloak of deepest black. His eyes, those piercing green orbs, seemed to glow with an otherworldly light, as if reflecting the fires of hell itself.

"You..." I began, my voice trembling with a mixture of fear and accusation. "You did this."

Hyde's lips curved into a slow, predatory smile, his teeth gleaming like a wolf's in the dim light. "Come now, my dear fellow," he purred, his voice a silken caress that sent a shiver down my spine. "You know as well as I that this city is a jungle, and only the strongest, the most cunning, can hope to survive."

He took a step closer, his gaze holding mine captive, like a snake mesmerizing its prey. "You have a choice to make, my friend. You can stand with me, embrace the darkness that courses through your veins, and together we shall rise above the rotting corpse of this city. Or..." He paused, his eyes flicking briefly to the mutilated corpse that lay between us. "Or you can join the ranks of the weak and the foolish, those who cling to their pathetic illusions of morality and virtue, even as they choke on their own blood."

I stared at him, my mind a whirlwind of conflicting emotions. Revulsion, terror, and, beneath it all, a sickening, insidious fascination. Hyde was a monster, a predator who reveled in the suffering of others. And yet, there was a part of me, a dark, hidden part, that understood his allure, that felt the seductive pull of his power.

"Think on it," he murmured, his voice a low, hypnotic purr. "But do not take too long, my friend. The shadows are growing darker, and the time for choosing sides is drawing to a close."

With that, he turned and melted into the night, leaving me alone with the corpse and the chilling echo of his words. As I stood there, the first tentative rays of dawn beginning to creep across the sky, I could not shake the feeling that this was but a prelude, a grim overture to the symphony of horror that was yet to come.

For in that moment, as the blood of Hyde's victim congealed on the cobblestones and the gas lamps flickered and died, I understood that the true darkness had only just begun to descend upon the streets of Mayfair. And with it would come a reckoning, a brutal, bloody purging that would leave no soul untouched, no secret unexposed.

The game was afoot, and we were all players, willing or not. The only question that remained was this: who among us would survive the night?

CHAPTER 19

In the chill of the evening, the fog rolled through the streets of London like a spectral tide, obscuring the grimy cobblestones and clinging to the worn heels of my boots as I approached the Mayfair mansion. The gas lamps flickered, their sickly light casting eerie shadows that danced macabrely on the weathered facades of the grand houses. The stench of the Thames, that putrid artery of the city, was mercifully dulled by the crisp autumn air, yet the memory of its foul embrace clung to my senses, a reminder of the murders I had committed mere hours before. The blood of my victims still lingered beneath my fingernails, a crimson crescent moon embedded in the beds of sanguine filth, I could still feel the warmth of the lifeblood as it sprayed against my skin, the coppery tang filling my nostrils. Their screams echoed in my mind, a symphony of terror and agony that stirred my soul.

Lady Elizabeth Thornwood greeted me with a practiced smile, her ice-blue eyes calculating as she extended a gloved hand. "Mr. Hyde, how delightful to see you again," she purred, her voice a silken whisper that belied the steel within. Her gown, a rich emerald silk, shimmered in the candlelight, the color of poisonous envy and verdant decay.

I took her hand, my thumb tracing the delicate veins that pulsed beneath her alabaster skin. "Lady Elizabeth," I murmured, "the pleasure is mine." My green eyes held hers, a silent battle of wills waged in the space of a heartbeat.

Her lips curved in a knowing smile as she extracted her hand from my grasp. "Do come in, Mr. Hyde. The others are most eager to make your acquaintance."

As I stepped into the grand foyer, the chatter of the assembled guests washed over me like a discordant melody. Their eyes turned towards me, a ripple of unease palpable in the air. I could see the flicker of recognition in some, the widening of eyes in remembrance of hushed whispers and lurid tales of the dark deeds committed by Edward Hyde.

My gaze swept over the gathered finery, the silks and laces that adorned the posturing peacocks of high society. And then, my eyes met hers. Isabella Blackwood, her deep blue gaze locked onto mine, a knowing darkness reflected in their depths. Her gown, a confection of midnight silk and shimmering jet beads, hugged her form like a lover's embrace, the stark black a startling contrast to her pale skin.

"Mr. Hyde," she acknowledged, her voice a low purr that sent a shiver down my spine. I could see the pulse that fluttered at the base of her throat, the delicate beat of life that called to the darkness within me.

"Miss Blackwood," I replied, my voice a velvet caress that belied the predator within. "How enchanting to see you again."

Her lips curved in a subtle smile, a silent acknowledgment of the game we played. "Indeed, Mr. Hyde. I have heard much of your... exploits. I trust your journey here was uneventful?"

I allowed my lips to curve in a slow smile, the memory of my bloody deeds still fresh in my mind. "Quite the contrary, Miss Blackwood. The streets of London are a veritable treasure trove of delights for those who know where to look."

Her eyes narrowed slightly, a gleam of interest sparking in their depths. "You must regale us with your tales, Mr. Hyde. I am certain we would all be most fascinated."

As I moved further into the room, I could feel the weight of their gazes, the subtle shift in the air as they parted to allow me passage. The scent of their fear was intoxicating, a sweet perfume that mingled with the cloying aroma of their expensive colognes and powders.

Their eyes followed me, their whispers a soft hiss that trailed in my wake. I could feel the darkness within me stirring, the beast that bayed for blood and reveled in the screams of the dying. This night was far from over, and the games had only just begun.

The opulent dining room sprawled before me, a grotesque feast of wealth and indulgence. The table, a vast expanse of polished mahogany, was laid with such an abundance of fine china and silverware that it seemed to groan under the weight of its own decadence. Candlelight flickered from ornate sconces, casting macabre shadows that danced across the walls like the twisted spirits of the damned. I could not help but compare this vulgar display to the stark brutality of the streets I had prowled mere hours before.

As I took my seat, the remembrance of my night's work played out in vivid hues against the backdrop of this gaudy spectacle. The alley behind the Ten Bells had been slick with rain and fresh blood, the latter courtesy of my blade and the unfortunate soul who had crossed my path. I could still see the terror in his eyes as I had descended upon him, the satisfying crunch of bone as I drove my knife into his flesh. His screams had been a symphony to my ears, a brutal melody that played out in stark contrast to the polite hum of conversation that now surrounded me.

Lady Elizabeth, ever the consummate hostess, presided over the gathering with an elegance that belied the calculating gleam in her eye. Her voice, as sweet and cloying as the perfumes that filled the air, cut through the chatter with practiced ease. "I do hope everyone is finding the evening agreeable thus far," she remarked, her gaze sweeping over the assembled guests like a general surveying her troops.

My eyes were drawn to Sir Maximillion Worthington, seated across from me. His rigid posture and meticulously groomed appearance were a study in controlled elegance, yet there was a subtle tremor in his hands that betrayed the turmoil roiling beneath his composed facade. His silver beard, neatly trimmed, framed a face that was a mask of rigid self-control. As he engaged in polite discourse with the lady to his left, I could not help but wonder at the demons that plagued him, the dark desires that lurked beneath his moralistic veneer.

"Indeed, Lady Elizabeth," he responded, his voice a measured rumble. "Your hospitality is, as ever, beyond reproach." His fingers gripped his wine glass with a white-knuckled intensity, the slight tremble in his hand causing the ruby liquid to shiver within its crystal confines.

I leaned back in my chair, my lips curving into a slow smile as I regarded him. The memory of his secret indulgences, the opium dens and

The Devil of London

hidden vices, were a delicious secret that I held close, a weapon to be wielded at my leisure. The thought of his carefully constructed facade crumbling under the weight of revelation was a tantalizing prospect, one that I intended to savor.

As the first course was laid before us, a delicate consommé that seemed to mock the raw, visceral hunger that gnawed at my core, I let my gaze wander over the assembled guests. Each one a pawn in this deadly game, each one harboring secrets that I intended to expose, to exploit. The room was a powder keg of tension, the fuse already lit and burning steadily towards the inevitable explosion. And I, Edward Hyde, would be the one to strike the match.

The candlelight flickered like a dying man's eyelids, casting macabre shadows upon the gilded wallpaper as the first course was laid before us. The consommé steamed gently, the scent of it mingling with the thick perfumes worn by the ladies, a futile attempt to mask the stench of London's streets that clung to our clothes. I, Edward Hyde, watched with keen interest as Lady Elizabeth leaned towards Isabella Blackwood, her voice a low hum, like the distant rumble of a storm.

"Miss Blackwood," Lady Elizabeth began, her eyes reflecting the dance of the candle flames. "You seem rather acquainted with our Mr. Hyde. Pray, tell me, what is your impression of the man?"

Isabella turned to her, a small smile playing on her lips, her deep blue eyes glinting with a shrewd intelligence. "Mr. Hyde is a man of... singular passions," she replied, her voice as smooth as the silk of her gown, a rich burgundy that shimmered in the light. "He possesses a certain... intensity that is as unsettling as it is captivating."

Lady Elizabeth raised an eyebrow, a subtle gesture that spoke volumes. "Captivating, indeed? And tell me, dear Isabella, do you find his intensity... alluring?"

Isabella laughed softly, a sound like distant music. "Alluring is a dangerous word, Lady Elizabeth," she said, her gaze flicking to me briefly, a silent acknowledgement of the power struggle between us. "I would say, rather, that he commands attention, much like a storm on the horizon."

Lady Elizabeth smiled, a cold and calculating curve of her lips. "A storm, you say? How very poetic. And tell me, have you ever seen what lies in the wake of his... storms?"

I knew what she was doing. She was probing, fishing for information, trying to gauge how much Isabella knew of my true nature. I had seen the remnants of my storms, as she put it. The bloody remains of my indulgences, the torn flesh and shattered bones, the screams echoing in the dark alleys of London. The memory of my last victim flashed before my eyes - a prostitute, her throat slit from ear to ear, her body convulsing as I bathed in her warm blood, her eyes wide with terror and pain. The thought sent a thrill of pleasure coursing through me.

Isabella's smile never wavered, but her eyes hardened, like ice over a frozen lake. "I have seen the aftermath of his passions," she said, her voice barely above a whisper. "The blood, the horror... the utter devastation."

Lady Elizabeth's smile faded, her expression turning pensive. She leaned back in her chair, her fingers drumming softly on the table. The room fell silent, the air thick with tension. The other guests watched, their eyes darting between us, their expressions a mix of curiosity and unease.

As the second course was served, Lady Elizabeth turned her attention to the rest of the table, her voice light and breezy, a stark contrast to the heaviness of the conversation that had just transpired. "Tell me, Sir Worthington," she said, her eyes gleaming with a wicked delight. "How fares your dear sister? I heard she was quite taken with that young poet, what was his name? Ah, yes, Samuel Hartley."

The air around us seemed to drop, like the barometric pressure before a thunderstorm. Hyde watched the room around him, the web of secrets and lies growing thicker, each character tied to the other in a tangled knot of deceit. In my mind's eyes I could see the blood flowing freely from the throats of my victims, the crimson rivers cutting through the cobblestone streets of London. I pictured the aristocracy and the lower class alike, bathed in red. The thought warmed me from inside out. The power struggle at hand was not unlike the ones I dealt with on the streets of London, and I was ready to claw my way to victory, no matter how much blood was shed.

The candlelight flickered, casting macabre shadows on the walls as the second course was cleared away. I, Edward Hyde, sat at the table, a wolf among sheep, their silken finery a pitiful armor against the blade of my intellect. Lord Frederick Pembroke, a paragon of military virtue, turned his steely gaze upon me, his scar a pale crescent above his eyebrow. His voice, a measured drumbeat, cut through the chatter.

The Devil of London

"Mr. Hyde," he began, his fingers tracing the stem of his wineglass with martial precision. "You speak of societal ills with such fervor. Pray, what remedies do you propose?"

I smiled, a slow curl of the lips, calculated to unnerve. "Why, Lord Pembroke," I replied, my voice a low purr, "I believe in excising the corrupt tissue, much like a surgeon with his scalpel. Would you not agree that sometimes, the only cure is to let the bad blood flow?"

His jaw tightened, a minute twitch beneath his neatly trimmed sideburns. "A drastic measure, Mr. Hyde. Surely, reform can be achieved through more civilized means."

I leaned back, swirling the claret in my glass, watching the legs drip like blood down the crystal. "Civilized, Lord Pembroke? Like the magistrates who line their pockets with bribes while children starve in the gutters? Or perhaps you refer to the noblemen who indulge in their pleasures, leaving bastards to fill the poorhouses?" I let my gaze drift to Lady Elizabeth, her ice-blue eyes meeting mine over the rim of her glass.

Pembroke's hand trembled slightly, a faint rattle of his silverware against the fine china. "You paint a grim picture, Mr. Hyde. But I maintain that the rule of law—"

I cut him off, my voice a whip-crack. "Law? You speak of law in a city where a man can buy a child for a shilling? Where a woman's screams are drowned out by the clatter of carriage wheels on cobblestones?" I leaned in, my eyes locked onto his. "I have seen the underbelly of this city, Lord Pembroke. I have waded through the blood and filth, the stench of decay choking my lungs. I have heard the cries of the innocent, and the laughter of the guilty."

His face paled, but he held my gaze. "And what of you, Mr. Hyde? Where do you stand in this sea of corruption?"

I chuckled, a low rumble like distant thunder. "I, Lord Pembroke, am the storm that will wash it all away."

Lady Elizabeth, ever the puppet master, interjected smoothly, "Gentlemen, such weighty topics on a night meant for merriment. Let us turn our thoughts to more pleasant matters."

But the seed was planted, the tension in the room taut as a hangman's noose. I could feel it, the barely concealed panic, the quickened pulses. They were mine now, these puppets in their silks and laces.

As the dessert course was served, Lady Elizabeth began her dance of revelations. "I must confess," she said, her voice a sweet poison, "I chanced upon the most curious rumor the other day. Something about Lord Harrington's eldest and a certain gambling debt?"

Gasps rippled through the room, eyes widening in shock. I watched, amused, as the color drained from Harrington's face, his fork clattering to his plate.

"Lady Elizabeth," he stammered, "I assure you, it is merely a misunderstanding—"

But she was already moving on, her barbs sinking deep. "And dear Lady Worthington, how fares your charity for the poor? I heard the most distressing tale of funds gone astray..."

The room was a tableau of disbelief, mouths agape, hands trembling. I could see the blood flowing, not the polite trickle of a gentleman's duel, but the gushing spray of an artery severed, the hot rush of lifeblood fleeing the body. I could hear the screams, the futile pleas for mercy. I could feel the blade in my hand, the warm slickness of blood on my skin.

I reveled in it, the symphony of horror playing out before me. This was my stage, my grand theatre of the macabre. And I, Edward Hyde, was the maestro, conducting the performance with a wave of my bloody baton.

The room had become a powder keg, the air thick with tension and the acrid scent of fear. Lady Elizabeth, the grand puppeteer, had pulled the strings with masterful precision, setting the stage for a spectacle of aristocratic carnage. I, Edward Hyde, sat amidst the chaos, a wolf in gentleman's clothing, my bloodlust stirring as I watched the assembled lords and ladies squirm beneath the weight of their exposed sins.

As the last echoes of Lady Elizabeth's revelations faded, all eyes turned to me. I could feel the accusations forming on their lips, the silent condemnation in their gazes. They thought me cornered, a beast caught in their web of civility. Little did they know, I was the spider, and this was my web to spin.

I rose from my seat, the scrape of my chair against the polished floor echoing like a gunshot. The room fell silent, the very air seeming to hold its breath. I could see the pulse of Lady Worthington's heart fluttering in her throat, the bead of sweat trickling down Lord

Harrington's brow. Their fear was palpable, a symphony of panic that sang to my dark soul.

"Ladies and gentlemen," I began, my voice a smooth, commanding baritone that cut through the tension like a blade. "You gather here, cloaked in your finery, hiding behind your titles and your wealth. You judge me, condemn me as a monster." I paused, my gaze sweeping over the assembled guests, lingering on the trembling form of Margaret Winters. Her gray eyes met mine, wide with fear and a spark of defiance. I could see the pulse in her neck quicken, her breath hitch in her chest. She was a songbird, trapped in a gilded cage, her wings clipped by the weight of societal expectation.

"But tell me," I continued, "who among you is without sin? Who has not dabbled in the darker pleasures of life, only to hide behind a facade of piety and virtue?" I could see the color drain from Sir Worthington's face, his hands trembling as he fought to maintain his composure. His secrets were a cancer, eating away at his rigid exterior, threatening to consume him from within.

"You speak of my crimes," I said, my voice a low growl, "but you know nothing of the artistry involved. You have not seen the beauty of a perfectly executed slice, the crimson spray of an artery severed, the delicate dance of blood as it drips from the blade." I could see the horror in their eyes, the revulsion twisting their features. But beneath it all, there was a spark of fascination, a morbid curiosity that drew them in like moths to a flame.

"Take Lord Harrington, for instance," I said, turning to the man in question. His face was a mask of terror, his body frozen as if facing the executioner's axe. "You think me a monster, yet you gamble away your family's fortune, leaving your wife and children to suffer the consequences. You, sir, are a coward, a parasite feeding on the misery of others."

I turned to Lady Worthington, her cheeks flushed with shame. "And you, dear lady, so pious, so charitable. Yet your hands are stained with the blood of the poor, your charity a farce to line your own pockets."

The room erupted into chaos, the carefully constructed facades of the aristocracy crumbling like a house of cards. Lord Harrington lunged at me, his face contorted with rage. I sidestepped his clumsy attack, grabbing his arm and twisting it behind his back with a satisfying crunch.

He cried out, his body convulsing with pain as I leaned in, my voice a low whisper in his ear.

"You are a pathetic worm, Harrington. You deserve to be gutted like a pig, your entrails spilled out for all to see." I released him, letting him crumple to the floor, a sobbing, broken mess.

Margaret Winters watched me, her eyes wide with horror and a spark of something more. She saw the monster within me, the beast that reveled in the blood and the screams. But she also saw the truth, the hypocrisy of the world she inhabited, the rot festering beneath the gilded surface.

Sir Worthington, ever the rigid soldier, stood tall, his voice a trembling growl. "You are a madman, Hyde. A monster that needs to be put down."

I laughed, a deep, resonant sound that echoed through the room like the tolling of a funeral bell. "A monster, perhaps. But I am the monster you created, the embodiment of your darkest desires, your most twisted fantasies."

The room was a symphony of chaos, the guests turning on one another like rats in a sinking ship. Their alliances shifted like sand beneath their feet, their carefully cultivated friendships crumbling under the weight of the truth. I stood amidst the carnage, a conductor orchestrating the descent into madness, my dark soul singing with the music of their screams.

As the chaos reached a fever pitch, I could see the fear in their eyes, the realization that they were not safe, not even in the heart of their precious society. They were sheep, ripe for the slaughter, and I was the wolf, ready to feast on their flesh.

I could see the blood, the crimson tide that would wash away the sins of the past, the rot that festered beneath the surface. I could see the blade, the cold steel that would sing with the symphony of their screams. I could see the future, the dark path that lay before me, and I embraced it, the monster within me rising to claim its throne.

For I was Edward Hyde, the maestro of the macabre, and this was my grand theatre of the grotesque. And the show, dear friends, was just beginning.

The grandeur of the dining room, once a stage for my meticulously crafted dramas, now seemed to close in around me, the flickering candlelight casting monstrous shadows that danced macabrely on the walls. The room, so recently filled with the cacophony of shocked voices, now hummed with a tense, anxious silence, broken only by the hurried footsteps of guests desperate to quit the scene. My breath came in short, sharp gasps, my stays suddenly too tight, as if the very air in the room had grown thick with the stench of secrets laid bare.

"Lady Elizabeth, are you quite well?" Isabella's voice cut through the fog of my thoughts, her eyes searching mine with an intensity that made me uncomfortable. Her dark blue gown, which had seemed so elegant at the evening's commencement, now appeared almost funereal in the dim light.

"Indeed, Isabella," I lied, my voice steady despite the tempest within. "It is merely the heat of the room. I find I am a touch overwhelmed."

Her eyebrow arched delicately, a gesture that spoke volumes of her disbelief. "Of course, Lady Elizabeth. The evening has been... trying." Her gaze shifted to Hyde, his tall frame leaning against the mantel, his green eyes gleaming with malevolent delight as he surveyed the carnage he had wrought.

I followed her gaze, my stomach churning as I recalled the vivid images Hyde's revelations had painted. Lord Harrington, his bloated body fished from the Thames, his throat slit from ear to ear, the water around him stained a sickening crimson. Lady Margaret, her lifeless form sprawled in the filth of a Whitechapel alley, her fine gown in tatters, her vacant eyes staring accusingly at the heavens. Each murder more grotesque than the last, each victim a pawn in Hyde's twisted game.

My mind raced, a whirlwind of thoughts and fragments, desperate to salvage some remnant of my crumbling plans. I had underestimated Hyde, a mistake that had cost me dearly. I had believed myself the puppet master, pulling the strings of London's elite, yet in reality, I was merely another dancing marionette in Hyde's grand theatre of the grotesque.

Around me, the remnants of the evening's festivities lay in ruins. Fine china shattered upon the floor, trampled underfoot by fleeing guests. The once-immaculate tablecloth now stained with spilled wine, the red liquid pooling like blood across the pristine surface. The sight sent a shiver down my spine, a grim reminder of the violence that lurked just beneath the surface of our polite society.

Sir Maximillion Worthington paused by my side, his normally rigid posture stooped, his meticulously groomed appearance disheveled.

"Lady Elizabeth," he began, his voice barely more than a whisper, "I must apologize for my hasty departure, but I find I am urgently needed elsewhere." His hands trembled visibly, his composure shattered by the evening's revelations.

"Of course, Sir Maximillion," I murmured, my voice barely audible even to myself. "I understand completely." A bitter laugh threatened to bubble up from within, the irony of the situation almost too much to bear. Here I stood, the once-great Lady Elizabeth Thornwood, reduced to platitudes and empty reassurances as my world crumbled around me.

As the last of the guests filtered out, the room seemed to grow colder, the shadows darker, as if the very house mourned the loss of its former glory. Isabella remained, her eyes locked on Hyde, a silent communication passing between them. The air crackled with tension, their connection palpable, a tangible force that sent a shiver of unease down my spine.

Hyde pushed away from the mantel, his movements languid, predatory, like a great cat stalking its prey. He crossed the room, his gaze never leaving Isabella's, until he stood mere inches from her, his breath hot on her cheek. "A fascinating evening, would you not agree, Miss Blackwood?" he murmured, his voice a low purr that sent a chill down my spine.

Isabella's lips curved in a slow, calculated smile, her eyes gleaming with a dark hunger that made my breath catch in my throat. "Indeed, Mr. Hyde," she replied, her voice barely more than a whisper. "Most... enlightening."

Their exchange sent a wave of nausea crashing over me, the realization of my own folly threatening to overwhelm me. I had believed myself a master of manipulation, a puppeteer pulling the strings of London's elite. Yet in my hubris, I had failed to see the true master at work, the dark heart that beat at the center of our twisted web.

As the door closed behind the last of the departing guests, I was left alone in the echoing silence of the dining room, the flickering candlelight casting long, dancing shadows across the walls. Shadows that seemed to twist and writhe, forming grotesque images of blood and death, a grim portent of the horrors yet to come.

My mind raced, a desperate litany of plans and schemes, each more futile than the last. I had gambled and lost, my carefully laid

The Devil of London

strategies crumbling to dust in the face of Hyde's machinations. Yet even as the bitter taste of defeat filled my mouth, I could not bring myself to surrender, to accept the fate that loomed before me.

For I was Lady Elizabeth Thornwood, the Widow Thornwood, a woman who had clawed her way to the heights of society through cunning and guile. I would not go down without a fight, would not surrender my hard-won independence to the whims of a monster.

Even as the shadows closed in, even as the dark storm gathered on the horizon, I stood tall, my chin held high, my eyes fixed on the gathering darkness. For in the end, I was a survivor, a woman forged in the fires of adversity, tempered by the trials of a life lived on the edge of ruin. And I would not go down without a fight.

The heavy oak door groaned shut, echoing through the vacant dining room like a dying man's final breath. I, Lady Elizabeth Thornwood, stood rooted to the spot, my silk skirts rustling softly as a chill wind swept through the room. The once-grand space now felt cavernous and hollow, a mocking reflection of my own emptiness. The flickering candlelight cast long, twisted shadows across the walls, their forms contorting into grim tableaux of blood and death, echoes of Hyde's gruesome deeds.

I could see them now, the vivid memories of his victims haunting my vision: Lord Harrington, his throat slit from ear to ear, the gaping wound a obscene smile beneath his lifeless eyes; Lady Margaret, her body drained of blood, the pallor of her skin a stark contrast to the crimson streaks painting her bedchamber; and poor young Thomas, his intestines splayed out like some grotesque parody of a pagan ritual, the stench of his viscera choking the air. Each murder more brutal than the last, each a testament to Hyde's psychotic delight in suffering.

My gloved hands clenched around the edge of the mahogany table, the delicate lace trimming grazing the polished wood. A shudder ran through me as I recalled Isabella's face, pale but resolute, her eyes locked onto Hyde's as she departed. Their connection was palpable, a tangible thread of darkness binding them together. What had transpired between them? What twisted alliance had been forged in the crucible of this nightmare evening?

"You played your hand too soon, Elizabeth." The echo of Hyde's smooth, commanding voice resonated in my mind, a mocking refrain that sent a shiver down my spine. His hypnotic green eyes seemed to bore into me even now, their intensity a palpable force. He had outmaneuvered me, turned my carefully laid plans against me with a masterful precision that left me reeling.

I pushed away from the table, my heels clicking sharply against the parquet floor as I paced the length of the room. My mind raced, a whirlwind of thoughts and calculations spinning through the fog of defeat. The social landscape of London would shift dramatically in the wake of tonight's revelations. Alliances would crumble, new factions would rise, and the criminal underbelly would churn with fresh blood.

The image of Nathaniel Wake, stoic and unyielding, flashed before my eyes. His thick, scarred knuckles, the silent testament to his fighting days, clenched around a tankard of ale. Would he stand against the tide of chaos, or be swept away by it? His neutrality had always been his strength, but in these uncertain times, such a stance might prove untenable.

A sudden gust of wind rattled the windows, the panes shuddering against the encroaching storm. The candles flickered wildly, their flames casting macabre shadows that danced and twisted along the walls. I paused before the hearth, the dying embers of the fire casting a feeble glow against the encroaching darkness.

"London will burn," Hyde had promised, his voice a low, seductive purr. And I believed him. The city was a tinderbox, its streets teeming with poverty and despair, its noble houses rife with corruption and deceit. It would take but a single spark to set it all ablaze.

I turned to face the empty room, my chin held high, my eyes reflecting the gathering storm. For I was Lady Elizabeth Thornwood, the Widow Thornwood, a woman who had risen from the ashes of her past to claim her place among the elite. I would not cower before the tempest. I would not surrender my hard-won independence to the whims of a monster.

No, I would stand tall, my spirit unbroken, my resolve unshaken. For in the end, I was a survivor, a woman forged in the fires of adversity, tempered by the trials of a life lived on the edge of ruin. And I would not go down without a fight.

But first, I needed a plan. A means of navigating the treacherous waters that lay ahead, a strategy to turn the tide of chaos to my advantage. I needed...

The Devil of London

The sound of distant thunder rolled through the night, a low, ominous rumble that seemed to shake the very foundations of the house. The storm was coming, its dark clouds blotting out the stars, its chilling winds sweeping through the streets like the breath of Death itself.

And with it, Edward Hyde would rise, his reign of terror eclipsing all that had come before. The city would be his playground, its citizens his pawns, and I... I would be the only one standing in his way.

God help us all.

CHAPTER 20

In the fetid heart of London, where the cobblestones were slick with more than just rain, I, Edward Hyde, made my entrance into The Crimson Lantern. The heavy oak door creaked shut behind me, sealing me within the den of iniquity, the air thick with smoke and the stench of unwashed bodies. The dim light flickered from grimy lanterns, casting eerie shadows that danced macabrely on the worn walls. The patrons, a motley crew of thieves, prostitutes, and cutthroats, paused their debauchery to cast wary glances my way. I could feel their eyes on me, a mixture of fear and respect that I drank in like the finest wine.

My gaze swept over the crowd, taking in the ragged attire and the gleam of dirty coins exchanging hands. The tavern was a pit of despair, a place where hope came to die. I reveled in it, my senses heightened by the palpable desperation that hung in the air like a miasma. My eyes settled on a secluded table in the far corner, where a familiar figure sat surrounded by her unlikely allies. Isabella Blackwood, her deep blue eyes meeting mine with a composed smile that did little to mask the tension beneath.

I moved through the crowd with a predatory grace, my elegant attire a stark contrast to the squalor around me. The patrons parted like the Red Sea, their murmurs of unease a symphony to my ears. As I approached the table, Isabella rose to greet me, her tall, graceful form a beacon of aristocratic refinement amidst the filth.

"Mr. Hyde," she said, her voice a melody of cultured tones. "How delightful to see you again."

I offered her a bow, my eyes never leaving hers. "Miss Blackwood, the pleasure is all mine."

Thomas Harding, the gaunt undertaker, sat stiffly, his pale hands clasped tightly on the table. His dark circles and slightly trembling hands betrayed his inner turmoil. His eyes flicked to mine, a mix of apprehension and resolve in his gaze. I could almost see the secrets he harbored, the burden of his knowledge weighing heavily on his shoulders.

Victoria Sterling, her honey-blonde hair catching the dim light, watched me with a steady gaze. Her clear blue eyes held a fire that spoke of her unwavering belief in justice. She sat with a quiet authority, her fashionable but conservative dress a stark contrast to the tavern's grimy surroundings.

Edwin "Flash" Barrett, the youngest of the group, fidgeted nervously. His large brown eyes darted between me and the others, his hands in constant motion. His slight build and youthful appearance belied the shrewd mind beneath. I could see the loyalty warring with doubt in his eyes, a battle I found most amusing.

As I took my seat, I could not help but recall the last time I had seen Isabella. The memory of Lady Thornwood's dinner party was still fresh in my mind, the scent of blood and fear lingering like a perfume. The lady's screams as I had carved into her flesh, the warm spray of blood on my hands—it was a symphony of sensation that I craved like a drug. The memory brought a smile to my lips, a smile that did not go unnoticed by the coalition before me.

Isabella's smile faltered for a moment, a flicker of unease crossing her features before she regained her composure. "You seem pleased, Mr. Hyde," she remarked, her voice steady despite the tension that hummed in the air.

I leaned back in my chair, my eyes never leaving hers. "Indeed, Miss Blackwood. The night is full of possibilities, is it not?"

The tension at the table was palpable, a living thing that seemed to pulse with the beat of the tavern's heart. I could feel the weight of their gazes, the mix of apprehension and resolve that hung in the air like a storm about to break. And as I sat there, surrounded by my allies and my enemies, I knew that the night was far from over. The game had only just begun, and I was the master of the board.

Blood still lingered beneath my fingernails when I entered the Crimson Lantern, the grime of London's underbelly clinging to my boots. The stench of the place was a pungent mix of cheap ale, unwashed bodies, and the faint tang of vomit—a symphony of scents that was as comforting as it was revolting. The dim light cast eerie shadows on the worn faces of the patrons, their eyes reflecting the flickering flames of the tallow candles like some grotesque tableau of the damned.

My eyes scanned the room, taking in the usual assortment of thieves, whores, and beggars. Their gazes met mine briefly before darting away, like rats scurrying from the light. I could feel their fear, taste it on the air like a sweet perfume. It was intoxicating, a sensation that never failed to stir the darkness within me.

And then I saw her—Isabella Blackwood, seated at a secluded table with her coalition of fools. Her back was straight, her dark hair piled atop her head in an elegant coiffure that was at odds with the squalor of our surroundings. The deep blue of her gown shimmered in the candlelight, the color of a bruise, a stark contrast to the pale column of her throat. She was a vision of refinement amidst the filth, a diamond gleaming in the rough.

As I approached their table, Isabella rose to greet me, her smile as polished as her appearance. Yet, I could see the tension lurking beneath her calm exterior, a tightness around her eyes that betrayed her unease. "Mr. Hyde," she said, her voice a melodious blend of charm and subtle threat. "How delightful to see you again. I trust you've been keeping yourself... occupied?"

I returned her smile with one of my own, a slow, predatory curve of the lips. "Indeed, Miss Blackwood. I've had the pleasure of indulging in some of my favorite pastimes." I let my gaze drift to Thomas Harding, who sat rigid and pale beside her. His eyes met mine briefly before flicking away, a nervous tic playing at the corner of his mouth. He knew what I was capable of, the secrets I kept buried beneath the surface. I could see the knowledge weighing heavy on his shoulders, a moral burden that threatened to crush him.

Isabella's smile never wavered, but her eyes held a cold light as she continued. "I must admit, Mr. Hyde, your recent actions at Lady Thornwood's dinner party have caused quite the stir. Such a display of... enthusiasm. One might even call it reckless."

The Devil of London

Her words were a challenge, a subtle chastisement cloaked in the guise of polite conversation. I could feel the edge of danger beneath her refined speech, the hint of a threat that was as enticing as it was infuriating. I leaned in closer, my voice a low rumble. "Reckless, Miss Blackwood? Or merely the actions of a man who knows what he wants and takes it?"

As I spoke, I let my mind drift back to the night in question—the way Lady Thornwood's blood had sprayed across the pristine white tablecloth, the crimson droplets stark against the fine china. Her screams had been music to my ears, a symphony of pain and terror that had stirred my soul. I could still feel the warmth of her blood on my hands, the way it had coated my skin like a lover's caress.

I reveled in the memory, letting it fuel the darkness within me. By the time I returned my attention to Isabella, I could see the slight widening of her eyes, the almost imperceptible intake of breath. She was not immune to my charms, no matter how much she might wish to be.

I turned my gaze to Thomas Harding, whose pallor had taken on a grayish hue. His hands trembled slightly as he reached for his glass, the liquid sloshing within as he brought it to his lips. I could see the memories haunting him, the ghosts of the past that refused to be laid to rest. He was a man on the edge, a fact that pleased me more than it should.

"Harding," I said, my voice a low purr. "You look unwell. Something troubling you?"

He set his glass down carefully, his eyes darting to mine before flicking away again. "Merely the... demands of my profession, Mr. Hyde. The hours are long, the work taxing."

I smiled, a slow, knowing curve of the lips. "Yes, I imagine dealing with the dead can be quite... draining. Especially when they refuse to stay buried."

His gaze snapped to mine, a spark of fear igniting in their depths. I could see the struggle within him, the battle between his professional discretion and the moral quandary that plagued him. He was a man haunted, a fact that I found endlessly amusing.

As I watched him squirm, I let my mind wander back to the countless bodies I'd left in my wake—the blood, the gore, the sweet symphony of screams that echoed through my memories like a lover's serenade. The recollections were vivid, a tapestry of violence and depravity that never failed to stir the darkness within me.

And as I sat there, surrounded by my allies and my enemies, I knew that the night was far from over. The game had only just begun, and I was the master of the board.

The Crimson Lantern's air was thick with smoke and the stench of unwashed bodies, the dim lighting casting eerie shadows that danced macabrely on the walls. I, Edward Hyde, sat at the table, my eyes fixed on the pulsating vein in Thomas Harding's neck as he struggled to maintain his composure. The recall of my past exploits still fresh in my mind, I could almost taste the blood, feel the warm, sticky liquid on my hands as life drained from my victims. The memory of their pleading eyes, the gurgling sounds they made as they choked on their own blood, was a symphony that fueled my dark desires.

As I reveled in these thoughts, Victoria Sterling interjected, her voice a clarion call cutting through the din. "Mr. Hyde," she began, her tall, graceful form leaning forward, eyes ablaze with a self-righteous fire. "You have been quite the talk of Mayfair lately. Pray tell, what are your intentions for our fair district?" Her honey-blonde hair caught the faint light, creating a halo effect that was almost laughable given the circumstances.

I turned to face her, my expression a careful blend of amusement and curiosity. "Intentions, Miss Sterling?" I repeated, my voice a low rumble. "Why, I merely seek to... enliven the neighbourhood." I let my gaze drift to the stains on my cuffs, remnants of my last encounter—the beggar's blood had been a vivid red, his screams echoing through the alley as I carved his flesh like a roast.

Victoria's clear blue eyes narrowed, her passion undeterred by my nonchalance. "Enliven?" she challenged. "Your actions have caused nothing but fear and distress. The people of Mayfair deserve better than to live in terror of your... enthusiasms." Her voice was steady, but I could see the pulse in her neck quicken, betraying her nervousness.

From the corner of my eye, I saw Edwin "Flash" Barrett fidgeting, his large, expressive brown eyes darting between Victoria and myself. His loyalty was a delicate thing, a balance I intended to tip in my favour. He wiped his hands on his breeches, a nervous habit that betrayed his discomfort. His sandy hair was tousled, his clothes a blend of servant's attire and street urchin—a chameleon in his own right.

The Devil of London

Flash's internal struggle was written plainly on his face. He watched Victoria with a mix of admiration and fear, her words stirring something within him. Yet, his allegiance to me was strong, forged in the fires of necessity and survival. I could see the war within him, the tug of conscience against the chains of loyalty. He laughed nervously, a sound that grated on my ears, but I let it slide, knowing that his turmoil would ultimately serve my purposes.

Victoria continued to press me, her voice filled with a misguided sense of justice. "You cannot continue to prey upon the innocent, Mr. Hyde. The people of Mayfair will not stand for it." Her hands were clenched in her lap, her knuckles white with tension.

I leaned back in my chair, a smirk playing on my lips as I recalled the vivid tableau of my last kill. The whore's body had been a masterpiece, her entrails strewn about like garlands, her blood a vivid contrast against the snow. I had left her in the alley, a gruesome surprise for the morning light. "The people of Mayfair," I said, my voice a low purr, "have little say in the matter, Miss Sterling. They are sheep, and I am the wolf that stalks them." I let my gaze drift to Flash, watching as his eyes widened at my words. His unease was palpable, a delicious scent that hung in the air like a promise.

Victoria's breath hitched, her resolve faltering for a moment before she rallied, her voice steady despite the fear that lurked in her eyes. "You are a monster, Mr. Hyde," she said, her voice barely above a whisper. "And monsters must be stopped."

I chuckled, a sound that held no mirth. "Indeed, Miss Sterling," I agreed, my mind already spinning with the possibilities that lay ahead. "But who, pray tell, will stop me?" My gaze drifted to Flash, his internal struggle a beacon that called to the darkness within me. I knew that his loyalty would be tested, that his allegiance would ultimately be decided by his fear. And I intended to use that fear to my advantage, to twist and shape it into a weapon that would serve my purposes. For in the end, all men were pawns in my game, and I was the master of the board.

The Crimson Lantern's air was thick with smoke and the stench of unwashed bodies, the flickering flames of candles casting macabre shadows upon the walls. I, Edward Hyde, stood at the table where Isabella Blackwood and her companions sat, their faces a picture of tension beneath their carefully composed exteriors. Victoria Sterling's cheeks were still flushed from her outburst, her bosom heaving beneath the modest lace of her gown. Thomas Harding's fingers drummed nervously on the table, while Flash Barrett's gaze darted between us all, his loyalty a pendulum swinging in the breeze.

"Come now, Miss Sterling," I began, my voice a soothing balm upon the charged atmosphere. "Your passion is commendable, but it clouds your judgment. You speak of monsters, yet you know not the true face of horror." I leaned in, my eyes locked onto hers, my voice dropping to a low, hypnotic timbre. "Have you ever seen a man's entrails steaming in the cold night air, Miss Sterling? Have you watched the light fade from a victim's eyes as their lifeblood pools beneath your feet?"

Her face paled, the blood draining from her cheeks as she grasped the table for support. I could see the images playing out in her mind, the gruesome tableau I had painted with mere words. I let her suffer a moment longer before turning my attention to Harding.

"And you, Mr. Harding," I continued, my voice like silk. "A man of science, are you not? You seek to understand the world through reason and logic. Yet, you cannot deny the darkness that lurks within the human heart. You've glimpsed it, haven't you? In the quiet of your study, in the whispers of your conscience."

Harding's fingers stilled, his breath hitching as my words struck a chord within him. I could see the memories surfacing, the experiments he'd conducted in secret, the moral lines he'd crossed in the name of knowledge. His gaze met mine, and in his eyes, I saw a reflection of my own darkness.

Then, I turned to Flash. Poor, torn Flash. His face was a battlefield of emotion, loyalty warring with doubt, fear clashing with hope. I reached out, clasping his shoulder in a firm grip. He tensed beneath my touch, his eyes wide with apprehension.

"Flash," I murmured, my voice a gentle caress. "My loyal friend. You've stood by me through thick and thin, haven't you? You've seen the things I've done, the lives I've taken. You've watched as I've bathed in the blood of my enemies, as I've reveled in their screams. And yet, you remain. Why is that, Flash? Is it fear that stays your hand? Or is it something more?"

His breath came in ragged gasps, his body trembling beneath my touch. I could feel his pulse racing, his heart pounding like a drum in his chest. I leaned in, my lips brushing against his ear as I whispered, "You cannot save them, Flash. You cannot save any of them."

The Devil of London

As I straightened, I saw Isabella watching me, her eyes narrowed, her lips pressed into a thin line. She was a formidable opponent, this one. Beautiful, cunning, and ruthless in her own right. I admired her, truly I did. But she was a fool if she thought she could best me.

"Enough, Hyde," she said, her voice cutting through the tension like a knife. "You seek to divide us, to turn us against one another. But we will not falter. We will not yield. We stand united against you, and together, we will see you brought to justice."

Her words were a rallying cry, a beacon of hope amidst the despair. I saw the others straighten, their resolve strengthening as they drew strength from her conviction. It was a magnificent sight, truly. A shame it would all be for naught.

"Justice, Isabella?" I chuckled, the sound low and menacing. "You speak of justice as if it were a tangible thing, a prize to be won. But justice is a fickle mistress, my dear. She favors the strong, the cunning, the ruthless. She favors me."

The air in The Crimson Lantern was thick with smoke and the stench of unwashed bodies, the dim light flickering from the hearth casting eerie shadows on the worn faces of the patrons. I, Edward Hyde, stood tall and elegant amidst the squalor, my sharp eyes fixed on the table where Isabella and her motley crew convened. The tension in the room was palpable, a tangible thing that seemed to hum in the very air we breathed.

Isabella's eyes flashed with a mix of anger and resolve as she held my gaze. "Your words are as empty as your soul, Hyde," she declared, her voice steady despite the slight tremor in her hands. "We will not be swayed by your poisonous tongue."

Thomas Harding, seated beside her, shifted uncomfortably in his chair. His gaunt face was pale, and his dark circles more pronounced, making him appear almost corpselike in the dim light. His trembling hands betrayed his nervousness, a stark contrast to Isabella's composure.

Flash, standing slightly apart from the group, looked from one face to another, his large brown eyes wide with uncertainty. His tousled sandy hair fell into his eyes, and he brushed it away with a jerk of his hand. I could see the conflict within him, his loyalty to me warring with the doubts that had begun to gnaw at his conscience.

I turned my attention back to Isabella, a slow smile spreading across my lips. "You speak with such conviction, my dear," I said, my voice a low purr. "But tell me, are you truly united? Or are there cracks in your little coalition that you dare not acknowledge?"

Isabella's lips pressed into a thin line, but before she could respond, Flash spoke up, his voice barely above a whisper. "They know about the shipment, Mr. Hyde. The one coming in from the East India Company."

The table fell silent, the shock of Flash's betrayal hanging heavy in the air. Isabella turned to him, her eyes wide with disbelief. "Flash, what have you done?" she gasped, her voice barely audible.

Harding's face paled even further, his hands gripping the edge of the table until his knuckles turned white. He looked as though he might be sick, his eyes darting from Flash to me and back again. Flash shook his head, his eyes filled with a mix of fear and regret. "I'm sorry," he stammered. "I didn't mean to... I just..."

His words were cut off by Harding's sudden exclamation. "This is your doing, Hyde!" he cried, his voice shaking with emotion. "You've poisoned his mind, just as you've poisoned everything else you've touched!"

I chuckled, the sound low and menacing. "Poisoned, Mr. Harding? That's a strong word, coming from a man who's made a fortune burying the secrets of the dead." I leaned in closer, my voice dropping to a conspiratorial whisper. "Tell me, how many bodies have you disposed of on my behalf? How many throats have you slit in the name of discretion?"

Harding's face twisted in anguish, and he looked away, unable to meet my gaze. "Too many," he admitted, his voice barely a whisper. "Far too many."

The room seemed to grow colder, the shadows darker, as the weight of Harding's confession settled over the group. I could see the mistrust and uncertainty growing in their eyes, the seeds of doubt that I had planted beginning to take root.

Suddenly, Harding pushed back his chair and stood, his body shaking with barely suppressed emotion. "I can't... I won't be a part of this any longer," he declared, his voice trembling. He turned to Isabella, his eyes filled with a desperate plea. "You have to understand, I never wanted any of this. I never wanted to be a part of his world."

Isabella looked at him, her expression a mix of sympathy and disappointment. "None of us did, Thomas," she said softly. "But here we are, nonetheless."

The Devil of London

I leaned back in my chair, a satisfied smile playing at the corners of my lips. The coalition was crumbling before my eyes, their unity shattered by the weight of their own secrets and fears. And as I watched them struggle to hold onto their resolve, I knew that it was only a matter of time before they fell completely under my sway.

As I reveled in the chaos I had created, my mind drifted back to the countless victims who had fallen prey to my blade. I remembered the warm, sticky feel of their blood on my hands, the way their eyes would widen in terror as they realized that death had come for them. I remembered the thrill of the hunt, the exhilaration of the kill, and the satisfaction of watching the life drain from their eyes.

Yes, I thought to myself, this is what I live for. This is what I was born to do. And as I looked around the table at the faces of my would-be adversaries, I knew that it was only a matter of time before they, too, fell prey to my dark desires.

The Crimson Lantern seemed to close in around me, the air thick with tension and the reek of spilled ale. The flickering flames of the tallow candles cast monstrous shadows on the worn timbers, reflecting the turmoil that roiled within our coalition. My heart pounded like a drum in my chest, echoing the relentless rhythm of the rain lashing against the grimy windows.

Victoria's face was pale, but her eyes blazed with a determination that cut through the gloom. She rose from her seat, her skirts rustling like autumn leaves, and fixed her gaze upon Hyde. "Mr. Hyde," she began, her voice steady as a rock in a stormy sea, "your words are as poisoned honey, sweet to the taste but deadly to the soul. We will not be swayed by your machinations."

Hyde's green eyes glinted like a cat's in the dim light, his lips curving into a slow, sinister smile. "Ah, Miss Sterling," he purred, his voice a low rumble like distant thunder. "Ever the beacon of virtue. But tell me, how does your righteousness taste when mixed with the blood of those who stand in your way?"

I watched as Victoria's hands clenched at her sides, her knuckles white beneath her gloves. "You speak of blood, sir," she retorted, "as if it were a trifle, a mere plaything for your amusement. But we know the truth of your games. We have seen the remnants of your 'amusements' - the torn flesh, the shattered bones, the eyes forever frozen in terror."

Hyde's smile never wavered, but his eyes... oh, his eyes held a chill that could freeze the very marrow in one's bones. "Indeed, Miss Sterling," he replied, his voice soft, almost caressing. "I have seen such sights as well. I have stood over the lifeless bodies of my enemies, their blood warm and sticky on my hands. I have watched as the light faded from their eyes, and I have reveled in their final, gasping breaths."

He leaned forward, his shadow stretching across the table like a dark stain. "But tell me, dear Victoria, have you ever felt the thrill of the hunt? Have you ever known the exhilaration of the kill? Have you ever taken a life with your own hands, and felt the power, the godlike power, of deciding who lives and who dies?"

His words painted a vivid image in my mind's eye: Hyde, his elegant form silhouetted against the moonlit night, his hands dripping with crimson gore. I could see the lifeless body at his feet, the flesh rent and torn, the eyes staring blankly at the heavens. I could smell the coppery tang of blood, could almost taste the metallic bite on my tongue.

Victoria did not flinch, but I saw the revulsion in her eyes, the horror that echoed my own. "You are a monster, Mr. Hyde," she whispered, her voice barely audible above the pounding of my heart. "A monster who preys on the weak and the innocent."

Hyde's laughter was a low, chilling sound, like the rustling of dry leaves in a graveyard. "A monster, perhaps," he acknowledged, his voice as smooth as silk. "But a monster who knows his nature, who embraces it. Can you say the same, Miss Sterling? Can any of you?"

His gaze swept over us, lingering on each face in turn. I felt the weight of his scrutiny like a physical touch, cold and unsettling. "You play at righteousness, at nobility," he continued, his voice laced with contempt. "But you are all hypocrites, hiding behind your facades of virtue. You are no better than I, no better than the lowest criminal in this godforsaken city."

He paused, his eyes narrowing as he leaned back in his chair. "But mark my words, dear friends. Your hypocrisy will be your downfall. Your precious coalition will crumble, and you will fall, one by one, like rotten fruit from a diseased tree."

His words hung in the air like a shroud, a grim portent of the horrors that awaited us. And yet, as I looked around the table, I saw not despair, but resolve. Victoria's eyes burned with renewed determination, and I felt a spark of defiance kindle within my own heart. We would not fall so easily, not while there was breath in our bodies and fight in our souls. For we were not merely playing at righteousness; we were fighting for it. And in that moment, I knew that we would stand against Hyde, against the darkness that sought to consume us. We would stand, and we would fight.

The Crimson Lantern's air grew thick with tension, a palpable miasma that seemed to cling to our skin like the damp fog of London's streets. Hyde's threats lingered, a spectral presence that chilled the very marrow of our bones. Yet, within me, a fire burned, fueled by Victoria's unyielding spirit and the grim determination that passed between us like a silent vow.

Isabella, her eyes glinting like polished steel, abruptly leaned forward. Her voice sliced through the gloom, as sharp and deadly as a stiletto. "You speak of hypocrisy, Edward," she began, her lips curving into a smile that held no warmth. "Yet, you omit your own sins. Shall I remind you of them? Shall I paint a portrait of your past in shades of red and black?"

Her words struck Hyde like a physical blow. His green eyes flashed, a fleeting glimpse of the monster that lurked beneath his polished exterior. For a moment, his mask slipped, revealing the twisted creature that reveled in blood and terror. I saw it then, the image of his victims—limbs askew, throats gaping like obscene smiles, their lifeblood pooling in crimson halos around their shattered forms. Their glassy eyes stared accusingly, a silent chorus of the damned, crying out for justice from their cold, unmarked graves.

Hyde's lips curled into a snarl, a primal, feral thing that sent a shiver down my spine. But Isabella did not falter. She pressed on, her voice a relentless, driving force. "Tell them, Edward," she demanded, her voice a low, dangerous purr. "Tell them of the beggar boy in Seven Dials, his throat slit from ear to ear, his blood mingling with the filth of the gutters. Tell them of the woman in St. Giles, her body broken and bruised, her life snuffed out like a candle flame. Tell them of the countless others who have fallen prey to your... appetites."

A heavy silence hung over the table, broken only by the ragged sound of our collective breath. Hyde's eyes bore into Isabella, his gaze a tangible, malevolent force. Yet, she held firm, her chin lifted in defiance, her dark hair framing her face like a raven's wing.

Beside me, Thomas shifted uncomfortably, his fingers worrying at the worn cuff of his sleeve. His eyes darted between Isabella and Hyde, a silent battle playing out in his gaze. Victoria, her cheeks flushed with righteous fury, watched Hyde with the keen, unblinking stare of a bird of prey. And Flash... poor Flash seemed to shrink into himself, his eyes wide with a mix of fear and guilt.

Hyde's lips twisted into a cruel parody of a smile, his composure regained, but the edge of his control frayed. "You are clever, Isabella," he conceded, his voice a low growl. "Too clever for your own good. But you forget, my dear, that I am not the only one with secrets."

His gaze swept over us, a predator assessing its prey. I felt the weight of his scrutiny, the cold, calculating intelligence that lurked behind his eyes. And in that moment, I knew that we stood on the precipice of a great and terrible storm, the outcome uncertain, our fates hanging in the balance.

The Crimson Lantern seemed to hold its breath, the very air growing thick with anticipation. The flickering lanterns cast eerie, dancing shadows on the worn wooden floors, and the distant hum of the city seemed to fade away, leaving only the pounding of my own heart in my ears.

Each of us was poised, ready to spring into action, our muscles taut, our nerves strung like the highest note on a violin. We were players in a deadly game, the stakes higher than any of us could have imagined. And as I looked around the table, I knew that we were bound together, our fates intertwined like the threads of a tapestry, woven in blood and shadow.

The storm was coming, and we would face it head-on, our resolve unbroken, our spirits undaunted. For in that moment, we were not mere pawns in Hyde's twisted game. We were fighters, warriors armed with truth and justice, ready to stand against the darkness that sought to consume us all. And so, we waited, the tension a living, breathing thing, the outcome uncertain, the future shrouded in mist and shadow. But we were ready. And we would fight.

CHAPTER 21

The carriage rumbled to a halt, and I, Isabella Blackwood, stepped out onto the cobblestone streets of London. The fog swirled around my feet like a spectral serpent, its tendrils reaching out to embrace me as I adjusted my cloak against the biting chill. The city exhaled a breath of decay, the stench of the Thames mingling with the acrid tang of coal smoke. My mind was a tempest, a whirlwind of thoughts that reflected the power I had gained and the grim currency at which it had been bought. The memories of recent weeks clung to me like a shroud, the echoes of screams and the coppery tang of blood a constant companion.

My boots clicked against the cobblestones as I walked, the sound echoing through the dimly lit streets like the ticking of a clock, counting down to some unseen doom. The gas lamps cast flickering shadows, their dance macabre a grim reminder of the darkness that had befallen this city. The once-bustling thoroughfares were now desolate, the few remaining souls scurrying like rats through the labyrinthine alleys, desperate to avoid the lurking shadows.

As I turned a corner, a figure caught my eye. Sir Maximillion Worthington, once a titan of society, now leaned against a lamppost like a common drunkard. His tall, weathered frame was adorned in the finest tailoring, but the cut of his coat could not disguise the diminishment of his spirit. His ebony walking stick, once a symbol of his authority, now seemed little more than a prop, the silver handle tarnished and dull.

"Sir Maximillion," I acknowledged, my voice cutting through the fog like a knife.

He looked up, his eyes meeting mine with a hint of desperation. "Lady Blackwood," he began, his voice a shadow of its former resonance. "A moment of your time, if you please."

I paused, my gaze sweeping over him. His breath misted in the cold air, the scent of alcohol clinging to him like a miasma. "What is it that you desire, Sir Maximillion?" I asked, my patience already wearing thin.

He straightened, a feeble attempt to regain some semblance of dignity. "I find myself in a state of... uncertainty," he admitted, his voice barely above a whisper. "My standing in society, once so assured, now seems... tenuous."

I raised an eyebrow, my gaze piercing. "And what, pray tell, has brought about this sudden change in fortune?" I inquired, though I knew full well the cause of his distress.

He looked away, his grip tightening on his walking stick. "The recent... events," he said, his voice faltering. "The murders, the scandal... it has shaken the very foundations of our society. And I find myself... displaced."

I could not help but feel a twisted sense of satisfaction at his discomfort. This man, who had once wielded power like a bludgeon, now stood before me, chastened and desperate. I knew that I held his fate in my hands, a pawn in the game of shadows that had consumed this city.

"Displaced, you say?" I echoed, my voice cold. "And what would you have me do about it?"

He looked up, his eyes wide and pleading. "A word, Lady Blackwood," he begged. "A mere whisper in the right ear, to assure those in power that I am still a man of influence, a man to be reckoned with."

I regarded him for a moment, my mind flashing back to the scenes of carnage that had become all too familiar. The bodies, twisted and broken, the blood pooling on the cobblestones like a grotesque parody of a painting. The stench of death, cloying and sweet, clinging to the air like a shroud. And standing amidst it all, Edward Hyde, his eyes wild and his hands dripping with gore.

"I will consider it," I said finally, my voice devoid of emotion. "But know this, Sir Maximillion. The London you once knew is gone, swallowed by the darkness. And in this new world, there is no room for weakness."

With that, I turned and walked away, leaving him to his desperation. The fog closed in around me, the tendrils reaching out like spectral fingers, beckoning me deeper into the heart of the nightmare that had consumed this city. And as I walked, I could not help but feel a sense of anticipation, a dark excitement at the horrors that lay ahead. For in this world of shadows, I was no longer a mere pawn. I was a queen, a puppet master pulling the strings of the damned. And I would stop at nothing to see my ambitions realized, no matter the cost in blood and souls.

The cobblestones, slick with moisture and other less wholesome fluids, seemed to stretch out before me like a pathway to the abyss. The fog was a living thing, wrapping its tendrils around me, drawing me deeper into its embrace. The marketplace, once a hub of vibrant activity, now lay in ruin, the stalls reduced to rotting wood and tattered canvas. The silence was oppressive, as if the very air was holding its breath, waiting for the next horrifying spectacle to unfold.

As I walked, the faint scent of decay wafted through the air, a grim reminder of the bodies that had been left to rot in the streets. The memories of Hyde's gruesome deeds were etched into every cobblestone, every brick wall splattered with blood and viscera. I could still see the remains of his last masterpiece, the entrails of some poor wretch strewn about like garlands, the cobblestones stained a deep, rusty red.

It was in this tableau of despair that I saw her—Annabelle Blake. She stood amidst the wreckage, her pale golden curls a stark contrast to the gloom, her delicate features set in a expression of quiet contemplation. Her gown, a soft blue silk, was untouched by the filth that surrounded us, as if the grime itself did not dare to mar her pristine appearance. Yet, her large, doe-like eyes held a depth of understanding that belied her innocent facade.

"Annabelle," I acknowledged, my voice cutting through the silence like a knife. "What brings you to this forsaken place?"

She turned to me, her eyes meeting mine with a directness that was almost unsettling. "The same curiosity that draws you, I imagine, Isabella," she replied, her voice as soft and sweet as ever, but with an undercurrent of steel. "The world has changed, and I find myself compelled to understand it."

I raised an eyebrow, my gaze sweeping over the desolation. "And what have you gleaned from this... exploration?"

Annabelle's lips curved into a small, enigmatic smile. "That even in darkness, there is opportunity. And that the line between innocence and cunning is as thin as a whisper, as fragile as a silk thread."

Her words sent a chill down my spine, a sensation that was not entirely unpleasant. I felt a kinship with her in that moment, a recognition of the shared darkness that lurked beneath our polished exteriors.

As I left Annabelle to her contemplations, I paused, the eerie silence of the fog-laden streets enveloping me. The memories of the past months flooded my mind, a grotesque parade of blood and terror. I recalled the screams that had echoed through the night, the pleading cries for mercy that had been met with cruel laughter. Hyde's influence was a poison, seeping into the very heart of Mayfair, corrupting all that it touched.

Yet, amidst the chaos, I had risen. I had seized the reins of power, guided by a hunger for control that burned within me like a dark flame. The old guard had crumbled, their weakness laid bare in the face of Hyde's relentless brutality. And in their place, a new order was emerging —one shaped by my will, tempered by my ambition.

But with power came responsibility, a burden that weighed heavily upon my shoulders. For every action, there was a reaction, a ripple effect that spread through the labyrinthine streets of London like a plague. And as I stood there, the fog swirling around me, I could not help but wonder —had I become a monster in my quest to control them?

The thought lingered, a bitter taste on my tongue, as I resumed my journey. The streets seemed to close in around me, the shadows whispering secrets and accusations in equal measure. But I pressed on, driven by a force that was as irresistible as it was terrifying. For in this world of shadows, there was no room for doubt, no place for weakness. There was only the path forward, and the dark delights that awaited me at its end.

As I stepped away from the ghost of the marketplace, the echoes of former vitality seemed to cling to my skirts, whispering tales of better days. The fog had grown denser, as if the very air conspired to shroud the horrors that had befallen Mayfair. My boots clicked against the cobblestones, a steady rhythm that belied the tumult within me.

A figure emerged from the shadows, tall and imposing, his once-pristine greatcoat now bearing the slightest hint of disarray. Lord Frederick Pembroke, a man whose name was once synonymous with virtue, now wore an expression that was far from the staunch moralist I had known. His eyes, haunted and hollow, met mine with a flicker of recognition.

"Lady Blackwood," he began, his voice a low rumble, devoid of its former conviction. "A chilling night, is it not?"

I paused, turning to face him fully. "Indeed, Lord Pembroke. The chill seems to have seeped into the very marrow of Mayfair."

He stepped closer, his scar a pale crescent against his brow. "You've seen it, haven't you? The darkness. It's touched us all." His gaze flicked to the shadows, as if expecting something to lunge from the gloom. "Hyde's influence... it's like a stain that cannot be cleansed."

I watched him, my curiosity piqued. "You speak as if you've seen his handiwork firsthand, Lord Pembroke."

His eyes met mine, and in them, I saw a reflection of the horrors he had witnessed. "I have," he admitted, his voice barely above a whisper. "I saw what he did to Lady Worthington. The blood... it was everywhere, like a grotesque painting. Her face... unrecognizable. And the scent—God help me, the scent of it."

I could picture it vividly—the crimson spatters against the pristine walls, the lifeless body sprawled like a broken doll. Hyde's brutality was legendary, his murders a symphony of blood and terror.

Frederick's gaze hardened, but there was a new gleam in his eyes, a tarnished edge that had not been there before. "He must be stopped, Lady Blackwood."

I offered him a small, enigmatic smile. "And who is to bear that cost, Lord Pembroke? Are you prepared to sully your hands with the same blood that stains Hyde's?"

He did not answer, but his silence spoke volumes. I left him there, a solitary figure swallowed by the fog, his moral compass spinning wildly.

As I continued on, the houses grew sparser, the streets more narrow and twisted. The fog thickened, clinging to my cloak like a shroud, as if attempting to obscure my path—or perhaps, to hide the secrets that lay ahead. The gas lamps flickered feebly, their light barely piercing the gloom. It was as if the very air was alive, pulsating with a dark heartbeat that echoed my own.

The house that was my destination loomed suddenly before me, a small, unassuming structure tucked away from prying eyes. Its façade was plain, almost nondescript, but the fog seemed to curl around it protectively, a serpent guarding its nest. The windows were dark, offering no glimpse of what lay within. Yet, I knew that behind those closed doors, the true face of Mayfair's horror awaited.

My heart pounded in my chest, a drumbeat of anticipation and dread.

The house loomed before me, a silent, hulking monster in the gloom. My hand hovered mere inches from the weathered wood of the door, yet I found myself unable to close the distance. Within my gloves, my palms were slick with sweat, and my heart thudded against my ribcage like a trapped beast. The fog had followed me, its tendrils caressing the worn stone of the facade, as if beckoning me to enter—or perhaps, warning me to stay away.

What secrets lie beyond this threshold? What horrors have been witnessed by these walls? I could not help but recall the whispers that had reached my ears, tales of Hyde's predilections—the blood, the screams, the endless nights of terror. I had seen the remnants of his handiwork myself, the grim tableaux he had left behind in those dark alleyways, limbs askew and blood painting grotesque patterns upon the cobblestones. A shiver ran through me, and I clenched my jaw, steeling myself against the memories.

This is the path you have chosen, Isabella, I reminded myself sternly. *There is no turning back now.*

Taking a deep breath, I rapped sharply upon the door. The sound echoed through the night, harsh and abrupt, like the crack of a judge's gavel. I waited, my breath misting in the chill air, as the seconds ticked by with agonizing slowness.

Then, at last, the door creaked open, revealing a sliver of dimly lit hallway. The scent of beeswax candles and something darker, more metallic, wafted out to greet me. And there, standing in the entryway, was Edward Hyde.

The Devil of London

His tall, elegant form was silhouetted against the faint glow of a candle, his sharp features cast in stark relief. His green eyes seemed to burn with an inner fire, like the embers of some ancient, malevolent force. He was impeccably dressed, as always, his dark coat and waistcoat tailored to perfection, his cravat a stark white against the shadows. Yet there was something wild and untamed about him, a sense of barely restrained power that made the hairs on the back of my neck stand on end.

"Lady Blackwood," he murmured, his voice a low, seductive purr. "How delightful to see you."

His gaze held mine, and I felt a strange, unsettling sensation, as if he were peering not merely at my face, but into the very depths of my soul. I knew then that he could see my fears, my doubts—and that he reveled in them.

"Mr. Hyde," I replied, my voice steady despite the turmoil within me. "I trust you have been well?"

His lips curved into a slow, predatory smile, revealing a glimpse of white teeth. "Indeed," he said. "My pursuits have kept me...invigorated."

He stepped aside, gesturing for me to enter, and as I brushed past him, I could not help but notice the dark flecks upon his cuffs—flecks that bore a striking resemblance to blood. A grim reminder, if ever I needed one, of the monster that lurked beneath his polished exterior.

I steeled myself and continued inside towards the house, a sudden image of a decapitated head resting in a pool of blood, intestines ripped from a stomach, and the look of terror forever frozen in the eyes of the victim flashed through my mind, for I knew Edward Hyde was capable of such slaughter.

The heavy oak door closed behind me with an ominous thud, sealing me within the dimly lit vestibule. Hyde's residence was a study in darkness, the air thick with the scent of beeswax candles and something more sinister beneath—the coppery tang of blood. I could not ignore the crimson smears marring the wainscoting, nor the discoloured patches upon the floorboards, evidence of Hyde's brutal proclivities.

Hyde led me into the parlour, where the flickering flame of the hearth cast macabre shadows upon the worn velvet furniture. Above the mantel, a grotesque display—a row of glass bell jars, each containing a grisly trophy: a dismembered hand, a section of spinal column, and worst of all, a human heart, suspended in clear liquid. The organ bore a jagged tear, as if it had been crudely ripped from its owner's chest.

"You admire my collection, Lady Blackwood?" Hyde inquired, following my gaze. His voice was a low rumble, like the distant echo of thunder.

"A peculiar hobby, Mr. Hyde," I replied, tearing my eyes from the morbid spectacle. "But then, you are a man of peculiar tastes."

He smiled, a slow, cruel curve of his lips. "Indeed, I am. But tell me, what brings you to my humble abode this evening? Surely not merely to critique my decor?"

I met his gaze, steeling myself against the malevolence I saw there. "I came to discuss the state of affairs in Mayfair," I said. "The shifts in power have not gone unnoticed."

Hyde raised an eyebrow. "Ah, yes. The delicate dance of society. How fares Lady Grenville? Still clinging to her title like a drowning woman to a piece of driftwood?"

I thought of the lady in question, her once-haughty demeanour now little more than a brittle facade. "She maintains her station," I said carefully. "Though her influence has waned."

"Waned indeed," Hyde agreed. "And what of Sir Reginald? Has he recovered from his...illness?"

I recalled Sir Reginald's pale, sweating face, the tremor in his hands as he clutched his glass of fortified wine. "He rallies," I said. "Though I fear his spirit is broken."

Hyde chuckled, a sound like distant thunder. "Broken spirits are my particular talent, Lady Blackwood. You would do well to remember that."

I felt a chill run down my spine, but I refused to let him see my discomfort. "You take too much credit, Mr. Hyde," I said. "Not every misfortune in Mayfair can be laid at your feet."

He stepped closer, his eyes gleaming in the firelight. "Can they not?" he murmured. "I wonder, Lady Blackwood, if you truly understand the extent of my reach."

I held my ground, even as my heart pounded in my chest. "I understand more than you think, Mr. Hyde," I said softly. "I understand that you are a monster, a creature of darkness and blood. I understand that you revel in the suffering of others, that you feed upon their pain like a vampire."

The Devil of London

His lips curved in a slow, predatory smile. "Ah, Lady Blackwood," he said. "You understand nothing at all. But I admire your spirit. It will make your eventual surrender all the sweeter."

He turned away then, gesturing to the grisly display above the mantel. "Each of these trophies tells a story, Lady Blackwood. A story of power and weakness, of victory and defeat. Tell me, which story do you think yours will tell?"

I looked at the jarred remains, the silent testament to Hyde's brutality. "I think, Mr. Hyde," I said softly, "that my story is far from over."

He laughed then, a harsh, barking sound. "Well played, Lady Blackwood," he said. "Well played indeed. But remember this—in the game of shadows, there can be only one winner. And I do not play to lose."

As I left Hyde's residence, stepping out into the fog-laden night, I could not shake the image of those grisly trophies, nor the chilling words that had passed between us. The game of shadows was far from over, and I knew, with a cold certainty, that the worst was yet to come.

The room seemed to close in around us, the air thick with the scent of beeswax candles and something far more sinister. The flickering flames cast grotesque shadows on the walls, where the mounted trophies of Hyde's past conquests loomed like specters. I could feel his eyes on me, those piercing green orbs that seemed to strip away all pretense, leaving me bare and exposed.

"You speak of victories and defeats, Mr. Hyde," I said, my voice steady despite the churning in my gut. "Yet you fail to see that I am not some pawn to be trifled with."

Hyde's lips curled into a smile that was more a baring of teeth. "Ah, Lady Blackwood," he replied, his voice a low, dangerous purr. "You misunderstand me. I do not see you as a pawn, but rather a worthy opponent." He gestured to the gruesome display above the mantel, where the severed heads of his victims floated in glass jars, their eyes clouded and lifeless. "Each of these poor souls thought they could outplay me. They were wrong."

I forced myself to look at the grim tableau, to meet the empty gazes of those who had fallen before me. The room was a macabre museum of Hyde's brutality, each jar a testament to his ruthless pursuit of power. The bloodstains on the floorboards were a grim reminder of the fate that awaited those who dared to cross him.

"You think to frighten me with these... trophies?" I asked, my voice barely above a whisper. "You forget, Mr. Hyde, that I have seen the dark heart of London. I have walked its shadows and heard the whispers of its secrets. I do not fear you."

Hyde's smile widened, and he took a step closer, his voice dropping to a conspiratorial whisper. "Oh, but you should, Lady Blackwood. You should."

A heavy silence fell between us, a chasm of unspoken understanding. In that moment, I saw the truth of Hyde's power, the depth of his influence. He was a spider at the center of a vast web, each thread a life he had ensnared. And I was but a fly, drawn ever closer to his deadly embrace.

The realization made me shiver, a cold certainty that the game of shadows was far from over. Hyde's influence was a potent force, a dark tide that threatened to engulf us all. I had been a fool to think that I could challenge him and emerge unscathed.

I turned away from him, my mind racing with the implications of our meeting.

As I stepped back into the fog-laden night, the chill air seemed to seep into my very bones. The cobblestones were slick with moisture, the gas lamps casting eerie halos in the mist. The once-familiar streets of London now seemed alien, a labyrinth of shadows and secrets.

My thoughts were a whirlwind of dread and anticipation. Hyde's words echoed in my mind, a chilling promise of the darkness to come. I could feel the storm gathering on the horizon, a tempest that threatened to consume us all. The game of shadows was far from over, and I knew, with a cold certainty, that the worst was yet to come.

The fog closed in around me, the tendrils of mist reaching out like spectral fingers. As I walked, the hem of my cloak brushed against the cobblestones, the sound a whispered echo of the turmoil within me. The night was alive with the promise of violence, the air thick with the scent of blood and rain.

I could not shake the feeling of unease, the sense that unseen eyes watched my every move. The streets were deserted, the usual bustle of London life replaced by an eerie silence. It was as if the city itself held its breath, waiting for the storm to break.

The Devil of London

The gas lamps flickered in the mist, their light casting eerie shadows on the cobblestones. I quickened my pace, the sound of my footsteps echoing through the empty streets. The fog seemed to close in around me, a shroud that obscured the path ahead.

As I walked, I could not help but glance over my shoulder, half-expecting to see Hyde's spectral figure emerging from the mist. But there was nothing, only the empty street and the echo of my own footsteps. The night was alive with the promise of violence, the air thick with the scent of blood and rain.

The game of shadows was far from over, and I knew, with a cold certainty, that the worst was yet to come. The storm was gathering on the horizon, a tempest that threatened to consume us all. And I, Isabella Blackwood, would be at its very heart.

The fog enveloped me like a spectral embrace, its tendrils clinging to my cloak as if eager to reclaim me. The night air was thick with the stench of the Thames and the faint, coppery tang of blood—a grim reminder of Hyde's recent indulgences. My mind was a whirlwind of thoughts, each one darker than the last, as I tried to piece together the fragments of our conversation.

The cobblestones beneath my feet were slick with moisture, and I could feel the chill seeping through my thin, silk gloves. My breath misted in the cold air, mingling with the fog as I hurried away from the house. The gas lamps cast flickering shadows on the deserted streets, their light barely piercing the dense mist.

I could not shake the image of Hyde's eyes—those cold, calculating orbs that seemed to bore into my very soul. His words echoed in my mind, a symphony of veiled threats and dark promises. "The dance of power is not for the faint of heart, dear Isabella," he had said, his voice a low growl that sent shivers down my spine. "And I do so enjoy a good dance."

As I walked, I noticed the faint outline of a figure slumped against the wall of an alleyway. The sight was not uncommon in these parts, but something about it gave me pause. I approached cautiously, my heart pounding in my chest. The figure was that of a man, his body contorted at an unnatural angle. As I drew closer, I saw the gash across his throat, a grotesque smile carved into his flesh. Blood pooled beneath him, staining the cobblestones a deep, viscous red. His eyes were wide open, frozen in a perpetual state of terror.

I pressed a gloved hand to my mouth, stifling a gasp. This was Hyde's work—a brutal, savage display of his power. I could almost hear his laughter echoing through the streets, a chilling accompaniment to the grisly scene before me.

Turning away from the corpse, I quickened my pace, my thoughts racing. Hyde's influence was spreading like a plague, infecting the very heart of London. The game of shadows was far from over, and I was caught in the midst of it, a pawn in his twisted dance.

The fog seemed to thicken as I walked, obscuring the path ahead. I could feel the weight of unseen eyes upon me, watching my every move. The city felt alive, pulsating with a dark energy that sent a thrill of fear and excitement coursing through my veins.

As I reached the end of the street, I glanced back over my shoulder. The house was now barely visible, its outline blurred by the mist. A single light flickered in the upper window, a lonely beacon in the darkness. I knew that Hyde was there, watching me, his presence a malevolent force that lingered in the air like a poison.

With a deep breath, I turned away from the house and stepped into the fog. The mist enveloped me, swallowing me whole as I disappeared into the night. The silhouette of my form faded into the darkness, leaving behind only the echo of my footsteps and the haunting memory of Hyde's laughter.

The game of shadows was far from over, and as I melted into the mist, I knew that I was stepping ever deeper into the abyss. The storm was coming, and I, Isabella Blackwood, would be at its very heart.

CHAPTER 22

The fog was thicker than before, swallowing the gaslight glow in ghostly tendrils as Isabella Blackwood approached Hyde's residence once more. The house loomed before her, a silent, hulking beast in the gloom. The darkened windows were like unblinking eyes, void of warmth, yet watching her all the same. Her breath was steady, her heart was not.

Inside her cloak, the cold steel of the dagger pressed against her side, a cruel reminder of what she had come here to do. Edward Hyde had ensnared this city in his grotesque dance of blood and terror, and tonight, she would end it. He would never expect it from her. That was his fatal miscalculation.

Her gloved fingers curled into a fist before she rapped on the heavy wooden door. The sound echoed into the silence of the street, swallowed quickly by the omnipresent mist. A long moment stretched into eternity, then the door creaked open with a groan. There he was.

Edward Hyde stood in the dim glow of a single candle, his sharp green eyes burning through the darkness. He was dressed as impeccably as ever, his waistcoat crisp, his cravat perfectly tied—but there was something off tonight. Something… restless. A shadow lurked behind those piercing eyes, an unseen storm brewing in the depths of his mind.

The air inside smelled of damp wood, blood, and something faintly metallic.

"Lady Blackwood," he murmured, his voice a velvet caress, rich with amusement. "Back so soon? I must admit, I find your presence most intoxicating."

She stepped inside without invitation, the door whispering shut behind her. The weight of the house settled around her, pressing into her bones. Every creaking floorboard, every flickering candle seemed to hold its breath, waiting for the inevitable.

"I had unfinished business," Isabella replied, her voice smooth, unshaken.

Hyde chuckled, low and knowing. "Do you now?" He poured himself a glass of deep crimson wine from the decanter on the mantel. "I had wondered when you might return. Tell me, dear lady, what specters haunt you so that you seek my company again?"

Isabella took a measured step closer, her boots barely making a sound against the wooden floor. Her senses sharpened, drinking in every detail. The scent of bergamot and sandalwood clung to him, beneath it the faintest trace of iron.

"I wanted to understand," she said, tilting her head, her fingers grazing the back of a chair as she circled him, a predator disguised in satin and lace. "The nature of power. The kind that makes men kneel and beg for their lives."

Hyde smirked, taking a slow sip from his glass. "Ah, power," he mused. "The one true currency in this world. And tell me, Isabella—do you find yourself longing for it?"

She let his name linger between them, a whisper of intimacy. He liked that. He thrived on the illusion of control. She could feel it in the way his muscles tensed ever so slightly, the way his grip around the glass tightened. He thought himself the puppet master, when all the while, she had been slowly, meticulously, twisting the strings.

She stepped closer still, her fingers trailing lightly over the mantelpiece. Her pulse pounded against her ribs, but her face remained impassive, her movements fluid. She knew she had his full attention now.

Hyde exhaled a slow breath, his lips curling in amusement. "You intrigue me, Lady Blackwood." He set his glass down, stepping toward her, his shadow stretching long and jagged across the floor. "Tell me—do you know why I allow you to return to me?"

The air between them tightened, charged with something dark and hungry.

She met his gaze, unwavering. "Because I am not afraid of you."

His smirk faltered for half a second. Barely perceptible, but enough.

In that moment, she moved.

The dagger flashed in the candlelight as Isabella struck, swift as a viper, aiming for the space between his ribs. But Hyde was fast—too fast. He caught her wrist in an iron grip, twisting her arm sharply, sending the blade clattering to the floor.

A breathless silence stretched between them, the only sound the flickering of the fire.

Then, Hyde laughed. A deep, genuine laugh, rich with delight and something else—something dark and unhinged.

"Oh, Isabella," he breathed, pulling her flush against him, their faces mere inches apart. "You wound me—almost literally. And here I thought we had an understanding."

His fingers trailed lightly up her arm, the ghost of a touch sending ice down her spine.

"I understand you perfectly," she murmured. "That's why you have to die."

Hyde's expression flickered, a hint of something unreadable passing through his eyes. Then, before she could react, he slammed her back against the wall, the breath forced from her lungs.

His fingers curled around her throat, not tight enough to choke—just enough to remind her of his strength, of the game he thought he was still playing.

"But you won't," he whispered, his lips ghosting near her ear. "Because you're not like me."

A slow smile curled Isabella's lips, even as she gasped for breath. "No," she rasped. "I'm worse."

And then she drove the second dagger, hidden beneath her sleeve, deep into his stomach.

Hyde's eyes went wide, his grip loosening as a strangled gasp left his lips. He staggered back, his hands flying to the wound, crimson blooming against his waistcoat like an inkblot spreading on silk.

A shuddering exhale left him, his smirk returning, albeit weaker. "Well played," he murmured, before his knees buckled beneath him.

Isabella stood over him, watching as the great Edward Hyde crumpled to the floor, his breath coming in wet, ragged gasps. The dagger's hilt protruded from his abdomen, slick with his own blood. His hands trembled as they reached for it, a dark laugh bubbling from his throat even as life drained from his body.

She knelt beside him, her lips close to his ear. "You were right about power," she whispered. "It is the only currency that matters."

Hyde's fingers twitched, his emerald gaze losing its sharpness as his body sagged against the floorboards.

For the first time, he had no reply.

The house was silent.

Isabella stood, wiping her hands on a silk handkerchief before stepping over his lifeless body. The weight that had pressed against her for so long had lifted, replaced by something colder. Something final.

She did not look back as she slipped into the fog-drenched night, the city stretching before her like a kingdom waiting to be claimed.

Edward Hyde was dead.

And Isabella Blackwood had won.

The fog was thicker than before, swallowing the gaslight glow in ghostly tendrils as I approached Hyde's residence once more. The house loomed before me, a silent, hulking beast in the gloom. The darkened windows were like unblinking eyes, void of warmth, yet watching me all the same. My breath was steady; my heart was not.

Inside my cloak, the cold steel of the dagger pressed against my side, a cruel reminder of what I had come here to do. Edward Hyde had ensnared this city in his grotesque dance of blood and terror, and tonight, I would end it. He would never expect it from me. That was his fatal miscalculation.

My gloved fingers curled into a fist before I rapped on the heavy wooden door. The sound echoed into the silence of the street, swallowed quickly by the omnipresent fog. Seconds dragged into eternity before the latch clicked and the door creaked open.

Hyde stood there, his emerald eyes gleaming like a predator's, an amused smirk curving his lips. "Lady Blackwood," he purred, stepping aside. "You do keep such interesting hours."

I met his gaze without hesitation, tilting my chin slightly. "I thought we might finish our conversation from before."

His grin widened, the wolf scenting blood. "How deliciously unexpected." He gestured for me to enter with a flourish. "Please, do come in."

I stepped across the threshold, the door whispering shut behind me, locking me inside with him. The air was thick with candle smoke and something more metallic—blood, old and new. The parlor was unchanged from before, the grotesque display of trophies on the mantel still leering at me from their glass prisons.

Hyde's presence filled the space, a storm bottled into the shape of a man. He was taller than he seemed in the dark, his silhouette a shifting shadow against the candlelight. He moved like a serpent, fluid, deliberate, his presence coiling around me.

"You've been thinking of me," he said, pouring two glasses of absinthe, his voice as intoxicating as the liquor itself. "I can always tell."

I took the glass he offered but did not drink. "Perhaps I have." I let the words settle between us, waiting for him to believe his own vanity.

Hyde chuckled, watching me over the rim of his glass. "It's the danger that draws you in, isn't it? The thrill of it?"

I took a careful step closer, keeping my movements slow, deliberate. "You think you understand me so well."

He tilted his head. "I know what drives people. Fear. Power. Desire. They all blend together, forming something exquisite." He reached out, tracing the edge of my cloak where it rested over my shoulder. "You, my dear, have a darkness in you. It calls to mine."

My pulse was steady. He was close now—so close I could feel the warmth of his breath against my skin, laced with absinthe and something darker.

Now.

With a flick of my wrist, the dagger slipped from the folds of my cloak. Hyde's eyes flickered downward just as I drove the blade deep into his abdomen.

His body jerked. The sound he made was not one of pain, but of surprise, a choked, breathless laugh. His fingers curled around my wrist, tightening like a vice, but I twisted, wrenching the blade deeper, feeling it scrape against bone.

"Clever girl," he rasped, blood trickling from his lips, his grin still in place. "I didn't think you had it in you."

I twisted the blade again. "You never did."

Hyde's knees buckled, and he crumpled against me, the weight of him dragging us both down to the floor. His breathing came in wet, ragged gasps as his grip on my arm slackened. He stared at me, eyes unfocused, yet still glinting with something almost like admiration.

"You win," he murmured, his smirk faltering. Blood seeped from his lips, painting his teeth crimson. His fingers twitched, then stilled.

I did not move, my own breath coming in measured beats as I watched the life drain from him. The shadows in the room seemed to recoil, the monstrous presence that had filled every corner now collapsing inward, emptying with him.

I stood, prying the dagger free, wiping the blade clean against the fabric of his coat. The silence in the house was deafening. The trophies on the mantel bore witness, their lifeless stares fixed on their creator's final moments.

I stepped back, surveying my work. Hyde lay still, his infamous green eyes dulling to nothingness. The great beast of London was dead. And I had slain him.

With one final glance at the corpse, I turned, crossing the threshold and stepping out into the night. The fog curled around me, parting like a curtain, guiding me back into the city now free of its monster.

I did not look back.

The night swallowed me whole, the city stretching out before me, indifferent to the act I had just committed. My hands still trembled beneath my gloves, though not from fear. A strange exhilaration coursed through my veins, an unfamiliar taste of victory.

I moved through the fog like a shadow, my pace unhurried yet deliberate. The streets were near-empty, save for a few stragglers huddled under gas lamps, their faces gaunt with hunger or despair. The stench of coal smoke and refuse thickened the air, clinging to my cloak as I drifted toward my townhouse. Each step carried the weight of finality, of change.

When I reached my door, I hesitated. The lock turned easily beneath my gloved fingers, and I slipped inside, pressing the heavy wood shut behind me. The house was quiet, the kind of silence that stretched, waiting to be filled. My breath came slower now, steadying, but my heart still raced. I removed my cloak, my dagger still warm beneath its folds. The blood had dried in dark rivulets along the blade, a stark contrast against the polished steel.

The Devil of London

I set it down upon the table, staring at it as though it might stir, as though Hyde's final breath still lingered upon its edge. I had done what I came to do. I had ended the reign of terror that gripped London. And yet, standing in my dimly lit parlor, the weight of my actions pressed down upon me in ways I had not anticipated.

No triumphant cries would sound in my name. No justice had been declared. The city remained as it was—bleeding, rotting, waiting for its next nightmare to rise.

I sank into a chair, my limbs suddenly heavy. I had won. I had survived. But at what cost?

As the first tendrils of dawn curled through the curtains, I let out a slow breath. I would not look back. Hyde was dead. And I remained. Whatever that meant for London, or for me, would soon reveal itself in the days to come.

For better or worse, the shadows had swallowed him whole. Pity, he never knew I loved him. The Devil of London, imagine that.

And nowI, Isabella Blackwood, was still standing.

Patti Petrone Miller

ABOUT PATTI

Ladies and gentlemen, step right up to "Where the Magic Happens" - a literary circus that'll make your bookshelf do backflips!

Meet Patti, the ringmaster of this wordy wonderland! She's not just an Executive Producer; she's a word-wrangling wizard, conjuring up an animated TV series based on "ELLIOT FINDS A HOME." It's the tail-wagging tale of a thumbs-up pup and his silent sidekick, proving that you don't need words when you've got opposable digits and a heart of gold!

Hold onto your bestseller lists, folks! This Polygon Entertainment superstar has hit the USA TODAY jackpot and Amazon's #1 spot more times than a cat has lives. With 7 dozen books under her belt, she's got more genres than a chameleon has colors. From Urban Fantasy to Horror, she's been spinning yarns longer than your grandma's knitting needles!

But wait, there's more! Patti's life is like a celebrity bingo card:

She rocked "Romper Room" at 4, probably making the other kids look like amateur rompers.

She rubbed elbows with Captain Kangaroo and Mr. Green Jeans. (No word on whether the jeans were actually green.)

She shared a train ride and a sandwich with Sidney Poitier. Talk about a meal ticket to stardom!

She high-fived President Nixon at the circus. Who knew the circus could get any more political?

She went to school with David Copperfield. We assume she didn't disappear during attendance.

She roller-skated with pre-famous John Travolta. Grease lightning, indeed!

She sipped cocoa with Abe Vigoda. Fish never tasted so sweet!

When she's not busy being a literary legend, Patti's juggling roles faster than a circus performer. Teacher, grandma, furparent - she does it all with a smile that could light up a haunted house.

knitting needles!

But wait, there's more! Patti's life is like a celebrity bingo card:

She rocked "Romper Room" at 4, probably making the other kids look like amateur rompers.

She rubbed elbows with Captain Kangaroo and Mr. Green Jeans. (No word on whether the jeans were actually green.)

She shared a train ride and a sandwich with Sidney Poitier. Talk about a meal ticket to stardom!

She high-fived President Nixon at the circus. Who knew the circus could get any more political?

She went to school with David Copperfield. We assume she didn't disappear during attendance.

She roller-skated with pre-famous John Travolta. Grease lightning, indeed!

She sipped cocoa with Abe Vigoda. Fish never tasted so sweet!

When she's not busy being a literary legend, Patti's juggling roles faster than a circus performer. Teacher, grandma, furparent - she does it all with a smile that could light up a haunted house.

Speaking of haunted houses, meet the "Queen of Halloween" herself! This Wiccan High Priestess is stirring up stories spookier than a skeleton's dance moves. Her books are flying off the shelves faster than witches on broomsticks, so follow her on social media or risk missing out on the hocus-pocus!

So, come one, come all, to Patti's phantasmagorical world of words! It's more exciting than a roller coaster, more magical than a rabbit in a hat, and more diverse than a box of assorted chocolates. Don't be shy - step into the spotlight and join the literary party where the pages turn themselves and the stories never end!

The Devil of London

www.ingramcontent.com/pod-product-compliance
Lightning Source LLC
LaVergne TN
LVHW041801060526
838201LV00046B/1081